I0825588

CAGE OF SECRETS

An Empire of Blades Novel

Book Three

Nicole Conway

No AI was used in the creation of this book, its text, or content.

This book is a work of fiction. Names, characters, places, and incidents are either products of the author's imagination or used fictitiously. Any resemblance to actual or fictional persons, living or dead, business establishments, events, or locales is coincidental. The author makes no claims to, but instead acknowledges the trademarked status and trademark owners of the word marks mentioned in this world of fiction.

Cover illustration by Lulybot

Interior illustrations by Covered by Nicole

For T

Thank you for tolerating all Jerran's shenanigans.

N
W
E
S
GAVRAL TUNDRA
WHITE WASTES
ETHALAN
ICEDRIFT SEA
WESTERN OCEAN
WHITECROWN MOUNTAINS
VORDEGA
HALONAR
VAARNA
DAN

AVORA
FORRAN PLAINS
TIBRUS
HOLVRADIX
VOCRAN OCEAN
BRASKOL
NOLTHAM
ELONDIA
LUNTHARDA
MALDOBAR
OUTHERN SEA
ELONDRAN OCEAN
RIENKA
NAR'HALEEN

N
W
E
S
LUNTHARDA
MALDOBAR
Halfax
SOUTHERN SEA
Almo
RIENKA
Brazur's Point
Ipsol
Sal'Karr
Derith
Salodurn
Banaris
Tkyeran
Kosaar
Malis
Kua'Tar
Mathros
Detharkis
Pithan
Soman Taal
Esfolar
Savarian Mine
Obsidian Ridge
DAMARIA
Fallern
Faladurn
Ollenvale
Alsferth
Hallowdu

VOCRAN OCEAN
BRASKOL
NOLTHAM
ELONDIA
Palodurna
ELONDRAN OCEAN
Compendium Library
Kansir
Uru'Nai
Valley of the Gods
Jagged Isle
Gate of Proleus
Kau'Pani
NAR'HALEEN
Tolem
Redwater
Dumathis
Lahn'Siir
Temple of Adiana
Temple of Undae
Pitch Graves
Obsidian Pass
Eternal Ruins
Pass of Jansar
Endsoldan Forest

PANTHEON OF REATIA

FOREGODS

Itanus
Enais
Milontos
Vescor*

OLD GODS

Giaus
Astaris
Avgior*

LESSER GODS

Paligno
Clysiros
Undae
Proleus

GODLINGS

Ishaleon
Adiana
Tykeron
Iksoli

** deceased or banished*

Part One
Violet

One

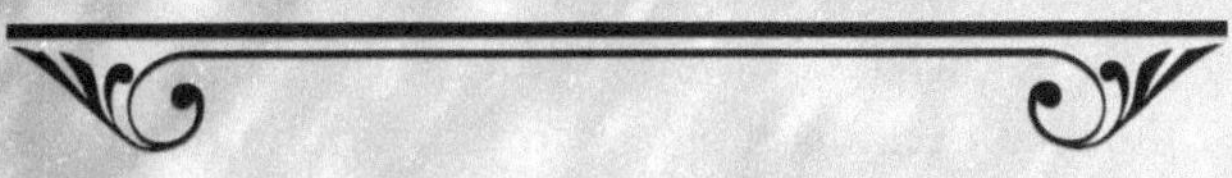

They were kicking me out of the Zenith's Call.

That was the only reason I could fathom that Mistress Orvana would call every senior agent into her chambers this early in the morning—including my own tandem, Roxus.

To exile someone from the order, you had to have the unanimous agreement of every senior agent and the elders. Normally, that wouldn't be an easy feat, especially since I was now a member with a successful mission under my belt. But the elders already hated having a Viperi slithering around in their midst.

So, she just had to get the rest of the senior agents on board, too.

Sitting beside the fountain in Krin'Moir, I watched the hallway that led into Mistress Orvana's private office. My stupid leg wouldn't quit bouncing, and I'd already gnawed away all the calluses around my thumbs.

Gods, this was taking forever. They'd been in there for hours already. How much longer would it be? Would they call me inside? Let me argue my case? Or would they want to wait and make my exile more public?

Ugggh. I couldn't take much more of this.

"Here. You should eat something," a smooth, masculine voice spoke up right before a fist-sized loaf of butterbread appeared in front of my face. The aroma of fresh buttercream, whipped and sugared to perfection that would melt on the tongue like snowflakes, filled my nose.

I flinched back, flashing a glare of warning up at the tall, leanly muscular half-elven young man grinning wolfishly back at me. Axien's broad smile crinkled the corners of his slightly upturned eyes and dimpled one of his cheeks. That look alone would've turned any other girl in Arx Eburna into a pile of quivering mush.

He was, by far, the most handsome young man strolling these halls. Not even I could argue that fact. Unfortunately, he also knew it. It made him far too smug for my liking as he waggled those perfect dark brows and dangled the fresh bread in front of me like he was taunting a dog.

Idiot. I ought to bite him, just for spite.

I hadn't even heard him approach. How long had he been standing there watching me anyway?

"I'm not hungry," I grumbled and glared back toward the hallway. Still no movement.

"Liar." He gave a noisy, dramatic sigh as he spun on a heel and plopped down beside me, tearing the loaf in two and cramming half in his mouth. "You're always hungry. Maybe that's why you're always angry."

I pursed my lips, hating that he was right—about the hungry part anyway.

The aroma of butter and sugar wafting off that little hunk of perfectly toasted bread already had my stomach doing somersaults. Heat bloomed across my cheeks when it gave a loud, angry *growwwwl.*

Axien just chuckled and held the other half out to me again.

I scowled and swiped it out of his hand.

"The meeting isn't about you, you know," he quipped as he went on chewing his half, joining me in staring at that empty, torch-lit hallway across the vestibule.

"You don't know that," I said around mouthfuls of bread. "What else would all of them be in there talking about? Mistress Orvana has been giving me dirty looks for two months—ever since we got back from delivering the Moonscape staff. You should have seen her when Roxus told her about what I did in the Viperi city. I thought she was going to dive over her desk and throttle me."

He gave another deep, melodious laugh. "Don't be so vain. Not everything's about you, you know. There's a war on. Mistress Orvana has more to worry about than whatever new disaster you've kindled."

I elbowed him in the ribs, making him choke on his bread.

Axien was insufferable enough when he wasn't trying to cheer me up. This was even more irritating. And ... sort of nice.

But I'd die before I ever told him that.

There was no escaping his sly, roguish grins and endless teasing now that he had officially joined the Zenith's Call. With his phialim—the arcane device that the Aurati had used to control and track him—now destroyed, Axien was free to choose his own path going forward.

And he'd chosen to stay here, with us, and become a proper member of the order.

Granted, it hadn't been easy to convince any of the elders that he could be trusted, but having Roxus and Curator Vanora stand and vouch for him had helped. It also didn't hurt that he was a novice sorcerer. Adding a half-Avoran to the ranks promised to be a big, shiny gold star for Mistress

Orvana. And having him also be capable of slinging spells around?

Well, that must have been too good for her and the rest of the elders to pass up.

Not that I knew all that much about Axien's magical abilities. I'd seen him cast plumes of flame and open ancient portals, but not much else. He still kept a tight lip about that sort of thing around me, and not even Curator Vanora would discuss it. Frustrating. They were both obviously holding back something important.

And for what? Why was it such a secret? All Avorans had magic, didn't they? What could be so special about his abilities that he wouldn't tell anyone else about them? Besides, we were all supposed to be on the same team here.

I didn't know what secrets they were keeping, or why. And I *hated* not knowing.

"Look there," Axien said, nodding to the hallway.

My face flushed with heat again. Oh, gods, had I been sitting there staring at him the whole time? Talk about pathetic.

I whipped around to find all the senior agents making their way out of the hallway back into the main vestibule of Krin'Moir. My stomach clenched and my heartbeat raced like mad as I bounded to my feet, leaning to catch a glimpse of a familiar face in the crowd.

Roxus and Curator Vanora emerged together, talking quietly and not seeming to notice either of us at first. Their somber, no-nonsense expressions and stiff body language were easy to read, even at a distance. That was how they seemed to regard one another all the time—as though there were a rift neither one of them knew how to cross or an invisible forcefield neither wanted to break.

But I saw Vanora's eyes linger on Roxus's back a second after he turned away. I saw his gaze slip along her profile whenever she spoke, his expression distant with thought, as though he were trying to read her mind. The energy between them practically sizzled and snapped like cold fire, and it was enough to make anyone standing too close shiver.

I didn't dare ask about any of that, though.

Clearly, they had some sort of long and complicated history, one that likely predated my existence altogether. But Roxus would have to work out his lady-problems all on his own.

"Well, I don't see any torches or pitchforks," Axien said with a deep, satisfied sigh as he stood beside me, arms crossed and hips cocked in a casual stance. "I think you might be in the clear."

"I will throat-punch you," I promised.

He just laughed again. "You'd have to find a stool to stand on first."

Moron.

My heart jolted, leaping into my throat when Roxus finally turned my way. Our gazes locked, and my scruffy tandem gave me a tired smile that never quite reached his warm, oak-brown eyes. He rubbed at the back of his neck as he ambled toward us, Curator Vanora still in step next to him.

Vanora, however, remained expressionless as she stood beside my tandem. She seemed to float there, effortless and graceful in a way that bordered on the divine. Her curator's robes were neat, without a single fleck of dust or wrinkle out of place, and all her silvery white hair hung loose and free around her, a flawless curtain of satin that rippled with every tiny movement.

"You didn't have to wait for us," Roxus said.

"What was the meeting about? What did Mistress Orvana say? Does it have anything to do with our last mission? Is she still angry about us going through the Viperi city?" The questions burst out of me like bees pouring from a hive.

Roxus's eyes went wide, brow skewing up in bewilderment before he flicked a suspicious, accusing glance at Axien. "Did you put that nonsense in her head?"

"She is fully capable of her own nonsense, sir," Axien replied, raising his hands in a gesture of surrender.

I shot him another venomous look, licking my teeth behind my lips. If I tripped him at just the right time, maybe he'd break a few of those pretty white teeth on the floor when he fell ...

"Come, Axien. We have work to do this morning. Violet, I'll have to postpone our next lesson, I'm afraid," Curator Vanora spoke up at last, as though she could sense how close I was to lunging at her tandem like a rabid wolverine.

But there was something else in her tone—a subtle touch of resigned heaviness. She flicked Roxus a quick, pointed look with her delicate brow crinkled before she turned and glided out of the vestibule like a weightless, ethereal nymph.

Axien deflated some, shrugged, and shuffled away behind her without another word.

Hmmm. We had been meeting for my etiquette lessons three times a week, and she never canceled. Not once.

Gods. Something really must be wrong.

I frowned up at my tandem, waiting until they'd crossed the room and were well out of earshot before I muttered, "It's bad, isn't it?"

Roxus shifted uncomfortably and put a hand on my shoulder.

"It's ... complicated," he replied. "Let's get something to eat at home and talk it over."

I clenched my teeth, fighting the urge to shrug his hand off and make a scene right here in the middle of Krin'Moir.

"Just tell me what's happening, Roxus," I demanded. "If they're going to expel me from the order because of what happened in the Viperi city, then I should at least be allowed to explain my side of things. I should get to speak before—"

"It has nothing to do with that, Vi," Roxus interrupted, his tone quiet but firm. Even his expression had gone stony, as though he didn't like that I was still ruminating on everything I'd been forced to do during our last mission.

How could I not though? Especially when I knew it painted me in a certain light?

I'd been forced to walk the streets of my kin and pretend to be one of them. And not a night had gone by since then that I wasn't dragged into an abyss of nightmares because of it. The whispers at my back here at Arx Eburna had always been bad, always accusatory, but now they were vicious. Conspiring.

Just waiting for me to prove that I was part of the same conspiracy as Sanja and Chrysa.

The only thing I knew to do was throw myself straight back into a rigorous training routine that didn't leave me a lot of spare time for personal matters—not that I had many to begin with. But if I worked hard, if they saw me doing my job nonstop, at least they couldn't accuse me of anything.

So all my days over the last eight weeks had been filled with training to regain the strength in my injured leg, carefully journaling everything I'd seen while I was in that Viperi city for the order's records, and more intense lessons with Vanora.

Then this meeting came out of nowhere. Well, okay, not nowhere. I should have known that any involvement with my kin would catch up with me. I just hadn't expected it to involve every single senior agent.

"The meeting was about me," Roxus said suddenly.

My body flinched hard as panic jolted through me. I stared up at him, all the breath leaving my body so quickly that I couldn't even make a sound.

"Well, me—and several of the other senior agents," he

amended quickly, sinking into a more casual stance with all his weight on one leg and his hands on his hips. His shaggy brown hair swished over his brow as he shook his head.

My mouth opened, but I still couldn't force out a single word.

"Let's go home, Vi. There's a lot we need to talk about, and I'd rather not do it here," he said, his gaze drifting down to catch mine again. His gentle smile was dimmed with lines of exhausted worry, like he'd spent all morning in mental warfare.

And lost.

Gods and Fates. Something had happened in that meeting with Mistress Orvana. Something bad. Surely they wouldn't kick him out of the order, too, would they? After everything he had done for them? He was irreplaceable. He was an Ursinaar.

Roxus's demeanor gave nothing away as he ambled toward the exit. His easy, casual smile never faltered. It didn't matter though.

Even if he wouldn't say it out loud, I knew all of this mess had to be because of me.

I was putting my mentor, the one man in the world I knew I could count on, at risk. He might never blame me, but he didn't need to. I knew who was at fault, even if he was the one suffering the consequences now.

And there was nothing I could do to stop it.

Two

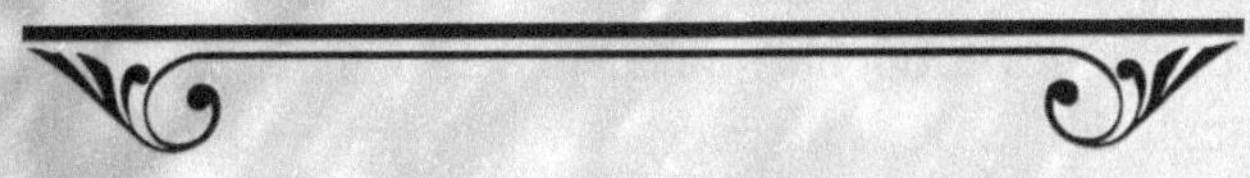

I was going to throw up.

Not because of the food, though. Delthene, Roxus's live-in housekeeper and the anchor of our little sort-of family, never disappointed when it came to cooking.

But the tension around our table was enough to make me want to gag.

Delthene had rushed through preparing a light, early lunch for us. She rushed around the table, carefully placing platters of smoked fish on thin, toasted slices of bread topped with capers and goat cheese, where we could all help ourselves. She poured cups of spiced tea into our cups with slices of orange floating on top before finally settling into her place across from me.

The instant I caught her glance, my stomach clenched hard again and my pulse fluttered. She wore the same worried, uncertain smile on her lips that Roxus had. Like she knew what was coming.

But how could she?

Unless something like this had happened before.

I stirred in my chair, watching the little curls of steam rise from my teacup, while Roxus piled food onto his plate and started eating. Delthene filled her plate as well, but only sat there taking little anxious sips from her teacup while her gaze flicked back and forth between Roxus and me.

"Mistress Orvana is calling a meeting of the elders and a few select senior agents from all across the Southern Kingdoms," Roxus announced at last.

I froze, my thoughts immediately racing like wind stirring through dry leaves, scattering everywhere. A meeting? Why? Where?

"When do you leave?" Delthene asked, somehow managing to sound calm and composed.

"Tomorrow morning at first light," he replied between bites of food. "I'll start packing after we finish here. We're to leave in staggered intervals, so we don't draw as much attention from any spies that might be watching the order."

"Tibran spies, you mean," I said, not meaning for it to sound as accusing as it probably did, like he was intentionally withholding details.

I just wanted to be sure we were all on the same page.

He nodded slightly.

"I assume you can't tell us where you'll be going, then." Delthene seemed to shrink in her seat, her shoulders falling and her lips pressed together tensely.

Roxus put a hand on her arm. "I'm sorry, Del. I shouldn't be gone more than a week, though."

A week? Gods.

This wasn't at all what I'd expected. Could this really be because of me? Or something worse?

"Is Vanora going, too?" I stared back down at my teacup, braced for the answer. My insides clenched and twisted, my stomach swimming like I'd swallowed a cup full of worms. Maybe this was why she'd canceled our next lesson.

If they both left, I would be utterly alone and exposed.

They were the only ones who cared to shield me from Mistress Orvana's hatred. If she turned on me while they were away ...

I shuddered.

"No," Roxus said with a sigh. "Eight have been chosen to attend from Arx Eburna, Mistress Orvana and myself included. There hasn't been a meeting like this since the War of the Stones. It's got everyone on edge. But the stronghold won't be left unattended or unguarded. Curator Vanora and a few others will be staying behind. The Vindexori will be on high alert, as well. Try not to antagonize them. They'll be looking for excuses to prove their capability."

Relief washed through me like a cool spring rain. Every tense muscle in my body relaxed at once, and I sank forward in my seat to rest my elbows on the table. I would at least have one ally in Arx Eburna until he got back, even if the Vindexori were more on edge than usual.

Thank the gods for that.

"All of this because of that tyrant, Argonox?" Delthene guessed, still taking little nervous sips of her tea as her lovely dark eyes flitted between us.

"He's more than a tyrant now—he's a problem. Knowing he has been brokering deals with the Viperi has raised alarms throughout the Southern Kingdoms. And given what we witnessed at the Levanurith temple, I'm confident they're not the only ones he's bargaining with for aid in his campaign." Roxus crammed another piece of fish-topped bread into his mouth.

"You mean those fighters who were helping Sanja," I said, taking up the tiny spoon in my teacup and stirring around the slice of orange to make it spin. "The ones wearing the symbols of the white hand with the eye in the center, right?"

I hadn't given them much thought at the time. There had been other, bigger problems to deal with—like not dying and

Axien dragging us through an ancient magic portal—and that symbol wasn't one I'd recognized.

Now that the dust had settled on all that, however, I could see the threads of influence that had been revealed in that skirmish. In that moment, Sanja had shown her hand—and by extension, Argonox's.

"White hand with an eye?" Delthene perked up, her gaze sharpening on Roxus.

He took a noisy sip of his tea, draining the cup before he put it down and answered, "The Hands of Fate seem to be allying with Argonox, as well."

Delthene dropped her cup with a yelp. Tea splashed across the table, and she immediately scrambled to start wiping it up. Her hands shook, face blanching as she scooped up the dirtied napkins and hurried to put them in the laundry before they stained.

I stared after her, my heartbeat quickening. She knew who that was? I'd never heard of the Hands of Fate before, not even in all my studies.

By the time I managed to drag my attention back to Roxus for an explanation, his entire demeanor had darkened. He sat back in his chair, arms crossed over his chest, jaw tight. His deep brown eyes smoldered as he stroked his stubbled chin with one hand, seeming to stare straight through me.

"The Hands of Fate are the Emperor of Nar'Haleen's private guard, Vi," he said in a low, bristled tone before I could even ask. "They've served him for thousands of years and are seldom seen outside of the palace—let alone in a remote temple at the service of a foreign agent. It is ... an alarming revelation. One that was not lost on Mistress Orvana or the elders. That's why we have to meet. We have to find out what is happening and how far Argonox's hand now reaches."

I didn't dare to say it out loud, but I knew exactly what he meant—the true meaning woven carefully in between those words. If Argonox had somehow infiltrated Nar'Haleen's royal court, either by force or treaty, then we stood on the precipice of invasion. The Tibrans would come like an unending flood, their ranks filled with brand new slave-soldiers.

Damaria didn't have the numbers or the resources to counter an attack from Nar'Haleen of that scale, not with the Tibran Empire backing them. The war between Damaria and Nar'Haleen had gone on for, well, as long as most people here could recall. Hundreds of years, maybe. It was more or less at a stalemate now, with Rienka caught in the middle since it technically belonged to Damaria but was the biggest trade port in either kingdom.

But this would tip the scales. And in the end, regardless of what deal the Emperor of Nar'Haleen might have made with Lord Argonox to keep his little throne, it would all belong to the Tibran Empire. They would bow to a foreign power, obey their new tyrant's whims, and fill his coffers with gold and his ranks with conscripted soldiers.

Because if history had taught me anything over my last two years of study at Arx Eburna, it was that no matter what they claimed ... tyrants and dictators did not share power.

Ever.

"You're going to be fine, Vi," Roxus murmured, almost as if he were trying to convince himself of it, too. "Vanora will look after you. I know you think Mistress Orvana despises you, but you might be surprised to hear that she spoke your name with praise at the meeting. She knows it's because of you and Axien that we now know the Tibran Empire is moving unseen across the desert."

My mouth quirked to one side, and I went back to fidgeting with my little teaspoon. "She'd probably have liked it better if I'd died in the effort, though."

His gaze softened with a crooked, disarming smile. "I'm

not so sure. The order is stretched thin. She's not in a position to be so discriminating when it comes to her agents, and you've proven yourself to be capable even in the face of what she would consider intense temptation to go back to old habits."

I snorted and rolled my eyes. Of course, she'd assume I would be tempted to rejoin my kin. What monster doesn't crave a den of its own kind?

"Have a little faith," Roxus coaxed. He picked up a piece of bread topped with fragrantly smoked fish and slid it onto my plate with a wink. "We're living in strange and desperate times. The allies we need don't always arrive looking the way we expect. It's best to keep an open mind."

I lifted a brow, giving him a challenging smirk. "Is that what you told Mistress Orvana about me?"

"Maybe." He laughed as he ran a hand through his shoulder-length, unkempt brown hair. "Like it or not, you two are very similar. Stubborn. Ruthless. Smart. It's a potent and exhausting mix. But it might actually be worse if you got along. I shudder to think of what havoc you might inflict on the order together."

I made a face, sticking my tongue out at him before I finally picked up the piece of crumbly, toasted bread to take a bite.

"Just do a tired old bear a favor, would you?" he asked, his expression tensing some. His eyes closed, and he bowed his head. It made all of his shaggy hair sweep forward, brushing along his shoulders. He wasn't *that* old, but tired lines creased the corners of his eyes.

I frowned around my bite of savory, smoky fish and airy, warm bread. "Let me guess—stay out of trouble?"

Roxus shook his head slightly.

Uh-oh. This was something serious, then.

I stiffened and stopped chewing, waiting for him to continue.

"Keep your eyes and ears open. I meant it when I said you were clever. You've got good instincts—better than mine, I suppose. You knew something was off about Sanja, but I ... I let the past cloud my judgment," he said. "I need you to be my eyes when I can't see clearly."

I swallowed stiffly, almost choking on my bite of food. "It wasn't your fault, Roxus. The same thing happened with me and Chrysa. I can't see any more clearly than you can, apparently."

His brow furrowed in a dissatisfied frown. The table lurched as he leaned against it, propping both his elbows and rubbing at the sides of his forehead with a slow, deep sigh.

"Twice now we've both been deceived by someone close to us. Someone we should have been able to trust," he murmured, almost as if he were talking to himself. "I've never heard of outside forces targeting the Zenith's Call so directly. It's unprecedented. And to be honest, we aren't prepared for it. Our mark used to mean something, even to kings. It used to be respected. But this fellow, Argonox ... he's a different breed. I suspect that's why Mistress Orvana is so worried."

Just the mention of that name—Argonox—seemed to make the surrounding air grow cold. I shivered and looked down at my half-eaten lunch. The Tibran Empire's newest dictator had taken his homeland by force. Now, he was making headway across the entirety of Reatia, ruthlessly seizing every kingdom he crossed. He seemed to fear nothing and no one, and apparently, he held no esteem or respect for the gods.

He craved only their power.

"It can't happen again, Vi," Roxus said. "The order is in a delicate state. We all look at one another with suspicion now, wondering who else among us has been bought with Tibran coin. Who will be the next to betray? To hand over divine secrets and artifacts we've all sworn to protect?"

I sank deeper into my seat, letting his words wash over me like the crash of icy waves. No wonder Mistress Orvana wasn't all that worried about me anymore. She had other, much closer enemies to worry about. At least I had spilled blood on the right side, even when given the chance to rejoin my treacherous kin.

But had that finally been enough to convince her I wasn't a traitor?

"We have to get it right this time." Roxus's voice had gone tense and sharp with urgency—desperate with determination. "We have to trust one another. We have to speak up when we see something that doesn't seem right. And most importantly, we have to believe one another, even if it seems far-fetched. Agreed?"

"Agreed. Trust for trust." I nodded, but dread was already sinking deep into my chest as though I'd been stabbed with an icy blade that slowly melted and spread chilly tingles through my body.

He wouldn't be saying all this unless he believed there were still traitors in our midst. I knew that.

And now he had to leave.

Roxus forced a reassuring, half-grin at my response, but it didn't even come close to reaching his eyes. Worry still shone there, reflected in varying hues of warm oak and amber brown flecked with gold. The little crease right between his eyebrows and the way he drummed his heavy fingertips on the table made my muscles grow tense, like someone slowly drawing back a bowstring to fire.

If something else went wrong, if someone came after the Whispering Vault or attacked Arx Eburna outright, I would have to stand up and defend it. Not alone, of course. But Axien and I would have more insight into our enemies than anyone else in the order. We'd already seen them in action once, and Axien had experience moving in their midst.

When and if they made another move against Arx Eburna, it would be up to us to see it coming. We'd have to find some way to stop it.

And this time, there would be no reinforcements coming to save us.

THREE

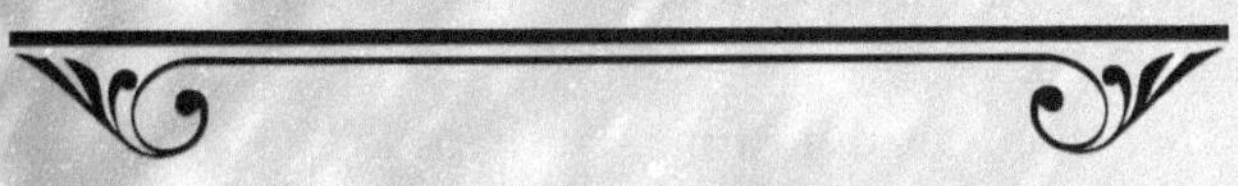

I had never seen Delthene cry before.

But after Roxus left the table, going up to his room to begin packing for his trip, I drifted through the house until I found her on the floor in the washroom. With her face in her hands, she sobbed quietly over the napkins that floated in the washbasin. Her shoulders shook as she gasped and sniffled, not seeming to realize I was gaping at her from the doorway.

Oh no.

Panic tangled my thoughts like tripwires, rooting me to the spot. I didn't know what to do. What to say. How to comfort her.

I'd never comforted anyone before.

All I could do was copy what others—Leruna, Roxus, and even Axien—had done for me in the past. Delthene had comforted me plenty of times, too, and my heart shuddered with terror that she might recognize her own words as I crept close and knelt beside her.

"It's going to be okay," I whispered as I slowly and awkwardly put an arm around her. "It's just a few napkins."

But this wasn't about the napkins. I knew that.

Gods, I was so bad at this. I sounded stupid, even to myself.

I just didn't know how to say the real thing. The thing that mattered.

Roxus was leaving us. These situations were getting more dangerous. She must have felt so vulnerable. So helpless. So afraid for him.

Delthene leaned into me, her head lolling to the side to rest on my shoulder as we sat on the washroom floor together, watching the napkins float in the little basin of water she'd drawn. She trembled and sniffed, wiping at her eyes and pushing loose strands of dark hair away from her face.

"I know he'll come back," she whispered brokenly. "He always does. But I always worry. And now the war ... gods above, please watch over him. I can't believe it's come again so soon." There was a weight to her words, like a burden she'd carried for years without daring to set it down.

A weight like memory.

I swallowed against a rising knot in my throat.

"Have you seen it before? War?" I dared to ask.

Delthene's whole body swelled and shrank with a deep, heavy breath before she replied. "When I was a girl not much older than you. I lost my family to it. Our farm, all our little sheep, and ... my babies."

My heartbeat skipped sharply. *Babies?* Did she mean ...?

"I had two sons," she confessed tearfully. "My family was poor, so my father married me off young because he couldn't afford to feed me. My husband and I were little more than children ourselves when I had our first baby. And before I was eighteen, I had two children. Two beautiful little boys."

Two children? When she wasn't much older than me? Gods and Fates. I'd never even held a baby, let alone thought about having one.

I sat still, struggling to wrap my mind around it, to comprehend how it might have felt to have two little ones I had to protect and feed. I'd never even tried imagining something like that before.

It was ... terrifying, honestly.

"The Nar'Haleenans invaded south of Faladurn," Delthene murmured, her voice strangely hollow, as though she had to let her soul slip free of her body just to speak the words aloud. "They killed my husband and burned our little house. They butchered all our sheep. I took my babies and fled into the mountains with some of the other village women."

I stared at her, not daring to blink or even breathe. It was hard to imagine, and it hurt to try.

"But those mountains are cold and bitter. We weren't prepared for it. A heavy freeze came in the night, and by dawn, many of us had died," she continued, her expression glazed with memory that seemed to have snatched her all the way back to that bitter night. "My babies froze in my arms."

I had to look away. Those words, wrung with sorrow, made all the light in her soft golden eyes snuff out.

"I would have happily died along with them if a company of priests from the Calo'Durn temple hadn't found us. They carried us back to their temple. Nursed us back to health," she said. "Let us stay and weep and grieve for what we'd lost."

"Was that where Roxus found you?" I guessed.

She bowed her head slightly, some of her long dark hair spilling free of its braid and framing her face. "Months later, yes. The priests let a few of us widows stay in the temple and work as maids, since we had nowhere else to go and the Nar'Haleenan armies were still attacking villages in the area. Then the Zenith's Call came to give them reinforcements, just in case the armies decided to breach the sacred treaties and attack the temples, too."

My mouth twisted, a bitter flavor rising in my throat as I

recalled what Varren had told me once about soldiers attacking temples. That had been what drove him to join the Zenith's Call. He wanted to make sure things like that didn't happen anymore.

Now, watching the fires of memory smolder in Delthene's eyes, I felt that, too. The primal, violent urge to protect.

"Roxus isn't even all that much older than me. We were both teenagers when we met," Delthene said, a ghost of a smile brushing her lips as she finally turned to look at me with a strange, tender warmth I didn't understand. "But he was so gentle and kind. Odd as ever, and a Vordegan accent so thick I could hardly understand him, but good. He invited me to come back with him to Rienka. He wanted someone to take care of his house while he was gone on missions. I guess he could see that the temple wasn't much of a comfort to me anymore. The rest, as they say, is history."

Part of me wondered if that's all she'd ever been to him—a live-in housekeeper. Had they ever been lovers? Why hadn't he just taken her as a wife, if they were both so young? Did Zenith's Call take wives?

Asking about any of that seemed like a terrible and incredibly awkward idea, though. Some things are better left unsaid, and it wasn't any of my business, anyway. Even if they had been lovers once, they didn't seem like it anymore. If anything, Roxus seemed to regard Delthene like a sister.

And me? Well, I'd become his wretched little would-be daughter.

"You never went back? To your old village, I mean. Or the temple?" I asked.

She shook her head slightly. "Some things are better left to time, my dear. I didn't get to bury my poor husband or my children. And the thought that the same could happen here, or that Roxus might be—"

Her face contorted as she fought back another sob, her eyes squeezing shut and her hands clenching hard in her skirts.

I should have reassured her. Whispered soothing words and promises that Roxus would always come back. He was made of tougher stuff than most of us, and not just because he was a Vordegan Ursinaar.

But no sound came from my screwed-up, pinched-together lips as I watched her cry softly. Because deep down, I didn't know what would happen to him. This wasn't like the war between Nar'Haleen and Damaria. The Tibrans were a new breed of evil, and they were actively recruiting. They were tunneling their way through the world like poisonous roots, undetected.

Unstoppable.

We'd only narrowly escaped them before.

How could I promise Roxus could do it again—especially if I wasn't there to help?

I couldn't.

Minutes dragged, and Delthene gradually pulled herself together. She shooed me from the washroom, assuring me she'd be fine, even though her eyes were still puffy and her chin trembled some.

She was a terrible liar, but maybe it was best to give her some time to herself.

My entire body had gone numb when I wandered back into my bedroom and shut the door. Delthene's big, orange, three-legged cat yawned at me from where he'd stretched out across the foot of my bed, basking in the rays of midday sunlight that bled through the drapes pulled over the windows. They rustled in the breeze that blew in from the ocean, the same breeze that filled my room with a heavy, briny smell.

That aroma soaked into everything—the sheets, blankets,

rugs, even my clothes. I drank it in, sighing into it, and let my head drop back to rest against the door.

At least here, nothing had changed. The world outside could spin out of control, but this place—my home—was still here.

For now, at least.

If the Tibrans came for Rienka next, where would we go? Where would we live? We would have to find somewhere safe for Delthene. Somewhere far away from Rienka, where the Tibrans might never reach.

But I didn't know if a place like that even existed.

I'd seen how far they'd spread already, how they could move practically undetected. They could be under my feet right now, and we'd never know it until it was too late.

I blew out another deep breath.

No, like it or not, Roxus had to go to this meeting. We needed to know how bad this was. How far they'd spread. We needed to get as much information about their movements as possible before it was too late.

By dinnertime, the tension in the house had eased into a bittersweet calm. Roxus had two leather bags stacked by the front door—one with his belongings and another packed with scrolls, books, and notes he must have been organizing all day. Evidence and historical records.

Just seeing those bags put my teeth on edge and made my skin itch. Had he included the journal entries I'd written about what happened in there, too? I'd spent hours scribbling down every shred of memory I had of what happened after the temple was attacked and Axien snatched me through that portal. I didn't want to leave anything out—about the Viperi, the Tibrans, the switchbeasts, all those strange war machines, and everything we'd seen and heard.

One tiny detail might make the difference.

"I was thinking we'd give Delthene the night off," Roxus

announced as he swaggered down the stairs, already dressed in his boots and long, weather-beaten coat.

I turned to face him, unable to disguise my surprise. "Is she okay?"

"She's a little shaky, but I think some time in her tea garden with some of the new books I got her will help," he said with a sly wink.

"Really? You're buying her more of those ridiculous romance books?" I curled my lip.

"Hey, everyone's entitled to a guilty pleasure," he chuckled. "She likes them, and it's the least I can do to make up for leaving her alone with you for a week."

I wrinkled my nose at him. "Right. I'll try to be less problematic than usual, then."

Roxus gave another deep, rumbling chuckle as he nudged me toward the door. "Don't make dead promises, girl. Go on. We'll head to the Rook's Roost and see if that big idiot friend of yours is still dealing out the wrath of Proleus."

My heart gave a sudden, fluttering jolt. He wanted to go check on Declan?

It ... had been a while. Too long, probably. I hadn't seen him since we'd been back, mostly because I'd immediately gotten my nose shoved back into the grindstone of training as soon as we hit the door.

Sure, I'd asked Leruna to look in on him, but I needed to see him myself. I needed to know he was okay and that Sulam hadn't targeted him again.

"R-Right, okay," I managed, my voice catching as I fought to keep any traces of the hailstorm raging in my head from reaching the surface.

I didn't do a great job.

Roxus's eyes squinted up at the corners as he focused on me. If he suspected anything, though, he didn't bring it up.

Probably biding his time, watching me sweat, and hoping I'd come clean on my own.

Too bad that wasn't an option. I would *not* be telling Roxus, or anyone else, what had happened with Declan. I had enough problems, enough scrutiny from stuffy senior agents scowling at my back, ready to accuse me at the first misstep.

I did not need my own tandem to know I'd poked the proverbial hornet's nest with Sulam and that Declan had been the one to pay the price for it.

Eventually, maybe, we could discuss it.

For now, though, I had to handle this on my own. I'd keep watch from afar, stay out of Sulam's disgusting business, and hope none of this got back to, well, anyone.

Hah. Right.

As if I'd ever been that lucky.

Four

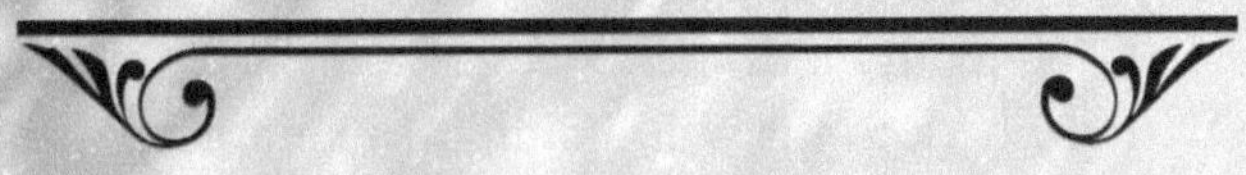

I had never felt so small in my life.

Clinging to Roxus's arm, I cringed as we waded into the crowds packed wall to wall in the Rook's Roost's notorious secret pit-fighting arena. The roar of conversation, laughter, and shouting from the fight-caller hit me like a punch to the gut.

Fates, I'd never seen it like this.

The tables were packed with all manner of vagrants, merchants, mistresses, and foreigners—all dressed in their finest, gaudiest ensembles. They drank from tankards and wine goblets, feasted on platters of fruits and cheeses, and piled heaps of golden coins into the porcelain bowls set at the end of their tables. Bowls meant for placing bets on whatever fight was going down in the pit below.

Lines of patrons stood along the bars on the first level, shouting orders to the sweaty, frantic barkeepers. The stench of a hundred different pipe tobaccos hung in the air as thick as sea fog. My eyes watered, and I coughed into Roxus's shoulder as he ushered me forward.

"Must be some big fights tonight," he muttered, voice tight with unease. He didn't like crowds like this either.

"Will we even be able to get a table?" Looking around, it seemed unlikely. Our usual spot was already taken, and I didn't see any other empty seats.

"I'll see what I can do," he huffed and slipped his arm out of my grasp, herding me toward a corner just inside the front entrance. "Sit tight. I'll be back."

With my back to the wall, I didn't dare move an inch as I watched the roiling sea of people moving along the steep staircases and down the line of tables that stood all around the central pit. I didn't recognize any of the flushed, gaudily painted faces, and they didn't spare me even a second glance.

That was probably for the best.

"What are you doing here?" a soft voice hissed in my ear so suddenly I almost shot straight out of my boots.

I snatched away, whirling to find a pair of familiar, sea-green eyes peering at me from under the deep hood of a pale blue cloak.

Leruna?!

"I-I came to check on Declan," I stammered. "What's going on? It's never like this here."

Her expression darkened, her lovely oval face going as cold as a winter's full moon as she reached out to wrap her arm around mine. "Come. We need to talk."

I let her tug me along into the crowds, up the stairs to the very top. There, the level was somewhat less packed, and the tables had a few open seats scattered around. Shadowed figures draped in heavy dark robes that covered their clothes stood along the back wall, lips pinched tight around long pipes. Their eyes followed us as we passed, but only for a few seconds.

Leruna chose a corner well away from anyone to stop and

face me at last, curling a finger to call me in close enough that we both had our heads underneath the large hood of her cloak.

"I was going to come see you at the house, but perhaps this is better," she said, talking fast and using the Rienkan tongue. Trying to keep others from eavesdropping?

"Why? What's the matter?" I asked.

Her full lips pressed together grimly, eyes searching mine for an instant as though she were struggling to find the right words, a gentle way to say what she needed to.

"Something is wrong with Declan," she whispered at last.

My stomach clenched hard, seeming to rise to the back of my throat and choke the breath right out of me.

"What do you mean?" The words left me, but my lips were so numb I didn't even feel them move.

She took my hand, turning with me toward the base of the sweeping, underground amphitheater. This was Sulam's nasty little kingdom where, in a sunken pit filled with blood-spattered sand, the figures of two men wrestled and exchanged blows.

I almost didn't recognize him.

Declan moved fast, each swing of his arms sending a spray of sweat from his exposed upper body as he bore down with relentless punches against his opponent. His teeth were bared, hair a tangled mess, and his nose oozed blood that ran down his neck, chin, all the way to his chest.

But where he'd once been a tower of thick, hard muscle ... I could see every one of his ribs. His deeply tanned skin was a patchwork of bruises that covered every part of him. His face had been bashed until all his features were so swollen, I hardly recognized him. If not for the tattoos and those pointed, Holvradix ears—I would have mistaken him for some new fighter Sulam had dragged in here.

His skin looked paler, almost ashen in the torchlight. His cheekbones were more pronounced and his collarbone stood out. His hips, too. Every inch of him was battered, his skin splotched with yellow, green, blue, and black bruising,

My neck throbbed, aching as I clenched my teeth so hard I thought my jaw might break. Declan had dropped a substantial amount of weight.

What, by all the gods, was Sulam doing to him? Was this some new twisted strategy to get back at me for interfering with his slavers—by making Declan slowly wither away while he fought for his life every night?

Or was this something else? Something far worse?

"Is he sick?" It was a stupid, desperate, hope-fueled question. Maybe this had nothing to do with Sulam, me, or anything intentional.

"Not that I can tell," Leruna replied from where she stood right beside me. "I haven't approached him, yet. Only observed, as you requested. But I'm worried, Violet. He was still in such poor shape when he left the temple, and I don't think he was given enough time to recover. He hasn't been coming by for potions or salves, even though he obviously needs them."

That was an understatement. He needed to stop this before he pushed his body beyond its limit. He needed a way out.

I just ... had no idea how to even suggest that. What could I do? Last time I had stuck my blade into Sulam's affairs, it had almost gotten someone close to me killed. Who would Sulam target if I tried intervening on Declan's behalf? His little sister? Delthene?

I couldn't risk that. No, I had to think. I had to come up with a plan.

There was a way out of this—there had to be.

"Roxus is leaving for a mission tomorrow morning," I said quietly. "He'll be gone for a week, and I can slip away and meet with you. Gods, Leruna, I'm so sorry I didn't come to speak with you sooner. After we got back, everything was just—"

"It's okay," she interrupted, her hand tightening around mine. "You're Zenith's Call now. What you're doing is important." Her tone faltered some and she looked away from the pit.

Away from where Declan had stumbled and was taking blow after blow to his face. Each one hit with a thud that I felt like a crushing hand tightening on my throat. His blood spattered onto the sandy arena floor.

I had to look away, too. My eyes welled, and I blinked hard, forcing the scorching heat of shame and anger back beneath the surface.

"I heard about what happened at Levanuris," Leruna said. "Many of the priestesses are worried about something similar happening here."

"It won't." I couldn't keep my lips from curling back in a defiant snarl at the thought. "I'll come to the temple as soon as I can, maybe even after Roxus leaves. We'll discuss it and come up with a plan to help him. Okay?"

Leruna nodded slightly, making some of her long, tightly curled dark hair spill out from under her hood. "What should I do in the meantime? Do you want me to keep watching him?"

"Only if it's not going to get you in trouble with the priestesses at the temple," I replied.

Her shoulders drew up, lips parting slightly as she took a deep, trembling breath. She blinked hard as she exhaled, seeming to relax into herself. Then she flicked those vibrant, sea-glass eyes back to me and forced a thin, fragile smile.

"He's a good man," she murmured.

I squeezed her hand, letting her feel a hint of my strength. Of my surety.

"He is," I agreed.

"I'll do whatever is necessary, then," she promised.

And I could have sworn there was a flicker of something darker, something as sharp as abyssal steel, in her eyes.

Five

Roxus was furious.

His nostrils flared as he puffed and snorted, glowering at me when I made my way back to the corner he'd left me in earlier. He scowled down at me, arms crossed and head to the side, one eyebrow arched expectantly.

"So much for staying put," he grumbled.

Gods, sometimes it felt like he still saw me as that feral, starving little child he'd scraped out of a prison cell. Never mind that I was wearing another one of Vanora's diabolical corsets that mashed my breasts up into pleasing shapes and told all kinds of lies about how much cleavage I really had. I still didn't like them.

The heels, however, were growing on me. I savored every inch of new height I could get. But the corsets restricted my flexibility especially in combat situations. A steep price for the sake of fashion, but Vanora insisted.

"I had to find a place to relieve myself that wasn't the stair-well—although that seems to be the prime location for every drunk in here to piss," I said, waving him off. "I didn't think it was something you'd be interested in, but if you'd like to hear about my lady-ailments—"

He rolled his eyes and moved closer, planting a hand on my shoulder to begin steering me toward the exit. I guess he wasn't buying an inch of that.

Smart man.

"There's nowhere to sit," he muttered sourly.

Ahh. So that's why he was so irritated.

"Did you see Declan?" I asked carefully, sneaking a glance up at his profile.

"I did." His scowl hardened further, darkness gathering in the edges of his rugged features as he dipped his chin slightly.

He'd noticed it, too, then.

Good.

Maybe, when he came back from this trip, we might actually be able to convince him to help. On our own, Leruna and I didn't stand much of a chance of twisting Sulam's arm—or breaking a few of his bones—until he let Declan and his sister go. But if I could recruit a few more people to the cause, including Roxus, and form a united front ...

That hope put a fresh spring in my step as we walked back home in silence. Roxus kept the pace swift, his hands deep in the pockets of his coat, as the wind teased through his mop of wavy brown hair. We'd almost reached the front of the house when he finally slowed, gradually easing to a halt across the street.

His gaze traced over the front of it as though he were memorizing every detail, the lights from the windows catching over his ruggedly handsome face. For a moment, it was as though the years peeled back like layers of pain, sweat, work, and worry. A smile ghosted over his lips, and he slowly panned his gaze down to where I stood beside him.

"I love you, Violet," he said.

Everything went still—my whirling, plotting thoughts, my

heartbeat, even the night wind. It all seemed to stop instantly. I gaped at him, watching and trying to figure out what he meant.

No one had ever said those words to me. Not my mother. Certainly not my father.

What was I supposed to do? Should I say it back? Was that what people did in these situations?

"You and Delthene are my family. You mean more to me than anything else. You know that, don't you?" he continued before I could come up with any kind of response. "I will always do everything I can to make sure you are both taken care of."

"I know," I managed to rasp stiffly.

Gods, why was he saying all this? And why did it feel so much like a goodbye?

"Good." He nodded firmly.

"You're, uh, scaring me," I admitted, looking him over to try and read any body language that wasn't being obscured by that ratty old longcoat.

As usual, he gave very little away. His casual, easy demeanor was a balm to the raging storm of worry that passed through my body and left me trembling.

"I'm sorry," he said, reaching over to ruffle my hair in a way that he knew good and well would piss me off immediately. "Nothing's wrong, I promise. I just realized I don't tell either of you that often enough. I mean to do better."

"And you're leaving tomorrow, and something might go wrong and we'll never see you again, and your last dying thought will be regretting that you never told me," I filled in, biting angrily at each word as I tried to smooth my hair back down.

He threw his head back, loosing a reckless laugh to the starry night sky. "Oh, my wicked little ward," he sighed as he stepped off the curb and started for the front door. "You always did have a way with words."

Nice. Way to dodge the issue.

I glared at his back, following a few steps behind him all the way inside. Roxus wasted no time disappearing back into his office upstairs, and I made my way to my room, making sure I stomped extra hard all the way up.

What was he thinking? Saying something like that right before he was about to leave? Gods, at least he hadn't said it to Delthene. Maybe I should have threatened him not to, especially after she'd spent the morning crying into a washbasin of napkins.

Ugh. Men.

No wonder he was still single. He'd die a bachelor at this rate.

Shutting my bedroom door behind me, I stood at the dressing mirror to unlace the corset that had begun digging into my hip bones. I threw it aside, stretching my back out before I sank down on the edge of my bed and started unlacing my boots.

I'd just thrown them into a pile and gone to fish my sleeping chemise out of my wardrobe when a flash of movement caught my eye, moving past the gap in the drapes that covered my balcony's doors.

My pulse hammered hard against my ribs as adrenaline poured through me, lighting every nerve on fire. My daggers were beside the bed. Too far to reach. I'd have to—

Thunk, thunk, thunk!

I hesitated. Was ... was someone knocking on my balcony doors? At this hour?

Scowling, I prowled over and yanked the drapes back.

A strangled yelp left my lips as I cringed backward, almost tripping over my own feet.

Axien had his face right up against the glass, hands cupped around his eyes as he peered back in at me.

What the—?! What was he doing here? And why hadn't he used the stupid door like a normal person?

"You!" I snarled, adding a Viperi curse I knew he wouldn't understand as I snatched one of the balcony doors open, ready to throttle the life out of him.

Even if I had to stand on my toes to reach him.

"Sorry, sorry!" he immediately apologized, wincing back. "I knocked downstairs, but no one answered. I got worried."

What? Oh, right. It was late—too late for normal visitors, and Delthene and Roxus were probably upstairs and hadn't heard the door.

I blew out an angry breath and crossed my arms, cocking my hips as I glared at him. "So your next idea was climbing up to my window and peering in here like a creep?"

He shrugged. "Sorry. It couldn't wait."

"What couldn't wait?" I fumed. Get to the point, man.

"I, well, that is ..." he started, but seemed to think better of it. He rubbed at the back of his neck and scratched behind one of his pointed ears before he finally continued. "I got a missive from Mistress Orvana."

I blinked, drawing back like he'd just pinched the end of my nose. "What? A mission for you and Curator Vanora?"

His expression tightened, almost as if he were bracing for impact. "No ... it's, uh, just for me, actually."

My jaw dropped.

He had been given a *solo* mission? Already?!

SIX

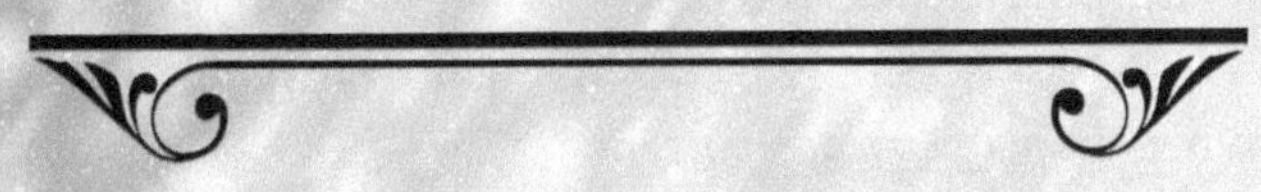

Nothing—absolutely nothing—about this was fair.

Axien had only been in the order for two months! I had been in it for two years and had never gotten a missive with my name on it.

In fact, the only reason I'd gone on any missions at all is because Roxus took me along as his tandem, not because I'd been personally requested.

Anger kindled in my chest, heating my face and turning my expression sour as I glared up at him. Big, stupid, too-handsome elf man. I should have known Mistress Orvana would trip all over herself rolling out a red carpet for him. Ugh.

"Wait! Just wait a second," Axien blurted, reaching toward me like he was going to grasp my shoulders. He must have thought better of it, though, because he froze an inch away from touching me and winced again. "Before you start punching things—or me—just hear me out. It's not a big mission. It's a glorified errand, actually. I have a feeling the only reason she's sending me is because she'd rather not spare someone more important for it."

I tensed and drew back slightly, already choosing which side of his face I'd smack if he dared to cross that last inch of distance and touch me.

Ever since that kiss in the back of the wagon on our way back from Dumathis, I'd established firm no-touching boundaries. I'd already had to smack him a couple of times for it, just to get the point across.

No way was I going to let any man treat physical contact with me like some sort of currency.

"I came here to ask you to come with me," he said, arms dropping back loosely at his sides. The wind rustled through his long, dark brown hair, teasing some of it over his brow. It gave him a roguish, perfectly disheveled look that pissed me right off.

No one should have been able to look so pretty without any effort whatsoever, elf or otherwise.

I tore my gaze away from his and picked at my nails. "And why would you want to drag me along, hm?"

"Because I'd rather not go alone," he admitted, cheeks flushing a little. "Even if it is just an errand, I'd like someone to be there to watch my back."

"So why doesn't Curator Vanora go with you?" I challenged. "She's your tandem, isn't she?"

"She's going to be overseeing some of the classes for the new prospects, since the usual instructors are gone," he said.

I arched an eyebrow, watching the way he shifted his weight from foot to foot and kept avoiding eye contact. Something wasn't right. He was holding back information—information he knew I wouldn't like.

So I went straight for the jugular. "And what is this mission, exactly?"

Axien sank back onto his heels, shoulders dropping some. "It's retrieval. Apparently, there's a noble down in Esfolar who has a divine artifact in their estate's private collection. With tensions rising and armies moving, they want it moved to a more secure location. Namely, Arx Eburna's Vault of Whispers."

Hmmm. All that sounded legitimate. Very routine, mundane, and simple.

Esfolar wasn't that far, and it was a place we'd both been before. It was still within Rienka, so the likelihood of running into invading Tibran armies was minimal. We could manage it in a couple of days.

So why was he squirming around like he had a pinecone in his pants?

"And?" I narrowed my eyes, tilting my head to the side and angling my chin upward expectantly. "What's the artifact? Something dangerous?"

Maybe that was why he was acting so squirrely all of a sudden.

"I, well, I'm not sure about dangerous, to be honest. It's something called Tykeron's Puzzlebox. I haven't been able to read the brief on it yet," he rambled on. "I doubt they'd send me after something problematic or life-threatening, though. Not without my tandem or another senior agent going."

Hmm. True. But still ...

I pursed my lips, watching him fidget and panic. He was practically sweating now.

Finally, Axien's chest heaved in a defeated sigh as he threw his head back, looking skyward as though making a last-second plea to the gods for help.

"It requires attending ... a soiree," he confessed at last, mumbling the words like he was half-hoping I wouldn't hear.

I frowned. "A what?"

"A soiree," he said, a little louder this time.

"And what is that, exactly?" I went back to picking my nails. Whatever game he was playing, I wasn't about to fall for it.

Axien pursed his lips, staring at me hard, as though he were trying to figure out whether or not I was joking around. "It's a fancy party. You know, like a ball? Dancing? Drinking? Painfully boring small talk with half-drunken nobles wearing far too much perfume?"

It took a few seconds of choking for me to finally put a sentence together. "You want to take me on a mission to a fancy party?"

"Well, uh, yes, I do." He winced.

"In front of nobles? On purpose?" I had to be sure I had heard him right.

"That's the idea," he confirmed again.

"Why, by all the gods, would you think that's a good idea? Look at me? Do you have any idea what will happen if you trot a Viperi into a ballroom full of nobles?" I gestured to myself, then planted my hands on my hips. "Unless you intend on walking me in on a leash."

One corner of his mouth quirked into a dangerous, devious smirk that made his eyes glitter. "Are you offering?"

"I'll make you eat those words while they're still in my fist," I warned, narrowing my eyes.

"It'll be fine. We're not there to socialize," he fumbled, showing me his palms in surrender. "All we have to do is find our contact, receive the artifact, and leave. That's it. In and out. Easy."

"Nothing is ever easy with you, Axien." I pinched the bridge of my nose, right between my eyes, where a little pulse of pain made me wonder if I was suffering from an aneurysm.

"You don't even have to talk if you don't want to." He took a step closer, his tone suddenly pleading. "I just ... I-I find it very difficult to be in settings like that. I'd rather not do it alone."

Cracking an eye open, I stole a glance at his worry-ridden face. His gaze bored into mine, brow drawn in desperation and mouth open slightly, as though he were hanging on my every gesture.

Then it all made sense.

This wouldn't be the first time he'd been subjected to noble events. In fact, there was a possibility he might even run into some of the figures from his past. People who had used and abused him. People who would assume he was still a slave on the end of a real, albeit gilded leash, unable to refuse anything they demanded of him.

He'd only been free of that life—of the chains that had bound him since birth—for a few short weeks. No wonder he looked like he might start throwing up on my boots at any second.

He must have been absolutely terrified.

"Fiiine," I surrendered, already hating myself for being such an insufferable sap. "I'll go."

Axien's entire body seemed to melt in on itself, broad shoulders sagging and head bowing for a moment. His hand drifted to the crossed leather straps on his chest that held his sheathed scimitars to his back, fiddling with the fine golden buckles.

"Thank you," he murmured. "I know what I'm asking of you."

No, he most certainly did not. But we'd cross that bridge later. Poor dope. If he thought for a second that parading me into a ballroom like that was going to keep him anonymous, he was in for a horrific surprise.

He'd probably be better off walking a switchbeast in.

It took everything I had not to reach out and give him a little consoling pat on the head. I settled for kicking him in the shin instead. Then I whirled around and stepped back into my bedroom.

"Don't start thanking me just yet," I growled back at him over my shoulder. "When do we leave?"

He swallowed hard. "Uh, well, that's the thing. We need to leave tomorrow."

I stopped, shutting my eyes tightly as I felt my very last nerve snap like a kite string. Gods, Fates, and all things holy. This man ...

I whirled to face him again. "*Tomorrow?* Are you completely insane? This may come as a shock to you, but I don't have a wardrobe full of pretty ballgowns to choose from! I can't get anything made that soon!"

"I am aware of that, yes." He gave a cringing half-shrug and backed away a step, moving out of throttling range. "That's why you'll be borrowing one from Vanora. I've already got it all sorted. She's got one that she's sure will fit you, and ... well ... it's all taken care of. Shoes. Jewelry. You just need to bring your makeup, since she mentioned you already have the right sort."

I scowled up at him, not liking the mental image of him and Curator Vanora discussing dressing me up like some sort of plaything. Before I could get another angry, seething word out, Axien waved his hands in a dismissing gesture and stood a little straighter.

"Listen, there's nothing for you to worry about. I'll have everything ready to go tomorrow morning. Just be out on your doorstep and I'll pick you up. Deal?"

I studied him—the way his blue-glowing eyes lit up like pale amethysts in the night. His flawlessly tanned skin shone a deep bronze, making all those sharp, half-elven features seem like they'd been cut from the same cloth as the young gods.

Yeah. He'd fit right in amongst a ballroom full of nobles.

I would be a complete disaster, though—more so than usual.

The prospect of being sneered at by a ballroom full of wealthy nobles and their well-armed guards made my stomach squirm and sour, shame already settling around my neck like an iron-wrought collar. It would be humiliating. Dangerous, even.

And it meant I had to wear an evening gown. Probably some of those especially tall heels Vanora made me practice in, too.

Fates, just cast me down.

"Deal," I grumbled, and before he could say anything else, I turned away again and shut my bedroom door between us.

I only had a few hours left to prepare for this nightmare. Might as well try to make the most of it ... and pack every single blade I owned.

Seven

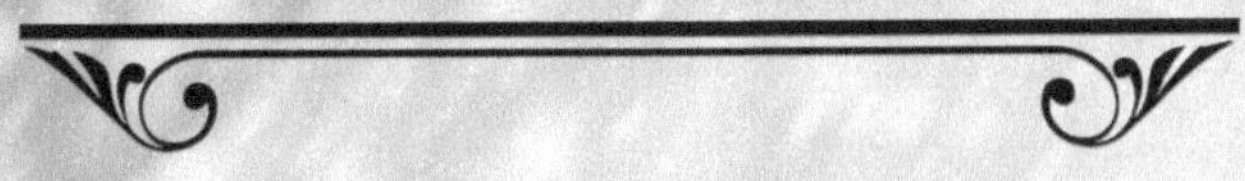

My hands wouldn't stop shaking.

Throwing my haversack over my shoulder, I started down the stairs to the front door before the sun had fully risen. The sky shone a pale, pastel pink, and a sliver of moon hung as clear as crystal against a few lingering flecks of stars. I shivered as the crisp morning air tingled over my cheeks and along the nape of my neck.

Or maybe that was just from the fact that I was a walking bundle of raw nerves this morning.

I clenched my teeth so they wouldn't chatter as I donned my favorite traveling cloak. I should be calm and collected. Confident, even. I should put on a brave face, if only for the sake of appearances. I didn't want Axien or anyone else to see me shaking in my boots over a simple mission like this.

But, gods, I hated leaving Delthene on her own.

Roxus seemed equally unsettled, his expression creased with deep lines around his eyes, nose, and across his forehead. He stomped around the sitting room, muttering to himself, and grabbed random things to shove into his bag at the last minute. A small, pocket-sized knife. A bundle of clean paper squares for letters. An extra tin of his favorite pipe tobacco.

Finally, he snatched his long, worn-out longcoat off the hook by the door and threw it on. Standing beside me, I caught him studying me with a cryptic, pensive frown.

I'd told him about the mission with Axien over our very early breakfast, and he hadn't stopped looking at me like that since. I couldn't tell if it was worry or just blatant disapproval, though.

"Everything okay?" I dared to ask.

His lips thinned, and he turned away to grab his two bags before he opened the front door, holding it ajar so I could go out ahead of him.

"Fine," he barked gruffly. "You sure about this? About going off with that boy?"

"No," I admitted. "But Zenith's Call shouldn't travel alone, right? Vanora is indisposed, so I guess it's me or no one."

"He could find someone else at Arx Eburna," Roxus growled low.

"Not this late notice," I countered. "Besides, I already told him I would. It'll be fine, papa bear. It's just a quick retrieval."

Roxus didn't reply, but his expression darkened with a fierce, bitter scowl aimed out the doorway ahead of him—right at Axien, who'd just rounded the corner and was fast approaching our house.

"The last one was supposed to be a quick retrieval, too," Roxus muttered bitterly.

My skin prickled at the memory. At everything that had gone wrong.

"Remember what I said." Roxus turned his coat collar up and adjusted the strap of his bags over his shoulders, carrying one on each side. One of his hands drifted down, brushing the pommel of the longsword belted to his hip, and his eyes never left Axien.

Almost like he was waiting for him to make a wrong move.

Strange. We'd been around one another plenty over the last few months. Arx Eburna wasn't that big, after all, so it was only natural we'd cross paths. In all that time, Roxus hadn't given Axien much more than a sideways glance and a dismissive snort.

Why the change? Was it just because now I'd be going off with him alone?

Or did Roxus know something I didn't?

No, I couldn't afford to start jumping to conclusions like that—especially after what Roxus had said yesterday about us keeping the air clear between us. No secrets. No holding back information, no matter how bizarre.

If something was going on with Axien that Roxus didn't like, I had to believe he would let me know.

"Oh! Good morning, Axien!" Delthene called out, appearing behind us in the doorway. Her watery smile was as thin as rice paper as she waved to him.

Axien just nodded with his own tired smile as he made his way over to stand on the doorstep with us, his dark hair tied back into a braid and faint dark circles under his eyes. Hadn't he slept at all last night?

That made two of us, I guess.

"You went over everything with Vanora?" Roxus opted to skip all pleasantries and went straight to interrogation. Fantastic. Not awkward at all.

Axien tensed before him, but didn't cower. He kept his posture straight and his gaze direct as he answered, "Yes, sir. Everything's ready."

Roxus's jawline hardened, gaze sweeping over the young half-elven man several times before he made a low, grunting noise of approval.

"Don't be so fussy," Delthene scolded gently as she patted Roxus's arm. "You've trained her well."

"It's not *her* I'm worried about." Roxus's voice was so low I could barely hear him. He turned to face me, giving me a quick hug as an excuse to mutter against my ear, "Eyes open."

I nodded as I pulled back, holding his gaze for an instant and pouring every ounce of will and confidence into it I could muster.

That must have been enough to soothe the grouchy old bear, because he blew an exasperated sigh, hugged Delthene tight, and started away without another word.

We stood together on the doorstep, watching his tall frame retreat into the early morning streets. No one said a word until he vanished around a corner.

"You two ought to hurry on, as well, before the market traffic picks up," Delthene coaxed, but I could see the corners of her forced smile beginning to wobble. Her golden eyes were misty as she hugged me, kissed my hair, and reminded me how lovely I was.

Her words from yesterday still replayed in my head. It made me search her wan, round face after she let me go.

Would she really be okay here by herself? Should I have refused to help Axien and stayed to watch over her?

Knowing what she'd been through, how she'd lost her own children, made those last few seconds with her squeeze tightly around my heart. She wasn't my mother, and I hadn't really considered her a substitute in that respect, but it was easy to draw parallels between the way she treated me and how she had probably doted on her own babies.

And, gods, that hurt *so* much.

It made my eyes sting and water as I forced a smile back at her.

"I'll be okay," I assured her, knowing full well I couldn't guarantee that. I shouldn't be making empty promises.

"I know you will," she said as she tucked a stray lock of my hair behind my ear. "Don't turn your back on that boy, though. He's a little too slick for my liking. Handsome ones like that tend to attract trouble."

Behind me, Axien coughed and blushed.

She winked at him, and he turned away, the tips of his pointed ears now bright pink.

I grinned at that.

"I can handle him. Oh, but here! I almost forgot." Digging through my haversack, I pulled out a crisply folded piece of parchment and handed it to her.

Delthene eyed it curiously. "Another letter?"

"I didn't get a chance to talk to Declan last night. He's been pretty busy with his pit fights, I guess. It didn't seem right to interrupt him, especially since it was so crowded," I said.

"Oh, I see," she said and pocketed my letter. "It's for him, then?"

"No, for Leruna again, actually," I clarified. "I just asked if she'd look in on him like last time. You know, to make sure he's not getting into any more trouble than usual. She likes hearing about what I'm doing in training, too."

Gods, I hated lying to her. It made bile rise in my throat as I forced a smile at her—one I knew she'd believe.

The letter was to Leruna, yes. But it was more of a desperate, slapped-together apology that I had to leave and couldn't meet with her for a few days. When I got back, however, I promised I would go and see her.

We'd find a way to settle this situation with Declan once and for all.

Delthene nodded. "Of course. I'll see she gets it, then."

"Thank you." I took a step back, bumping against Axien.

"Ready?" Axien asked.

No. Of course not. But I was out of time, and dragging this out any longer would be excruciating.

I waved to Delthene, casting one last, long look over our modest little house on the corner, before I turned to follow Axien away toward the south end of the island. Toward the harbor, markets, and whatever else awaited us.

I would come back. So would Roxus. We'd all be together again. Everything would be fine.

I had to believe that.

Axien and I could handle this and return in a couple of days. No drama. No foul-ups, nasty surprises, or Tibran soldiers lurking around shadowed corners. Just a clean, simple, business-as-usual retrieval.

I frowned at the back of Axien's head, following along behind him like a duckling toddling after its mother. The hand that wasn't holding onto the strap of his bag hung at his side, shaking slightly. I could have sworn faint dark veins stood out against his tanned skin, disappearing beneath the cuff of his leather vambrace.

Just like before.

My tongue suddenly felt dry, and I couldn't shake that clammy, tingly coldness that settled over my skin and made my insides feel crampy and achy, like I was starving but too queasy to eat anything. That feeling usually meant I was getting in way over my head.

And this time, more than ever, I probably should have listened.

Eight

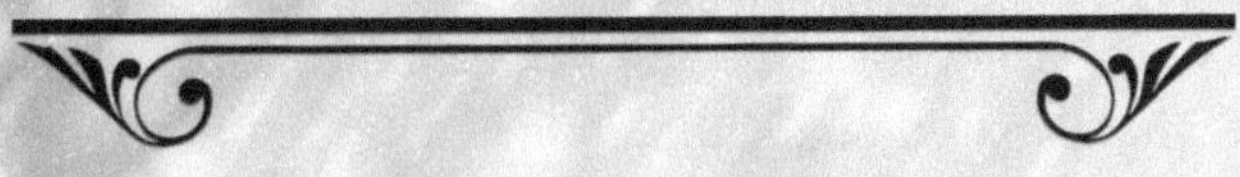

This wouldn't be like before.

Last time we'd left for Esfolar for our mission, we had taken hippocampi and ridden out discreetly. But that wasn't an option now.

This time of year, the currents had shifted and intensified. It was too much for even the strongest of those aquatic steeds to handle, and even the wild hippocampi had moved southward into the shallows to find calmer waters.

I tried not to let my disappointment show as Axien led the way along the crowded, early morning docks to a line of sizable ferryboats that rocked at their moorings. All three of them buzzed with activity, preparing to take their first haul of passengers to the various islands scattered in Rienka's massive, crescent-shaped bay.

Men, women, and children stood in long lines, coins in hand, ready to claim their seats. We joined the line for the nearest of the boats, one headed for the island of Kosaar. The first leg of our journey.

I let out a groan and let my bag slide off my arm while we waited for the crew working the ferries to begin letting folk onboard. I barely had time to get in a few twisting stretches before boarding began, and our line started shuffling up the steep gangplank.

"Roxus hates me, doesn't he?" Axien asked suddenly.

I hesitated, almost tripping over one of the warped wooden boards as I followed him onto the crowded deck of the ferry.

What the—? Was he being serious? Since when did Axien care what Roxus thought about him?

I watched him trudge on ahead, head down and back hunched under the weight of the much larger travel bag he had slung over one shoulder. He wove through the crowd, never looking back until he'd found two open seats along the bow of the ferry.

"I-I, uh, I don't know," I stammered as I sat down and put my bag between my knees. "He's complicated."

It was the truth, at least. I'd never considered how Roxus felt about Axien until recently. Sure, he snapped at him now and again, but I always chalked that up to him being protective of me, as strange as that was.

But this morning, Roxus had been moodier than usual. He'd been downright cold to Axien. It made my mouth scrunch as I mulled it over.

"I've been thinking of apologizing to him directly for everything that happened," Axien said as he sank into the seat directly beside me and leaned forward, resting his elbows on his knees.

"You already apologized to Mistress Orvana, all the elders, and the senior agents," I reminded him. "You were pardoned. Obviously, they have moved on from what happened, or they wouldn't even be considering you for a mission like this."

"I know. But none of that matters. They don't know me," Axien replied, shaking his head. "Roxus does. And I broke his trust. I put you in danger. He may never forgive me for that. I just … I had hoped he would see that I …" His voice trailed off, and his mouth twisted bitterly to one side.

"That you're trying to make up for it?" I guessed.

"Gods, it sounds even more pathetic out loud," he muttered.

It was, sort of.

I understood where he was coming from, though. I just couldn't wrap my mind around why he valued Roxus's opinion more than anyone else's. More than Mistress Orvana's. More than his own tandem's.

Sure, it might have bothered me if Curator Vanora didn't like me—but most people didn't, so it wasn't going to keep me up at night. Axien, on the other hand, must have been far more accustomed to people instinctively liking him. That, or he felt like he owed Roxus now.

And I seriously doubted Roxus would be accepting kisses as apologies or repayment.

I certainly wouldn't have, either, but Axien hadn't really given me much of a choice. Now, it was best to keep a healthy distance and not think about it.

"Is that why you look like crap today? Staying up all night fretting over what a grumpy old bear thinks about you?" I jabbed, trying to change the subject. If I teased him a little, maybe he would lighten up.

It usually worked with Declan, anyway.

Axien snorted and straightened, his arms draped limply across his lap. My gaze caught on those strange, dark veins that spread out over the tops of his hands. Granted, they were faint. Barely noticeable unless you knew what you were looking for.

But I'd seen them too many times now to mistake them for anything else.

Had he been practicing his magic? Using too much of it? I wanted to ask, but all the words seemed to tangle in my throat.

"The not sleeping is part of it, I suppose," Axien admitted. "Look, I know you're not happy I'm being handed personal missions, but to be clear, I did not ask for this. The only reason I agreed to it at all is because Curator Vanora insisted. According to her, I'm not in a good position to be refusing anything that's asked of me just yet. Not when it comes directly from Mistress Orvana, anyway."

Ah. Fair point.

"What's the other part, then?" I asked.

Using too much magic again—that had to be the real reason. He wouldn't admit it, though. He'd never liked talking about his magic, and not much had changed on that front.

"I'd rather not go into that," he mumbled, angling his face away. His hands squeezed into fists for a second, making the muscles of his forearms flex against his dark leather bracers. Veins stood out against the exposed skin of his elbows, although they weren't dark like the ones on the tops of his hands.

"We're a little beyond you keeping secrets at this point," I snapped. "You've asked me to come along, wear a fancy gown, and watch your back. The least you can do is level with me."

Axien didn't reply or even face me again. He just sat there, giving me the back of his head like a sulking child. Unbelievable.

I resisted the urge to yank on that braid of his.

"Fine. Keep your stupid secrets, then," I fumed and turned away, too.

Ridiculous—this was ridiculous! Why was he still throwing up walls like this? Hadn't I earned more? Idiot. Better just to drop it. Pushing the issue with him only made things worse, and I was not up for an argument this early in the day.

"I will level with you, Violet," he answered at last. "Just not now. Not yet."

I rolled my eyes. Whatever.

I panned my gaze across the docks, watching the sailors pull in the gangplank and begin calling orders. Below the passenger deck, fifty oarsmen slid their long, broad wooden paddles through portholes on either side of the ferry. They bristled outward like spines on a lionfish, rippling and moving as one.

My mind slid into numbness, surrendering to the warm tug of the sea breeze that teased through my hair and brushed over my skin. The boat rocked, forging out of the shelter of the harbor and into the strong currents as the oarsmen below chanted to keep the rhythm of their rowing synced.

Salty spray peppered my lips and misted over my face and neck, and I closed my eyes to drink it all in. To feel the rock and sway of the boat's hull under my feet. To breathe in the heavy, damp sea air and let it saturate me inside and out.

The mournful cries of gulls followed us all the way out of Sol'Karr's busy bay, past the colossal stone replica of Undae, Goddess of the Sea, that stood guard at the entrance. With her face pointed into the strong northern wind and a conch shell to her lips, it was as though she'd risen from the sea floor and been frozen in place there.

Beyond the bay, the waves intensified. The oarsmen chanted louder, stomping their feet as they battled the swift current that immediately swept us to the west. Our ferry, along with all the other ships navigating Rienka's waters this time of year, had no choice but to cooperate with the powerful currents. To use them rather than fight a losing battle against them.

It made the journey go faster, though.

We made good time across the open water, passing smaller fishing boats and majestic merchant galleons with their sails spread to the morning sun. It didn't take long for Kosaar to rise into view as we cruised south, and the ferry's crew began shouting orders to prepare for arrival.

They walked the rows of passengers with little baskets, collecting payment and tips for passage. Axien tossed two coins in for us, but didn't say another word until our boat had finally sidled up to a dock in Kosaar's marketside harbor.

Overall, Kosaar was about the same size as Sol'Karr, but it was far flatter and had more level ground for buildings. The largest of them all rose at its center like a giant, round bowl made of smooth, golden-colored stone. The sight of it put a stab of unease through my chest.

I'd never seen it before. At least, not this closely. But there wasn't a soul in Rienka who didn't know what that building was ... or what it represented.

Everyone called it the Caldera, and its high walls were lined with sweeping staircases and endless rows of steeply sloping seats around a central, circular colosseum. There, on a battlefield of blood-soaked sand, gladiators, criminals, war prisoners, and runaway slaves were set against one another in fights to the death.

Sometimes they were fed to monsters or strange beasts from foreign lands. Sometimes they were made to run gauntlets of traps. But according to Declan, no matter what the poor souls sent to fight in that arena were forced to do, the ending was always the same: they died, the crowds cheered, and an old man named Amandris, who owned it all, made mountains of coin.

A man who had one son, set to inherit it all.

Sulam.

I'd heard that Sulam's family owned a massive estate that butted up right against the Caldera, with a grand balcony that overlooked the arena floor so they could drink expensive wines and watch every fight. I'd never seen it, of course—the estate or the Caldera. Not up close, anyway.

Hopefully, I never would.

Declan had mentioned how much he feared the place. How he dreaded that, one day, Sulam might get tired of him and throw him in that arena for one final battle. The one that would end his life … and by extension, his little sister's.

The idea stung at my mind like a hornet trapped under glass, frantic and angry and attacking anything it could. Any shred of my sanity would be a swollen, throbbing blister until I got back and figured out what to do with him.

After what had happened before, when Sulam nearly killed him to send a message to me, I'd stayed well away from Sulam's slavers. I had no choice. As much as I despised it, Sulam's show of strength had worked. I couldn't risk him going after Declan like that ever again. It had only been chance—pure dumb luck—that I'd gotten to him before he died.

And Leruna was the only reason he was still alive at all.

Sulam had found a weak spot in my armor, so I had no choice but to keep a distance. I'd left Sulam's disgusting slave traders alone. And things had been quiet on that front ever since.

Too quiet.

But when I got back, I'd be making plenty of noise.

Nine

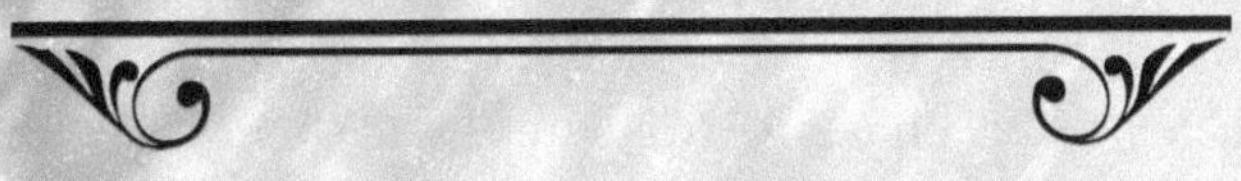

"Time to move," Axien said.

He nudged my arm, jostling me back to reality. I cringed away from the contact, and he gave me a tense, almost curious look as he stood and picked up his bag again.

Oh. Right. I guess I'd been too caught up in my own head to realize we'd passed the entire journey without saying another word.

I gathered my things, too, and followed him off the ferry and onto the crowded harbor of Kosaar's northern docks. The midday sun was high in the sky, and the heat wavered off the cobblestone streets as we moved inland. The smell of sizzling street meats, baskets of fresh spices, and the ever-present pungent brine of freshly caught fish poured over me in waves. The chatter of shoppers and merchants, haggling over prices, was a constant buzz.

All of it seemed to converge, crashing in on me all at once. Too late, I realized it had been a long time since I'd left Sol'Karr—since I'd left Arx Eburna or Roxus's house, actually.

By the time we wriggled free of the crowds, my head was

spinning, and I could barely keep up with Axien's longer strides. After a few minutes, he seemed to notice that, as well. He stopped, turning back and offering a hand to pull me along.

I frowned at it, then up at him, and shook my head.

We did not touch. Not after last time.

Axien's face slowly melted from a look of roguish amusement to confusion. His hand fell back to his side, and I could feel his gaze still on me as I fell in step beside him.

But I didn't look back.

It took a few hours to walk to the other side of the island along the crooked, twisty rat's nest of ancient roads that were thrown like a tangled net over it. Little streets seemed to double back on themselves, or dead-end out of nowhere, and we got turned around a few times and had to stick our heads into shops to ask for directions.

Or, rather, Axien stuck his head in.

That stupid, broad, handsome smile of his always won people over. I did well just keeping my head down and my red Viperi eyes out of sight. No need to terrify the locals just to figure out whether we needed to take a left or a right at the next intersection.

By the time we reached Kosaar's eastern shore, my clothes were damp with sweat, and my vision was swimming. My throat scraped with every breath, raw with thirst. My feet slid inside my boots, my socks drenched through.

Axien must have noticed, because he made a big show of finding us a spot in the shade in a small park about a mile from the main harbor. He threw down his stuff and announced he was going to find us something to eat before he strode off.

I watched him go, hating the way his every movement seemed so assured, smooth, and quietly powerful. That quiet elven grace seemed to come so naturally to him. I wondered if he even realized how people stared at him when he passed, as though his presence alone was enough to bewitch them.

A magic that oozed out of his every pore and drew people in like ants to sugar.

Fates, I just hoped I didn't stare at him like that. Embarrassing.

Sitting in a grassy spot in the shade of a little tree, I peeled off my boots and sweat-soaked socks so I could let my feet breathe a bit.

Ugggh. So much better.

I wiggled my toes in the cool grass and spread my socks out so they might dry a little before we had to get moving again.

We had one more, slightly longer ferry ride to reach Esfolar. But if everything went according to plan, and no one tried to kill us, we should get to the city and settle into an inn tonight. Then, tomorrow, the real work would begin.

Hopefully, we could find a bathhouse so I could get myself cleaned up from travel, and I'd put on whatever nightmare of a dress Curator Vanora had sent along for me to wear. We'd attend the soiree tomorrow evening, receive the artifact, and be gone like fog at sunrise before anyone was the wiser.

"I hope you like lamb," Axien said as he returned with four hand-sized meat pies wrapped in waxy paper. "I got two for now and two for later."

He handed me my share, and I wasted no time cramming my face full of flaky, buttery pie crust that was folded like a pocket filled with slow-roasted lamb, gravy, and spiced potatoes. I downed half my waterskin before I finally flopped back onto the grass with my arms, legs, and pasty bare feet spread wide.

"If you were that hungry, you should have said something," Axien chuckled as he nibbled away at his own lunch.

"According to you, I'm always that hungry," I deadpanned, closing my eyes to bask in the cool breeze that tickled through my pruny toes.

"And angry," he added, his tone prickly.

Minutes slipped by in silence, and I'd almost convinced myself I could steal a quick nap while he finished eating. After all, it wasn't like anyone would mess with us out here in the open. There were other couples and families seated around the park, having their lunches, too.

Not that, uh, we were a couple. Nooo. Not even a little.

"So you're worried about that Holvradix fellow, eh? Is that what's got you so snappy lately?" Axien blurted, his tone so painfully awkward it made me crack an eye open to peer up at him.

He'd already turned his face away again, hiding his expression from my view. Gods, that was getting old.

I'd show him snappy.

"Half-Holvradix," I corrected, since he was always so quick to make that distinction about his own heritage. "And yes. Sort of."

"He seemed fit enough the last time we saw him fight," Axien mumbled around a mouthful of his food. "But you sent that healer woman, Leruna, to look in on him?"

"I did." I didn't want to give him any ammunition to lob back at me, so I kept my answers short. To the point. No lies, but also no extra details or justifications, just like he did with me and his magic.

He seemed dead set on keeping his secrets, so I'd keep mine.

It's not like he knew Declan anyway. As far as I knew, the last exchange they'd had was when Declan had punched him across the face.

Gods, I wish I could have seen that.

"Violet, if something is going on with him—" he started to speak.

I cut him off quickly. "There isn't."

"Then why—?"

"I don't want to talk about it," I snapped, pushing myself upright and beginning to slide my slimy, sweaty, cold socks back onto my feet. Gross.

Axien sat still, half his meat pie in his hand, as his blue-flame gaze held squarely on me. I could practically feel it, like a ghostly brush against my skin, as he watched my every move. Every twitch in my brow. Every pulse in the angry vein that was probably standing out against the side of my neck.

Varren had teased me about that before.

Apparently, that's how he could tell when I was about to start taking cheap shots during our sparring matches, so he had to tap out or get ready to visit the healer again.

Hah. As if I needed to take cheap shots to put him on his rear.

"How long has it been since you last saw him?" Axien asked quietly.

I flashed him a glare of warning. "I said I don't want to talk about—"

"How long?" he demanded again, matching the venom in my voice drop for drop.

Anger rippled through my body, but I kept my expression empty. Why was he pushing this? Why did it even matter to him? Was he jealous?

No, of course not. That was idiotic. This was something else.

But what?

"Right before we left," I growled bitterly. "Roxus and I went to see him fight."

"And? How did he seem?" he pressed.

"Not good." I frowned down at my boot, jerking the laces roughly into place.

"Not good how?" Axien asked, lips pursing thoughtfully.

"He's lost a lot of weight," I replied dryly, hating that I'd let him wring this much of the truth out of me so easily. "I don't think Sulam is feeding him enough. Or letting him rest between his matches."

I doubted Sulam actually fed Declan anything, let alone let him rest. I kept that thought to myself, though. The more I volunteered, the more Axien would ask. The more he'd want to know about Declan's past, his current situation, and my involvement in all of it. And I would not tell Axien—or anyone else—about what had happened right before our last mission.

Not even Leruna knew the full extent of it. Yes, she'd been there when he was injured. She was the one who had saved his life—giving him that thornwine potion had undoubtedly dragged him back from the gods' doorstep. But she didn't know why he'd been targeted in the first place.

She didn't know it was my fault. No one did—except Sulam. And all I could do was pray he never breathed a word of it to anyone.

Or found a way to use it against me.

Axien stayed quiet while I finished lacing both my boots. He stared down at the half-eaten meat pie in his hand, studying it like he was trying to read divine omens in the arrangement of the potatoes and slivers of roasted lamb.

"Violet, if there's anything I can do to help—" he started to speak.

I didn't let him finish that thought.

"There isn't," I said sharply and got to my feet. "I'll handle it. It's not your problem."

"If it bothers you, then yes, it is my problem." His tone was firm. Resolved. Relentlessly defiant, as though daring me to argue otherwise.

It dragged my gaze back to his like gravity, forcing me to turn so I was facing him again.

"Why?" The question broke past all my better judgement.

Still seated on the grass, not two steps away from me, his expression dissolved from that razor-edged frustration to a soft, knowing smile that tilted the corners of his mouth crookedly.

I wasn't his problem.

And I'd make sure I never was.

Ten

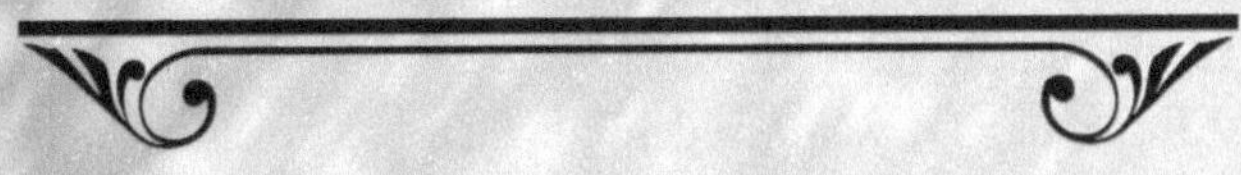

I couldn't breathe.

Standing at the bow of our second ferryboat, I stared out across the deep, white-capped waves at the monument of dark stone that rose from the depths like a spire of black crystal as the rhythm of chants and stomping thrummed under my feet like a pulse.

Just the sight of it made my blood run cold. Made every muscle in my body lock up solid and all the wind rush out of me at once.

Necrolis Prison.

I'd glimpsed it before, months ago. That had been at night and from much farther away, though, so there wasn't much to see. Now, it felt close—too close. Like I might be able to catch the echoes of screams on the wind that tore ruthlessly across the surface of the water.

I gripped the boat's railing until my knuckles blanched and my fingertips went numb, searching every hard edge of the huge, windowless fortress for some sign of life. But there was nothing. No lights or torches burning anywhere. No guards patrolling. No banners flying. Not even the gulls dared to land on any of the exposed reef surrounding the base of the structure.

Just a spear of dark stone against a blood-red sunset.

My heart twisted deep in my chest. I bit down hard.

Chrysa was in there, caged in the darkness. She'd spend the rest of her life there. Unless, of course, the Tibran Empire invaded Rienka. They might set her free. Or, they might kill her for her failure instead.

After what I'd witnessed High General Crassus do to his soldiers and to Sanja, it seemed like a toss-up.

"I heard some of the senior agents talking about what happened with her," Axien said as he wandered over to lean against the railing beside me. "About what happened when they brought her to trial before Mistress Orvana and the elders. They said she was utterly expressionless the entire time. No tears. No begging or pleading. She didn't even say a word to plead her case."

Somehow, that didn't surprise me.

Chrysa had been that way—cold and distant—even when she was pretending to be my friend. As though the tether between her and all of her emotions had been cut a long time ago.

"Do you still dream about her?" Axien asked, his tone cautious. "Before, you would whimper in your sleep. Sometimes you'd even cry out. Usually, it was her name."

"Sometimes." My throat burned as I swallowed hard.

"What does she say to you in your dreams?" He sounded genuinely curious, and his arm brushed against mine. It might have been an accident because of how the ferryboat was bobbing and fighting the late evening wind.

But I wasn't taking any chances. I took a side step away from him, just for good measure.

Axien's jawline tensed. He looked down, brow furrowing in a pensive frown as he watched the rippling line of long oars below us, all moving together against the wind and waves.

"I, uh, I'm sorry. I shouldn't ask personal things like that," he said.

"No," I agreed. "You shouldn't."

His lips thinned as he turned to face me, one hand still gripping the rail. His chest rose and fell in slow, deep breaths, as if he were mustering the nerve or the anger to say something else. A storm of emotion flickered in his bright, gleaming eyes.

I braced for it.

A second passed. Then another.

"Vedra'tavas ..." he finally cursed in Damarian, hissing the word under his breath and shaking his head. He pushed away from the railing and walked away, his tall frame disappearing into the crowds of other passengers huddled on deck.

My heart gave another painful twist, making my mouth screw up as I watched him go. We couldn't go on like this. I knew that. Sooner or later, we'd have to clear the air and figure out how to work together.

But whatever tentative bond we'd begun to forge deep in the ruins beneath Dumathis had snapped. I wasn't even sure precisely when. Maybe when he'd thrown me down at Sanja's feet? Or when he'd kissed me and called it payment?

I could at least understand why he had pretended to betray me. But that kiss ... and calling it something he owed me? Like he hadn't wanted to but had no other choice? Gods, just thinking about it made my insides squirm and cramp. It felt dirty, shameful, and wrong—especially since I'd actually *enjoyed* it.

Shuddering, I pulled the hood of my cloak down to hide my face.

Whatever it was that had broken that bond between us, I had no idea how to start rebuilding it.

Or if I even wanted to.

For now, it was better to keep a distance. No touching. No personal talks about feelings. No sharing secrets.

Axien might not understand or like it, but that was too bad. He should have just kept his stupid lips to himself. The least he could do now was give me the space to figure out what was going on in my own head.

He did owe me that much.

I didn't see him again until the ferry docked at Esfolar's grand port. He stood at the end of the gangplank, searching the crowds of other passengers with his expression much softer and his dark eyebrows raised. With every group that passed, his demeanor seemed to stiffen and his features drew more tense. More anxious. As though he was worried I'd ditched him altogether.

Then our gazes locked, and my heartbeat gave a frantic little flutter.

His posture relaxed, and his mouth opened as though he were going to speak.

I quickly looked away.

Axien never said a word as I approached, sliding free of the traffic still exiting the ferry so I could stand beside him. He jerked his head to the side, gesturing for me to follow, and I fell in step as we dove headlong into the sprawling city.

The sun had already set behind us, but the horizon still glowed deep scarlet, orange, and purple as the last few rays of light gave way to a canopy of glittering stars. The failing light made the white stone streets and buildings shine like a tapestry of soft, warm pastels, and the countless twinkling lights of windows in sweeping estates and grand temples made it hard to tell where the sky ended and the buildings began.

We left the harbor along a broad avenue that sloped to the north, passing grand townhomes and elegant shops that lined either side of the sidewalk. All were closed for the night, lights only glowing through the drapes in the upper-floor windows.

No one else walked the sidewalks, and we didn't pass any carriages or wagons until we reached a square that was flanked on all sides by inns and upscale lounges.

There, the soft murmur of conversation and the aroma of tobacco smoke drifted out through open windows, mingling with the rush of water from the fountain in the middle of the square. Fine little carriages were parked along the curbs, with drivers in silk tunics sitting idly and puffing on their long pipes while they waited for their patrons.

We were a *long* way from the Rook's Roost.

I kept my head down and my hood pulled low as we made our way toward one of the inns. An intricately carved wooden sign hung over the door, depicting a crossed sword and feather in gold paint. My gaze caught on the sword, noting the symbol painted very carefully onto the pommel.

A crescent moon.

That couldn't be an accident, right? That they would include that on a sword that also happened to look a lot like the one in the Zenith Call's symbol?

A silver bell tinkled overhead as Axien pushed the door open, and I breathed in the fragrance of rich, spiced tea that filled the dim entryway. A large chandelier with a dozen colored glass globes hung overhead, and a fine wool rug stretched across the floor, ending at the base of a sweeping staircase that must have led up into the rest of the inn.

Fancy. Maybe a little *too* fancy for us.

My pulse fluttered, and I stole a glance at Axien. Was this really the right place? How could we even afford this? Had Curator Vanora made this reservation for us? Was she the one paying?

Gods, I hoped so. I only had a few coins on me, and I doubted that would even pay for a pot of tea in a place like this.

A plump little woman in a clean, white linen dress greeted

us from behind a tall counter, taking Axien's name with a bright, albeit cautious smile. Something secretive twinkled in her golden Damarian eyes as he pulled a coin from his pocket and slid it across the counter to her. The faint blue glow gave it away even before I saw the mark of the Zenith's Call etched into its surface.

A stemma.

She took it and immediately whisked it away, too fast for anyone to notice.

"Ah, yes. I see. We received your letter early this morning," she said as she pretended to check a large, red leather-bound book for our reservation. "You've got a lovely suite on the third floor. I'll ring a maid to show you up. Will you be wanting a bath drawn tonight? Or a meal? We also offer a full service for tea and wine, if you like."

"A bath and wine, if it's no trouble," Axien said, flashing one of those dazzling smiles that seemed to work like a magic all its own.

It certainly worked on her, anyway.

Her full cheeks went rosy, and she stumbled all over herself as she called for one of the maids to show us upstairs.

The maid, who looked like she might be close to my age, didn't seem as enthralled with him, though. She kept her head down and gaze averted as she bowed and led the way to the third floor, giving soft instructions about where the dining hall and washrooms were, how we could call for any service we might need, and that they would be happy to clean our traveling clothes if we wanted.

Fates, was this how all the nobles lived?

I gaped at the long halls lined with polished, dark wood paneling, glittering chandeliers with dangling crystals of colored glass, and plush wool carpets. Even the door to our room looked like something pulled from a castle, with an ornate golden knob adorned with filigree wreathed around the face of a lion.

The young maid unlocked it and stood aside, waiting for us to enter before she held the key out for Axien to take.

I almost crashed into his back when he suddenly stopped short in the doorway, blocking my view. What the—?

"Uhh, there ... there must be a mistake," Axien stammered.

I peered under his arm, squinting into the gloom of the room. It was wide and spacious, just as grand as the rest of this place. A fire already burned low in the marble pit set into the floor to the left, giving off a radiant glow that filled the space with deep shadows. Large animal skin rugs stretched across the floor, and fine velvet cushions were placed for seating around a low table under the wide window.

To the right, a massive bed spanned nearly the entire wall. Claw-footed nightstands stood on either side, and a lavish canopy of draped deep purple silks hung over it, suspended by golden ropes and loops.

A mistake? Had he completely lost his mind? This was the most beautiful suite I'd ever seen in my life. Fates, I wasn't even sure if I was allowed to touch any of it, let alone sink into that plush, downy-stuffed bed, and—

Oh.

Oh no.

"There's only *one* bed," Axien said, facing the maid with a frazzled look of panic.

"Yes, sir," the maid said as she dropped the key into his hand and gave a low curtsy. "Please let us know if there is anything more you require."

Axien and I both stood, mouths open, watching the maid speed away back down the hall without another word. She disappeared into the gloom of the stairwell, footsteps all but soundless on the fine carpets.

Then, slowly, I dragged my gaze over to meet his. Heat flooded my cheeks, blazing down my neck, over my chest, and tingling all the way to my scalp.

A joke. This had to be someone's idea of a terrible, disgusting joke. Vanora's? No, no—she wasn't the type to scheme like this. Axien's, then?

The slack-jawed, pasty look of horror on his face made it hard to tell. Either he was the best actor in all of Reatia, or he had not planned for this either.

He blinked owlishly a few times, mouth slowly closing. Then his back went straight, and his expression drew into a tense, wild-eyed look of determination.

"No, this ... this is fine. Just fine," he said, nodding and muttering like he was trying to convince himself. "It's a huge bed. And it's only for one night."

"I am *not* sleeping with you," I growled, crossing my arms.

"No, no. It ... it won't be like that. I'll stay on top of the blankets. We'll be far apart," he reasoned, tone still fast and frantic as he stepped into the room ahead of me. "If you think about it, we've slept much closer together in bedrolls in the back of wagons, right?"

I narrowed my eyes, not budging from the doorway.

"And we can build a wall between us," he added quickly.

I arched an eyebrow. "A wall of what?"

"Cushions. Pillows. Our bags. Whatever it takes," he said as he wandered to the middle of the room and dropped his belongings in a heap at the foot of the bed. His face was still pasty, and he scratched at the back of his head as he turned in a slow circle, taking in the rest of the lavish space.

"It'll be fine," he repeated. "Just fine."

"I hate you sometimes," I muttered as I stomped into the room after him, closing the door with my foot.

"This isn't my fault!" Axien blurted. "I'm not trying anything, I swear! I told them there would be two of us! I just assumed they'd know that meant we needed two beds. For two people—two *separate* people. And it is a nice room, isn't it? Vanora said this was an excellent place to stay, and ..."

I quit listening as he rambled on and on, making long strings of panicked excuses while he walked the perimeter of the room like a chicken being chased around a yard.

Gods, spare me. Deliver me from this idiotic man.

Otherwise, this might be his last night alive, because if he dared to set so much as a toenail over the wall of pillows I would be building between us—I would murder him. I'd tell everyone back at Arx Eburna that he'd run off into the night and disappeared without a trace.

And no one would ever be the wiser.

"Give me the brief on the artifact," I said as I chose one side of the bed, the one closest to the door, and threw my bag down. Might as well get to work. "I want to look over it while I'm in the bath."

"You're really okay with this?" Axien asked, eyeing me suspiciously as he began to rummage through his belongings. He pulled out a small, yellowed scroll of old parchment and held it out to me.

Already armed with a silk chemise to change into after my bath, I faced him with a cold, disapproving scowl of warning —just in case he decided to look for any false hope in this mess.

"With sharing a bed with you? No. But I'm not a child. We're here to work. That's it," I said and swiped the scroll from his hand.

"And what is that?" He nodded to the chemise.

"A broken nose, as far as you're concerned," I warned.

"You're not sleeping in your fighting leathers?" His throat bobbed, mouth scrunching to one side uncomfortably.

"Should I be? You're the one who said this mission wasn't dangerous," I reminded him. "If you were lying to me—"

Axien drew back a step, shaking his head and waving me off. "No, no! It's not that. You're right. I just ... well, it doesn't matter. We can discuss the mission later."

"You're not taking a bath?" I wrinkled my nose. I'd spent the day sweating puddles into my boots. My skin was caked with grit and sea salt. My hair was practically crunchy now because of it.

I could not fathom that he wasn't in a similar state.

"I will," he hedged, avoiding eye contact. "Eventually."

Oh. Right. He'd always been weird about bathing—something I'd written off as a strange, probably foreign preference. He was originally from Tibrus, after all.

Or was he? I'd never asked about that, or where the Aurati had raised him initially.

Whatever the case, it wasn't my problem. He could look after himself.

"Suit yourself," I said and spun on a heel, leaving him standing in the room alone.

The instant the door clicked shut behind me, I heard the creak of the bed like he'd sat down on the edge of it, followed by a long, low, growling breath.

I froze, holding my breath to listen. Nothing. No movement. No sound at all.

Nearly a minute passed before I dared to lean down and peer through the keyhole, back into the room.

Okay, fine. It was creepy. Invasive, too, probably. But something about the weight of that silence beyond the door made my skin prickle with unease. I needed answers.

I needed to be sure he wasn't deceiving me again.

Squinting through the keyhole, I spotted Axien sitting on the edge of the bed, hunched forward with his head in his hands. He rubbed his temples and jaw, his features drawn into a fierce, intensely focused frown. It was almost a grimace of pain.

He muttered something so faint I couldn't make it out, then began unlacing his vambraces one at a time. He threw them down onto his bag and rolled up his sleeves, hands shaking and breath hissing and catching as he did.

Black veins covered his forearms, spreading and growing gradually darker as they snaked up to his elbows. I'd only spotted a few of them faintly mottling the tops of his hands, and it seemed like most of them had been covered. Gods, I hadn't realized how bad they were or how far they'd spread.

He let out a gasping whimper as he flexed his hands, clenching and unclenching his fists. His expression seized, and he finally let his arms fall limp into his lap again. His chest heaved deeply, nostrils flared, brow glistening with a sheen of fresh sweat as he stared into the glowing coals that smoldered in the fire pit.

My stomach clenched hard. I gripped the scroll of paper in my hand tightly, resisting the urge to fling the door back open and storm in so we could work this out.

Sooner or later, we had to talk about it. Whatever was happening to him, whatever had put those marks on his skin, it was getting worse. It was causing him pain.

It might even be killing him.

And we had to find a way to stop it. I needed him to at least talk about it.

We had to find some path back to trusting each other again ... before his time ran out.

Part Two
Declan

Eleven

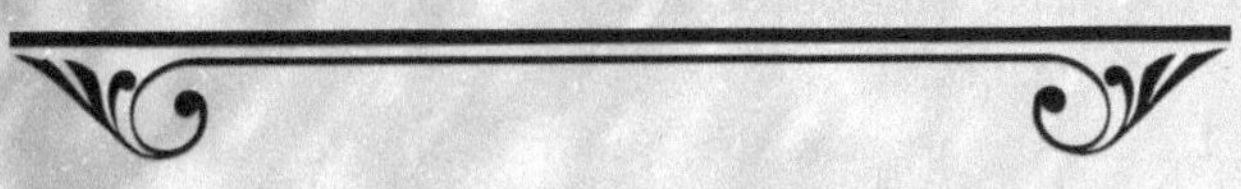

Every breath was agony.

My head swam, and there wasn't a single part of my body that wasn't throbbing.

A sharp pang of pain shot through my chest as I shambled to my feet. Probably another fractured rib. The constant ache in my jaw from a hard right hook yesterday likely meant I'd knocked something loose there, too. And my stupid leg—curse it—still felt stiff and numb from the break. It threatened to buckle if I put too much strain on it.

But all of it was drowned out by the pounding, aching, and relentless hammering of my pulse in my temples as I slowly raised my head. I squinted into the glare of the ambient torchlight, turning to look across the roaring crowds seated all around the pit.

Nobles, aristocrats, fat merchants, and their dolled-up mistresses and courtesans threw fistfuls of gold coins down on the tabletops. They chanted my name. They loved it all—the way my bare upper body was dappled in bruises, the way my freshly busted lip and nose bled, and how I raised my battered fist to them in victory.

They screamed louder. More coins flew.

Sick freaking monsters, all of them.

I sucked in a ragged breath, nearly choking on the pipe smoke that hung as thick as fog in the room. A few hundred unfamiliar faces turned into a writhing blur until I shook my head, forcing my vision to clear. Curse it. I'd taken a few solid hits to the face. One of them had my left eye pulsing and probably turning black.

I cut a glare toward Sulam's private box, where he normally sat like a bloated toad king on a too-small throne. It was empty tonight, though.

I frowned and spat into the sand before turning back to the crowd.

Good. Maybe I'd finally catch a break.

A few more easy matches and I'd get my pathetic ration of coins for my trouble, barely enough for a meal and a bath. Then I could go back to the rotting, soggy hole I called a home. Debt paid. Night over.

I'd settle for that and a bottle of cheap wine. It was the best I could hope for these days, unless Sulam was here. Lately, he'd been pushing me harder than ever. More fighters. Meaner opponents. Sometimes he even allowed weapons.

So far, he hadn't forced me to outright kill anyone, thank the gods. I wasn't an executioner. I'd beat someone all the way to the god's doorstep if that's what it took to keep Sulam's slimy hands off my little sister, but no one died in the pit.

Not intentionally, anyway.

Accidents happened, of course. I couldn't say for sure that no one I'd beaten didn't succumb to their injuries later, but that was never my intent. Whatever happened after they left this pit was out of my control.

A busty young woman in a red velvet corset leaned over the edge of the pit, offering a tankard of frothy, lukewarm ale down to me along with a very generous view of her assets. I took it, downed a swallow, and poured the rest over my head. It made her giggle, cheer, and bounce—which made for an even nicer view.

I still had a pulse, after all.

She joined in the chanting of my name as I handed the empty tankard back and strolled to the middle of the pit, shaking out my arms and adjusting the bloodstained wraps on my knuckles.

Back to work.

The security guards were already dragging my last victim away by his heels, his face swollen beyond recognition. He'd need a healer unless he wanted to lose the arm I'd broken at the elbow. Somehow, I doubted anyone would offer him that courtesy, though. Not here.

Here, help only came if you were the last one standing.

I flexed my shoulders, using the back of my hand to wipe the sweat from my brow as the fight-caller began announcing the next round. No break this time, apparently.

Fine. Better to get this over with as soon as possible.

"Tonight, we have a special treat for all of you," the fight-caller crowed as he spread his arms wide, waving for the crowds to hush. "You all well know what evil threatens this land! The beast in the north hungers, spreading tendrils of his wicked schemes throughout the world. You know of whom I speak."

The cheering faded, replaced with a cacophony of disgusted hisses and boos.

"Argonox, Emperor of Tibrus, has already begun his vicious siege of Nar'Haleen. Soon, we know he will turn his gaze upon us. He would seek to ruin us all. And what message shall we send in return? That we cower in fear?" The fight-caller paused for a beat of heavy, uncomfortable silence.

Then a cruel, wide smile curled up his lips. "Well, I, for one, propose we send him this!"

He flung a hand toward the entrance, where a few of Sulam's personal guards were wrestling someone through the crowd toward the pit. The booing and hissing grew louder, then turned to angry shouts and spitting. Someone threw a tankard.

The crowd parted and I finally saw him.

The man dangling between Sulam's guards already looked half-dead. By the time they dragged him to the edge of the pit, he'd quit struggling and stared down at me with wide-eyed horror.

My lip curled. My shoulders bowed, hands clenching at my sides as I studied him.

A Tibran.

Not just a runaway or refugee, though. Not in that armor.

One glimpse of that black scale mail, the sharply angled pauldrons, and red-trimmed jerkin hit me like a punch to the throat. Every muscle locked up solid. My ears rang.

Th-that was ... the same armor my father had worn when I'd last seen him, nearly eight years ago.

This man was Darksteel Guard. High-ranking Tibran Infantry. Had they captured him somehow? Or just dressed up some poor idiot and turned him into a scapegoat for everyone here to take all their hate and rage out on?

No—that couldn't be it.

The man looked older than me, probably somewhere in his mid-thirties, and he had the telltale Tibran mark branded into the side of his neck. A former slave-soldier? Or had Argonox always marked all his followers that way? Had he done it to my father, too?

I didn't know, but his brand was old and faded. Regardless of how he'd wound up here, this man had been in the Tibran ranks longer than most. And if that pasty expression of terror on his face was any indication, he knew exactly what was coming next.

"Captured from the front lines at the siege of Kansir, we present for your entertainment and just vengeance, a Tibran Field Captain. The fates may show mercy on his soul, but he will find none here! Only justice!" the fight-caller roared.

The crowd went mad, screaming and hurling insults at the captured Tibran.

The man shut his eyes, expression scrunching as though he were fighting to keep his composure as Sulam's guards stripped away layer after layer of armor, tossing it into the crowd like prizes, leaving him in nothing but breeches. Beneath it all, he was a decent size for a human—but so skinny you could count every rib. Argonox didn't see fit to feed his own men well?

I licked my teeth behind my lips, the coppery tinge of blood flavoring every swallow.

They forced him to his knees, revealing where Sulam stood right behind him, watching with a sickening smile. His beady eyes gleamed, glittering with wicked delight as they slowly panned to me. His wide lace collar framed his flabby neck, making him look like the world's most disgusting flower.

I knew what that look meant.

My stomach soured. I bit down hard against the urge to gag.

"Tonight, our champion will demonstrate what divine vengeance really looks like." The fight-caller gestured to me with a flourish. "This fight ... is to the death."

My stomach rolled again, and I dropped my gaze away—away from that Tibran man. Away from Sulam, who was grinning wider than ever. Away from the writhing hoard screaming for blood and loving every second of this.

Damn all of them straight to Vescor's abyssal pit.

"For this fight, we take no bets," the fight-caller announced. "But should you fine folk feel led to show your gratitude to the one who has supplied this opportunity, we do humbly accept! And may it afford us more opportunities in the future to send our message to the throne of that beastly tyrant. Rienka spurns you! We reject you! And we join the voices of all the Southern Kingdoms to curse you!"

The guards seized the man by each arm, lifting and tossing him forward into the pit. He hit the ground with a thud, kicking up sand and sputtering as he scrambled to his feet not fifteen paces from me. His chest rose and fell with frantic, gasping breaths, and he whirled in a circle, eyes wild and shaking like a newborn fawn, searching for a way out.

But there was only one way out of Sulam's pit.

And that was through me.

"Face me," I growled low in the Tibran language. It felt strange and twisted, nearly foreign on my tongue.

It must have been years since I'd spoken it aloud, but no one would hear me over all the chaos from our captive audience. They'd assume I was taunting him.

He spun, backing up a few more steps as he took me in—my half-Holvradix height, my many scars, bruises, and all the blood spatter on my skin from tonight's previous matches.

Fates, to him, I must have looked like a towering, primal beast.

Or certain death.

"Wh-What is happening?" he gasped hoarsely.

"You're going to fight me," I growled, stretching my neck from one side to the other and making a show of prowling in a slow circle around him. "One of us is going to die. I don't really care which, but I can assure you ... I will do what I can to make yours quick. I'd appreciate it if you'd return the favor."

His whole body tensed, arms locked at his sides and hands curled into tight, shaking fists. He stared at me, expression skewing with panic. His mouth opened and closed, like he might try to speak or beg.

But he didn't get the chance.

From up on his raised platform, the fight-caller shouted over the noise, "FIGHT!"

My pulse kicked hard, wild and frantic, as adrenaline poured into my veins like cold fire. All the pains and aches of old injuries faded to numbness. My muscles twitched. My whole body flexed, bracing for what came next.

I stole a final glance at Sulam, standing between the two armor-bound thugs that served as his guards. His nostrils flared, as though he were drinking it all in. Relishing the bloodlust that hung thick in the air. His eyes squinted, narrowing slightly at me in unspoken threat.

I had no choice.

It was this man's life ... or my sister's.

Twelve

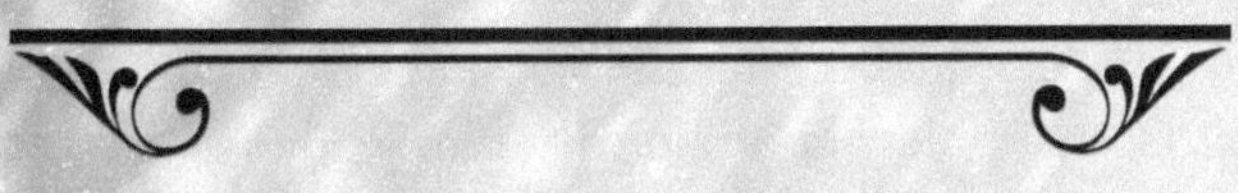

I had to hit first.

Move quick. Draw blood. Start the frenzy. End it fast. Get it done.

Nora's face flashed through my mind—her tear-filled eyes desperate and pleading as Sulam held her by a fistful of her long, dark red hair. So much smaller than I was. She was only six years old and I ... I'd stood there, fighting to get free. To get to her. But I had been too weak.

A useless, pathetic child of eleven years. All I could do to save her was offer myself in exchange. I'd sworn to do whatever Sulam wanted if he would just let her go.

My jaw clenched. My body was steel, blood burning hot in my veins as I stared at my opponent.

Kill him. Kill him now. If you do it quick, you won't remember it. Don't think, idiot, just do it!

I lunged, a primal cry ripping from my throat as all the bonds of my sanity snapped at once. I swung two sharp jabs, keeping my arms in close and my weight grounded in my heels.

He floundered, barely managing to feint back from the

blows. His whole body trembled as he drew his arms up, taking a defensive stance.

Interesting. So he had a little skill. He wasn't just some refugee they'd slapped in armor.

I moved in again, faster this time. My pulse thrashed, booming so loud it nearly drowned out the screams of our audience.

I struck again, ducking and weaving in for another punch at his face and a low hook aimed at his side. He dodged again, but staggered when the second hit made contact.

BAM!

Something crunched under the impact against my knuckles. Bone. Probably a rib or two.

He sucked in a ragged gasp and faltered, barely staying on his feet as his face went white with pain. He pitched forward, guard down.

BAM!

I hit him again. Another hook aimed at his jaw. His head snapped back, arms flailing wide as he fell like a freshly cut tree.

My opponent hit the sand flat on his back. His chest rose and fell with panicked breaths as I prowled in, still on the defense, with my weight in my heels.

"Get up," I snarled and spat on the ground next to his head.

He blinked slowly, blood running from between his lips as he stirred. He looked up at me, expression dazed.

Curse it.

I bared my teeth, stepping in and reaching to drag him up by the hair. "Get up!"

CRACK!

Pain exploded through my abdomen as he brought a knee up into my gut, right under my ribcage. Probably aiming for my groin, but missing by a hand's length.

Lucky me.

My vision spotted and I staggered back, wheezing through the waves of agony that threatened to drag me to my knees. My side. My ribs. They were broken. Broken badly. Any contact to that area—I couldn't stand it.

I fought for breath. My eyes watered. My vision tunneled.

The crowd screeched. They stomped their feet and beat on the tables.

When my vision finally began to clear, my opponent was on his feet again. He stared at me with his knees still shaking, keeping a distance as he watched me struggle, blood still dribbling down his chin.

"W-We don't have to do this," he gasped in Tibran. "We can get out of this. We can fight our way out together. We can be free."

My heart gave a violent twist. It made every muscle tense and my spine go stiff.

Hope—Fates, I hated it.

I clenched my jaw against the throbbing agony and forced myself to stand straight. To face him. To put my fists back up.

I was already injured. Surely he had noticed. He could kill me.

Do it. Just do it, you idiot!

I dove for him, fists flying. He scrambled away, able to evade my blows when the pain slowed my strikes. We whirled and spun, evading and striking, dipping and dodging. Moves and countermoves. A jab to his chin. A sad attempt to trip me with a foot hooked around mine.

Idiot. I was too big. Too heavy. He had seen my weakness. Why wouldn't he just exploit it? End this?

End me?!

The stench of sweat and blood saturated every desperate gasp for air. The noise of the crowd melted to a fuzzy, pulsing roar in my ears. The drumming of my heartbeat and the scrape of my breathing seemed so much louder.

"We can't keep this up forever!" The Tibran man stared at me, giving me that same awful, pleading stare she had.

Nora...

"THEN DO IT!" I roared louder.

He staggered back, withdrawing as his gaze darted down to my injured side. The awful black and purple bruise. Obvious swelling. One hit was all it would take. I would go down. He could choke me out, break my neck, whatever he wanted.

I'd be helpless to stop him.

Nora would forgive me. I'd done everything I could. I'd fought for so long, until the taste of blood in my mouth might as well have been water.

She had to forgive me ... for finally giving up. She would understand.

"Suit yourself," the Tibran man muttered through his teeth.

I braced for it. For him to rush in. Another kick or hit to my side. Pain. And then the end.

It would hurt. But so had everything else. At least this would be the end, and I could finally—

The Tibran man whirled on a heel and ran for the edge of the pit. His feet flew over the sand, face twisted in wild determination as he jumped with arms reaching up. He caught the edge of the pit with his fingertips. Just enough purchase to begin scrambling over the edge.

No. Oh, gods, no. No, no ...

NO!!

I started after him, staggering into a frantic run. Ten steps away. Six. Five.

Sulam's guards pushed through the crowd just as he got his upper body over the edge. The scrape of steel rang out as one of them drew his sword. Torchlight shimmered off the blade as he flipped it, caught it by the blade, reared back, and swung.

CRACK!

The crunch of bone on metal instantly froze me in place—three paces away.

The Tibran man's head snapped back. Blood sprayed through the air, spattering my face. He hit the ground in front of me, eyes open. Mouth agape.

The crowd went silent.

He started to shake all over. Seizing harder and harder. His eyes were wide as bloody foam came from his mouth.

Then he went still.

His eyes, still wide open, stared up at me. Unblinking. Empty.

A second passed. My heart refused to beat. All I could do was stand there, utterly paralyzed, and gawk down at him.

Then the crowd around the pit began to cheer again. Over the noise, the fight-caller declared me the victor. Coins fell like glittering rain. They chanted my name again and again.

But I couldn't move.

I couldn't think. Fates, I-I couldn't even—

"JUSTICE! JUSTICE!" the crowd screamed.

I blinked, my body jerking as the word struck me like a blow to the back of the head. My knees wobbled as I turned to stare out at the crowd. At hundreds of red, drunken faces I didn't know. Nobles. Aristocrats. Courtesans and mistresses. Merchant lords and their cold-eyed guards. Someone in a pale blue hooded cloak that didn't seem to fit in with the rest of the audience.

My eyes instinctively landed on the empty table where Violet and Roxus should have been.

I … needed her to be there. One look would be enough. I'd be grounded. Anchored to someone who saw this filth for what it was. Who wasn't afraid to recoil at it. To acknowledge it.

But she wasn't here. She hadn't been for weeks now.

Her seat was empty.

And, gods, so was I.

Thirteen

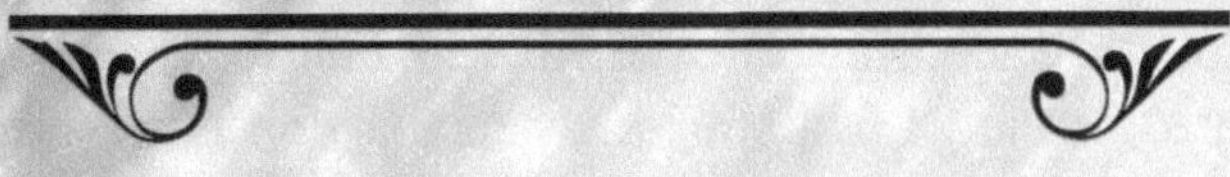

I shouldn't be alive.

Not if the gods had any sense of honor. Not if anything in this world was just and good.

The corpse Sulam's henchmen dragged out of that pit should have been mine. But it wasn't. I was still here.

Sitting alone in the dark, cramped staging room, I stared at the bloodstained strips of cloth wrapped around my knuckles. It wasn't mine. Neither was the spatter on my chest and arms.

My stomach lurched, and I clenched my teeth against a cold shudder that crept up my spine. It left my ears ringing as flashes blurred through my mind. Visions of what had just happened replayed like a scream echoing through the depths of a cave.

His face frozen in a look of terror. The way he had convulsed. The gurgling of his death rattle through bloody foam. The silence of the crowd watching, while not a single soul made a move to help him.

Not even me.

I was no better than them.

At least that Tibran man had possessed enough mad

courage to try to escape. What had I done? Nothing, that's what. I'd played this disgusting game over and over, knowing it was all in vain. Eventually, I'd lose. And then my deal with Sulam would be over.

And my baby sister, Nora—she would be at Sulam's mercy.

I hung my head, shame like a cold hand squeezing my lungs. I had given up. I'd wanted it to end, for that Tibran man to end me. I had been ready to abandon Nora just for rest.

My mouth screwed up. Blinking, breathing, my own heart beating—all of it hurt. Every part of me seemed to throb with agony. Streams of sweat ran from my hair, down my cheeks, and dripped off the end of my nose.

I couldn't keep doing this. But I couldn't stop, either. There was no escape. No mercy. No end.

"Well, well. Here he sits, victorious yet again. How's my favorite blunt instrument doing?" Sulam's throaty voice hacked a chuckle as he stepped into the staging room.

The bulging velvet purse on his belt clattered with every lurching step he took toward me. Probably packed full of coins. Blood money.

I didn't look up from where I sat on an old wooden bench set against the wall when he stopped before me. Normally, I'd have a line of other fighters sitting next to me, ready to take our turns as the fight-caller arranged the matches.

But today was a new nightmare. Sulam was apparently hand choosing my opponents now. He'd put that man into the pit to send a message. He'd claimed it was justice against the invading Tibran Empire. But I wasn't stupid. Sulam never did anything without an ulterior motive. He always had an angle, an end goal, and ten ways of screwing with everyone so he wound up on top.

I just had no idea what his game or goals were this time.

"Got off easy with that one, didn't you, boy?" Sulam jabbed when I didn't speak up. "I wouldn't call that a victory or even a fight. More like a pathetic display."

"You're the one tossing terrified Tibran soldiers into the pit. I doubt that will earn you much in bets if you keep that up. People pay to see a real fight, not mindless slaughter," I muttered. My nose scrunched as I caught a whiff of him—that sickly sweet cologne mixed with sour sweat and wine.

Putrid.

He made another phlegmy, hacking noise and spat on the ground right next to my foot. "Bold words from the coward who let him run. But then, I suppose I should've known a deserter wouldn't have much fight in him. He pissed himself the second we put him in chains."

I didn't reply, gritting my teeth as I waited for him to get to the point.

A startled groan leaked past my lips as Sulam suddenly grabbed a fistful of my hair and jerked my head back, forcing me to meet his gaze. Those black, empty eyes bored into mine, bottomless and unfeeling like a shark. His lip twitched and his cheeks above his sparse, oily beard flushed purple with anger.

"Don't think for one second I didn't see you holding back," Sulam seethed. "What's wrong? Not quite man enough to stomach real combat? All these fights, beating and breaking one man after another, but deep down, you're still nothing but a useless child."

I forced myself to think past the rage that scorched my tongue like hot cinders. Past the urge to throttle him to death with my bare hands and sling his carcass into the middle of that pit for all his beloved patrons to see.

Gods knew I wanted it. To be the one watching him draw that final breath. For him to know it was my doing—that I had been the one to send him to Clysiros's feet.

But I couldn't. Not when he still had Nora locked away in his estate.

"You want me to end it quick?" I rasped. "Fine, then. But we both know your customers like a show. I was doing my job, doing you a favor by—"

He jerked my hair harder, dragging me from my seat onto my knees before him.

"A show? Hah! Haven't you heard? War is coming, boy. The Tibran armies advance closer by the day. Having a few of their captured deserters put down is good for public morale, and my patrons appreciate the patriotism," he sneered. "They want to see them crushed like roaches. So next time, don't play with your food. Got it? Not unless you want me to start playing with mine."

My lip curled. My fists tightened until they shook. But I didn't move. I didn't resist.

"Eight years I've put up with you—only because you made decent money. The betters like you. But now I wonder how they would feel about you if they were to learn that you were also a Tibran, hm? Would they still cheer and chant your name? Or would they wish to see your brains spattered all over my arena floor? Maybe they'd prefer to see you in the Caldera, eh?"

My stomach turned to lead.

Sulam's beady eyes glinted in the weak light, alight with glee as they held my gaze. Waiting. Examining every twitch and subtle expression on my face.

But I wouldn't respond. I couldn't. No reaction. No fear. No weakness ...

Other than her.

Slowly, I turned my face away.

"Don't worry, boy. Your secret is safe with me, for now." Sulam chuckled darkly, his grip on me finally loosening. He stood back, wiping his hand off on his finely tailored jerkin like I was something filthy.

I swallowed hard, still on my knees before him. Waves of heat rolled through me, so strong it made my stomach curdle and my vision swerve in and out of focus.

I could do it. Right now. I could lunge for him. Kill him. End this.

But what about Nora?

I knew his men had orders. If he died at my hands, she would suffer and die at theirs. There was no escape. No hope.

Not for either of us.

Sulam nudged me with the toe of his finely polished boot. "Get up. I want you back in the pit. And I promise, this next fight will be a much more suitable challenge for you."

I gasped in a halting breath, the pain in my side flaring as I leaned back to stare at him again. "But ... but I already went two rounds."

"And now you'll do a third, especially since that last one was so pathetic." He snapped his fingers, and two of his favorite henchmen—muscle-bound thugs armed with shortswords and crossbows—stepped through the doorway to flank him.

They were big enough to make him feel safe, apparently. But neither one of them could match my height as I forced myself to stand. My bad leg trembled, threatening to give under my weight.

I wasn't an idiot, though. I couldn't take them both. Not while I was already injured. Not exhausted. Not unarmed.

One of them still had fresh blood on the pommel of his weapon and a glint in his eye, like me getting a bad idea would absolutely make his night.

I swallowed against the thick, coppery flavor of old blood and the burn of bile in my throat.

Once again, I had no choice.

"There's a good beastie," Sulam purred as he slapped my back and immediately made a face, wiping his hand off on his pant leg. "Go on. Your audience awaits."

His voice held an excited edge—a tone that sent a chill straight to the pit of my stomach. He was never excited. Not unless he knew what the outcome was going to be. That it was going to benefit him somehow.

But if he put me up against even a half-decent fighter, he had to know I couldn't win. I'd lose, and lose him money in the process. My leg was so weak I could barely put weight on it. My side throbbed with sharp, punishing agony that made bright spots dance in my vision.

I-I couldn't do it. I couldn't go another round. Not and live to see the other side of it.

I was going to ...

Oh, gods.

"If you want me dead," I realized aloud, the thought hitting me so suddenly it knocked the wind right out of me, "just do it. Have one of your thugs gut me right here. Don't make it a spectacle."

Sulam stopped, his expression going eerily blank as he stared up at me. Then the wheels began turning again behind his dark eyes. Calculating. Trying to sort out how I knew and how he could work this to his advantage.

"Now, what in the world would I stand to gain from that?" he chuckled darkly.

My stomach clenched hard. Bile rose in my throat.

"Y-you want me to die in the pit, don't you?" My voice was broken, halting, and disgustingly terrified. Small.

Childish.

The smile that curled over his mouth seemed to snuff all other sounds in the room. Everything except his rough, throaty voice hissing, "No, beastie. I want you to die in just the right way."

Fourteen

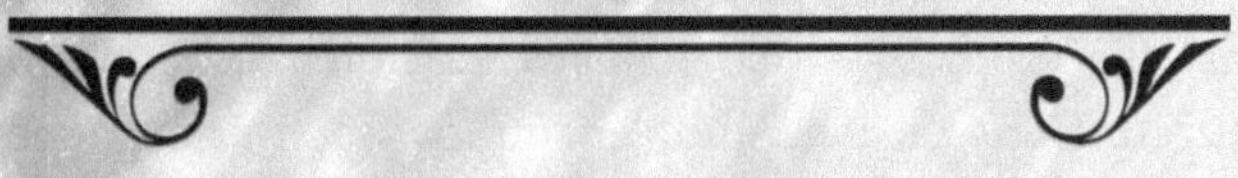

I would not go quietly.

Dropping back down into the pit, I set my teeth against the agony and forced my body to stand tall. Shoulders back, head up, fists clenched. If Sulam wanted me to die here in this miserable, putrid hell, then there was nothing I could do. It would end here.

But I wouldn't give him the satisfaction of seeing me cower. No crying. No begging. No pleading. And absolutely no running away.

I would go down swinging—fighting to the last breath.

Across the arena, my new opponent was already pacing. A hulking tower of a man, his bald head seemed a little too small for the rest of his body. Like someone had balanced a cannonball on a mountain of muscle.

Fates, where had Sulam found this guy? Some pirate ship moored out in the harbor?

His skin was a sunbaked bronze that had blown out the ink on all his tattoos and left his skin looking like old leather. He wore nothing but a ragged pair of stained linen breeches torn off at the knee.

His bloodshot eyes were wild with rage as he stared at me, shifting his weight and practically salivating at the promise of violence. No mercy. Barely any humanity at all.

I made a crude gesture with a finger at him and turned my back, wincing through the bolt of white-hot pain as I flexed my shoulders and paced to the other end of the arena.

My ears rang so loud I couldn't make out anything the fight-caller said. Not that it mattered much. The gist never changed. I was the defending champion. He was my enemy, a usurper come to challenge me.

But this time … I would lose.

I might be taller than the human practically snorting steam on the other side of the arena. I might even be stronger. But he wasn't injured. He was fresh for the fight.

I turned to face him—the man who would be my end. The monster Sulam had summoned to break me, once and for all. My pulse thundered deep in my chest. I took in a deep, steadying breath.

The fight-caller raised a fist and screamed, "FIGHT!"

The crowd erupted, and that monstrous man charged headlong for me like a bull.

The arena floor shuddered with every step. But it took effort to move that much muscle. He was committed.

I had to use that.

I dropped back into a defensive stance, keeping my injured leg behind me. My opponent roared in, sailing into my space like a boulder flung from a catapult. I dipped, ducking under his bone-crushing punch, and whirled to the side with my own fist already cocked.

I drove it into the side of his face with every ounce of strength I had left.

BAM!

My knuckles cracked under the force. Pain shot up my arm.

His head jerked to the side, and something in his jaw snapped under the impact.

He staggered, yelling in pain and fury. The crowd hissed as he slammed into the arena wall, unable to stop his momentum before he reached it.

I scrambled back a few paces, desperate to put as much distance between us as possible. The more time I had to prepare, the better. Fates knew I needed every second I could get.

The hulking man whirled, eyes bulging and blood drizzling from his mouth, and shoved away from the wall. He rushed for me again, roaring like an animal.

And the dance began.

He swung, launching hit after hit, while I dodged and ducked. The first time his fist made contact with my chin, my head snapped back, and my vision went dark for an instant. Good gods, he hit hard. Blood filled my mouth, and I barely managed to dip under his follow-up.

Dazed, I sprang back, keeping my weight on the balls of my feet as I kept my arms up to protect my face from another blow.

Then he rammed a hit straight into my gut, right below my sternum.

Instantly, all the wind ripped from my lungs. I sagged forward, seeing stars, as my ribs sang in agony. My entire body seemed to fold in on itself, and I wheezed.

His hands gripped the sides of my head suddenly, and I barely glimpsed his knee coming up to crush directly into my face.

Darkness swallowed me. Blessed silence.

Then everything snapped into focus again. Blinding light filled my eyes. Screams and shouts from the crowd. Something crunching.

Lying on my back in the sand, I couldn't move or make a sound as a huge fist slammed into my head over and over.

Then I was airborne, being thrown across the arena like a ragdoll. My arms and legs flailed. I couldn't catch myself and hit the ground hard. My body rolled a few times before I lay still on my side, my vision swerving in and out.

The monstrous bald man stalked toward me, pumping his arms in the air. The crowd chanted. They stomped their feet and slammed their tankards against the tabletops—the sound like war drums beating in the depths of my despair.

I couldn't move.

Tears welled in my eyes.

This was it, wasn't it? The end. Bathed in blood and humiliation, I would go to the gods' doorstep like a coward.

And Nora...

A strange hush fell over the room suddenly. No more stomping or cheering.

Not twenty feet away, my opponent stood frozen, his expression a skewed mixture of confusion and fury. He stared, dull cow eyes wide as they tracked something moving behind where I lay.

What was happening? Why wasn't he advancing? Why didn't he finish this?

Shakily, I forced myself up to my elbows ... and barely glimpsed a figure standing right beside where I lay sprawled in the sand.

A figure in a cloak made of pale blue fabric that shone with a silvery gleam in the torchlight.

"Audience interference is strictly forbidden," the fight-caller shouted. "Whoever you are, get out of the pit or fall victim to the brawl!"

The figure cruised forward a few more paces and stopped, standing between me and the monstrous thug who was gaping like he thought he might be hallucinating.

"Don't be stupid," a smooth, feminine voice snapped. A slender arm emerged from beneath the cloak to point a finger straight at my opponent. "I invoke the rite of Komu Rakt. You've drawn first blood against one of mine. Now you'll duel me or submit."

Wh-What? What did that mean? Who was this woman?

She unfastened her cloak and let it fall.

The bald man tensed, lip curling in a defiant snarl as he recoiled a step.

I couldn't look away, my mouth screwing up as I willed myself to stay conscious. It couldn't be her.

Leruna stood, head high and muscular shoulders back, the torchlight gleaming off her smooth, light brown skin. But the slender, Rienkan elven woman wasn't wearing her traditional healer's garb this time.

Dark tattoos ran from the back of her neck down her spine, disappearing beneath the dark leather harness that bound her breasts. More swirled up from her hips to her ribcage, emerging again from beneath that corseted harness to spread across her collarbone.

My pulse skipped.

There, right at the center where her cleavage began, all her tattoos merged into one central design. The image of a sea serpent stared out from just below the hollow of her throat, fins flared across her chest and jagged fangs bared.

No. That wasn't just any sea serpent.

Holy gods.

She was a Skyhart.

A pirate.

No ... pirate royalty.

My heart slammed to the bottom of my stomach so hard I nearly gagged. No. No—this wasn't right. Leruna was a priestess. A member of Undae's holy order. She couldn't be a member of Rienka's most powerful, brutal, and notorious pirate family! There would have been signs. Hints. I would have seen it. Sensed it somehow.

Right?

Leruna panned a cool, slightly annoyed glance down at me. Like this entire mess had been avoidable.

The chamber was completely silent. No one dared to move. Not in her presence.

Because not a soul lived in all of Rienka without hearing the Skyhart name whispered like a curse. Their legacy was as long as it was bloody—but more than that ... they were god-touched. Stone-speakers.

Hand-chosen by the sea goddess, Undae, to carry her essence, speak for her, and even control her seas.

Chills swelled through my chest, prickling over every raw nerve. Legend said Undae had taken two of the Skyhart ancestors—a pair of twin brothers—and transformed them into monstrous sea serpents.

The drakkons.

They were legendary monsters of the deep that only their family could control. Even to this day, every sailor—pirate or otherwise—feared them. The Skyharts were not mere vagrants. They were pirate kings and queens. Unrivaled. Unchecked.

Unstoppable.

My thoughts scrambled. Why? Why would she ever come to a place like this, let alone put herself in the path of my enemy? Why would she disguise herself as a healer and live in the temple?

And why, by all the gods, did she care what happened to me?

Yes, she'd saved my life once before. She had even supplied me with healing materials now and again. All of that, however, was probably at Violet's insistence. Leruna had ties to Roxus, somehow. The two had known each other for a long time.

But this woman had no real allegiance to me.

"Well?" she demanded, tilting her head to the side. "Do you accept my challenge? Or do you submit?"

The bald-headed thug glanced between us, as though debating how much crushing the life out of me might be worth to him. A duel against a Skyhart? A lifetime of being hunted and then a grueling, torturous death if he somehow managed to win?

Priestess or not, Leruna was not standing in that pit alone. She had generations of brutality backing her—a literal pedigree written in the blood of every sorry soul who ever tried to stand against her family.

And that thug must have known it.

Whispers stirred through the audience like wind through dry leaves as he dropped down to his knees in the sand and put his head down and groveled.

My head dropped back to the sand, a breath escaping me in a rasping rattle. It made my vision wink in and out again, darkness choking out the light as a strange tingling cold climbed my body from my toes, up my legs, all the way to my neck. Almost as though I were being slowly dipped in frigid water that numbed away everything.

Was this death?

Is this what it felt like to die?

I didn't know. But, gods, part of me hoped it was. I needed all this to finally be over. To escape.

To rest at last.

As everything blurred to shades of gray, I spotted the fight-caller up on his lofty stand. He stared, mouth agape, in silence. And right beside him, his flabby cheeks puffed like an angry toad and his dark eyes narrowed to glittering slits of malice,

Sulam glared at Leruna like he was already plotting his revenge.

Like somehow, someday, he would make her pay for this humiliation ... Skyhart or not.

Part Three
Violet

Fifteen

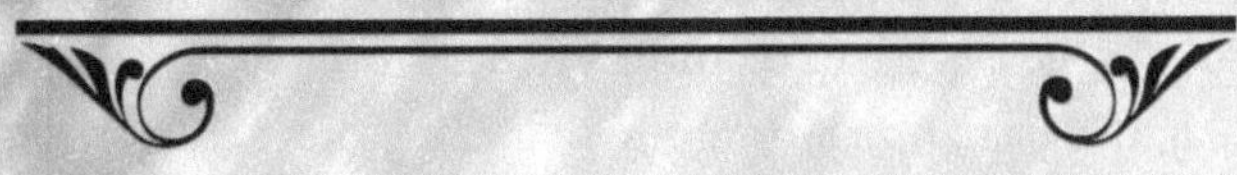

I'd never seen this street before.

The city rose around me, dark towers of shadow in the night, veiled by the pouring rain. The stormy wind snatched at my hair, stung at my skin like the piercing of a thousand icy needles. My bare feet slipped and faltered on the rain-slicked stone streets.

But I did not slow down. Not for a single, frantic, gasping breath.

I pumped my legs harder, head down, gaze scanning frantically for the next turn, the next narrow alleyway, the next obstacle I could put between myself and them.

Slurring male voices howled and whooped behind me—no, us. She was still with me, stumbling along a few yards behind. She sobbed and whimpered, wheeling her arms to keep from falling as we darted through the city's soggy streets.

She was too slow. She tripped and wobbled, crying out with pleading, frantic words in a language I didn't understand. Each step dragged her farther and farther behind, but I didn't dare stop or even glance back.

There was only forward. Only running.

Only survival.

If she fell behind, she stayed behind, to whatever end. That was the law of my kin. The only law I understood. You didn't have to be the fastest. You just couldn't be the slowest.

We scrambled around another tight bend in the road, feet squishing over the muddy, sandy sludge that filled the streets this close to the harbor. The smell of rotting fish saturated every wild gasp as I hauled myself forward.

Lighting snapped tongues of white fire across the sky, followed swiftly by the relentless snarling of thunder. My pulse skipped, feeling the closeness of that primal, elemental energy like a shudder on my skin.

Faster, faster, faster.

The voices were louder now. So close. Something shattered behind us in the dark. Glass? Were they throwing bottles?

THUD!

The girl bleated like a frightened lamb as she fell face-first onto the ground.

No—no, no, no. I could not stop. Not even to look.

I sprinted forward, adrenaline surging through me like I'd been struck by one of those lightning bolts as she began to scream.

The men's voices crowed with delight.

Ahead, a teetering tower of old crates stood against the side of a building. I darted for it, scaling the heap to the top and cramming my soaked, shaking body into one of them. They were old and warped from moisture, the planks so bowed and split that I could peer through them. My heat-vision saw it all; saw the sheets of cold rain as a grainy background to the warm bodies writhing in the street below.

The men on her, weapons in their fists.

Her still-hot blood pooling and mixing with the rain.

A few of them circled the area, looking all around. Calling

for me like a dog. They whistled and taunted, promising they wouldn't hurt me. Lying. Lying while they beat her.

I clamped both of my freezing hands over my mouth and shut my eyes tightly. I didn't want to see. I didn't want to hear, but I couldn't plug my ears.

So I heard the rush of the rain on the cobblestones and the rumble of thunder. I heard the clubs swinging, bashing, and cracking. I heard them laughing.

And I heard it when her cries finally went silent.

* * *

"NO!" I screamed at the top of my lungs.

My cry hung like the shattering of glass in the still, warm air of the suite as I bolted upright in bed. A low, growling rumble of thunder rattled the windowpanes as though in answer. Rain pattered against the glass with soft thumps.

I sat still, my back ramrod straight and my entire body shivering in the downy duvets and fine satin sheets. My hair clung to my skin, still damp from the bath, and now the fresh cold sweat that made my entire body shudder.

A dream. Just a dream. A nightmare.

It was so long ago. I'd almost forgotten. I *had* forgotten, until a few months ago. This same dream had come to me once before, surfacing like a bloated corpse left to rot in the sea.

The memory of the night I had escaped Sulam's grasp.

I rubbed at my arms and stole a glance over the wall of pillows I had built down the middle of the bed. Axien's side was empty. The blankets were rumpled, but when I swapped to my heat vision, the mattress wasn't even warm.

He'd been gone a while.

I frowned, my insides immediately twisting into a thousand throbbing knots as I scanned the rest of the room. The embers smoldered low in the fire pit, but he was nowhere to be seen. No traces of him apart from his large bag of belongings that sat where he'd dropped it earlier.

Why would he leave? Where would he go? Downstairs?

Was he up to something? Had he been playing me and everyone else at Arx Eburna for a fool again? Was he still siding with the Tibrans, even after—

I flinched, whipping around and reaching for my daggers I kept under my pillow, as the door suddenly clicked open.

Axien's tall frame filled the doorway, silhouetted against the light from the lamps in the hallway behind him. His gaze locked with mine, and he hesitated. His glowing eyes narrowed slightly, and he slowly eased into the room, shutting the door behind him.

"Violet? What's wrong?" he asked, tone hushed and tense.

"Where have you been?" I demanded. No point in mincing words.

He stopped again, standing within the glow of the fire pit. His long dark hair dripped, sticking to the darkly tanned skin of his jaw, neck, and collarbone. His pale green nightshirt was untucked, the light fabric clinging to the moisture on his skin. Bathed in the glow from the embers, it offered glimpses of the hard planes of his abdomen, hips, and chest beneath.

All of him was leanly muscular, solid, and pleasingly toned. Beautiful in a way I doubted a human man could ever dream of being.

Curse that half-elven blood.

"I couldn't sleep. So I went to the bath," he said simply.

I studied the way his lips formed each word, the way tension played over his features like ripples on a pond. Not a lie, but there was something beneath it. Something more he wouldn't admit.

"Why are you awake?" he countered as he strode closer, stopping next to my side of the bed. "I heard you shout."

I could smell the bath oils on him. Rich, sweet, and with a hint of something sharp like anise or clove. It sent waves of warm, tingling shivers over my skin.

I swallowed hard and immediately looked away, barely managing to squeak, "It's nothing."

Gods, why was my face so hot?

"Are you ill?" he asked, not buying an inch of my excuse. "Was it another nightmare?"

Visions of that girl lying in the street flashed through my mind again. My throat went dry, and my expression seized. Too late, I turned my face away.

The bed shifted as he sat down next to me, careful not to touch me as he let his hands rest on his knees. "We can talk about it. Sometimes that helps."

I snorted. Really? Because he was so eager and open with all his issues—he would know all about the power of sharing?

Yeah. Right.

"Tell me why you snuck off to have a bath in the middle of the night, and maybe I'll consider it," I said.

As if he would.

"You never go to the public baths. You never even use the private bath if someone else is in the room," I continued. "Is this because they don't have public baths where you lived before?"

Axien's features skewed some, drawing up into a look of discomfort that put deep lines between his eyebrows. As though he were trying to think past something painful. Finally, his wide, densely muscled shoulders rose and fell with a deep, surrendering breath.

"It's because for the majority of my life, I never had a choice about who saw my body or when, let alone what I did with it," he explained quietly. "I realize it is strange to the people in this region that I don't enjoy public baths. To some of them, it's probably even insulting. But it's not something I do out of spite to your traditions."

My heart sank some, realizing far too late what should have been obvious. He'd been Aurati. Not a courtesan, like Vanora or Sanja. They'd always had some semblance of choice about what they did.

Axien had never had that kind of control over his life, his body, or anything that happened to him. He'd been a slave. Worse than that—he'd been treated like he didn't even have a mind, spirit, or will of his own.

He wasn't private about his bathing because he was being modest or suspicious—he was doing it out of fear.

Knowing that someone had done something so bad to him that now he didn't even feel safe to be in a common public bath set all the cinders of my rage ablaze. My pulse quickened, blood burning hot, as I stared up at him. My throat burned, but I couldn't speak. Not yet.

Seconds dragged by in agonizing silence broken only by the occasional distant growl of thunder and tapping of rain against the windows. Gusts of wind blasted the panes, making them rattle again.

"I apologize if I made you suspicious. I should have explained soon—" he started to speak again, but I cut him off immediately.

"Don't," I snapped. "Do not apologize for that. Not to me. Not to anyone."

He slowly closed his mouth, eyes wide as he returned my stare.

"You never have to apologize for that kind of thing to me —for trying to heal the damage other people did to you," I clarified, forcing calmness back into my voice.

Every word stung though. Gods, saying that made my eyes water and my hands clench in the sheets as I tore my gaze away from his.

It felt too real. Too close.

Too much like something I'd desperately needed to hear, as well.

He slid a hand across the bed, inching slowly closer until he took one of mine. It made my face burn again and my heartbeat skip and stall sloppily. We hadn't touched like this since ... well, since he'd kissed me.

But this didn't feel like that moment.

His fingers wove through mine, grasping firmly like someone holding onto something solid to steady themselves. Like a tether to reality he was terrified of losing.

I squeezed back.

"You don't have to tell me about your nightmares if you don't want to, Violet," he whispered, his voice nearly lost to the storm still raging outside.

"I will," I murmured back. "I will, just ... not yet."

He nodded once. "When you're ready, then."

I wanted to tell him not to get his hopes up. I didn't know when that would be. Maybe I'd never be ready to talk about the things I saw in my dreams.

All those memories had been buried so deeply in my wicked brain, I'd assumed they'd never resurface. They'd just slowly melt away, fusing with every other twisted thought and idea, until they were so melded they'd never be recognizable again.

But that night—that girl who had tried escaping Sulam with me—she was now a prisoner in my mind. She was locked away in my internal asylum along with Chrysa and my mother. I had no idea what had happened to her, though.

My mother was dead. Chrysa was in Necrolis Prison. But when Sulam's men dragged that girl away into the dark of that rainy night ... I had never seen her again.

I didn't know if they'd really killed her, or if by some divine miracle, she had survived. I didn't know what I'd say to her if I ever saw her again, or if I'd even recognize her if we passed in the street. Her hair had been a ruddy color, but that was all I could remember about her.

"Are you hungry?" Axien asked suddenly, jarring me as he carefully withdrew his hand from mine and cleared his throat. "It's just ... well, we skipped dinner. I could go down and get us something. We can discuss the mission while we eat."

I nodded, waiting until he'd stood and gone to the door before I dared to let out a slow, shaking breath. My hand tingled with warmth from where he'd held it, and the soft fragrance of his bath oils still hung in the air. It sent shivers through me and made my legs clench together.

I hated it—the way he made my body betray me. The way his energy drew me in, seeping through all the cracks in my mental fortifications, and lulling me into a sense of calm and comfort that made me drop my guard entirely.

I didn't want to trust him. I didn't want to like him.

But it was far too late for all of that.

Axien was a dangerous man.

And I needed to feel his hand around mine again like I needed air.

SIXTEEN

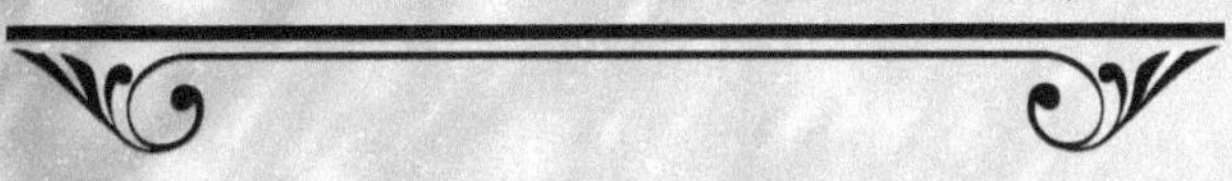

I'd never be able to sleep.

Not with the storm growing more intense outside, the lightning flashes so constant it was disorienting as I slipped out of bed and made my way to the fire pit.

Dressed only in my thin, white chemise, I stoked the embers, adding a few more pieces of wood, and coaxed the flames back to life before I settled into one of the cushions to finish reading our mission missive. I'd only scanned it in the bath, thanks to the low candlelight in there.

But as the flames licked higher in the fire pit, I held up the crinkled pages scrawled with neat lines of Mistress Orvana's tight, curling lettering.

Only ... there wasn't much to it—just as Axien had said.

The details were brief and vague when it came to the artifact itself; just that it had been a family heirloom in this noble family's estate for generations, and they didn't want to see any of their treasured items falling into Tibran hands. Understandable.

The family name, Ragentrude, wasn't one I recognized,

but the missive indicated they were an old, well-established house originally from the western coast of Damaria. They were well-connected traders who had built their fortune hundreds of years ago, and they were hosting the soiree in honor of their youngest daughter's debut to the rest of the court. There would be nobles from all over Damaria, Rienka, and even a few from Maldobar in attendance.

It would be a grand, glittering affair. The perfect backdrop for a little bit of espionage. The missive advised that we keep our eyes and ears open for any murmurings that had to do with the Tibran movements.

Interesting. So Mistress Orvana was fishing for rumors in the noble court now?

That couldn't be a good sign.

Flipping through the pages, I scoured for any little details I might have overlooked about the artifact—Tykeron's Puzzlebox. The most I found was a description of a small, fist-sized icosahedron made of dark gray metal. Less than ideal, considering it had Tykeron's name attached to it.

He was one of the more obscure, lesser-known gods. Not one I had spent a lot of time studying, honestly. I knew he presided over luck, fortune, and chance. He also had an affinity for gold, jewels, and riches. He loved secrets, reveled in games, wine, riddles, and debauchery, and was the twin sibling of Iksoli, goddess of mischief. They made quite a potent pair, in what little lore I'd read about them.

But a puzzlebox named for him? I hadn't seen mention of that anywhere. Was it something he'd made himself? Or something infused with his power?

Regardless, it was an odd choice of name, given the description in the missive. An icosahedron meant it would have twenty faces, all triangular. Not a box. So why call it that? Boxes held things, but this sounded more like a foci—something the ancient Avoran sorcerers used to store their magic for use in powering other, larger artifacts.

Bizarre.

I rubbed my chin as I flipped through the pages, reading them over and over. Scouring for any minuscule hint of what we might be dealing with. Nothing seemed out of place, though.

Maybe it was just as simple as Axien claimed. If it was a relic—magical or not—that bore Tykeron's name, the wealthy merchant family of Ragentrude may have only kept it because they thought it might bring them good fortune. A lot of merchants paid homage to Tykeron, after all.

But if it was just a good luck charm, why were they so worried about the Tibrans taking it?

None of it made sense.

I'd practically memorized the entire missive by the time the door clicked open and Axien reappeared with a tray of food and wine balanced in each hand. He gave a broad, proud grin and strode in to set them on the low table.

It scrambled my brain immediately.

"Well? What do you think?" he asked as he settled onto a cushion beside me, holding out one of the glasses of wine.

"What, um, what do I think about what?" My thoughts were chaos—useless mush. I almost dropped the missive in the fire pit as I reached to take the wine glass from him.

He nodded to the papers. "They didn't give us much to go on, did they?"

Oh. Right. Work.

"No," I admitted, forcing my concentration back to the entire reason we were here to begin with. "Something about it doesn't feel right."

"How so?" He frowned over the rim of his glass as he took a sip.

"It's rare to find any artifacts affiliated with Tykeron, and there's so little information about this one. The family seems very eager to get rid of it," I said.

Axien shrugged. "I imagine having any artifacts would make them a greater target for Argonox," he suggested.

"True," I considered aloud. "But it seems like no one understands what it is or even knew they had it until now. Even the Zenith's Call had nothing on record to offer about it. So why worry about it being taken if no one knew it existed to begin with?"

His mouth scrunched thoughtfully, and he gazed into the flames in the fire pit, the light dancing in golden flashes across his blue eyes.

"I suppose you're right about that," he said at last. "I hadn't considered they were showing their hand by even admitting they had something the Zenith's Call had no record of. What do you suspect then? You must have an idea."

"I think it must be something dangerous." I sighed into my wine glass before taking a long sip. The rich red liquid burned a trail from my tongue, down my throat, all the way to my stomach.

Axien arched an eyebrow, silently urging me to go on.

I huffed. Wasn't it obvious?

Apparently not, because he just pursed his lips impatiently.

"Why else would they go to such lengths to hide it, even from the Zenith's Call?" I asked. "If it's something that could be used as a weapon, the Ragentrudes must have realized they have no hope of keeping it from the Tibrans if they were to be invaded. They're a merchant family, after all. They probably have guards, sure, but no armies."

"Ahh," he replied, realization dawning on his expression at last. "So the only way to keep it from falling into Tibran hands is to give it to us and hope the Zenith's Call can defend it, or hide it away well enough that Argonox never finds it."

I snapped my fingers. "Exactly."

"That just begs one question then," he mused, taking another sip of wine.

I frowned. "What?"

"Why send two green tandems to fetch it?" He held his glass up to the light of the fire, squinting critically as he swirled the blood-red contents. "Even if they are short-handed now, sending us to retrieve something that dangerous is a risk."

I smirked. "Because if it explodes and we both die in a ball of divine fire, they won't have lost anyone important?"

He choked, almost spitting his wine back into his glass as he tried to take another drink.

I laughed.

"You're terrible," he chuckled.

"I'm realistic," I corrected, and grinned as I downed the last of my wine. "And hungry."

"Shocking," he quipped.

"But not angry," I pointed out proudly as I stood to investigate the plates of food he'd brought back.

"Not currently, but give it time." Axien waggled his eyebrows.

I hated that I liked it so much.

Gods, I really was in trouble.

I settled at the low table nearby, turning all my focus to the spread of roasted lamb, curried potatoes, and thinly sliced, roasted eggplant over slices of toasted bread he had brought up for each of us. I could argue with a lot of things, but food this good was rare. Curse Axien for knowing how to get me in a good mood. And curse my own stomach for being an accomplice to his schemes.

Breathing a silent apology to Delthene, I dove into the feast without holding back. Tomorrow would be busy, after all. I might not have time for another meal until the mission was over, even if it all went off smoothly. We would need to return to Arx Eburna as quickly as possible once we had the artifact in hand.

No time for picnics by the harbor.

So I picked up my fork and prepared to do battle.

Seventeen

I was going to need a *lot* more wine.

If I were going to survive tonight, mentally and spiritually, being a little tipsy might be the only solution.

The only way to make it through without putting my fist through someone's face.

Standing before the tall dressing mirror, I stared at the gown Vanora had sent for me as two of the inn's maids helped me into it. Sheets of liquid-smooth silk the color of fresh blood formed a voluminous skirt that spilled from my hips to the floor. It was split so high up one of my legs I had to mind how I stepped and moved, or I'd be showing a lot more than too much thigh.

Fates help me. It was diabolical.

I absolutely *loved* it.

The bodice hugged my body tightly and was made of a sheer, flesh-colored fabric studded with hundreds of tiny diamond-like crystals. I might have looked entirely naked, except that more of that deep crimson silk wound over my breasts and off one shoulder, almost like bandaging. It connected to one sheer sleeve that went down my right arm with hundreds more of those little silver crystals—just enough to hide my oathmark.

My back was exposed all the way down to the curve of my hips, and the maids had spent hours washing, combing, and styling my long, silvery-blond hair into a plait that hung down my back. They'd woven more of those sparkling crystals into it that sparkled and glittered whenever I moved.

I'd never worn anything so light, fine, and utterly revealing. Roxus would have been ready to spit fire if he'd seen it. Delthene would have blushed ten shades of pink.

But something about it made me smirk as I eyed my reflection, admiring how it hugged my body like a sheath. I'd fixed my makeup exactly as Vanora had advised, outlining my eyes in sweeping strokes of dark black kohl and painting my lips with the deep red rouge she'd sent along with the dress that matched the hue of the gown.

I had three dangling jewel earrings in each ear and a choker of more glittering crystal and red glass—or at least, that's what I assumed they were.

Until I saw the letter.

The maid who had been pulling all my eveningwear out of Axien's bag produced a rectangular, black velvet box and presented it to me with a curtsy. Inside, a small, folded note sat atop a gleaming silver comb in the shape of a serpent with red-jeweled eyes.

I recognized Vanora's neat, intricate lettering immediately.

I received these as a gift from a grand duke when I was your age. I'm not sure his wife would have been pleased that he was dipping into her family jewels for a courtesan. All told, they are worth 6,000 gold. May they serve you well, little viper. ~ V

My heart stopped. My mouth went dry as my jaw dropped open, landing somewhere around my feet as I slowly panned my gaze back up to the mirror. They ... weren't glass and crystal then.

Real diamonds.

And rubies as big as my thumb.

Sweet, holy, jumping spirits—how could she just hand me something like this?!

I held perfectly still, trying to remember how to breathe as the maid slipped the comb into the braid at the back of my head and stood back. The second maid stood behind me and held up a good-sized hand mirror so I could see myself front and back.

Is it to your liking, miss?" she asked, keeping her eyes downcast. A gesture of respect I still hadn't gotten used to.

"Yes, it's ... beautiful," I admitted.

"You look so lovely, miss," the second maid volunteered. She was a little bolder and gave me a quick, blushing smile before she quickly looked down, too.

I did. Like it or not, and despite the shoes Vanora had picked—which were so tall and delicate they felt like a personal attack—I did look properly soiree–worthy. Lovely, even. And not at all like myself.

My stomach fluttered as I turned, glancing myself over from different angles and running my hands over the skirt. The cool, flawless silk flowed as smoothly as spring water between my fingers. Expensive and absurdly revealing.

I snorted at the thought. So much for discretion.

Swaggering in like this—a Viperi girl dressed in a Lunthardan-styled gown, dripping in diamonds and rubies—on the arm of a half-Avoran wouldn't be discreet at all. Just what exactly was Curator Vanora playing at?

Or was I entirely wrong? Would everyone be dressed like this, so I'd just be another gemstone in a gaudy, sparkling sea?

"Wow. Th-that's ... you look ..." a male voice stammered in the doorway.

I turned just in time to see Axien's face flush almost as red as my gown before he bowed his head and cleared his throat. "I should have asked if you were ready before coming in. My apologies."

"It's fine," I murmured, gesturing to the maids to dismiss them.

I waited until they had scurried from the room and shut the door, giving them a minute to get out of earshot down the hall, before I turned to face him. My skirts shifted and moved with me, and I kept my core tensed so I didn't wobble on Vanora's nightmarish, spindly heels.

Axien, on the other hand, seemed far more comfortable.

He'd dressed in a fine silk black tunic with a high neck, black breeches, and a dark teal overcoat trimmed in gold. With a black leather broadbelt bound over a waistwrap of gold, intricately embroidered silk, he'd opted for a more Rienkan style.

And it suited him handsomely.

His dark brown hair was brushed out smooth, partially pulled back to expose his pointed ears. He had kohl smudged around his eyes, as well, and a simple golden chain around his neck. His tall black boots were oiled to perfection, matching his belt, and he had a small golden pin in his hair in the shape of a feather.

"Now I know why Vanora wrapped that dress so carefully," he said as his molten, fiery blue gaze slid up and down my body, drinking in every detail.

My heartbeat skipped, and my face went tingly.

"Let's hope I don't have to do any fighting in it," I said. "I'd hate to ruin it."

He grinned and shrugged. "I'm sure you can manage either way. But if everything goes to plan, fighting won't be an issue. The Ragentrude's eldest son is going to find us in the ballroom and take us to the artifact. We'll do the handoff and quietly excuse ourselves. Easy in, easy out."

Yeah. Right. Because things always went like that—easy.

Hadn't he learned anything about working with me? Apparently not.

I needed to be able to fight, even if it was just hand-to-hand. The dress would slow me down. The heels had no tread, so I might slip in them. And where was I supposed to hide my daggers?

"Are we going in armed?" I asked, eyeing the pillow where my daggers were still tucked away out of sight.

"It would be difficult. They'll be doing weaponry checks at the door, no doubt. Any sword or dagger you might see would be purely decorative," he replied as he began digging through his nearly empty bag.

I frowned down at the dress, thinking it over. I might be able to strap one dagger to my other thigh—the one that wasn't exposed by the slit in the dress. That was better than nothing, but only if they didn't check me at the door. Would they check the ladies, too?

I had no idea.

"Theoretically, we shouldn't need weapons at all. But just in case, I brought this," Axien announced as he poured the contents of a small leather pouch into his hand.

A glittering gold ring tumbled out, shimmering and topped with a round-cut topaz. Stepping closer, Axien showed me how the jewel sat on a small, false-top that opened on a tiny hinge, revealing a needle-sharp barb hidden underneath. Not big enough to deal lethal damage, but it would certainly sting if I punched anyone while I wore it.

"It's poisoned," Axien clarified, reaching out for my hand so he could slip the ring onto my middle finger. "Prick someone with it, and they'll be unconscious in seconds, dead in a minute."

I stared at the ring, holding my hand up to admire how it shimmered so innocently in the light. Even the tiny hinge was hidden in the scrolling design around the soft blue topaz. Lethal and beautiful.

I loved it instantly.

"Not to keep though?" I just had to be sure. This was definitely something I'd be tempted to tuck away and forget to return later.

He smirked and tossed the empty pouch back on the bed. "It's an early birthday gift, actually."

I blinked at him, glancing him up and down a few times, as I tried to work out whether or not he was kidding. Nope. No traces of teasing glinted in his shining, magically hued eyes.

I squinted and pursed my lips.

"I don't know when my birthday is," I countered, testing him.

"I know. Delthene told me you had all decided on a day that suited—the day Roxus brought you home from the prison," he said. "That would have been three years ago, right?"

Gods ... had it really been *three* years now?

I sank back, my weight on those precariously thin heels, as the realization settled over me like the kiss of a winter's first frost. Time had seemed irrelevant when every day was essentially the same, filled with endless training and studying.

He was right though. It had been three years.

I was now seventeen.

Er, well, somewhere near it, anyway. We couldn't be precisely sure, since Viperi didn't care to mark those kinds of holidays with any special celebration, and I'd spent so long as a street urchin just trying to stay alive, I'd lost track of how old I actually was.

According to Leruna, seventeen or eighteen was a safe guess, though. We'd decided to err on the younger, thanks to my stature.

"I ... um, thank you," I stammered as I stared down at the ring again.

"I'd be lying if I said I didn't have help," he confessed with a nervous chuckle. "Just try not to stab anyone by accident. Or yourself, for that matter."

I flashed him a wry grin and spun away on one of my fancy heels. "No promises."

Eighteen

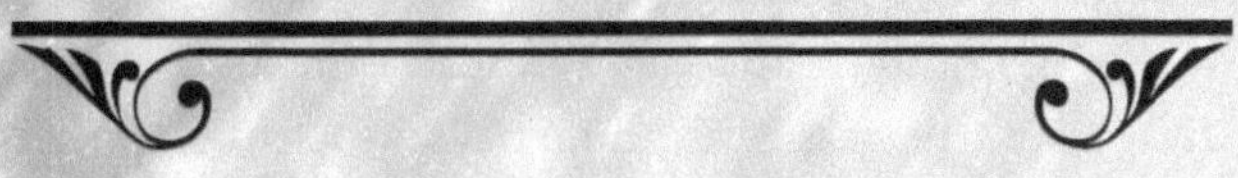

There was no escaping it.

The way my body fit perfectly against Axien's side as we strode up the front steps of the grand estate sent waves of buzzing heat all through me. With my hand around his arm, I forced my focus into my body language and every single shred of training Vanora had ever drilled into me.

How to walk with my shoulders dropped and back arched slightly, hips swaying into every step. Chin parallel to the ground. Neck curved elegantly. Eyes focused—no, smoldering—ahead. Every stride dripping with sultry, serpentine confidence.

Other couples we passed paused, watching us glide by. The women eyed my attire, whispering behind silk fans and blushing delicately as they watched Axien. The men did an immediate double-take, regarding me like a powerful predator cruising through the shoals—half in fear and half in pure, enticed exhilaration.

I let my gaze slip over them, meeting their eyes for a fraction of a second. Just enough to see their pupils dilate. To light the spark of curiosity.

Then I glanced away, expressionless, as though I'd never seen them at all.

We paused at the entrance, and Axien handed off our invitation to one of the doormen, who immediately bowed and gestured for us to go inside.

Music, laughter, and light spilled through the open doorway from the grand vestibule beyond. Up a sloping staircase flanked with white marble statues of angelic, winged women holding gilded candelabras, a pair of huge double doors opened into the ballroom.

We paused at the top of a second staircase that offered a lofty view of the space—a raised square balcony that overlooked a broad dance floor below. A massive chandelier hung in the center from four golden ropes—so huge it hung like a small crystalline moon over the space. Pillars of the same white marble flanked the walls, creating little alcoves and nooks where groups of guests gathered to converse.

The sight of it—the thrum of the music that vibrated up from the floor and through the very marrow of my bones—stole my breath immediately. I stared across a sea of glittering gowns and stately looking men in fine overcoats. Long tables of tiny sandwiches and cakes on pristine silver platters stood against the far wall, with maids standing at the ready with trays of fine wines, liquors, and champagnes in delicate glass flutes.

I squeezed Axien's arm a little tighter.

His body tensed in response, and he put his other hand over mine.

I didn't recognize the strange, vacant smile he wore as he gently led me out around the room one smooth, calculated step at a time. His lips stayed bowed at that slight, confident curve, but the light of real joy never touched his features, as though mentally he had sealed himself back behind that veneer of perfect composure.

Swiping a flute of sweet white wine off one of the maids who passed by, I held it daintily just like Vanora had shown me. Might as well. I'd need it if I was going to get through the next few hours without having a nervous breakdown.

Besides, maybe a little light drinking would numb the pain in the arches of my feet. I'd be lucky to be able to feel my toes by the end of the night.

"My, my. How all the gentlemen stare at you," Axien observed in a low, throaty purr against my ear. "I ought to be in a jealous frenzy. But instead, I'm imagining all the ways I'd like to show them who you belong to tonight."

Gods, I didn't recognize that voice he was using, but it sent a jolt through my body that nearly made my knees buckle. What game was he playing at, saying things like that?

Was this a show just to throw off anyone who might be eavesdropping? Or was he just toying with me again?

Either way, I wasn't going to let him win. If he wanted to make me blush and cringe, he'd picked the wrong girl in the wrong dress.

Vanora had taught me thoroughly ... and sent me to battle in full armor.

I willed my face to stay neutral, pulling all my emotions back behind my own mask of indifference as I flicked a glance up at him. I let my gaze pan across his face, flitting down to his lips for the briefest instant before returning to lock with his.

"And why aren't you?" I asked, feigning a doe-eyed expression of bewilderment. "Ah, right. Because who would ever be jealous of a Viperi girl, hm? That kind of sentiment would just be a form of madness, wouldn't it?"

I waited, watching his expression twitch as he fought the urge to let that mask crack. Did he even remember saying something like that to me before, when we were on the ship? He'd teased me about having rivals. About how futile it was for him to even imagine tossing his hat into the ring when it came to winning my affection.

But *I* hadn't forgotten.

His jaw worked from side to side as he sucked his teeth behind his lips. Something dangerous flickered in the shadowed corners of his features, lurking there like a wolf beyond the light of a campfire. Waiting. Biding his time.

I let a hint of victorious, wicked pleasure dance in my eyes before I tore my gaze from his and gave an exaggerated, bored sigh.

"Seriously, Axien," I murmured and took a sip from my wineglass. "How are we supposed to find Lord Ragentrude in all these people? There must be hundreds."

"I suppose we could make ourselves known," he said. "You know, let *them* find *us*."

"How? Do they know what we look like?"

He pursed his lips, scanning the surrounding room again. The upper level where we stood was thick with people chatting and drinking. The lower level was filled with swirls of glistening color as women in lovely ball gowns spun through dances with their partners.

"I believe Mistress Orvana told them what we looked like," he replied at last. "But in this crowd, I'm not sure that matters. They'd never pick us out from a distance, even with you in that dress."

I rolled my eyes. "I'm glad someone's enjoying it."

"Oh, I'm confident several other men are enjoying it, as well," he retorted, his tone a little prickly. "How's your dancing?"

I couldn't keep my lip from curling. "Decent, according to Vanora."

"That's quite a compliment coming from her," he marveled.

No kidding.

"We've only gone over basic waltzes, though," I clarified.

"Do you know how to follow a lead?" His demeanor had cooled again as he eyed the dance floor.

"Um, well, that depends," I hedged. "What exactly did you have in mind?"

"Something complicated," he said. "Something you won't like."

I frowned. "Why not?"

"It'll involve me touching you." He flicked me a devious, dangerous smirk. "A lot."

I gripped his arm tighter in warning. "It better not be inappropriate touching."

"I'll do my best." I didn't need any training in interpreting body language to spot that lie. "But I'm just a mortal man, after all."

Jerk.

"Right. Sure. Remember, I have a brand-new poisoned ring that I haven't had the chance to test out yet. I'd hate to slip up and have a terrible *accident*," I scoffed and downed the rest of my wine. "Besides, I doubt you groping me on the dance floor is going to get everyone's attention."

The wind rushed out of me so suddenly I couldn't even gasp as he caught me by the waist and pulled me in, his nose brushing mine as he dipped me backward. One hand brushed up my side, over my shoulder, and down my arm until he plucked the empty wine glass from my hand.

"We'll just have to see, won't we?" he purred, so close I could feel the vibration of each word in his chest.

Heat blazed in my blood, making my skin prickle wildly and my heartbeat bash recklessly against my ribs. He'd feel it. Or hear it.

But I couldn't push away. Not with him staring at me like that. Not with his lips so close and the memory of how they'd felt—how he had tasted—running laps through my twisted imagination.

Oh gods.

This was going to be a disaster.

Nineteen

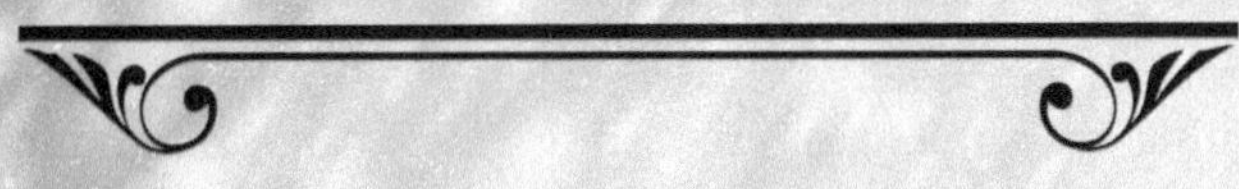

Yep. This was a huge mistake.

I had no idea what kinds of dances the Aurati taught their "products," but I was willing to bet it was a lot more than I'd learned over the last few months. They were supposedly trained to be proficient in all the courtly traditions, according to Vanora.

I probably should have demanded that he tell me what, exactly, he had planned. I didn't want to be a spectacle. Didn't want to be laughed at by a ballroom full of puffy nobles.

But as Axien led me out onto the dance floor, stopping by the group of minstrels to murmur a few words and slip them a handful of gold coins, it was far too late to back out now.

For better or worse, I was in this now. Stuck like a fly in sap.

I had to duel Axien again, and this time, I did not intend to lose.

"If you want to make me look stupid, there are easier ways," I fumed as he swept me out at arm's length, striding around to give a formal, courtly bow.

I bit back a startled noise as his lips brushed the top of my hand.

Bad. This was so, *so* bad.

What was he planning? Why was everyone else moving away, staring at us with mixed expressions of surprise, curiosity, and confusion? And what kind of song was this?

I'd never heard anything like it, each note sharp and pulsing like a heartbeat. Dramatic. Followed by surging, whining harmonies from the strings. It was an aching, hungry, furious song, and it set my blood on fire immediately.

"Just follow my lead and try to keep up," he said as he drew me in slowly, positioning a hand at my waist while he seized the other and pulled me in close against him.

There was a beat of stillness. A breath and pause. Just his strong, larger body held firm against mine.

Then the room was spinning, whirling, and slipping around me like a patchwork of color and shining glass. The only thing in focus, the only thing that remained clear in that whirlwind of color and light, was him. That slash of a roguish smile. That delighted, wicked light dancing in his eyes.

The feel of his body moving with mine, flowing through each movement. His hands on my waist, my arms, and brushing along my thigh where the slit in my dress revealed far too much. Every touch set my senses ablaze and made my heart quiver in my chest.

My pulse was a reckless flutter—light, frantic, and constant. A sharp contrast to the deep rhythm of the music and the heat of adrenaline in my veins.

He dipped me so low I was forced to balance on one of my thin, precarious heels and trust the strength of his arms not to drop me flat on the marble. I clung to him, breathing hard, my gaze ensnared with his.

"Not bad," he panted, his brow shining with sweat. "Don't tell me, you've been practicing with someone."

I let my eyes go steely, seizing his wrist as one of his hands slid up my side, going a little higher than I was prepared to allow.

"Who do you think would practice with me?" I hissed. "You think I'm cornering new prospects in the halls? Scaring them into waltzes?"

His laugh was deep and rich, hitting my senses like a sip of warm molten chocolate. It sent a shockwave through me, making every nerve extra sensitive to all the places we touched.

I hated it—especially since he seemed to somehow sense it.

His smile widened deviously.

"You don't seem to realize the effect you have on people, my dear," he said as he spun me around, catching me against his chest and dipping me low again.

I made a scoffing sound. Whatever.

I suppose he was right—beyond wanting to butcher me on sight because of what I was, I had no idea what other effects I had on people.

But based on the way his pupils stayed dilated, jaw clenched so tight a muscle twitched in his cheek, I could venture a guess at the effect I had on him.

The song ended so abruptly, with him still holding me in that final pose, I didn't realize we had been the only ones dancing to it until a smattering of light applause went up through the surrounding ballroom.

I stood straight again, still breathing hard, and stepped away from Axien. He offered a slight bow, but I didn't curtsy back. I couldn't.

Looking around, all the other stately couples who had been dancing before stood back and smiled widely, nodding and whispering to one another. Watching us. Speculating.

Oh, gods. How humiliating.

"Let's try something a little slower now, hm?" Axien

baited as he offered his hand again. "A nice, gentle waltz, so you can rest?"

Rest? I wasn't tired, what was he even—?

"If I may, I'd like to borrow the lady for the next dance," another masculine voice spoke up suddenly.

We both turned, facing a finely dressed man sporting a golden sash pinned to one of his shoulders with a silver brooch. He must have been somewhere in his mid-twenties, and the Ragentrude family crest was engraved on his brooch and on every one of the matching silver buttons of his dark blue waistcoat.

Axien and I swapped a sideways glance.

This was him? The son of the Ragentrudes?

I hadn't expected him to be so ... well, good-looking.

I'd imagined he might be polished and poised, like any man of noble birth. And he was. But his smile had a disarming easiness to it as he gave me a slight bow of greeting and offered a hand. His sandy colored hair was cut short, styled handsomely so it fell loosely over his brow and around his ears. He wasn't as tall as Axien, but he had a stockier build that reminded me a little of Varren. Thickly muscled and solid.

"If the lady is willing, of course. Would you indulge me?" he asked, still waiting for me to accept his invitation.

O-Oh. Right.

Dancing.

I slid back behind the mask, behind all the layers of training Curator Vanora had etched into my brain. My posture relaxed so that I settled my weight with a slight angling of my hips. I let my eyes smolder, looking at him beneath my lashes as I placed my hand on his. Only the tiniest bit of a smile touched the corners of my mouth, and I let my fingertips lightly graze his wrist beneath the cuff of his coat sleeve.

Skin-on-skin contact—just enough to kindle that flame of interest.

Axien cleared his throat beside me, prickly energy wafting off him past that veneer of charming indifference as he took a step back away from us. A scowl twitched as his brow for only an instant before it vanished behind a forced, thin smile. The corners of his eyes stayed tense as he gave Lord Ragentrude a once-over.

Sizing him up.

It made the hairs on my arms prickle with a little thrill of wicked delight.

"By all means, don't let me get in your way," Axien said stiffly, his gaze still lethally sharp on me for a second before he turned and made his way to the edge of the dancefloor.

I watched him go, noting how he reached up to rub the back of his neck and scratch under the collar of his overcoat. A nervous habit. Or, rather, an irritated one.

Interesting.

More couples filled the dance floor around us as a gentle waltz began, and Lord Ragentrude slipped a hand behind my back and eased me into the opening steps. He wasn't nearly as eager to press our bodies together and maintained an inch or two of respectful space as we twirled, gliding across the marble to the swell of the music.

Thank the gods for small mercies.

"I must admit, when the order wrote they would be sending a Viperi agent, I was intrigued. You'll have to allow me to apologize for stalling your mission to indulge my own curiosity, but I didn't want to miss the chance to meet you," he said.

My mask nearly slipped as I fixed my gaze upon him. Standing so close, the notes of his cologne—rich with hints of cedar, sage, and something citrus—sent a warm shiver up my spine.

He'd called me Viperi.

Not pitathi.

Even more interesting.

Usually, people used the two terms as though they were interchangeable. I wondered if some even knew the second was a slur.

But this man apparently knew the difference and cared enough to use the right one.

"Am I as terrifying as you'd hoped?" I teased lightly, offering a coy little grin before angling my face away over his shoulder.

"Oh, truly mortifying," he teased back as he swept me easily into a pose, his face suddenly very close to mine.

Near enough, I could spot hidden flecks of gold and green in his light brown eyes.

"And utterly bewitching," he added softly.

My stomach flipped, and my breath caught as he stepped us smoothly into another wheeling turn, my skirts fluttering around us. It wasn't the hungry, nearly desperate way Axien had danced. It was elegant, composed, and practiced.

Experienced and restrained in a way that made me conscious of all the tiniest errors in my steps. Would he notice how inexperienced I was? Or would he just chalk it up to my being a half-feral, red-eyed monster?

As the dance came to an end, I caught a glimpse of a familiar, disgusted scowl in the crowd behind us. Axien stood with his arms crossed, mouth now twisted sourly to one side, and gaze smoldering on Lord Ragentrude as though he were imagining all the ways he'd like to torture the man.

When he noticed me watching him, I smirked. Axien immediately dropped his hands back to his sides and straightened. All traces of that sulky scowl dissolved back behind his usual mask of cold-eyed indifference.

Too late for that, though. Idiot.

"Perhaps I can convince you to attend another ball as my guest, when we aren't so pressed for time?" Lord Ragentrude suggested as he offered his arm and walked me off the dance floor.

"As much as I would love that, I'm afraid it would take quite a convincing letter to the mistress." I gave his hand a light, consoling pat, letting my side brush his slightly.

"Keeps you lot on a short leash, does she?" He sounded genuinely disappointed.

"These are dangerous times," I said, feigning a little disappointment of my own. I didn't want to write him off completely.

Not when Vanora had advised me that having positive contacts in noble courts could be valuable cards to play later on. Better to keep myself in his good graces, kindle his interest and curiosity, than to shut him down completely.

"Perhaps I could write to you, then?" he suggested as we stopped in front of Axien.

I made sure he got a full view of my bright, flattered, blushing smile as I dipped my head in a gracious, elegant nod. "I would be flattered to hear from you again, my lord."

That muscle in Axien's jaw twitched again, gaze flicking between us before narrowing on me almost accusingly. If he had opinions about it, however, he kept them to himself—after a few deep breaths that must have been his attempts to collect his sanity.

"Well, then. I suppose we should get to business." Lord Ragentrude straightened his waistcoat. "I'll try to make this as quick as possible; I know you have a long journey home ahead of you tonight."

"Yes. We do." Axien bit at the words a little too sharply.

Lord Ragentrude gave him a solemn nod and motioned for both of us to follow. "This way. Keep close. We've got to go down to the catacombs. I hope neither of you are squeamish about the dead."

Twenty

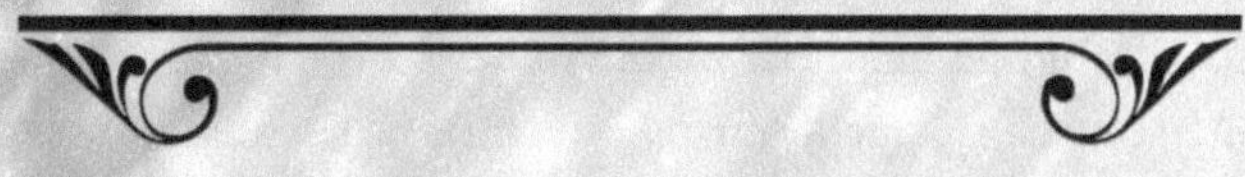

Corpses had never bothered me.

I'd been around plenty of them. Granted, they were usually fresh ones ... that I was somehow responsible for.

But as we stepped down into the dank, cavernous catacombs beneath the Ragentrude estate, a cold chill rose in my blood. My pulse sped off like a startled doe, knees wobbling a little as we descended a long staircase flanked on both sides by cracked and crumbling statues of jackals with glittering, red gemstone eyes.

The servants of Clysiros, Goddess of Death.

This place hadn't been made by human hands. The false arches engraved into the dark stone walls and ceiling, and intricate alcoves with gilded brass lanterns, were definitely Avoran in style. And the last time I'd stood in a place like this—in a crumbling ruin of their world—things had gone ... poorly.

I stumbled, one of my stupid spindly heels catching on a crack in the stone floor. Axien's arm was around my waist in a blink, holding me on my feet and steadying me against him.

"I've got you," he murmured low, his expression focused and fierce as he stared at the gloom ahead of us.

Lord Ragentrude paused at the base of the stairs, moving to one of the small bronze braziers that flanked either side of the railing. He pulled a small, brass-tipped torch from a sconce on the wall and lit it with the brazier's embers. The flames flickered and danced, casting wavering beams of light across a long, rectangular chamber before us.

My breath snagged, staring out into the silent stillness.

Four rows of stone sarcophagi stood on either side of a central aisle, each one adorned with sculptures of weeping winged figures, draconic beasts, and carved depictions of flowers. Some were plated in gold. Others were adorned with painted silver, encrusted with jewels, or tiled mosaics made of tiny glass shards.

All of it was immaculate. Not a fleck of dust out of place. The deep quiet sank into my bones like gentle snowfall.

I stared in awe, breathing in the heavy musk of the burning incense and watching the torchlight glitter over the gilded effigies. Some of them were so detailed I half-expected them to start moving. To rise and regard us with those eerie, jeweled eyes.

Fates, have mercy. Were all of these Avorans?

"We call them the dreamers," Lord Ragentrude explained as he stopped ahead of us, holding the torch higher so we could get a better view. "Your order has examined them all, of course. They concluded they were likely members of the same family, long ago. In fact, the entire structure was likely an above-ground mausoleum for them before the fall of their empire."

Axien's throat bobbed as he paused before one of the sarcophagi, one with a pair of black glass dragons crouched over the sculpture of an Avoran male, his eyes closed and hands clasped on the hilt of a sword. A thousand thoughts seemed to flash across his features as he studied it, lips pressing tighter and tighter into a thin line.

"Now, it lies below our estate, so we feel obliged to keep it maintained as closely as we can to their traditions." Lord Ragentrude gave a resigned sigh and turned to continue on. "Come. We're nearly there."

"Are you all right?" I whispered and took a step closer to Axien, sliding a hand down his arm to grasp his.

He grimaced and nodded. "Fine. Let's get this over with."

A lie.

But now didn't seem like the right time to push it. We still had a job to do.

Lord Ragentrude guided us onward, through two more rooms that were laid out the same way with rows upon rows of grand sarcophagi. My skin prickled as the air grew colder. Closer. More stagnant.

Every step and shuffle we made seemed to echo back a thousand times, and the smell of the incense seemed to saturate everything. I had to wonder if it was coming from the braziers that stood at every entrance, or if it was also inside some of those ancient coffins. Infused in them, somehow?

Finally, Lord Ragentrude stopped before the magnificent relief of a large stone door engraved into the wall. Lines of Avoran script lined the exterior, surrounded by the images of the Viepol—the two draconic beings that guarded the realm of the dead and presided over the souls who were allowed to enter the kingdom of the gods. There were trees with entangled branches that created an arch above the door, all made of pure white marble set into the black stone of the wall.

I'd never seen anything like it, but it definitely looked like another mausoleum entrance. The Avoran writing spoke about eternally honoring someone named Vesperus. They listed off his relatives, boasting his bloodline, which wasn't uncommon. But Vesperus wasn't a name I recognized on its own.

"Took your order a while to figure out this little trick," Lord Ragentrude quipped as he handed his torch off to Axien and reached to press both of his hands to the reliefs of the carved door handles. "You see how the leaves of the trees nearly touch some of the lettering above? It spells out the incantation. Clever, isn't it?"

I watched, sounding out the letters as I identified where the white marble leaves of the trees nearly touched letters in the inscriptions. It only took me a few seconds to translate it.

"Wealth in wisdom. Fortune in fortitude," I read aloud at the same moment he spoke the incantation in Avoran.

The handles of the door glowed a brilliant blue with the sudden swell of magic. Lord Ragentrude pulled them, the loop-styled handles moving like two huge knockers that were easily tugged open. The stone doors moved as though they were weightless, grinding and rumbling, until they revealed a small chamber beyond.

But there was no sarcophagus there.

Past the open maw of the chamber's two doors, a small altar of solid green glass sat in the very center. On top, two golden angelic beings bowed in reverence, their wingtips touching and cradling an icosahedron about the size of my fist.

My stomach dropped to the soles of my miserable shoes. Shivers ran wild over my skin.

It was made of metal, just as the missive had said it would be. But every one of its many faces was incredibly ornate, engraved with layers of runic marks and Avoran lettering, interlocking geometric designs, and a unique large symbol inlaid with gold.

Gods and Fates ... what was that thing?

I'd seen many Avoran relics over the last three years. But

never in any of my studies had I even read about something like this.

Axien and I swapped another wary, sideways glance.

Good thing we didn't have to do anything with it beyond carrying it in a bag. Something about it put a knot of dread in the center of my chest. Maybe it was that, despite being warned that it had some sort of magical significance, none of it glowed even the slightest hint of blue.

Was it dormant? Or had its magic already faded away?

It didn't matter—the feeling in my gut was loud and clear. We shouldn't be messing with this thing. We shouldn't even touch it. Something about it was wrong. Deceptive.

Axien shifted uneasily beside me, casting Lord Ragentrude a wary frown as he asked, "You really have no idea what it is?"

Lord Ragentrude shook his head, his expression almost bitter as he eyed the artifact. "No, although I'd bet good coin it's cursed to drive anyone who looks at it for too long absolutely mad. My uncle was absolutely obsessed with it. It's all he thought of day and night for forty years. My great-grandfather, too. They both claimed they heard voices coming from it. Because of that, my parents discouraged me from coming down here. If I were in their place, I'd have given it over to your order long ago. Good riddance."

"So you won't be terribly disappointed if we accidentally drop it in the harbor?" I said with a teasing smile, hoping it would disguise the way my insides had started quivering.

He chuckled and waved his hand. "I certainly wouldn't shed a tear for it. But in any case, whatever it is, it's in far better care with you lot for now. I'd rather not have the Tibrans be the ones to finally unravel its mysteries."

"Agreed," Axien said and stepped forward into the chamber.

All my focus settled on him, on his tall frame moving into

that little room as he reached for the artifact. Dread twisted in my belly like a cold knife. Every step seemed to echo too loud. My heartbeat drummed and throbbed in my ears, and my hands went clammy.

Wrong. Something was wrong. This thing—whatever it was—didn't want to be touched.

We should walk away. Leave it alone.

Right. Now.

I took a stumbling step forward, closer to Axien, instinctively reaching for the back of his overcoat. To stop him. To pull him back.

A gurgling, choking cry broke the silence suddenly.

I whirled just in time to see Lord Ragentrude crumple to his knees, hands reaching desperately to the arrow bolt sticking out of the side of his neck. Blood spurted from the wound. His eyes stared at me, wide and horrified.

"AXIEN!" I screamed as I dove for him.

More arrows pinged off the stone around me. Someone growled, biting words in a language I'd only heard spoken a few times in my entire life.

Was that ... Maldobarian? Here? Who? Why?

I seized Axien by the arm, trying to drag him out of the line of fire as the arrows kept coming. One whizzed past my face, slashing my cheek.

It was a second—maybe less. Not enough for a breath.

Axien's hand landed on the artifact and every one of the golden symbols on its many faces ignited with radiant blue light. The world seemed to slide sideways around us, ensnared in a smear of color and shadows. The earth fell away from beneath my feet as a void opened up beneath us, as though the fabric of reality had been torn away.

I stole one final glance up, past the chamber doors, where a company of dark figures dressed in dark leather armor rushed for us. They moved as one, fast and ruthlessly efficient, taking aim with their heavy crossbows again. Their faces were half hidden beneath dark shawls, and they all wore the same silver vambraces buckled onto their wrists.

Vambraces that bore the image of a snarling wolf's head. A wolf with three eyes.

The symbol of the Ulfrangar Assassins.

And then there was nothing but that void of endless dark ... and the feeling that we might be falling forever.

Or straight into a trap.

Part Four
Declan

Twenty-One

Mother wasn't moving.

Huddled together in the dark, I kept my arms tight around my little sister as the groan of the ship filled the stagnant air. The creaking of the ropes that held stacks of crates and barrels in place made me wonder if they might snap and we'd be buried alive. The smell of fouled saltwater and the acrid tinge of infection saturated every breath I took.

But we were together.

Wrapped up in a threadbare blanket that had once covered our shared bed in Tibrus, I held Nora close and covered her eyes. I didn't want her to see.

Mother had started to make noises again last night—coughing and gasping frantically until pink foam came out of her mouth. She'd tucked us in and gone to lie down.

She hadn't moved since.

"Is Mama still asleep?" Nora whispered, her voice trembling.

I stared at where our mother lay on a makeshift pallet not five feet away, surrounded by the bags of belongings we'd managed to lug aboard. Her skin had turned a strange grayish blue. Her eyes were open, but milky, and never blinked. Her lips were purple.

She wasn't breathing.

"Yes," I lied. "Be quiet. We don't want to wake her. She needs to rest."

"Because she's sick?" Nora asked.

"Yes," I lied. Dead people couldn't be sick.

A loud, hacking, wet cough sounded from somewhere in the maze of cargo around us. Someone else was sick, too. It put another pang of terror through my stomach, and I gripped Nora tighter.

What about us? Would we get sick, too? What if I died before Nora? Who would look after her? What would happen once we got ... well, wherever it was we were supposed to be going?

I didn't know.

My throat went stiff and I blinked hard, keeping the tears back. I didn't dare let my breath hitch or my body shudder. I couldn't let Nora see me get scared. She would be scared, too.

And it was my job to keep her safe now.

"I'm hungry, Dee," Nora whispered again, more quietly than before, as though she were afraid to admit it.

"Me, too," I said. "They'll bring down food soon. I'm sure they're just busy. It's a lot of work to run a ship."

She didn't answer.

Time crawled by. It could have been hours or days before a lantern appeared at the stairwell that led down from the ship's main deck. Four men stalked through the gloom, muttering and pausing at each group of refugees. I watched, holding my sister tighter and shrinking back into the shadows as they passed by.

The one with the lantern stopped over us, his face drawn in a grim scowl as he glanced between us and our mother's body. His mouth hardened. He curled his fingers, and two of the other men with him moved forward.

We watched, gripping one another tight, while they wrapped Mother's body up in her bedroll and carried her out. It took both of the men, grunting and heaving, to manage her weight.

Because she was Holvradix and would have been more than a foot taller than either of them standing.

Nora whimpered against me.

I put a hand over her mouth to stifle her sobs.

"Either of you coughing?" the man with the lantern demanded. "Feverish? Sickly?"

I shook my head.

He snorted, squinting his eyes like he didn't quite believe me. I must have looked healthy enough, though, because he lurched away—on to the next group.

"What are they doing with Mama?" Nora cried, squeezing me harder.

I couldn't hold back the tears then. They ran down my face, dripping from my trembling chin as I buried my face against her hair. She smelled like home.

"It's okay, Nora," I rasped weakly. "We're going to be okay. I'm going to take care of you."

Footsteps passed by again as the men carried out another body wrapped in old, stained linens. Then another.

And another.

"I swear it to the Fates, Nora," I murmured against her hair. "I'm your big brother, and I will always protect you."

My blood was acid in my veins.

The scorching heat of that pain, ripping through every inch of my body, snatched me from the smothering hell of my nightmare. I gasped frantically, like I was breaking the surface of a lake I'd been slowly drowning in. It burned through me, boiling every muscle and frying every nerve.

It hurt—gods, everything hurt so much.

I couldn't cry out, though. I couldn't even move. The world seemed muffled and far away, as though I were trapped under a blanket of smothering darkness. My eyes wouldn't open. None of my limbs would respond.

It didn't matter, though. I still knew where I was. The smell of the place, of citrine cleaning oils and faint traces of herbal tea, filled my nose as I took in a gasping, ragged breath.

I'd been in Roxus's house many times. Enough to recognize it on smell alone.

Never in a bed, though.

Sweet Fates, I could feel silken sheets and a feather-soft mattress beneath my back.

How? How had I gotten here?

There was no possible way Leruna had carried me, and the only reason Sulam's men would have carried me out of that arena was if I was a corpse they intended to dump in the harbor.

"I'm so sorry for troubling you like this, Delthene. I didn't know where else to take him," Leruna's voice pleaded from somewhere nearby. "Sulam's men watch his place almost constantly, and I don't want to bring any more trouble to the temple. The high priestess won't stand for it."

"Hush, girl, you have nothing to apologize for. Gods know Roxus would want him here, knowing he's in such a state," Delthene replied, but I could hear the tension in her tone. Worry drenched every word.

I just couldn't tell if it was worry for me, or that Sulam's men might have followed her here.

Maybe a bit of both.

"Get your tools ready, I'll see to drawing up hot water and

getting you clean rags. Gods, he's barely recognizable. His poor eyes—mercy be, they look ready to burst," Delthene fussed. "What did they do to him?"

"The same thing they've been doing for years," Leruna replied. "Although, now it seems Sulam might really be trying to kill him."

"Lucky you found him, then," Delthene murmured, her footsteps briskly tapping over the wood floor and fading in the distance.

Only once it was quiet, and we must have been alone, did I hear Leruna mutter dryly, "Lucky, indeed."

"You know, when you asked me to watch your back tonight, you might have warned me you'd be confronting one of Dah's biggest rivals," an unfamiliar male voice piped up suddenly. "He's not going to be pleased you provoked Sulam in his own lair."

Leruna puffed a deep sigh. "What choice did I have? You saw what was happening in there. Besides, I'm sure Dah will want to know about the Tibran soldier. If Sulam is getting involved in the war, that means it could come here more quickly than any of us bargained for. We need to be ready."

"Fair enough," the male voice agreed, albeit with a strong flavor of sour defiance in his tone. "Need anything else? Or am I free to go?"

"No, I can take it from here. Thank you, Elio. For carrying him here, I mean. I owe you one," she said quietly.

"You owe me lots, actually," he chuckled. "Don't think I forgot how you swiped my favorite blunderbuss."

"You always were a lousy shot anyway," she quipped. "Send the others my love."

His footsteps began retreating the same way Delthene's had. Then they paused.

"They miss you, you know," he added, his voice softer. Gentler.

"I know," she said.

"You could come back anytime. Dah would love to have us all in the business again. Just say the word," Elio suggested cautiously. Like he knew he might be overstepping.

Leruna didn't reply, though. After a few seconds of uncomfortable silence, he left and a door clicked shut.

The silence that swept in felt heavy.

I couldn't see her, but I could sense Leruna close by. She rattled and rummaged through what must have been her healer's tools. Instruments to try to put me back together again.

I wanted to tell her not to bother. I'd have to go back to Sulam. I'd have to go back to the pit.

But the words sat like anchor stones on my chest. I couldn't force myself to even try to speak.

"You have to take this," Leruna muttered under her breath as she pried my mouth open long enough to force a foul-tasting goo down my throat.

I gagged and choked until she followed it with a sip of water.

"You stupid, stubborn idiot. No wonder she wanted me to keep an eye on you," she seethed. "You must try to stay awake, Declan. Don't you dare die. Not now."

Die? Was ... was it that bad? Sure, I'd taken a good beating, but it couldn't be that—

Wait. Had Violet put her up to this? To watching me like some sort of babysitter?

The thought put a knot of anger in my gut, not that I could do anything about it.

Violet was a meddler by nature. I'd seen that play out first-hand with that Chrysa girl and getting far too involved in what turned out to be a complete disaster at Arx Eburna. She should have known better than to stand that close to the furnace, given who and what she was.

Having that energy now directed at me was infuriating, though.

I could handle my own business. I didn't need a keeper.

Er, well, I hadn't in the past.

Things were different now. And while it stung the ever-loving hell out of my pride, I now owed Leruna my life. Again. If she hadn't stepped in, I'd be a cold corpse, floating face-down in the harbor outside the Rook's Roost right now.

And gods only know what would have happened to Nora because of it.

Fates, I really was an idiot.

Leruna didn't say much else as she began cleaning me up. I managed a few semi-conscious groans through my teeth when she rolled me onto my side, moved my arms and legs, and began setting the knuckles I'd broken. I still couldn't will my eyes open, though.

Not until she began probing around at my ribs with her fingers.

One hard poke and I nearly bucked out of the bed. My eyes flew open and a weak cry leaked past my lips.

Leruna froze, staring at me with wide, startled eyes.

"H-Hurts," I managed to groan hoarsely as I sank back down into the mattress, my teeth chattering and my vision swimming.

"I'm sure it does. Hold still." Her expression fell back to that look of cold exasperation as she ran her fingers gently along each of my ribs. "Three severely broken ribs, two broken knuckles, a broken finger, a broken wrist, a fractured jaw and cheekbone, a possible orbital fracture, a severe concussion, and two of the worst black eyes I have ever seen in my life. Oh, and let's not forget another broken nose. At this rate, you'll be lucky if it doesn't rot and fall off your face altogether. It's a miracle you're not missing teeth."

I swallowed stiffly, wondering if that was actually possible or not. She was a healer, after all. Was it a joke? Did healers joke about that kind of thing?

"Your leg is still very weak. It looks like you have soft tissue damage that still hasn't healed fully," she went on as she scooted her chair closer to the bedside. "You shouldn't be fighting in that pit at all yet."

"I'll be s-sure to bring th-that up ... at the n-next meeting," I rasped weakly.

She shot me a withering glare and flicked the end of my very broken nose.

I nearly whimpered again. My eyes welled, and I glared back at the blurry outline of her. "I-I thought h-healers ... were s-supposed to ... b-be nice."

"Only to first-time offenders." She flashed a quick, sweet, dazzling smile and batted her eyes sarcastically.

"D-Does Vi ... Violet know?" I managed to croak weakly.

Leruna's vibrant turquoise eyes flicked up, meeting my gaze for a moment. "That I am a Skyhart? No."

Hmm. Interesting. "R-Roxus?"

"No," she answered quickly. "No one else did until tonight."

Oh. Well, crap. She'd given up her anonymity to save my sorry rear.

"S-Sorry," I rasped again.

"Doesn't quite cut it, does it?" she snapped without looking up from where she was still assessing my ribs. Every little poke lit my body aflame with a fresh rush of agony. My hands shook out of control and a cold sweat shivered from my head all the way to my toes.

Curse it, was I going into shock?

Leruna's full lips twisted to one side as though something about the sight troubled her.

"Don't get any wild ideas about me, though. I may have the Skyhart name, but I haven't set foot on a ship in five years.

I left that lifestyle behind," she said sharply. "Does it hurt when you breathe in?"

All I could manage was a trembling nod.

She hissed a soft Rienkan curse and turned to rummage through her medical tools again.

"D-Do you ... m-miss ... it?" I managed to grit the words out, but the more I spoke, the harder it was to breathe. My chest grew heavier and heavier, almost like someone was stacking bricks on my sternum.

Distraction—I needed her to keep talking, so I didn't think about it.

Leruna's expression was all focus and determination when she turned back to face me. "Every single day. I left the lifestyle, but not my family. My father doesn't hold it against me. He's only ever wanted us, his children, to be happy. And I suppose he's not foolish enough to imagine that all his children would dream of becoming nomadic, seafaring criminals."

Oh. Well, that explained why the man who had been here before was so keen to have her come back. I guess they hadn't stashed her away at the temple, serving the sea goddess, as part of some plot or ploy. She'd left on her own. And they were giving her the space and respect to make that decision.

But ... why? Why would she choose to live in a temple over sailing with her family's fleet? Freedom, power, prestige, wealth, adventure—she had left all of that behind. And for what? A life of prayer and selfless service?

It made no sense to me.

Neither of us spoke again as she continued her assessment. I couldn't stand to make eye contact with her. Not while she had stripped me down to my smallclothes and was running her hands over every square inch of me. It felt wrong to acknowledge or even think about it, especially while she was wearing those robes.

The instant she grabbed the waist-tie of my underwear and

started to pull it loose, I couldn't stop myself. I seized her hand at the wrist, gritting my teeth through the flare of scorching pain as I protested, "Th-That part's ... f-fine ... I p-promise."

Leruna arched a slender eyebrow challengingly. "You really think it's something I haven't seen before? I am a healer, you dolt."

"N-Nobody hit me ... th-there," I objected again, sounding even more winded and pathetic than before.

She narrowed her eyes. "Lovely. But you took several hard blows to your abdomen and have extensive bruising. If you're bleeding internally, it might also come from your nethers, and that would be a very bad sign. I might only have minutes left to save your life."

My face flushed hot, and I collapsed back onto the bed, my body shuddering as I fought for each breath. Gods, it was like I was drowning from within.

Focus. I had to focus. Calm down. Be still. Let her do her job.

It wasn't weird. She was a healer.

I shut my eyes and tried to send my mind somewhere else—somewhere far, far away where a pretty elven healer wasn't snatching my smallclothes down and examining everything underneath.

I tensed, gripping the bed as tightly as my shaking hands would allow until she finished and pulled my underwear back up onto my hips.

"No bleeding. Now, was that so difficult?" she muttered as she moved away, turning her attention to a collection of powders in small jars. She began measuring them out, adding them into a small mortar and pestle.

My face throbbed, half in agony and half from pure shame. I looked away, unable to muster the nerve to reply.

It wasn't that I suspected she was ogling. I just wasn't used to ... well, being touched. Not like that, anyway. Not by anyone who cared to see me put back together instead of broken down. And certainly not gently.

Delthene returned like a whirlwind, and they both took a long time washing me of all the dried blood and dirt. Hours dragged on, and Leruna cleaned my cuts and gashes, stitching them closed. I had a bad one on my brow now. She warned that even with the healing salve, I'd likely have a scar.

Just another one to add to the collection.

My freshly blackened eyes were swelling shut, and it was getting harder and harder to see anything. I could make out Delthene steeping more of that foul herbal remedy in a pot of tea. She poured a cup and began insisting I drink it.

I gagged again as I tried to drink it, so she spooned sugar and honey into it to help with the bitter flavor. It didn't make much difference.

I choked it down, sip by sip, and my head was swimming by the third cup—either from the healing remedies or the concussion. I couldn't tell.

Leruna and Delthene propped me up in bed, stacking pillows behind my back. They worked together, helping me sit upright long enough for Leruna to wrap thick layers of bandaging around my chest, right over my ribs.

Each time she so much as bumped my injured side, a whimper of pain seeped through my clenched teeth. My swollen eyes watered. I fought not to sob, because that would hurt far worse.

"Breathe, Declan. I know it hurts. Just breathe," Leruna murmured soothingly as she arranged a leather bladder filled with crushed ice against my ribs and secured it with a long strip of cloth.

It might have helped, except that every breath sent a bolt of pain through my body. No amount of tea or ice would help with that.

Or so I thought.

"Relax. You need to rest," Leruna said as she finished wrapping my hand and forearm, stabilizing my broken wrist with a piece of flat, thin metal. She'd taken her time splinting it because of the broken knuckles and finger. In all, that arm would be useless for a while.

Fantastic.

"I'm ... n-not tired," I slurred.

I was, though. Exhausted didn't even begin to describe it. My heart sat like a cold stone in my chest—heavy and petrified into something shriveled and unrecognizable.

"Take this," she said, pulling another vial from her kit and adding her little mixture of powders to it. A strange, reddish liquid swirled inside. Not thick like blood. More like a watered-down wine.

"More n-nasty ... r-remedies?" I arched a brow and took it from her with my good hand.

She nodded. "Chaser root extract. They typically use it in a tea. But you're a big boy. I'm sure you can handle it like this."

I scowled and pulled the cork off with my teeth, spitting it into my lap before I downed the vial in one swig. My mouth screwed up as the spicy, almost cinnamon-like fluid oozed down my throat. I coughed and sputtered.

A smug little smirk brushed over her features as she turned away, as though trying to hide it.

"Gods. That's w-worse than the other one," I complained and handed her back the empty vial. "Wh-Where do you get all this stuff? The temple?"

Leruna swiped it from my hand and rolled her eyes. "Some of it, yes. Servants of Undae are trained in extensive healing practices. We learn to make medicines, tonics, and potions from a variety of materials. But there are certain ones that are harder to get. They're rare or too expensive for the temple to keep in stock and have to be shipped from other kingdoms far over the seas."

I waited for her to explain, but she just went back to busily packing away all her tools, taking her time to clean and inspect each one before she put it into the leather pouches she had arranged on the bed beside me.

"And?" I pressed, ignoring how my lips had begun to go numb. "Where d-do you get th-those?"

She puffed an annoyed sigh. "My family gets them for me, if I ask. I try not to, though. And what they do give me, I use very sparingly. I try to make it last as long as possible, as getting more takes time and no small amount of coin."

There was no mistaking the stiffness of reluctance in her tone, like she was silently daring me to keep pushing the issue.

A new, astoundingly awkward silence filled the air between us with a tension so thick I could practically taste it. That is, until that extract finally burned a trail down to my stomach.

I slumped into the pillows as the room slowly began to spin. My head grew foggy, and my arms and legs were heavy and tingly. Even my fingers were numb.

Gods, was I drooling? I couldn't tell.

"Now maybe you'll do as you're told and rest," she muttered as she rolled up her kits, tying them into bundles and tucking them into a haversack. The bed lurched as she pushed off of it to stand.

Through the gathering haze, something struck me like an arrow to the chest. Panic. Fear. It consumed me, mind and body, like I'd just had my head forced underwater.

My hand darted out, and I grasped her by the arm tightly again.

She froze, staring down at me with her lovely face drawn into a shocked frown.

"P-Please don't ... don't l-leave me," I heard myself beg, my voice hitching with pain.

Her expression softened, eyes filling with something like concern. She nodded and eased back down onto the edge of the bed without a word.

I didn't need her to talk, though. I just needed someone to be there. I didn't even understand why. I was a grown man, and I hardly knew her.

But, Fates, I didn't want to be alone.

"You can't keep doing this, Declan," she whispered so quietly I barely heard her.

The room was spinning faster, and I couldn't keep my eyes open, let alone speak. As the chaser root extract pulled me down, deeper and deeper into slumber, I could have sworn I heard her smooth voice speak softly again.

"You can't make me watch you die, too."

Twenty-Two

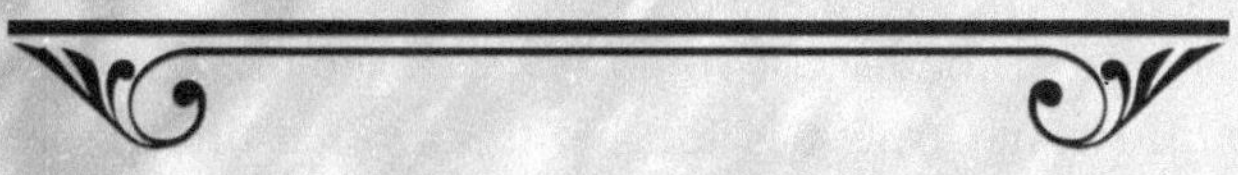

Death had become an old friend by this point.

I'd spent most of my life dancing with it, and I wore a mark for every one of those encounters. Scars, bruises, and broken bones were just the price of admission. Pain was the price I had to pay to claw my way back to life.

But, gods, I'd never felt anything like this.

Whatever remedies Leruna had given me right after the fight must have been powerful, because I had still been able to speak and think even while she worked on my wounds.

Once they wore off, however, I felt all of it. Every stitch. Every broken bone. Every throbbing bruise and torn muscle. The way my entire body seemed to throb in time with my pulse. My face was a broken mess. My chest still felt far too heavy, and every breath was a battle.

I wasn't ready to give up the fight though.

Time passed. Days—weeks—I wasn't sure. And I couldn't bring myself to care. Not when the pain was so relentless. Not when every tiny movement forced whimpering cries through my teeth.

I lay in the dim room, trembling and groaning. Slipping in and out of delirium. The sheets beneath me were soaked with sweat. I couldn't eat. I couldn't sleep.

All I could do was hold on, white-knuckling my way from one second to the next. Praying that the next breath wouldn't hurt so much, or that the gods would have mercy and just let me die.

Through the haze, I could barely make out the shape of Leruna sitting at my bedside, her legs crossed under her, and her face buried in a book. Her lips moved, like she was reading it out loud, but I couldn't hear it. Not with my ears ringing and my breath scraping like nails down a rusty sheet of metal.

Sometimes I could have sworn something soft and furry brushed against my shoulder or hand. Roxus's housekeeper had a cat, didn't she? A cantankerous orange thing with three legs? I think they called it Gibb.

I'd seen it once or twice when I'd come here to spar with Violet. It had never let me touch it before, though.

Now, I had to wonder if the tales I'd heard about cats being able to sense impending death were true. Maybe that's why the heavy, musty-smelling beast kept trying to lie on the pillow right up against my head. Whatever the case, the vibration of its deep, breathy purrs was a nice distraction. Soothing even.

No wonder Violet had developed a soft spot for it.

I survived from one agonizing breath to another until Leruna finally allowed me another dose of her medicines. She measured each out carefully, mixed it into teas, and helped me drink. She wiped my face and chest with damp cloths and helped me sit upright long enough to relieve myself into a chamber pot.

I couldn't decide what was worse—that a few broken ribs had me writhing around for days, or that this wasn't the first time Leruna had been forced to be my nursemaid.

Freaking humiliating.

The pain remedies helped, though. After each dose, I got a few hours of relief, and I was yanked down into a deep, dreamless sleep. I could hold down soup, mashed fruit, or porridge. But the pain was still there, lurking at the back of my mind. Waiting to roar back with a vengeance.

I had almost given up, almost accepted that I would have to find some way to end this the next time I got a good dose of those potions in my system. With those medicines working their magic, I might be able to drag myself to the balcony. And if I threw myself over the railing, a fall from that height would likely be enough to kill me.

Hopefully.

I'd decided on it, resigning myself to Clysiros's dark final judgement, when I opened my eyes and realized I could hear something other than my own pounding pulse and muffled cries. I blinked, trying to focus on that noise.

The faint rumble of the surf echoed in the distance.

I could hear it clearly. Gods, I could even smell it faintly on the wind.

Squinting around the room, I spotted where Leruna had left a window open. She was gone, her chair empty and the thick leather-bound book she'd been reading from left on the nightstand.

I frowned ... until another gust of the sea air blew in to kiss my sweaty skin. I shut my eyes and took in a breath, hands squeezing the blankets in preparation for the splitting pain that came each time those ribs moved.

Nothing. Just a dull ache.

I took in another, deeper gulp of that briny wind just to be sure.

No pain. Well, maybe a little, but nothing at all like before. More of a deep soreness and a pinch of discomfort.

It was over.

Gods, I-I was—

A rasping sob shuddered through my body before I could stop it. Tears filled my eyes. I put a hand over my mouth so maybe no one would hear.

Gods and Fates, it was over. I was alive.

All because of her.

The rush of adrenaline made my heartbeat kick hard in my chest. It lit a fire in my soul and sent a rush of energy through me.

Up. I had to get up. I had to move. To feel myself in control again.

My head swam a little as I sat upright, using my arms to balance while I swung my legs over the edge of the bed. My feet met the cool wood floor, and I wiggled my toes. No numbness. Still no pain.

It wasn't enough—I had to try standing.

Setting my jaw, I slowly pushed forward and kept one hand on the bed as I stood upright. My knees wobbled some, but held strong. Every muscle in my thighs and calves felt tight and sore. My skin was gritty from sweating. The room seemed to spin slowly for a few seconds.

I blinked hard and shook my head, taking a few slow breaths. Adjusting. Feeling the flex of each muscle and the stretch of tendons. Soreness still hovered at the back of my mind, but I was standing next to the bed, steady and clear-eyed.

I took a step, the floorboards creaking faintly under my weight. My knees still shook, and my bad leg was definitely stiffer than the other. It forced me to limp and favor that side.

I could do it, though. I could walk.

I hobbled a few more steps, and gradually my knees stopped trembling. I could hold myself up, standing tall, with only a faint pulling, straining discomfort in my side. Strange.

I ran my hand along the thick bandage still wrapped

around my torso, over the ribs I'd broken. That area still hurt the most out of everything.

Granted, it was bearable now, but I had to wonder why. I'd broken ribs before. Numerous times, in fact. What was different about this time?

Staring around the room, I took in the floor-to-ceiling bookcases crammed tight with all manner of books and trinkets, all covered with a fine layer of dust. An assortment of bizarre weapons hung along the far wall behind a washstand and armoire. A tall dressing mirror reflected the light that ebbed in from the open window.

My breath snagged in my throat at the sight of my reflection. Holy gods.

I lurched closer to get a better look.

It wasn't pretty. Horrifying, more like it. I might have felt worlds better than before, but I looked like a dead man walking.

My face was a bruised, swollen, barely recognizable mess. Granted, the bruises were now a sickly greenish-yellow, which was generally a good sign. That meant they were healing, at least. But I still wore a bandage over the bridge of my nose. Leruna had taped it down after she reset it and threatened me if she caught me trying to take it off.

Wearing nothing but my smallclothes and an assortment of other bandages offered a horrific view of the rest of my body, which was covered in more of those greenish bruises and raised, pink scars. So many that it was difficult to tell where the bruises ended and my tattoos began.

A few of my fingers were still wrapped, and I couldn't ignore the way my right arm tingled with a strange, prickling sensation that made me want to scratch at my palms. I couldn't move my wrist with it still splinted, but I managed to wiggle my fingers a little despite the wrappings. It only gave me a little of that achiness around my knuckles.

I turned, cringing at the soreness as I lifted my bandaged arm to get a better look at the biggest bruise—one that was still deep purple and black. It went from my pectoral down to my hip, all the way around to my lower back.

The sight sent a bolt of panic spearing through me. What the …? Was that from being kicked, or—?

"You were bleeding internally," a soft, feminine voice said from the doorway.

I flinched again and wobbled. Spinning around, I found Leruna watching me, her arms crossed and her expression a strange mixture of seriousness and apprehension.

"What?" I rasped, trying to wrap my mind around what that huge bruise really meant. Had I really been bleeding out from the inside? Didn't she normally do surgeries for that sort of thing?

"One of your broken ribs punctured your lungs and internal organs. You didn't even know it. And you were in such a fragile state, I wasn't sure you could survive surgery," she explained quietly, dropping her gaze to the floor between us. "All I could do was dose you with my strongest healing remedies, pray for Undae to spare you, and wait."

"That's why you were worried about me bleeding from, uh, down *there?* Right?" I guessed.

She nodded slightly. "I didn't know how bad it really was. But I knew you were already in shock and struggling to breathe. And giving you such a heavy dose of such powerful healing tonics too many times would be toxic. I had to be extremely careful with spacing out the doses. What you're seeing on your skin now is where the blood pooled inside you. It will take time for it to fade."

I had to swallow against a knot of anxiety in my throat as I turned, staring at the massive, dark, ominous-looking splotch on my skin. Knowing what it was—proof of how close I'd brushed with death this time—made my skin prickle like mad.

In the reflection, I caught Leruna's gaze flickering to me, panning over my body from head to foot, before she swiftly turned away. Her brow crinkled and she dipped her chin lower, expression closing as though some intrusive thought had consumed her.

The sight of me, of so many layers of scars, must have been horrifying for a healer to see.

"I went to your place to get you fresh clothes, but I couldn't find anything that wasn't sweaty, ragged, and stained with old blood. Roxus's things won't come close to fitting you, so I bought a few tunics and pants. Hopefully they're the right size," she murmured. Her face flushed a rosy color across her cheeks and nose. "I left them in the bathroom. You should take a bath while you've got the energy to stand."

Hobbling back around to face her, I rummaged through all my scrambled thoughts, searching for something intelligent to say. Gods, why was this so awkward?

"Oh, uh, yeah, thanks," I stammered stupidly.

Her mouth quirked to one side. "Think you can handle it on your own?"

"What?"

"Climbing in and out of the tub," she clarified.

Oh. Oh, that was ... hmm. I hadn't considered that. But that would mean stripping down again in front of her. It would also mean looking like a helpless weakling.

I'd done more than my fair share of that lately.

My whole head flushed, and I was suddenly acutely aware that I was still standing there in front of her, a priestess, in nothing but my smallclothes.

Gods just strike me down.

"Yeah, I'm good," I managed to reply and forced a crooked smile that probably looked as uncomfortable as it felt.

I was not, in fact, good. Not even a little.

But I wasn't about to subject either of us to that experience again. Especially since I was certain the tub in question was made for regular-sized folk, not Holvradix half-breeds. There would be no hiding anything under the water, even if I managed to fold myself up into the tub.

Leruna frowned like she wasn't buying it, but didn't press the issue.

"I'll make some tea, then. When you're finished, meet me on the rooftop garden. You could use some fresh air, and Delthene would like a chance to change the sheets in here," she added as she pushed away from the doorway. "Try not to hurt yourself. It's been over a week since I had to stitch some part of you back together. I'd like to keep it that way."

I almost missed it—the quick, cunning little smirk that tugged at her lips as she started away. Her tone betrayed it, though. There was no mistaking the flavor of smug sarcasm in her words, even as she swaggered off.

I just stared after her.

All that thick, dark, spiraling curly hair swished at her waist. The little tips of her pointed ears peeked out on either side of her head. Her robes were so loose and billowy, I only glimpsed a faint hint of her hips swaying with every step.

That's all it took to get my blood going, though.

The sight stole my breath for a second. No one would ever accuse Leruna of being plain, that's for sure. She was, well, exactly what you'd expect a pirate king's daughter to be. Unpredictable as the sea winds. As intense and mysterious as the dark ocean depths. And stunning, even in those healer's robes. Those turquoise eyes framed with long, dark lashes, full lips, and flawless bronze-brown skin would have any man on his knees.

Now that I'd seen what she was hiding beneath them—those tattoos and fitted leathers—it almost seemed like a tragedy that her strong, perfectly curved body was hidden under all that bulky, holy fabric.

Agh! No! Fates, what was I thinking?

I cursed through my teeth and started hobbling for the door.

Fates, maybe I'd knocked something loose in my brain this time. She was a holy woman! I was ... well, *criminal* seemed like a strong word. Definitely a thug, though. A useless, battered thug chained to Sulam's heel like a mongrel dog.

And Leruna had already seen the absolute worst of me. She had seen me broken and bleeding, begging for a death that would free me from this miserable hellhole I called a life.

There was no coming back from that.

Not for me. Not when nothing had changed about my situation.

I was still trapped. Still bound to Sulam. No one could break those chains, not without taking him on. Not without risking everything.

And not without sentencing my little sister to death.

Twenty-Three

The halls were growing longer.

That, or the house was cursed, so you walked for hours without ever reaching your destination. Yeah, that had to be it.

I couldn't think of another reason why I was sweating and wheezing as I made my way from the washroom to the short flight of stairs that led up onto the roof. By the time I arrived at the bottom of them, my head was swimming and my hair was damp with sweat instead of bathwater.

"You can do it," Leruna's voice called down from the top of the stairwell.

I looked up, squinting into the glare of the midday sun, to find her silhouette in the open passage that led out into the garden. With the sun at her back and the glare in my eyes, I couldn't make out her expression. Something about that challenging edge to her tone made me suspect she was smirking now, though.

"Yeah, yeah," I groaned and seized the stair railing to steady myself.

"Take it slow," she coached. "Breathe in deeply. Make sure

your footing is solid before putting your weight into each step."

"I know how to go up a few stairs, woman," I growled through my teeth, already shaking as I took the first two steps. My bones ached. Hints of pain were flaring up my legs and side. I could barely catch my breath, and my knees were beginning to shake again.

Curse it, was the pain remedy wearing off already?

"Your body has been through a lot. Frankly, a lesser man would still be lying in that bed fighting for his life from brain damage," she said. "Lucky for you, Holvradix elves have bone like iron. That extra-thick skull of yours did you some good, for once."

I shot her a haggard glare from under my sweaty bangs. "I'm only half Holvradix."

She shrugged. "Then you inherited some of the more useful traits. What is your other half, then?"

"Human," I grunted, lowering my head and taking a few deep, gulping breaths before I forced my legs to move again. Four more steps. Then I'd find somewhere to sit and suffer.

"From Tibrus, right?" she asked. "I thought I heard you speaking Tibran to that man in the pit. It was so noisy in that arena, though. I wasn't sure."

My shoulders tensed. I set my jaw and refused to look up. I didn't want to see her face. Not when I knew how everyone here in the Southern Kingdoms felt about Tibrans now. Not that it wasn't warranted, of course.

But still ...

"That was a long time ago," I muttered as I hauled myself the last few steps. I barely managed to catch myself as my knees threatened to give. Gods. If this was meant to be some sort of test or assessment of my recovery, I must have been failing miserably.

"Not that long," Leruna retorted, sweeping around me

and motioning for me to follow her through the raised garden beds and large porcelain pots. "It was bold of you to speak to him at all like that. Risky, considering your audience. What did you ask him?"

Panting and sweaty, I wiped my face on the sleeve of my new tunic and shuffled along after her into Delthene's meticulously manicured gardens. Even with the little flowering fruit trees offering some shade, the midday heat left my head pounding.

"Mostly, I was trying to get him to kill me. Sulam might have let him live to fight another day in my place, then," I said as I followed her along the landscaped path to a little table and chairs.

Leruna stopped ahead of me. Her head whipped around to glare at me, expression riddled with horrified disapproval. "You ... were ready to sacrifice yourself for him like that? A Tibran soldier?"

"Yeah, well, folks tend to forget that the first to suffer at the hands of tyrants like Argonox are their own people. He had already begun purging the senate of dissenters and consolidating absolute power before we fled the capital. All of Tibrus has been at war with Argonox for years before he ever set foot anywhere else looking to conquer." I rubbed at the back of my neck, not expecting her to understand any of that.

Few did.

Tyrants could happily torture, slaughter, and starve their own people without anyone in the outside world batting an eye. The rest of the world only cared when they raked their bloody claws over foreign soil. Then it was a problem.

Hell, no one beyond Tibrus had even known Argonox's name until he invaded Noltham years ago.

Now he was infamous, and every Tibran was guilty by association. Just like that man who had died in the pit today.

My stomach turned at the thought.

"A lot of people like him, soldiers with families to protect, had no choice but to stay even after things began to go wrong. Refusing orders, trying to escape—that sort of thing will have commanding officers making an example of you and your entire family in the city streets," I continued at last, finally daring to meet her stare.

Leruna blinked slowly, thoughts flickering behind those enchanting turquoise green eyes like shooting stars crossing a midnight sky. Fast and breathtakingly beautiful. Processing and weighing my every word. Her lips parted and she slowly turned to face me fully, her head only coming to the middle of my chest.

"But you escaped?" she asked hesitantly, like she was trying to understand how. Then she gave me a shoulder and pulled out one of the chairs, motioning for me to sit.

I swiped my tongue along the side of my cheek, tracing old scars there from past fights and trying to decide what to say. How to say it. If I even should.

I mulled it over as I limped for the chair and eased down into it. The movement still ached. Still made my breath catch as a little hint of that pain stung at my ribcage. I could bear it, though.

Even if I did have to try explaining the rotten way I'd wound up here in Rienka.

"My father sold off everything we had to barter secret passage for us. He sent my sister, Mother, and me here eight years ago. But he couldn't go with us. If he left his post, his commanding officers would have known we fled. They would have hunted us down along with all of our extended relatives." I couldn't look at her anymore as I forced out each word. Things I'd never said out loud before to anyone.

Not even to Violet.

"Like any self-respecting dictator attempting a rise to godhood, Argonox had set himself up to strike at just the right time. His followers slaughtered everyone in the senate and left the capital in ruin. They moved uncontested through the city, pillaging, murdering, and burning. We could see the plumes of smoke for miles, even at sea." I shuddered, squeezing my eyes shut for a few seconds.

It didn't help.

Gods, I'd never forget it—how my mother had clung to the ship railing and sobbed. She had screamed for our father and for her friends who hadn't been so fortunate. For our cousins and grandparents. Humans who, despite her origins, had welcomed her into my father's family with open arms.

They were her entire world.

That moment must have broken something deep inside her, because she was never the same. The light went out in her eyes, and her skin drained of all color. She barely spoke. Like a phantom had stolen her soul and left behind an empty husk.

It hadn't made sense to me then. Not when I was just a dumb kid. I couldn't understand that losing everything—her husband, her family, her home—had broken her. She must have felt like my sister and I were all she had left in the world.

My hands clenched so hard the veins stood out against my hands.

I jolted at the sudden scrape of Leruna's chair as she sat down and scooted it closer.

I looked up and found her sitting so close that our knees nearly touched.

Uh-oh. Was this some sort of follow-up examination?

It sure seemed that way with the way she kept peering at me like she was trying to decipher some secret code etched into the corners of my bruised-up face.

"Where are they now? Your mother and sister?" she asked cautiously, as though worried I might lash out.

My heart wrenched deep in my chest, twisting against all the memories that welled up like acid from deep in my soul.

"Plague took most of the refugees stashed below deck with us," I confessed, bowing my head. "Mother fell sick, and the Harbinger took her beyond the Vale soon after. She went in her sleep, so ... it was peaceful."

My throat went stiff at the word—peaceful—and I fought to swallow. She hadn't died screaming or seizing. But peaceful? I didn't know that for sure.

Maybe she'd been dreaming of home, of our father, and the life we'd had before. Gods, I hoped so. I hoped the Harbinger had come softly. That he had made sure she was reunited with Father so they could pass on to the afterlife together.

But there was no way to know what had happened. I'd woken up in the night to relieve myself and found her body already stiff and cold, still curled around Nora. Her lips were blue. Her skin was a strange, dusty gray. Her eyes were glassy and wide open.

I'd known right away, even as a dumb kid, that my mother was gone. Nora hadn't, though. She was too little.

And I'd been too much of a coward to tell her the truth before we were separated.

"After that, the captain ordered all the bodies to be thrown overboard so the infection wouldn't spread. No funeral. No priest to sing the old songs to beg the Fates to let her pass to paradise," I managed to continue, gritting out the words past the heaviness in my chest.

"Oh, Declan," Leruna whispered. She leaned in even closer and bumped her knee against mine.

It was enough to jar me from that trance—from being consumed by the dark flames of memory. My chest heaved in furious, deep breaths.

All I could do was stare back at her. None of the words spinning through my mind seemed right in that moment.

But then she asked *that* question.

She held my gaze as the words left her lips and speared me straight through the chest like a barbed pike.

"Declan, where is your sister?"

Twenty-Four

Something inside me shattered.

Heat and rage roared through my head. Shame scorched through me, singeing my throat and ripping every shred of strength from my body. My eyes welled. My chest split with pain like I'd been run through with a pike.

Nora. Where was Nora?

She ... she was all I had left. My only family. The only blood and flesh like mine still breathing in this world. She was mine. My responsibility.

Gods and Fates, it had been a week since I fought in the pit. Sulam would be furious. He wouldn't care that I'd almost died. I'd broken our bargain.

And she would suffer for it.

Flinging my chair back, I snapped to my feet. Fury roared in my ears. Fury ... and panic.

My body flashed hot and cold. My pulse raced.

O-Oh, gods.

What had I done?!

I'd been lying in this house, doing nothing, while Sulam

had my baby sister hostage. Had her in his hands like a toy he could pull apart any way he wanted.

I hadn't sent word to him about my condition. I hadn't done anything that might save her from him.

Too late—oh, gods, I was too late!

No.

NO!

My legs buckled, and I hit the ground on my knees. I cursed in every language I knew and slammed my fists into the pebbled pathway. Over and over.

Kill him. I *would* kill him. I'd beat him for every mark he put on her. For every drop of blood he spilt from her veins.

Sulam would pay.

I snarled as someone suddenly seized my arms and started fighting to hold me back.

"Stop it! Declan, you have to stop! Calm down!" Leruna shouted over me. "Do you hear me? Get a hold of yourself! STOP!"

I couldn't.

As long as Sulam still breathed, neither Nora nor I would be safe anywhere.

He had her. Had her right now in that fortress of a house. What had he done to her? Was she even still alive?

"Declan, look at me." Strong hands gripped the side of my face, forcing me to meet those sea-colored eyes.

Everything froze. The roaring in my ears faded.

I couldn't move. I couldn't even blink.

"You have to calm down. Focus. Breathe. Whatever is happening to you, you're not alone. I'm here. Do you understand me?" Leruna's stare bored into mine, intense and bright as a star. "You're not alone. I'm here. I'm right here."

The only light in the dark I could see.

It took all my strength to give a small nod.

"Good." Her hold on my face loosened and she sat back,

head tilting to the side as she kept those bewitching eyes on me. Boring into my brain like a worm into an apple. Like she could read every thought, every secret I'd never dared to speak aloud.

It made my skin prickle wildly. My pulse began to slow. My knuckles throbbed from where I'd hit the ground. Fortunately, it didn't seem like I'd reopened any of my wounds.

"Seems you inherited that Holvradix temper, too," she surmised and puffed a heavy sigh. "I suppose that does answer my question, though. Sulam has your sister, as well?"

My face heated and I looked down. "Y-Yeah."

"As a fighter, like you?" she pressed.

"N-no, she, uh," I hesitated, my voice catching in my throat. "She's one of his slaves. He keeps her locked in his estate. He won't let us ... I-I haven't seen her in years ..."

Awkward silence filled the space between us, making every gust of wind and tinkling of Delthene's carved shell wind chimes seem far too loud. There were a thousand things I should have told her. I should have been thanking her and kissing her feet. She'd saved my life ... again.

Granted, Violet had been responsible for it both times. Curse that little white-haired menace. She was meddling more than usual, all without bothering to visit or talk to me directly. I didn't understand why she'd suddenly made herself so scarce, but I'd have a few choice words for her when she dared to show her face again.

"So, this is why you've been fighting all this time," Leruna finally murmured, her lips pursed, brow crinkled with thought. "He's made you fight to keep her alive. Goddess, Declan, surely you see what's happening, don't you?"

I stiffened, my temper sparking some at the hint of accusation in her tone. Did I see? Of course I freaking saw. I felt it in every mark, every scar on my body.

Leruna's expression cooled, her shoulders drawing back

and her lips thinning when I didn't answer. "This can't go on, Declan. Your body can't take this kind of abuse anymore. It's already resistant to my healing remedies because you've been taking so many of them over the years. You've built up a tolerance to a point that would be lethal to anyone else. It's only a matter of time before they quit working for you altogether."

What ...?

My pulse skipped. I gaped at her and tried to wrap my mind around that.

I mean, of course, I had taken quite a lot of those remedies and tonics. I'd been stitched up and bound together countless times—and not just by her. But I'd always been able to walk it off in the end. Chalk it up to that Holvradix resilience my mother's blood had given me.

I had to believe that still counted for something.

"I have no choice," I countered, growling each word through my teeth. "If I don't go back, if I don't keep fighting, then who knows what he will do to—"

"How do you know she is even still alive?" Leruna questioned, her eyes cold steel in the sunlight.

All the feeling drained out of my body, rolling off my skin like falling rain.

How did I know? Because I felt it—felt her, felt our connection. It was soul deep. Nora wasn't dead.

And if that wasn't enough, I had evidence. I had the testimony from someone not even Sulam knew about—someone inside his house, who swore she was alive and well.

But that was a secret I'd never betray. I wouldn't breathe a word of it to anyone. Not when all our lives still hung in the balance. This web was fragile, and one wrong tug would tear everything apart.

I couldn't risk it.

My mouth mashed, teeth gritting to keep all the rage-fueled words in. That Holvradix temper, as she called it.

"I have to send word to Sulam as soon as possible," I muttered. "I have to let him know I'm coming back to fight. So he doesn't hurt Nora. I have to make sure he knows I didn't run away."

"Gods, you're so stupid," Leruna snapped bitterly, her brows knitting together as she glanced me up and down. "You really think you can keep doing this? Don't you see what's happening, Declan?"

I bit down hard and turned my gaze away.

"How could you even agree to this in the first place?" she went on, her words coming faster. "Didn't you set any sort of terms for how it would end? A set length of time you had to serve? A number of fights you had to win?"

I had to look away. I couldn't answer that. There was no good answer to any of those questions, anyway.

Just the ugly, pathetic truth.

When I still refused to respond, Leruna puffed another tight, angry breath and stood. "I will send word to Sulam, if you want. But you can't go back. Not yet. You won't make it to the front door, let alone down into that pit, before you collapse. Your body is still weak. Pushing it too far now, when it's just finally begun to heal, will break you. And what then? What happens to her if you really do die?"

I hated how right she was. More than that, I hated that I needed her to be the one to tell Sulam. To bargain for my time to heal. To make sure none of this impacted Nora.

I forced myself to nod slightly.

Leruna stood over me for a few, impossibly tense seconds. I could feel the sting of her gaze moving slowly over my body. But I didn't dare try to imagine what she must be thinking. How disgusting and pathetic I must have looked to her right then.

So much for the champion of the arena.

At last, Leruna grumbled something about helping

Delthene get the sheets changed on the bed I'd been borrowing. She started to leave and warned me not to dawdle too long up here on my own. Eventually, my pain would return. I'd struggle even more to get down those stairs and back to bed.

I didn't reply.

I waited until the sound of her footsteps disappeared into the house before I dared to look up. Wincing against the sting of pain in my side, I dragged myself back into the chair and sat, drinking in the salty breeze and warmth of the sun. My thoughts circled like gulls soaring around the masts of the ships that sailed by on the far horizon, just as noisy and relentless.

I couldn't shake the worry that trusting Leruna with all the gory details of my life might be a mistake. We were barely more than acquaintances. Sure, Roxus trusted her. Apparently, Violet did, too.

But could I? And more than that ... how could I ever expect her to understand any of it?

She wasn't there when it happened. She didn't know what it felt like to be powerless—not when she'd been born into a family like the Skyharts. She had a fleet of blades and teeth at her back, priestess or not.

Wherever she walked, she was never truly alone.

But when Sulam had found us, Nora and I were only kids. We were nothing but orphans lost in a kingdom where we couldn't even speak the common language. We were starving. Terrified. Desperate.

And I was the eldest. The only son. My father's heir. I was supposed to handle it, to find a way for us to survive and take care of my sister. I was supposed to make sure she was safe.

I hadn't known any better then. And when I realized what was happening to us, it was already too late. Sulam had Nora in his grasp. And my eight-year-old mind only saw one way out. One way to protect her.

I thought I had no choice other than to agree to whatever he said. To take Sulam at his word, because even then, I still didn't fully comprehend what he was or what that choice would mean ...

That I was making a deal with a man who might as well have been a demon cut straight from Vescor's own flesh.

My throat burned as the memories of that night danced through the back of my mind like shadows in candlelight. Yes, I'd made a terrible mistake. But I would fix everything. I'd find a way out for both of us.

I just needed more time.

My stupid body could hang on a little longer. It had to. I was down, but not out of the fight. Not yet.

Sure, Sulam was setting me up to fail. I wasn't sure what had changed and why he suddenly wanted me dead, and I doubted I'd be able to find out. Not unless I had some expensive help.

But if Sulam got his way, if I was finally going to meet the goddess of death face-to-face, then I'd do it carrying his head as my trophy ... one way or another.

Part Five
Violet

Twenty-Five

I couldn't breathe.

My eyes flew open to nothing but dark.

I tried to gasp, but something big and heavy crushed down upon me.

Was that ... a body? Had one of the Ulfrangar gotten to me? No—not an Ulfrangar. I knew the scent of eucalyptus and cedar that clung to his fine clothes.

Axien.

But he wasn't moving or making a sound.

Was he ... dead? Had the Ulfrangar shot him, too?

Oh, gods, what was happening?!

I squirmed, grunting and digging my fingers into Axien's torso. I pushed with all my strength, silently praying that all those cursed push-ups might finally pay off for once. My arms flexed, burning with effort.

His weight shifted, then he—moved.

Axien pushed off of me suddenly, sucking in a ragged breath and rolling over to lie sprawled out beside me.

Not dead, thank the gods. Just unconscious.

"What, by all the gods, was that?" He coughed and panted.

"U-Ulfrangar ... attacked," I managed to wheeze back. "I-I think they killed Lord Ragentrude."

No one took an arrow to the neck like that and walked it off.

"Are you all right?" Axien asked as he pushed himself upright.

I nodded, still trying to calm my breathing. "Yeah. I think so. You?"

He nodded back. "You're sure it was Ulfrangar?"

Gathering my hands behind me, I hauled myself into a sitting position. My head swam, making the whole room slosh sideways. I rubbed at my forehead, trying to force my vision to clear.

"They had silver cuffs with the three-eyed wolf on them. No mistaking that," I explained as I squinted around and blinked hard a few times. Slowly, everything steadily came into focus.

He made a disapproving sound in his throat. "Then they were probably following us the entire time, just waiting for Lord Ragentrude to take us to that room."

I had to agree.

Why else would they wait until that moment to make their move? The rest of the crypt hadn't even been guarded. If they'd known the incantation to make the magic door open, they could have waltzed in and out with the artifact without anyone being the wiser.

"So much for this not being complicated," Axien grumbled as he twisted back and forth, studying the room where we both sat unceremoniously on the floor like two newly born goats.

"Where are we? Did you pull us through another portal?" I asked as I wobbled to my feet.

Axien stood swiftly, offering a hand to steady me. "Not intentionally."

"Is that something you can do *un*intentionally?"

His expression steeled, brow setting in a furrow as his gaze roamed the area around us—a room that looked suspiciously like a fancy vestibule or entryway. Had we just been transported to another room in the Ragentrude estate?

The rectangular room had only one door, though. One fine, polished wooden door with a gilded knob stood directly across from us. A fine, dark green wool rug stretched the length of the space, and a round, claw-footed entryway table stood in the very middle ... directly beneath what I almost mistook for a chandelier.

Almost.

My lips parted, neck arching as I gazed at the shining glass sculpture of the icosahedron that hung—no, floated—directly above the table. It shimmered as it slowly spun, looking in every single detail like the artifact we'd seen only seconds before. Every surface bore a different golden glyph, and the beveled details that swirled over every surface had been written in the ancient Avoran language.

A brilliant bluish light pulsed gently from its center, and shadows of glass mechanisms seemed to click, whirr, and rotate like the innards of a clock.

"Incredible," I breathed.

Axien took a step closer to me, almost as though he were subtly trying to angle himself between me and the artifact. Was he worried about it exploding or something?

A horrifying thought.

"I think ... we're *inside* it," he murmured as he took another uncertain step closer to it.

"What?" I balked.

"I think we're inside the puzzlebox," he repeated, his tone more certain. "When I touched it, I felt something happen. It was almost as if it made a connection with me. I tried pulling back, but it was too late."

I hedged toward him, gnawing at the inside of my cheek as I kept my eyes on that hovering glass sculpture, just in case.

"Does it glow? Can you see any magic?" Axien glanced my way, his expression still tense.

"That thing is glowing, yes," I confirmed. "Especially a few of the larger symbols. But I don't see anything else doing it. Not yet, anyway. Look, if you're right, and we are inside the artifact ... how exactly are we going to get out? And what does that mean for the outside world? Do the Ulfrangar have it now?"

Axien's broad shoulders dropped slightly and he shook his head. "I don't know."

Well ... crap. My thoughts whirled, racing between all the possibilities of where we might be and what could possibly be happening somewhere beyond this room. What if we couldn't get out? What if we were trapped in here forever? What if the Ulfrangar or the Tibrans found a way in? What, by all the gods, did they even want with this thing?

We were missing something. Something important. But from where I stood, it didn't look like we'd be finding any answers in this particular room.

We needed to move. In my professional experience, it was always harder to hit a moving target. Any second, Tibrans could come spilling in around us.

"There must be a way out," I declared as I set my focus on the only door in the room.

Stepping past Axien, I made a wide berth around the round table and the hovering glass icosahedron with my back to one of the polished wood-paneled walls.

All magical strangeness aside, a door was a door. It had to lead somewhere. It could be just that simple.

Seizing the handle, I gave it a twist. The knob immediately

flickered blue, gleaming between my fingers, as it clicked. A wave of prickly chills climbed my spine as I pushed it open, peering into the dim room beyond.

It was a study, or some sort of office, with bookshelves spanning floor to ceiling on every wall. They reminded me a bit of Roxus's shelves, packed tight with finely bound leather books, odds, and ends. Little figurines stood alongside arrangements of different glass containers filled with strange things like feathers, dried flowers, and brightly colored liquids.

A lavish seating area was appointed around a large white stone hearth, and a commandingly large claw-footed desk was set with a red velvet, high-backed chair. All empty. Not a soul in sight.

The chills spread to my arms and legs, making my heart-beat skip.

If there was no one here, why was the fire lit and roaring like it had been tended? Why were there papers stacked on the desk, along with a fine golden feather quill and an inkpot? Why was a tea set placed on the table between all the delicately detailed furniture, complete with steam still rising from the spout?

Wrong—everything about this place was all wrong.

I pushed the door the rest of the way open so Axien could see, too. He poked his head through directly above mine, and for a few seconds, we just stood there peeking in at the next room like two children trying not to get caught eavesdropping after bedtime.

"The lamps are all lit," he whispered. "Someone must be home."

Gods, he was right. There were fine golden sconces built into the bookshelves, and every single one was lit. But the flames didn't burn red.

To me, they glowed as blue as his eyes.

"They're magic," I whispered back.

"And what about the fireplace?" he asked.

"That one seems normal," I answered.

He made another low, thoughtful, grumbling sound in his throat.

"I don't like this." My hands clenched into shaking, clammy fists in my skirts.

"I don't either," he said. "But we don't have much choice, do we? We can't just sit here. There must be someone here who can help. Someone who can send us back."

I drew in a shaking breath. He was right—as much as I hated to admit it. Gods, I wished I had my daggers. I'd settle for another dinner knife. Anything was better than being empty-handed.

I did have the new ring Axien had given me. It was a weapon of last resort, but it was better than nothing.

And it was more than enough to give me a flicker of confidence as I pushed the door open further and took a small, cautious step into the study.

Axien seized my arm, stopping me. Staring past me, his vibrant eyes narrowed as he surveyed the room again.

"There's no other door," he said.

I blinked, hesitating. Then I took another look around the lavish space.

Fates, he was right. We were standing at the *only* door.

But ... that didn't make sense. If this was the only way in or out, where had the water for the tea come from? And the firewood stacked neatly in the rack beside the hearth? And all the other items?

Had someone else been here only moments before? We would have seen them coming or going through the crypt, right?

My stomach flipped and swam. I drew my bottom lip between my teeth, trying to make sense of it.

But absolutely none of this made any sense at all.

"We go in and shove one of the chairs under the knob to keep anyone else from coming in," I plotted aloud, keeping my voice hushed. "That way, no one can burst in and surprise us. Then we investigate. We figure out who this place belongs to. If it's Ragentrude, then ... then maybe it does make sense for all of this to be here. Right?"

Axien's expression darkened, tension thick on his sharp features as he gave me a long, meaningful glance. Then he took a deep breath in through his nose and slowly blew it out, as though he was trying to mentally prepare himself for the worst.

"We stay close together," he replied.

"Agreed."

His throat moved as he swallowed and gave a final nod of agreement. His hand slid down my arm, taking mine again.

Then, together, we stepped into the study.

Twenty-Six

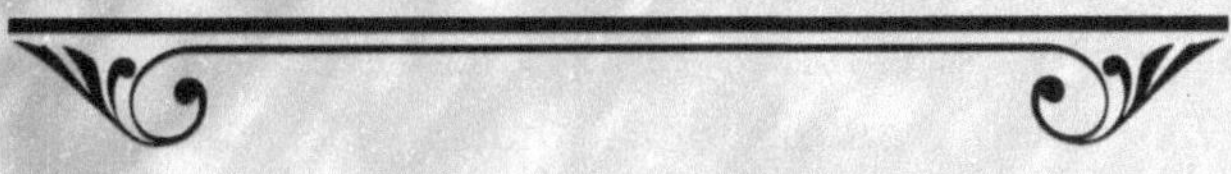

We moved as one.

Crossing the room, Axien and I picked up one of the small parlor chairs and lugged it to the door. I swung it shut and held it closed while he angled the back of the chair under the knob. He gave it a few hard shoves, just to make sure it was wedged in there tight.

Then we both stumbled back.

My heart pounded wildly, sweat now running down the sides of my face as I waited for anything to happen.

Seconds ground by like centuries. I held my breath, every muscle in my body braced for anything.

But there was nothing.

No pounding on the other side. No beastly growls or magical explosions. Just the comforting crackle and pop of the fire behind us and the soft fragrance of chamomile wafting from that dainty porcelain teapot.

"Right," Axien said, his voice hitching nervously as he took another step back from the door. "That should hold."

Who was he trying to convince? Me? Himself? Or the door?

I decided to remind him that if a small army of Tibrans *really* wanted to get in here, they would be able to knock down that door chair and all.

"Let's take a look around," I suggested as I moved away, the heels of my fancy shoes clicking off the polished wood floors. "Maybe there's something we're missing."

Gods, it sounded even stupider when I said it out loud. Something we were *missing?* Like, what? Everything?

Axien didn't call me on it, though. He must have been clinging to every shred of hope he could muster, too.

I started at the desk, rifling through the stacks of parchment that were placed neatly in a row across it as though someone had been sorting their mail. Some of them were creased, like they'd been folded, and had remnants of broken wax seals on them. None of the seals were anything I recognized, though. Certainly not the Ragentrude's.

So, I started casually flipping through the letters themselves.

"These are all written in Avoran," I realized aloud and frowned up at Axien in confusion.

He frowned back and immediately came over to look.

They weren't anything special. Most were letters written like correspondence between friends or relatives. They talked about dinner parties, meetings, and gossip.

But they all shared one feature: they were either signed by or addressed to someone named Vesperus Theoclordan.

The same name that had been on the outside of the chamber that held the artifact.

Another wave of queasy dread seeped through me from head to toe, and I put the last stack of letters carefully back down where I'd found them.

This was beyond strange.

"See what else you can find," I suggested as I continued going through the desk.

Axien's mouth pinched tight, brow now creased with worry, as he shuffled to the bookshelves.

I rummaged through all the drawers, finding more stacks of clean, unused parchment, older letters, extra quills, a golden seal, and a small box with sticks of sealing wax inside. Nothing out of the ordinary for someone's desk.

"Look here," Axien called suddenly.

I dashed over to find him holding an ornately carved wooden box. Inside, pressed between two folds of dark blue velvet, three glimmering rings shimmered in the firelight. These weren't ladies' rings, though. The bands were thick and wide, clearly made for a man's finger. The designs were odd, too, like nothing I'd ever seen before.

But they all glowed with a halo of vibrant blue light.

"Magic," I gasped.

Axien's grip on the box tightened. "All of them?"

"Yes."

Axien loosed a shaking breath as he stared at the rings again.

One looked sort of like a signet ring, but instead of a round top, it was cut to the shape of a shield. Tiny chips of red stone were inlaid in it, and the band had countless lines of Avoran writing so small I couldn't make out what it said.

The second was gold with a black gemstone cut in the shape of a fox's face. The band had the same sort of writing, all spiraling around the central stone, and studded with more small chips of the same black stone.

The last ring was made from flawlessly polished silver, crafted to look like two feathered wings wrapped around the finger. Where the two wingtips touched on top, a bright, diamond-shaped amethyst glittered and sparkled.

I stifled a gasp as Axien plucked it from the velvet cushion, holding it up to the ambient firelight.

"You're taking it?" I hissed.

"Borrowing," he corrected as he slid it onto his middle finger. His expression skewed slightly, and he flexed his fingers, studying the silver ring curiously.

"What is it?" I asked, half expecting his finger to suddenly rot off entirely.

It didn't, thank the gods.

"It's the same as when I touched the artifact," he said. "Almost like it … is a part of me. A new muscle I can flex at will."

I took a big step back. "Do it, then."

He flashed me a wide-eyed stare of shock. "Here? Now?"

"I'd rather know if you're going to suddenly explode into a magical inferno now rather than later when I might be dealing with other enemies," I snapped.

His lips pursed sourly. "Your concern for my well-being is truly overwhelming."

I crossed my arms and cocked my hips. "I'm not the one trying out someone else's magic rings."

"Look, in my very limited magical experience, I suspect that we've most likely just stumbled into what was once an Avoran sorcerer's private study. That's the only reason I can fathom that any of this is here, untouched, and still looking exactly like it did thousands of years ago," he said. "If this is some sort of arcanely crafted space, a pocket-dimension created between the fabric of reality and the realm of the gods, then there would be no passage of time here. It would be exactly as the sorcerer left it, frozen forever."

I stared at him, floundering in my head while I tried to make sense of that. A … pocket-dimension? Where had he come up with that theory? Or was this something all Avorans knew?

"Then … how do we get out?" I asked hesitantly. "You must have a theory about that, too, right?"

Gods, I hoped so.

He swept his tongue over his top lip, brows rumpling together as he glanced back toward the door.

"There's only one door," he reminded me. "But that doesn't mean it only leads to one place. Maybe it can lead us home."

A pang of dread jabbed at the pit of my stomach.

"It could also dump us straight into the eternal void," I retorted, scowling.

"We don't have much of a choice. We can't stay here forever." He crossed his arms, too, matching my energy with his own stubborn frown.

I hated it when he was right.

"Right. Lead on, then, Mr. Sorcerer." I side-stepped out of his way, tipping my head toward the door. "Let's see what you can do."

He snorted, rolling his eyes as he strode past me. It only took a few paces for all that arrogance and confidence in his demeanor to fizzle. He practically limped the last few feet before he stopped and started working the chair out from under the knob.

I followed, keeping a few paces back just in case, and watched as he flexed his hands. He clenched them, shifting his weight and muttering a few words before he swiftly grabbed for the knob and twisted it.

Blue magical light bloomed from under his hand, flashing brilliantly for a second before it faded.

I held my breath, inching closer to him. Just in case. Annoying as Axien could be, he was my—well, not my friend. Not really.

Or was he? Could you even be friends with someone you'd kissed like that?

The door groaned as he pulled it inward, and a rush of freezing air howled through the gap. The force of it snatched the door straight out of his grasp so hard it banged off the study wall and knocked over a few glass decanters.

I screamed, leaping to Axien's side as they shattered on the floor.

But he didn't move. He stared, mouth hanging open, as the wind snatched at his hair and overcoat. I shivered, ducking behind his taller form to shield myself from the frigid wind that gusted through the open doorway.

C-Cold. Why was it so cold?

Flecks of white swirled around us, blowing in through the open doorway.

Gods and Fates, was that ... *snow?*

Twenty-Seven

"I see something!" Axien called over the howl of the wind.

Peering from around him, I squinted into the wind—into the blinding torrent of snow that stuck in my lashes and melted on my cheeks. At first, there was only darkness and those endless flecks of white. Even my heat vision saw nothing but a black void.

Then, far in the distance, I spotted the ghostly shapes of mountains against a stormy night sky. They thrust upward at staggering heights, with jagged, snow-covered slopes flecked with aspens.

But that wasn't what made my pulse pound in my throat. Far on the other side of the open expanse before us, like a frozen lake that stood between us and those mountains, something warm glowed against the freezing storm.

Lights.

Another door?

No ... it was bigger. Much bigger.

"Is that a cabin?" I called up to him.

"I think so," he verified. "And there's smoke coming from

the chimney. We ... we should see what's there. Maybe there's someone else there who can help us. It's not that far. We can make it."

"Not in this dress, I'm not! Look at my shoes, Axien! I can't walk in snow like this!" I seized his forearm tightly, trying to hold him in place.

"Then I'll carry you." Before I could protest, he faced me and draped his overcoat over my shoulders, wrapping me up like an angry little sausage wrapped in a pastry roll, before he swept me up in his arms.

Humiliating.

"Stop it! We shouldn't go out there!" I protested, wriggling angrily inside his coat. "We don't even have any weapons! What if something goes wrong?"

"What other choice do we have? If there's even a small chance that the owner of this place is still here, we need to find them. They might be our only chance of getting out," he growled, holding me tighter. "We can't stay in here, Violet. You know it as well as I do. If the Ulfrangar are murdering nobles in Rienka, then—"

"I know," I interrupted. I growled a few angry, Viperi curses under my breath and held still.

Once again, Axien was right. Gods, that was becoming a really annoying trend in our relationship.

"I'm gonna run for it," he warned as he stepped into the doorway, the icy wind freezing snowflakes into his hair and eyebrows.

"The d-door—le-leave it open. Just in ca-case," I said, my teeth chattering.

What if it closed and disappeared entirely? What if we got stuck here? We'd die of exposure long before anyone even realized we were missing. What if we got all the way to that cabin only to find it was abandoned, too?

I cringed, turning my face into his chest as I felt Axien's strong body flex, his arms holding me tighter against him. His jaw clenched, eyes cold steel as he dove forward into the blizzard. With his head into the wind, Axien sprinted out across the flat expanse between the door and the distant glow of the cabin's windows.

A low cracking, splintering from underneath his feet made my heartbeat stammer. His footing slid some, and he nearly fell.

Ice—gods, it really was a frozen lake.

Axien hissed a curse, but he didn't stop.

Gripping me tighter, he poured on more speed, rushing straight for the cabin. His breathing deepened, coming in heavy gasps. In through his mouth, out through his nose. The wind snatched at his hair. Snow stuck to his brow and caked onto his eyebrows.

I stoled a glance ahead, squinting into the wind.

Halfway there. We could do this. We could make it. Just a little farther.

The cabin was only about half a mile away now. Two windows glowed promisingly, and black smoke belched from the stacked-stone chimney. Snow had blown up against the sides, almost burying the thatched roof entirely in a drift.

But it was there—and I could see the door.

Fates, I just hoped whoever might be inside would actually let us in.

A flicker of something caught my eye to the right, moving so fast I barely noticed. It stayed fast and low, like a wisp of shadow amidst the swirling white of the storm.

My head whipped around, but it was already gone.

Every nerve immediately drew tense and every sense opened, focusing on the storm around us. Out on the lake, there was nowhere to hide. Not for a normal creature.

But that shadow ... it hadn't moved like anything living.

"Axien." I squirmed to get his attention. "Axien, there's something—!"

"I know," he shouted back over the howl of the wind. "I can feel it."

He could *feel* it? What did that even mean?

I stared at him for a second, then tore my gaze away and searched the storm again. My eyes watered in the stinging wind. My nose and cheeks burned.

Then I saw it again, rising behind us, not sixty feet away.

A dark shape, that wavered and flickered, seemed to hover over the surface of the ice. The wind was too strong. The snowfall was blinding. I couldn't make out any details.

But I could feel it watching us. Observing. Waiting. Calculating.

I knew what it felt like to be hunted.

"I see it!" I shouted to Axien.

His face hardened with a snarl and he gripped me tighter, pumping his legs faster and faster. He didn't reply. He stared straight ahead, straight at the cabin.

Almost there. Almost there.

A scream tore from my throat as the shadowy creature appeared right behind us, not ten feet away.

I floundered in Axien's arms as panic snatched away every shred of my sanity. Fear took me like a riptide as I stared at the massive beast towering over us. Big as a nightmare. Dark as pure pitch.

A thing of purest nightmare.

The beast stood well over ten feet tall, considering us with a head like a bare, bleached animal skull. No eyes filled the empty sockets. Just tiny, pinpricks of flame-red. It rose on a spindly, gaunt body covered in shaggy, matted black fur—a body that I could have sworn looked almost humanoid, apart from its hooved feet. Bare bone spines ran down its back, and horns like jagged, sharply angled antlers spread out like a crown of thorns from its head.

It reached for us, stretching out a hand with too-long, claw-tipped fingers. Its bony jaws opened with a screeching sound like a chorus of screaming infants.

And then we were at the cabin.

Axien ripped it open, and golden light poured over us. He flung me down onto the floor and whirled around, slamming the door behind us. With his back against the wood, he stared down at me, eyes as wide as two glowing blue moons and face so pale I couldn't tell if it was because he was half-frozen or just terrified.

Both, probably.

"There's a plank! Above the door!" I said as I fought to get untangled from his coat and scrambled to my feet.

I helped him fit the long wooden plank across the door, sliding it into the two iron hooks that held it in place. Then we both stood, our backs against the wood, panting and shivering. Alive. Safe.

Hopefully.

My heart pounded in my ears, so fast and loud it was a constant hum. My body ached as the warmth of the cabin's interior began to thaw out all the places where the storm had nearly frozen me solid.

"Is it gone?" I whispered.

Axien stood shaking beside me, every muscle drawn tense, his jaw clenched. He blinked, not seeming to register that I'd even spoken.

"Axien?" I tried again.

He slowly shook his head. "I-I ... I don't know."

Someone had to find out.

Slowly pulling away from the door, I kept my body low as I crept to the nearest window and peered out into the dark.

White flakes swirled beyond the pane, but beyond that ... there was nothing. A void of darkness.

With a hard blink, I swapped over to my heat-vision. My heartbeat throbbed in my eardrums as I scanned the world beyond the frigid glass.

Nothing.

No signs of heat anywhere in that whirling vortex of white flecks.

"I think it's gone." I stepped back from the window.

Axien blew out a ragged, groaning breath and slowly sank to the floor. He sat with his back still pressed against the door and his head in his hands, his strong shoulders shaking. Or maybe he was shivering? Neither one of us was dressed for snow.

"What, by all the gods, was that thing?" he gasped, his voice cracking and frantic.

"I-I don't know," I stammered, easing down to sit beside him. "I've never heard of anything like that before. But something about it felt ... evil."

Axien didn't reply. He just dragged his fingers through his hair as he fought to catch his breath.

I stared down at my toes. They glowed a bright, angry pink from the wind. Stupid, useless shoes. Lovely as they were, they did nothing for me now.

I took them off and threw them aside. The fancy, glittering heels *thunked* across the wooden floor, landing at the foot of a narrow, roughly hewn bed.

My gaze wandered around the tiny, one-room cabin. Like the study, everything seemed pristine and neat, left in perfect order, as if the owner had only just stepped out a moment ago.

A fire roared in the stone hearth, with a big black cooking pot nestled over the red coals. It filled the space with a cozy, radiant glow and balmy heat. The bed had been made with quilts, blankets, and pillows. Animal trophy mounts hung on the walls—four wreaths of elk antlers, stuffed wolf and deer heads, even a bear skin had been stretched across the floor like a rug.

A large trunk sat against the far wall, with a weapon rack hung right above it, displaying a few swords in varying sizes and a crossbow and quiver. There were a few hatchets, the sort for throwing or cutting apart soft tinder, and a few large hunting knives for skinning game. Nothing out of the ordinary for a cabin like this.

The tiny kitchen area had a table built from crudely cut and trimmed logs, with two chairs on either side. The wood stove was lit, and a loaf of braided bread sat on a cutting board along with a wheel of cheese—none of it moldy.

But there was no one here.

Once again, Axien and I were alone.

"It's just like before," I murmured shakily. "Like someone was just here and we missed them."

"Perhaps they were," Axien mused as he pushed himself to his feet and began pacing the length of the cabin.

"A sorcerer who also enjoys the hunt?" I couldn't keep the skepticism from my tone as I joined him. The wooden floorboards creaked under my bare feet as I prowled toward the weapon rack, eyeing the simple wares on display.

Two shortswords. One longsword. Both were clearly Avoran in make, but surprisingly plain. No golden filigree. No etchings or sweeping designs that would mark them as a wealthy man's wares. Interesting.

"Now then, what have we here?" Axien said, leaning over the trunk. He'd already flipped back the heavy lid and leaned in, resting his hands on the rim as he peered at the contents.

I hurried to peek over his shoulder, mouth quirking as I surveyed the layers of folded fine leathers and furs.

Hunting attire?

"Here." Axien pulled a dark leather longcoat with a gray fox fur collar off the top and handed it to me.

I held it up, admiring it for a moment. Even if it wasn't ornate or grand, it still felt sturdy and well-made. More of the plush fox fur lined the inside, as well, so it would be incredibly warm. Even the sleeves were lined, and there were many deep pockets inside and out.

I offered it back to him. Clearly, it had been made for a man. It would be several sizes too big for me.

But Axien was already pulling more items out of the chest. Hunting leathers, pants, boots, belts, and even fur-lined socks.

"So now we're looting this place, too?" I frowned as he began dressing himself, pulling on another long leather coat over his shoulders and buttoning it all the way to the neck.

"One ring and a coat isn't looting," he countered and nodded to the coat in my hands. "But in your case, I'd suggest a full wardrobe change. You can't go out there in that gown, let alone in bare feet."

I pursed my lips, appraising the fur-lined coat again. "It's too big."

"We'll cinch it up. There are some belts in here." He tossed one at me.

I caught it and ran my fingers over the polished silver buckle. "It'll drag the ground," I grumbled weakly.

"Then I'll cut it. Look, we can't stay in here. We only have two choices. Either we stay here and pray someone eventually comes and finds us before we starve to death, or we try to get back to the door to the study and try something else. Unless, of course, you'd like to take our chances out on the tundra?"

I scowled, my gaze immediately drawn to the weapon rack. Going out there into that freezing wind would also mean facing that creature again. Just the thought made my stomach swim.

But what choice did we have? At least this time, we

wouldn't be unarmed. We could come up with a plan. We could prepare.

And maybe, we would stand a chance if that monster showed up again. We might not be able to kill it, but we might be able to hold our own until we got to the door.

A knot of dread twisted in my stomach, clenching and aching until it made me nauseous.

Something about that creature had felt wrong—ancient and ominous in a way that made me remember all the stories I'd read about creatures born of Vescor's malice. Monsters like switchbeasts and the pit demons of old.

But that wasn't possible.

A creature like that wouldn't be living in an Avoran puzzlebox. That made no sense whatsoever. The Avorans had warred against beings like Vescor. They wouldn't invite his offspring to live in their cozy magic studies.

Whatever was going on here, it was far beyond our understanding. So we needed to find a way out—soon.

Even if that meant braving the cold, and whatever other monsters lurked outside. We could make it.

We had to.

Twenty-Eight

This had to work.

If it didn't—if we got lost out on the ice or if that creature attacked us again—then we'd lose more than just the artifact.

We might die in here, and no one in the Zenith's Call would know what had happened to us. The Ulfrangar would make off with the artifact, and Fates only knew what would happen.

"Fine. Hand me the boots," I growled and swiped a pair of leather pants from the little pile he'd been making. "Gods, I'm going to look like a child playing dress up in her father's wardrobe."

"Better than freezing those lovely toes off," he chuckled, but it was a hollow, forced sound that did nothing to disguise the tremor of worry in his words.

This was madness. We both knew it. We didn't even know what sort of monster that skull-faced beast was, let alone what it might be capable of.

But staying here wasn't an option, either. Better to go now, to work through this as quickly as possible, and find a way out. Any seconds wasted might be costly on the other side.

So we armed ourselves as best we could—me with one of the shortswords and a hunting knife, and Axien with the other shortsword and the longsword. He threaded both onto a belt he fastened over his coat, then swiped the crossbow and quiver. The wind would be too strong to fire it with any accuracy, but we couldn't afford to be choosy.

Not when we had no idea of what we were really up against out there.

"Turn your back," I commanded as I prepared to change into the leather pants and a wool tunic he'd dug out of the trunk.

Not that nudity bothered me. I'd been raised in the Southern Kingdoms, after all. But knowing he wasn't as comfortable with it put a strange tension in the air.

Axien obeyed, keeping his nose to the door and his hands on his hips while I tried to wriggle free of Vanora's fancy dress.

Only ... I couldn't.

There were too many buttons in places I couldn't reach, and the stupid thing fit so tightly against my body that I couldn't even twist the fabric around to manage it. The buttons were tiny and impossible to slip through the silky fabric.

Curse it all. No wonder it had taken the maids so long to put it on me.

"I can't get this thing off on my own," I seethed, twisting and wrenching at the fabric. I tried bending over and pouring it over my head, skirt-first.

But the gown wouldn't give an inch.

"Do you want help?" Axien asked quietly.

I spat another string of Viperi profanities and finally dropped my arms to my sides in defeat. I couldn't even pull it over my head because of how tight it fit across my shoulders.

"Fine," I snapped. "But not all the way. Just until I can get the rest of it myself."

"On my honor," he swore.

I kept my back to him, face burning as his footsteps approached. His fingers grazed the nape of my neck, rough and warm against my skin, as he carefully brushed my hair aside and worked at the buttons one at a time.

With each inch of fabric loosened, my heartbeat quickened. I held the front of the gown against my chest so it wouldn't fall, since I had nothing underneath except a very dainty pair of underwear—the sort that was basically just a scrap of silk that wouldn't show a seam under the dress.

The sort of undergarment men found alluring, according to Vanora.

"You think Vanora will be upset about me losing her dress?" I asked, attempting to pry my thoughts away from what Axien might think about my undergarments.

Nope. I did not need those kinds of thoughts tumbling around in my head.

"I think she's welcome to come back in here and fetch it herself, if she is," he said, the heat of his breath puffing against the bare skin of my neck.

It made my pulse skip and stall, toes curling in and out against the floor. My stomach fluttered, spinning over and over like water swirling down a drain. My skin flushed, becoming extra sensitive at every place his rough, callused fingers touched.

The contact made memories dance through my mind, remembering all too clearly how it had felt to dance with him. To have him grip my body in places that stole my breath.

A sick, twisted, wicked part of me wanted him to do it again. Now, right here, where no one would see. Even if it meant absolutely nothing to him, because how could it? Our previous, er, physical contact had been purely transactional or his stealthy way of passing a key to me so I could escape. Not because he had wanted to.

But maybe that had changed? Did he want to?

Madness. Gods, what was I even thinking? Of course not. And I didn't want it, either.

Definitely not.

"There," Axien announced, his voice lower. Softer. Closer. "Think you can manage the rest?"

"Yes." My voice caught, the words tangling in my throat as I sucked in an unsteady breath.

Fates, I had to get it together. This was ridiculous. I'd cut the rest of the stupid dress off if I had to. Anything to get some distance between us again. I needed a few inches for sanity's sake.

Just to clear my head.

"Violet? What's wrong?" He put a hand on my shoulder and slowly turned me around to face him, brow drawn in a hard furrow of concern.

Our gazes locked, and I knew he would see it. The way my whole face was burning meant it was probably as red as a ripe tomato. The way my breathing had gone shallow and panicked. The way my skin prickled wildly under the feel of his palm. My pulse racing against the side of my neck. If the Aurati produced courtesans worth any inch of their salt, he would see it all.

And he'd know.

Axien's lips parted, expression smoothing from concern to something open, vulnerable, and awed.

His throat moved as he swallowed hard. His eyes flashed like cold blue steel.

One step brought him right up against me, his face turned down as he put two fingertips under my chin and tilted my head back. My hair slipped over my now-bare shoulders, and everything in the room faded away to a weightless haze.

Axien bent down slowly, his lips brushing against my cheek as he murmured, "Tell me to stop."

Oh, gods, what was happening?

"I thought I'd never feel it again—you touching me. You wouldn't even let me near you for the longest. And I hated it. Hated how much I needed it ... and how much I deserved your scorn." His voice was a feverish, rough whisper. "Now you look at me like that? Tell me to stop, Violet. Right now."

I held perfectly still, breathing in frantic gasps of his scent. Rich and deep like cedar, sharp like clove. Every taste of it dizzying and enough to bend my body closer to his.

Enough to drive me insane with a need to cross those last few inches of distance I barely understood.

He was right. I'd punished him with that distance because ... he'd hurt me. He'd made me feel so unworthy, calling that kiss some form of payment I hadn't even asked for.

How could I trust him now? What if he said something like that again? I wasn't some prize he could reward himself with for good behavior.

"Do it," he growled louder as his hand seized my chin tighter, lips ghosting over mine so close I could feel their inviting heat.

And I remembered exactly how they tasted. How they'd felt against mine.

I opened my mouth, but no sound would come out. I didn't want it to stop.

I wanted more.

"Do it now," he warned, voice now tight and furious, as though he were warring with himself, fighting tooth and nail to hold back.

My face flushed hotter, body vibrating against his. Half in rage. Half in terror.

Because I wanted to trust him, even if it made no sense.

But I couldn't do it. Not yet. He was right. I had to stop this.

"St ... stop," I managed weakly.

His hand dropped away, and he immediately pulled back, chest heaving with manic breaths as he stared down at me. He ground his teeth, jaw working furiously. Then he turned away and stormed for the door, stopping before it and bowing his head.

"Hurry up and change," he said, his tone almost pleading. "We need to hurry. We don't know how much time might be passing in the real world."

I turned my back, as well, and began shimmying the rest of the way out of the dress. My heart still hammered like it might burst straight through my ribs and land in my lap. Gods and Fates. What was happening?

Why did being close to him make me feel ... *everything?* Like the world was too loud, too bright, and far too close? When had it started? And what did it mean?

Breathe—I just had to breathe. Push it away. Don't think about it. Calm down.

Fates, smite me.

My head spun, hands tingling as I worked the leather pants up to my hips and rolled the waist down a few times so they wouldn't fall. The tunic hung off my shoulders like a nightgown, and I knew I'd look ridiculous when I faced Axien again and sighed.

"This isn't working," I fumed, fighting with the sleeves that hung off my hands like a poorly stuffed scarecrow.

Axien stole a glance over his shoulder and sighed. His eyes shone with a faint glimmer of sadness as he approached again. "Gods, are you even five feet tall?"

With heels on, maybe.

I narrowed my eyes at him. "Does it matter?"

"Here. Let me try," Axien laughed quietly and motioned for me to sit down on the lid of the trunk.

He wrestled with the sleeves of the tunic and coat, rolling them up four times so my hands could poke through. Meanwhile, I worked on layering up a few pairs of the socks so the oversized boots wouldn't fall off my feet. In the end, the whole ensemble was bulky and ridiculous.

But it was a lot better than traipsing through the winter storm outside in a silky ball gown and bare feet. I'd just have to figure out how to move and fight when and if the time came.

Lucky for Axien, all the borrowed clothes he'd swiped from the trunk seemed to fit reasonably well. The coat was a little snug across his shoulders, but the sorcerer responsible for this place must have been around his size. He had turned the collar up to block the wind from his pointed ears and stood waiting by the door, a steely-eyed glare focused on the knob.

I hastily unclasped Vanora's expensive jewelry and tucked it into one of the pockets of my new, too-big pants. I did the same with the fine silver brooch in my hair, making sure it was pinned in place inside the pocket so it wouldn't spill out.

Then I darted over to the kitchen area, snatching two of the kitchen knives off the cutting block and slipping one into my belt and the other into the side of my right boot.

"Stealing more cutlery?" Axien asked as I made my way over to stand beside him, hand already on the pommel of the shortsword I'd taken.

"Hey, it worked last time." I shrugged.

He snorted and shook his head. "I suppose it did."

"In my experience, you can never have too many knives." I drew the shortsword and gave it a testing, flourishing swing.

It might have been plain-looking by Avoran standards, but those crafty winged elves couldn't be matched for quality. The leather grip was soft and pliant in my palm, and the blade so balanced I could have stood it on its point. Excellent.

"Let's hope we don't need them," Axien murmured and straightened, rolling his shoulders before putting his hands under the thick wooden plank we'd used to bar the door.

I tensed, drawing every one of my senses into focus. That smoldering heat deep in my chest crackled and sparked, primed for the fight. For the bite of the wind. For the sprint.

"We run and don't look back." Axien's expression cooled with the same primal focus. "We make for the door. No stopping. We don't engage the creature unless we have to."

"And if the study door is gone?" Better prepared than sorry.

"Then we come back here and figure out our next move," he replied. "Ready for this?"

I nodded sharply, tightening my grip on the shortsword. "Do it."

Twenty-Nine

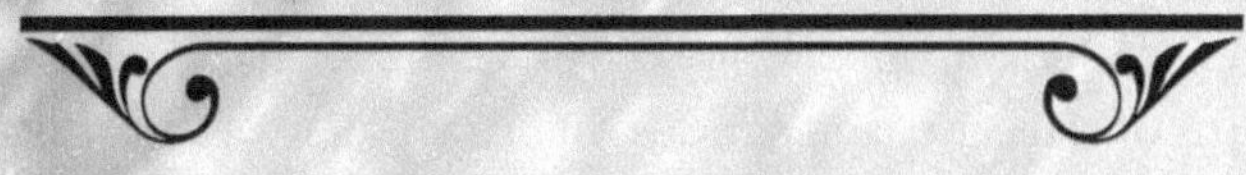

We ran for our lives.

Axien threw the wooden beam off the door and seized the knob. Immediately, the wind ripped it out of his hand and tore through the cabin, howling with a fury and cold that cut straight through all my leather and wool layers. My eyes stung. My chest seized on every freezing breath.

But there was no turning back now.

Axien and I dove headlong into the whirling snow and wind, boots flying over the powdery drifts until we reached the edge of the frozen lake. Every sprinting step crunched and sank deeper. My teeth chattered. My nose ran.

I clenched my teeth and squinted ahead, scouring the bitter night for some sign of the door as we took off across the ice. It groaned and popped under our weight. My oversized boots made my steps sluggish, and thanks to his longer legs, Axien pulled ahead right away.

I cursed, chasing his heels like a terrier until he stole a glance back and slowed down some so we were running side-by-side.

Idiot—what was he doing? What the heck happened to not looking back?

I wheezed and gasped on the icy wind that seemed to freeze my lungs from the inside. My face stung, and I had to steal a glance down to make sure I hadn't dropped the short-sword since my bare hand was completely numb.

An ear-splitting scream ripped through the whiteout, so close and loud it made me stagger. A noise like a disjointed chorus of screeches and squeals that made all my joints turn to jelly. It came from everywhere at once, so loud it made my eardrums ache and my vision swerve.

Oh, gods. That creature—it had found us again! Where was it?

I whipped my head around, but there was nothing. Only the storm. Only Axien, mere feet away, drawing his longsword.

Was it invisible? Or could it teleport somehow? Would it materialize right in front of us?

My stomach dropped as I drove my legs faster, fighting the slick surface of the ice and my too-big boots.

The door—gods, where was the door?!

I scanned ahead, eyes wide and desperate as I scoured the snowfall for something—anything.

Only darkness. Only the snow. The ice creaked and groaned under our feet. My panting breaths scraped my throat raw with cold. My eardrums still throbbed from the monster's cry. My pulse thundered in my head.

Then a flicker of bluish light winked in the distance, dead ahead.

Magic light.

The door!

"THERE!" I yelled back and pointed toward it.

"Go, go, go!" Axien urged as he reached his free hand out like he was going to take my arm and drag me along.

I reached back for him. His fingers brushed mine.

BOOM!

The ice exploded between us, bursting upward and flinging both of us sideways. I screamed, my body pitching end over end until I hit the surface of the ice and slid to a stop. My blade clattered out of my hand, sliding away over the frozen lake.

Sprawled on my back, I watched bright spots dance before my eyes as snowflakes hit my cheeks like the caress of freezing fingertips. My ears rang. Everything seemed to spin slowly.

Axien—gods, where was he? Where was the door? What was happening?!

A whimper leaked through my clenched teeth as I forced myself to roll over and sit up on my hands and knees. Fear split my chest like a pike as I gaped up at the tangle of huge dark thorns that had erupted from the ice like black spikes. It shuddered with a groan, and the ice beneath me rattled and splintered.

I staggered to my feet as the mass of black thorns crunched, twisting and unfolding into a pair of bony wings that erupted from the back of the towering skull-faced monster.

Wings—it had *wings* now.

Granted, they were mostly naked bone. The black leathery membranes were ripped and ragged, as though they were rotting away. I doubted it would be able to get airborne with them, let alone fight the fierce blizzard winds.

The beast rose before me, a twitching, blurring, smoking mass of matted black fur drawn over a giant skeletal body. Its jaws snapped, head still crowned in a wreath of spiny black antlers, long tail lashing like a whip of cracked leather and splintered bone.

Through the veil of wind-whipped snow, its red bonfire eyes focused on me, as bright as two hot coals in the storm. Something else glowed from the very center of its chest, a tiny pinprick of blue arcane light I could barely make out through the whorls of dark fog that curled around it. A gemstone embedded in its flesh, maybe? Or some sort of necklace?

I couldn't tell. And right then, it didn't matter.

The ice groaned louder, splintering under the beast's weight as it took a step toward me. Dark smoke rolled off its bony, tattered wings. Its jagged claws scraped and dug into the frozen surface of the lake.

I wobbled to my feet, slipping and sliding to keep my balance like a newborn fawn.

Run. I had to run.

Right now.

CRAAACK!

The ice rocked violently under my feet, tilting to the side as the creature took another step closer. A large portion had cracked free of the lake's solid surface, floating on the icy waters like a slick, snow-dusted raft. Any weight made it tip and wobble, and I wheeled my arms trying to stay on my feet.

The creature recoiled with a hiss, flaring those wings wider and blasting a sulfurous breath through the empty nostril holes in its bleached-bone head. It seemed to think, to contemplate where I stood on that hunk of floating ice, too far for it to reach with its long, jagged claws. Its weight might sink the ice with both of us on it.

This was it. My chance. I scoured the ground all around me. Sword—where was my sword?! I'd dropped it when I fell, but it couldn't have landed too far.

The monster unleashed another screeching bellow that vibrated through my body, right down to the marrow. My brain seemed to swell, like my entire head might explode. White-hot pain split through my chest like I had been gored open, and my vision scrambled. Something hot and thick ran from my nose and seeped into my mouth.

Blood.

I cried out, floundering back and covering my ears.

It didn't help. The sound permeated everything, tore through my flesh, and pierced my mind. It made my heart ache like someone had punched a fist straight into my chest and was twisting it over and over, trying to rip it from me.

The monster put another massive foot on my hunk of floating ice, making it rock beneath me again. It teetered, and I tumbled forward—sliding toward the creature as it crouched low, a bony hand outstretched to seize me.

I screamed, pitching wildly and clawing at the slick surface of the ice.

Closer to those glowing red pinprick eyes, snapping jaws bristled with fangs like pearl-white daggers, and raking claws as long as spear-points.

My fingers slipped and slid over the bitter cold ice. My heart pumped like mad. I just had to find something, anything, to hold on to.

But there was nothing. The surface of the ice was too smooth. No flaws or cracks. Nothing to grip, like a looming wall of glass.

I was sliding straight for the beast, with no way to stop it. Falling, falling, straight into doom.

Unless ...

I bared my teeth, reaching down to snatch the kitchen knife from my belt and slam it into the ice with all my strength. It lodged in deep, and I gripped onto the handle for dear life as the sheet of ice tilted higher and higher.

Dangling in the open air, I cried out again. A scream of frustration and terror tore from my throat and was immediately lost to the wind. I would not die like this. Not like prey. Not like a coward.

I kicked my legs, fingers already sliding off the metal handle of the knife.

I-I couldn't do this. I only had seconds, then I would fall.

Below me, the monster raged as it raked its talons over the wall of ice it had created, mere inches from my feet. Just out of reach.

But not for long.

Two of my fingers slid off the knife handle.

Then a third.

CRACK!

The knife snapped off at the hilt.

A frantic gasp left my body like an explosion as I plummeted down, down, down.

Straight into the monster's grasp.

Thirty

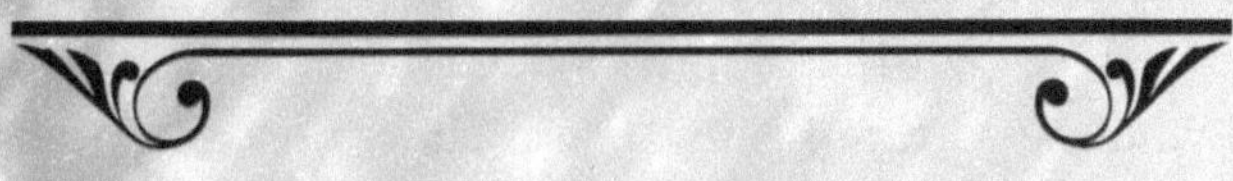

"VIOLET!" A desperate roaring cry broke over the wind as brilliant purple light exploded in my vision.

Axien.

I knew his strength immediately. The feel of his arms closing around me and snatching me out of the air.

Half a second too late.

Agony surged through my body, lighting up every nerve as something tore into my right forearm. One of the monster's claws raked over my flesh, tearing me open from my elbow to my wrist. My mouth opened, but no sound came out as my spine seemed to curl and my blood burned in my veins.

Then I was flying, racing through the snowstorm like an arrow. We zoomed skyward as one, Axien holding me tightly against his chest as he fought the storm with wings that shone like translucent purple glass.

He ... had wings, too?

H-how?

I couldn't ask—not when my throat closed around the fresh agony thrumming from my arm. It tore every thought to shreds and left me shuddering, teeth clenched so tight I thought my jaw might crack.

"Where is the door? Can you see it?!" Axien shouted frantically, his chest and shoulders flexing as he fought the wind on those glassy, glowing purple wings.

I squinted through the stinging, bitter air, my gaze hazy and swimming with pain.

But I saw it—the pinprick of blue light amidst the dark and whirling vortex of snow. It was closer now, but probably fifty feet below us.

"Th-There!" I managed frantically, pointing with my good arm.

WHOOOM!

An ear-bursting cry shattered around us. Shards of black glass flew like daggers.

Axien's flight wobbled, and he let out a barking cry of panic, floundering in the wind as he kept his face turned to the door.

His entire body seemed to glow, wreathed in a halo of purplish light that centered around those wings. His eyes were sunlight through arctic ice, brilliant and flickering with power—but his face was already streaked with black veins that climbed his throat and spread from his brow across his cheekbones. His jaw flexed, teeth clenched, as he held me tight against his chest.

Whatever those wings were, they were forcing him to use magic. Too much magic. I'd seen the veins spread that far and that fast only once before, and he'd been using a divine staff meant for a goddess.

A staff that had nearly killed him in the process.

"Hurry!" I pleaded as I looked back, my hair whipping around me as we tore through the gusting storm.

The monster galloped over the surface of the ice, moving with an almost apelike gait with its weight on its long, sinewy forelegs. The edges of it seemed to melt away into the night, as if the entire creature was just a trick of smoke and wind. Then, a few lumbering paces later, it solidified again. Closer.

Closing in fast.

Oh, gods—if it reached the door before we did ...

"You have to go faster!" I shouted again.

"You're more than welcome to do the flying yourself next time!" Axien huffed, his expression wild and desperate. His glassy purple wings flapped, fighting the wind with every beat.

The beast shrieked another piercing cry that made my spine lock up and my blood freeze. One swipe of its long-fingered paw flung another burst of dark power that froze into jagged black crystals that ripped through the gale straight for us.

Axien immediately snapped his wings in close and spiraled, dodging artfully and diving like a falcon for the door. Closer. Closer.

So close, I could see the light ebbing through the cracks along the edges—radiant blue, magical light.

It was closed now, though. Maybe the wind had pulled it in? We'd have to stop to get it open.

"Hold on!" Axien warned an instant before we hit.

I shut my eyes tightly, cringing into the warmth and strength of his body. He wrapped those brilliant wings around us and hit the door head-on, full speed, without holding anything back.

BAM!

We hit hard, slamming into the wood. He seized the handle and ripped it ajar, flinging us both over the threshold. He let me go and I floundered, wheeling back just in time to see him leaning against the door ... while a massive, claw-tipped hand reached in from the other side.

Oh gods! No!

The creature bellowed. It pushed against the door, trying

to force it inward. The wood groaned. A harrowing crack sent my heart plunging to the bottom of my stomach.

Oh gods—what if it broke the door?!

Axien pushed back, his snow-slicked boots skidding over the wooden floor as he yelled out a string of Avoran profanities.

I surged for him, putting my back against the door and pushing with all my strength. Closed—we had to get it closed!

I screamed as the door shuddered and cracked behind me. The beast's claws dragged over the wood, scraping mere inches away. Hungry. Relentless.

"As one! Get ready!" Axien managed, words gritting out through clenched teeth. "NOW!"

With both palms pressed to the wood, he bore in a sudden burst of unnatural strength. His palms glowed blue, eyes a flare like the final flash of sunlight over the ocean.

Together, we pushed with all our strength.

The monster on the other side let out a howling shriek of fury and pain, and its fingers withdrew suddenly.

It was all we needed.

BAM!

The door shut. Axien threw the lock, and immediately, all the raging monster's cries went silent.

Gone. It was gone. Sealed somewhere beyond that magical door.

I sagged to the ground, landing on my rear.

Axien stood like he'd been paralyzed in place, hands still pressed to the door, chest heaving with ragged, panting breaths. He blinked owlishly, gaze fixed on the door, as though he were pouring every ounce of his will into keeping that barrier between us and the monster in place.

"Axien?" I rasped brokenly. "Is it sealed?"

His knees buckled.

I barked a cry of alarm as he hit the ground next to me,

spilling into a pile of icy leather and frost-caked furs. The glassy purple wings of light winked out, and his whole body seized in response, mouth opening as he coughed and choked. His body shook as he rolled onto his side and spat a spray of thick, dark blood onto the floor between us.

"Axien?!" I crawled toward him, seizing his shoulder with my good arm and trying to steady him as he retched again.

Too much—he'd used too much magic again!

I had to help him. I had to find something, anything, to give him.

But I didn't have any of my Zenith's Call gear. No potions or tonics. No healing salves. I didn't even have bandages.

"Breathe, you've got to breathe," I coaxed as I held a shaking hand against his chilled cheek. "You'll be okay. We're safe now. Just breathe."

My words tangled and caught in my throat as my eyes welled. If he ... Gods, if he died in front of me ... I couldn't do this. I couldn't find a way out of here alone. I didn't understand any of this magic. I couldn't resonate with it like he seemed to be able to, as though it spoke to his instincts in a language only he understood.

The dark veins had spread nearly over his entire face. His eyes looked glassy, pupils blown wide, and his lips were blue. His body shuddered and shook, and he curled into himself with his knees drawn up and his arms clenched close to his middle.

"What can I do?" I asked, hating how small and terrified I sounded. "How can I help you?"

"I-I'm okay," he managed to grit out. "Really, I'm fine. Just a little winded. And cold."

"Cold? Seriously?" I arched a brow, unable to tear my eyes away from the black veins spidering over his skin. He was a lot worse off than just being a little chilled, even if he didn't want to admit it.

I looked up, eyeing the flickering flames that still danced in the hearth on the other side of the study. Focused calm took my brain like a rising tide, drowning out all the other noise. The worries. The doubts. Everything went silent except for one thing—one purpose:

Axien would not die here. Neither of us would.

I wouldn't allow it.

There had to be something in this miserable place that could help us, and I'd happily tear it all apart looking if I had to. For better or worse, we only had each other now.

And we were going to find some way to get out of here alive, whatever the cost.

Part Six
Declan

Thirty-One

Leruna was going to rip my head clean off.

—But only if she caught me first.

Granted, that wouldn't be very hard. After a few days, I could manage a walk around the room without limping. Running, though? Yeah, no. That wasn't going to happen. I wouldn't be winning foot races anytime soon.

Still, I couldn't afford to lie around and wait, which was exactly what Leruna wanted me to do. She'd assured me she sent word to Sulam, letting him know I was at death's door and if he wanted me back in the pit to fight, he'd have to give me a little more time to heal. According to her, Sulam had been his usual slimy, asinine self while threatening repercussions if I wasn't back within a week—his version of relenting.

Part of me wanted to hope that his little game of forcing me to fight until I died was finally over. He'd made his point. I was worth more to him alive, anyway.

But I knew better. I knew Sulam.

Given the fact that he had been all too happy to watch me die in that last fight, I doubted he was letting me off the hook out of mercy. He had a motive buried somewhere in all this. He always did. The game wasn't over.

I was willing to bet good coin I'd be figuring it out soon, too—the hard way.

That's why I had to be ready.

I had started yesterday with pushups and sit-ups on the floor in Roxus's room. It didn't take five minutes of it for my broken, battered body to start shaking, and the pain nearly had me puking into the chamber pot. My formerly broken ribs left me short of breath and in sweaty, shaking agony for hours afterwards. My wrist still threatened to give under the strain.

Too soon for that, I guess.

So today, I tried shadowboxing instead.

I made each jab and punch into the empty air, testing the strength in my arms and shoulders. But my swings were too loose. Too slow. Too weak.

My stupid arm had taken too much damage, what with the broken knuckles, finger, and wrist. I couldn't keep my core tight thanks to my broken ribs, so one good hit from an opponent would have me back face-down in the dirt, gasping like a freshly caught carp.

I wouldn't stand a chance in that gods-forsaken pit. Any soft-bellied noble in the crowd would be able to take me down.

I didn't have any other choice, though.

Every second I spent here was borrowed, and the threat to Nora hung over my head like a crown of iron thorns. Gods only knew what he'd done to her already.

I just couldn't lie around. I had to go back—soon. I had to show Sulam I wasn't done and take whatever he threw at me.

And maybe ... I could negotiate an end to this madness.

Leruna was absolutely right. I couldn't do this forever.

There had to be an end at some point, and the gods knew I'd paid my dues in sweat and blood ten times over.

But I had nothing to bargain with when it came to Sulam. No leverage of my own. No money. No family name to back me.

I did have an insane idea, though.

I just needed to talk it over with Leruna first.

The prospect of that conversation pushed a shaking breath past my lips. I staggered to a halt halfway down the last flight of stairs and leaned into the wall. My knees shook, body flashing hot and cold with fatigue.

Breathe—I just had to breathe.

Gods and Fates, never in my life would I have dared to imagine that going up and down stairs would demand every ounce of strength I had. But since shadowboxing and pushups were still out of the question, I had no choice but to settle for this. Even if it was utterly pathetic.

Thank the gods no one was here to witness it. Namely Leruna.

Just the thought of her face, pinched with disapproval that made her left eye twitch, and her lip curl a little at one corner, made my insides feel like mushed-up rotten meat.

We had not touched on the topic of my less-than-ideal arrangement with Sulam since she'd left me in the rooftop garden a few days ago. If anything, our conversations were even more clipped, tense, and awkward than ever. She avoided eye contact as though it might sting while she changed my bandages.

And I still couldn't come up with a single intelligent thing to say as I clenched my teeth and tried not to bawl like a fool whenever she probed at my broken bones.

Curse it all, I had no right to ask her for anything. She'd already saved my life, hadn't she? How could I ask her to use her family's name to pressure Sulam into letting Nora and me go?

I couldn't. Not for my own sake, anyway.

But for Nora ... I'd beg. I'd plead. I'd get on my knees and lick her father's boots—whatever it took.

I'd rather owe the Skyharts a dozen years of free labor on a ship than face an eternity in the pit ... or certain doom in the Caldera. So I'd do it. Today, maybe.

Yeah. Definitely today.

I could totally do it. Right after I got to the top of these stupid stairs, I'd get myself cleaned up and plead my case properly. I had to look the part of the obedient patient. Like I'd done nothing except rest and contemplate my pitiful existence, as ordered.

Delthene and Leruna had left hours ago for the market district. They'd be back any moment, and I had to make it all the way back to my borrowed room before then. Nothing to worry about. Leruna didn't scare me.

I totally had this.

A yelp tore out of me, and I almost tripped when the knob on the front door jiggled suddenly. Oh, gods, no! Not yet!

I floundered, trying to haul myself up the stairs two at a time.

Then the jiggling stopped.

I paused.

Chest heaving and sweat dripping down the sides of my face, I steadied myself against the wall and looked back. Down five or six steps and across the dim sitting room, I could see the front door plainly. A slim glass window beside the door revealed shadowy figures moving beyond the beveled pane.

Deep, masculine voices muttered from the other side.

I turned around slowly, every movement making the muscles in my thighs spasm in complaint.

BAM—BAM—BAM!

I startled as something slammed hard against the outside of the door. Too hard for a knock. Not hard enough for a kick.

What in the abyss was going on out there?

"Hey!" I shouted, hobbling down the steps again.

No answer.

It took far too long for me to make it back to the bottom of the stairs, dragging my hand along the wall so I didn't trip and fall. By the time I managed to cross the sitting room and reach the front door, the voices and shadowed figures beyond the windowpane were gone.

I seized the knob and tore it open, revealing ... nothing.

No one on the street in either direction. Just the glare of the sunlight and a soft sea breeze that left my sweaty skin chilled.

Huh. Strange.

I started to close the door again, but my bare feet slid on something wet that speckled the floor. Something thick and red.

Was that ... blood?

My heart dropped to the pit of my stomach so suddenly that my knees nearly gave as I turned, my gaze following the trail of blood droplets all the way to the front door. The knob slid out of my hand. I staggered back, all the wind leaving my body in a rattling gasp as I stared at the single, pale, severed hand that had been nailed to it.

A dainty hand. A *woman's* hand.

With a lock of long red hair tied around the middle finger.

The ground rushed up—or maybe I fell. I couldn't tell. Time seemed to stop and start in blinks and flashes.

On my knees, I stared up at the bloody, severed hand with a nail driven straight through the middle of the palm. My vision swerved in and out of focus, dark spots dancing everywhere I looked. My throat closed like I'd tried swallowing a fistful of dry cotton.

Nora's hand.

It was Nora's hand nailed to the door, with a lock of her red hair around it.

It was a message from Sulam. It had to be. He knew where I was. He knew I was dodging him, hiding out here, licking my wounds. He didn't care how injured I was, or even if I could survive a single round in that pit.

All he knew—all he cared about—was that I had failed to hold up my end of our bargain.

And now my baby sister had paid the price.

A cry ripped from my throat, half scream, half sob. But I couldn't hear it. My ears felt like they'd been stuffed with cotton, too. Every sound was muffled. Fuzzy. Far away.

G-Gods. I had done this to her. They had carved my debt out of her flesh.

And they would continue ... unless I returned. They'd deliver her to Roxus's front door piece by piece.

I had to stop it.

Nora. My Nora needed me. I had to leave.

Right now.

Thirty-Two

I was burning.

My blood ran molten. My heartbeat thrashed like thunder. My body shook, knees quaking as I willed my legs to move, to stand.

I had to. I had to go back right now. I had to prove I wasn't giving up. I wasn't betraying my bargain.

Pain rippled through me like lightning over a stormy night sky as I forced myself to walk, staggering down the front steps and leaving the door wide open. It didn't matter. Nothing did except going back to the Rook's Roost as fast as I could manage.

My bare feet dragged over the uneven cobblestones as I shambled away from the house and down the street, heading for the harbor. It was a mile, maybe a little more. The roads were steep, but I was going downhill.

I could make it.

The world around me shone in variations of red, as though everything had been stained in blood. Something echoed in the back of my mind like the constant, high-pitched shriek of a boiling teakettle.

But I didn't stop.

Crowds parted for me as I wove through the market district, leaning against merchant stands and catching myself against the side of parked carts. My vision swam and sloshed, the low afternoon sun seeming to spin around me amidst a sea of whitewashed stone buildings, cloudy sky, and tangled streets. I caught glimpses of unfamiliar faces, uncertain and riddled with a mixture of concern and disgust.

Then I saw it—the battered sign hanging above the old tavern's door depicting a crow with a mug clutched in its talons. The Rook's Roost looked like every other grimy pirate bar on the harbor side road, with windows so thickly smeared with smudges and yellowed by pipe smoke that you couldn't see anything but vague shapes beyond them.

I couldn't use the front door, though.

With a shoulder against the rough stone wall, I hauled myself down the narrow alleyway that ran behind the tavern. There, hidden behind a false front of stacked up ale barrels, a hidden hatch door led to a steep staircase that plummeted down into pitch blackness. That was how I had to come and go when I limped home every night, battered and bloody.

A coppery flavor rose in my throat, burning like venom, and I gagged as I swallowed it down. Closer. Almost there. I could see the barrels. I could make it.

My body flew forward, arms and legs flailing, as something slammed into the back of my head. My vision went white as I hit the trash-strewn ground, rolling until I landed flat on my back.

Wh-what?

Dark, shadowy spots danced before my eyes. I hacked and choked as I rolled over, spitting a mouthful of something hot and thick onto the stone.

Blood.

"He said you would come crawling back as soon as you got

our little message." A deep laugh broke over me like a clap of thunder. "The others said you were too weak, but I bet ten silvers you'd come back before sunset. Looks like I'll be drinking from the top shelf tonight, all thanks to you."

"M-my … pleasure," I rasped and spat a spray of crimson onto the stones again, my vision still swimming as I shakily raised my head.

Four blurry figures stood over me, but I couldn't make out any of their features. Nothing but the vague, smeared outlines of eyes, toothy grinning mouths, and the glint of sunlight off patchwork armor.

That's all I needed, though.

I'd seen enough of Sulam's hired thugs come and go from the pit fights to recognize the putrid stench of them—cheap ale, days of unwashed sweat and brine, bad tobacco smoke, and just a hint of piss.

It didn't take much to sort out what this was and why they were here.

Gods, I was such a damn idiot.

Fresh agony throbbed at the back of my head where one of them had struck me hard enough to leave me dazed. The whole world seemed to reel beneath me as I tried to push myself up again.

I had to stand. I had to fight.

Coming here had apparently been Sulam's plan for me all along. A trap—and I'd stumble headlong into it. There was no running. No hiding.

But I knew the long scrape and ring of a blade sliding out of a sheath all too well.

Curse it all.

On a good day, I could hold my own against an armed opponent. But today was not a good day. My knees buckled as I tried to get up, every muscle fiber ablaze with pain that had my body flashing between hot and cold.

"Pathetic," another one of Sulam's men scoffed. "Just run him through and be done with it."

"Fool, remember your orders," the first man snarled as the group surrounded me. "He goes to the pit. He dies there, or none of us gets paid a single copper. Get him up."

"Wh-where is Nora?!" I demanded, my voice hitching in agony as I took a sluggish, pitiful swing at the nearest of the figures. It threw me off balance, and I hit the ground face-first again, my cheek mashed into the cold, gritty stone.

No answer. Just a chorus of throaty, half-drunken laughs.

"Tie his hands," the first thug ordered. "Then gag him. We don't want him making a ruckus until the fights begin—if he doesn't die on his own before then."

Tears blurred my vision as I tried to stand again, hands splayed on the stones. But I couldn't push up. Couldn't force my body to move or rise.

Nora. Where was she? Had they killed her already? What was Sulam doing? Why was any of this happening? I'd fought for him for years. I'd held up my end.

What had changed?

A whimpering cry leaked through my clenched teeth as they wrenched my arms back behind me, beginning to tie them at the wrist.

"Well now, isn't this interesting?" a feminine voice echoed down the alleyway, carrying like the crack of a whip in the humid, salty air.

The thugs stopped, their snickering and jeering suddenly going silent. I willed my eyes to open, to focus on the silhouetted trio of figures that had appeared on the other end of the narrow passage.

I knew her immediately. The slope of her hips, cocked at that arrogant slant. The way the wind teased through her unruly mane of dark curls. The way the sunlight kissed over her sun-bronzed skin.

Leruna.

"You have something that belongs to me," she purred low, a lioness considering her prey as the other two figures behind her took an aggressive step to stand on either side.

Two men, one hardly more than seventeen, flanked her with blades already drawn. The younger, slimmer one had the same thick mop of dark curls that came to his shoulders like Leruna's.

He was all lean arms and legs, willowy and skinny like a young wolf, and had the same sea-green eyes and pointed Rienkan ears as Leruna. But his wide, cunning grin and freckle-dusted cheeks were different. More impish.

A younger brother, maybe?

The other man was ... definitely not a relative.

The sight of him, all brawn and sun-faded tattoos, sent a bolt of terror straight down to the very core of my soul. He wasn't even a Rienkan elf, even if the ears that peaked out of his dense, braided black hair were pointed. He stood like a colossus, a hulking giant of a man easily nine feet tall, gripping a claymore in his huge fist like it was a child's toy.

He was ... Holvradix.

Not a half breed, though. Full-blooded, like my mother.

His massive chest rose and fell in slow, steady breaths as he panned a cold stare over the group of Sulam's thugs as though he were waiting for permission to start crushing skulls like walnuts.

"Was my claim not clear enough to your master before?" Leruna mused as she slowly, lazily, drew the blunderbuss from the belt strung low across her hips.

"Now, hold on, woman, you can't just—"

"I can. I have. And I will as often as I wish," she promised as she wiped a smudge from the barrel of her weapon with the hem of her loosely fitted linen blouse. "Your master is more than welcome to duel me himself for my right. But until then ... you know the penalty for stealing from the Skyharts."

Footsteps scraped erratically behind me. The thugs hissed back and forth, whispering frantically. Trying to figure out their next move.

Leruna's gaze shot up suddenly, narrowing on them with an unfeeling, brutal edge that made my heartbeat come to a lurching halt in my chest. It wasn't the gaze of a healer.

It was the dead-eyed stare of a natural-born killer.

"Bring that one to me," she commanded, tipping the gleaming barrel of her weapon toward one of the thugs—the same one who had won ten silver betting on my desperate sprint here.

"And the others, dear sister?" the young elf beside her asked, twirling a long dagger through his fingers.

Leruna's lips twisted into a vicious little grin. "Waste not, Elio. The sharks hunger."

Thirty-Three

The screaming wouldn't stop.

I lay on my belly like a beached porpoise, hands bound at my back and blood oozing from the corners of my mouth, as chaos broke around me like a whirlwind.

One of the thugs tried to make a break for the hidden barrel-door, but Elio was as fast with those knives as any fighter I'd ever seen. He pulled them from a pair of baldrics crossed over his chest with a flick of his wrist and flung them end-over-end at his target in a blur. They flew like tongues of silver fire, and the fleeing thug let out a howling cry.

Until another dagger lodged right in the middle of his forehead.

Another of Sulam's hired fighters tried dodging around the Holvradix man, throwing down his shortsword as though he were hoping that gesture of surrender would buy him passage.

It didn't.

The massive elf grabbed him by the throat and lifted him off the ground, his nostrils flaring as he gave a slow, bone-crunching squeeze. The man kicked and fought, writhing like a caught snake. His eyes bulged, face turning purple as he clawed frantically at the pirate's giant forearm.

A gurgling, crunching, crack made bile burn at the back of my throat as the thug's body immediately went limp, and the Holvradix man dropped his lifeless body into a heap.

Only two left.

"N-now, wait! Please! We can come to an arrangement, can't we?!" the would-be leader begged as he backed away. A few paces, and I couldn't see him or his one remaining lackey anymore from where I still lay.

It didn't matter, though.

The Holvradix elf and dagger-slinging boy moved in, making quick work of their orders. The last lackey fell with a garbled cry, and I was glad I didn't see what had happened to him. The sound was more than enough.

The Holvradix pirate dragged the last of Sulam's men by his hair, kicking and screaming like a caught piglet, all the way to Leruna's feet. He held the man there on his knees, the lethal edge of that claymore pressed against his back.

"Now, then," Leruna crooned as she leaned closer to the thug's face, using the barrel of her blunderbuss to lift his chin so he had to look her in the eye. "Let's have a little chat, you and I."

"P-Please, lady, I-I was only following orders!" the man sobbed. A puddle formed on the ground between his legs.

"Shhh. None of that," she scolded as gently and evenly as a mother speaking to a sniveling, naughty child. "You take coin from Sulam. That means you're willing to get your hands very dirty. But your mistake was in thinking that Sulam is the most dangerous person walking these streets. That you were powered by the throne of his little empire."

The man broke down, weeping and wailing and making a loud ruckus as he begged for his life.

She crammed the barrel of her weapon into his mouth to silence him.

His eyes went wide, face paling as he froze. His pulse throbbed in the side of his neck, and his nose ran, hands spread and held out in total surrender.

"You're going to answer me with a nod or a shake of your head, are we clear?" Leruna ordered, all traces of that creepy, motherly calm gone as her finger stroked the trigger.

The thug nodded shakily.

"Did you nail that hand to my door?" she questioned.

He nodded again, expression twitching and spasming. Expecting any second, any tiny movement, to be the one that sealed his fate.

"And did you cut it off the girl yourself?" Her eyes narrowed to lethal, sea-glass slits.

He shook his head frantically.

"Did Sulam give it to you?"

Another nod. His throat bobbed as he swallowed and choked on the barrel of her blunderbuss.

"The lock of hair, too?"

Sweat ran in rivers down his face as he bobbed his head.

My mind reeled, thrown into a frantic tailspin of confusion.

What was she doing? Why was she asking him all this? What did she know that I didn't?

"And do you know why Sulam has suddenly decided to kill his favorite fighting pet?" she pressed in harder, venom in every word. "Seems like there is a very deliberate message he is trying to send. Did he discuss it with you? Or mention it where you could hear?"

The thug shook his head, gaze pleading as he sucked in frantic breaths through his nose.

Leruna licked her teeth behind her lips as she studied the

man, as though she were measuring every single inch of him against her own instincts.

Looking for traces of deceit. Or bits of truth he hadn't let go of yet.

Whatever she saw, or didn't see, I couldn't tell. My body chilled as the adrenaline seeped from my veins, leaving me trembling and my vision dimming in and out of focus again. Consciousness slipped from my grasp like sand through my fingers.

Fates, I wouldn't last much longer.

"There. See how helpful you can be? Just needed the right motivation," Leruna said as she gave her Holvradix companion a meaningful glance. "Send Sulam my regards."

The huge elf's expression darkened as he watched Leruna pull the barrel of the weapon out of the thug's mouth. She stood straight, a hand on her hip, as she scowled disapprovingly at the spit-smeared end of her weapon for a moment.

Then she moved like a striking viper.

CRACK!

The impact of wood against bone sent another jolt through me, and I gaped as the piss-soaked thug suddenly dropped unconscious at Leruna's feet.

One blow upside his head with the blunt end of her weapon knocked him out cold.

The big Holvradix man wasted no time picking him up by the collar of his shirt and dragging him over to the false-door front hidden amidst the barrels.

Whatever happened next, I couldn't see. But the screaming started again, louder than ever.

I shuddered. I was no stranger to brutality and blood, but these pirates were ... a breed unto themselves. They worked at violence like artists at a canvas.

"Get him up," Leruna ordered coolly, not even sparing me a glance.

I flinched, managing a moan of protest as someone grabbed hold of my arms and began cutting at the bonds on my wrists.

My pulse quickened, body tensing as the heat of adrenaline prickled at my skin and left my extremities numb and heavy.

"Easy there, big guy," Elio murmured as he worked at cutting me free. "You're safe. Stupid—but safe."

The idea of being safe with pirates was an irony I didn't have the strength or the will to argue.

I let out a rasping breath as one final twist of his deadly knife let my arms fall back to my sides, limp and useless. A shuddering, hitching groan left my throat raw as I tried to roll over onto my back, but my body wouldn't respond.

Curse it, he was right. I was an idiot.

But what other choice was there? They'd ... they'd nailed a hand to the door and made it look like hers. Made me think that Nora—*my* Nora—was ... No. Gods, no. I couldn't think it. That might make it real.

The thug had confessed he didn't know who the hand or lock of hair belonged to. It might not be hers. Just a trick to lure me here. Bait in a bear trap.

And I'd fallen for it. I'd almost walked right back into the jaws of Sulam's machinations.

The thoughts tangled like nets snagged in coral at low tide, fraying and torn between hope and a sinking feeling that threatened to drag me all the way under into despair.

"Declan," Leruna spoke over me, her tone sharp with annoyance. "Can you stand?"

I couldn't answer except to let out another long, low groan through my teeth.

"He's barely conscious," Elio reported matter-of-factly. "Doesn't look like they did much to him yet, though. A knock on the back of the head, but I can't find any other new injuries. Lucky fool."

Leruna snorted like a furious mare, every bit as wild and untamable as she crouched down beside me. Her warm, weathered palms slid over my face, forcing my eyes open wider one at a time and taking my pulse.

"Pupils are responsive. Pulse is fast, but normal. No concussion," she said. "Lucky is right—lucky once again to have that thick Holvradix skull."

"I can carry him," the giant elf loomed over me, a tower of sun-darkened muscle and swirling runic tattoos.

My mouth screwed up bitterly, my ego stinging like he'd just slapped me across the face. It was bad enough to know I was literally only half the man he was, but to be carried like a caught lamb?

Gods, they should have just let the thugs kill me.

"Fine." Leruna blew out a resigned sigh. "Hurry."

"What about the others?" Elio asked as he stood by, wiping down his daggers and slipping them back into his cross-buckled baldrics. "Want me to dispose of them the usual way?"

"Yes. Then post a watch. I want to know how Sulam responds to our little message," she replied. "Send word to Roxus's house, but don't come yourself. Delthene is troubled already. It's bad enough to drag the family name into this, but as far as Sulam knows, I'm the problem, not the rest of you. Perhaps he will second-guess involving any more outside parties."

"You know Dah won't see it that way," Elio countered, his tone cautious, as if he were stepping lightly around his elder sister's temper. Smart kid. "If you're involved, we all are. That's how family works, you know."

Her lips pinched tight, slender brows knitting as she turned and strode away, offering no response.

"I'll cut them into manageable pieces," the big elf growled and shuffled off. "Come on."

Elio nodded, making that mess of fluffy, dark curls swish over his eyes. He spared another quick, almost sympathetic glance my way before he disappeared, and I heard more shuffling and motion nearby.

Then the brutal hacking, crunching, and ripping of bodies being dismembered.

I shut my eyes tightly, not wanting to see or hear any of it. It was worse than the screaming, and there was no corner of my mind dark and distant enough to escape it.

I shook with a cold sweat by the time silence fell again, and the huge elven man reappeared to haul me over his massive shoulders.

Dangling from his grasp, my gaze caught on the carnage we'd left in the alleyway behind Sulam's tavern. Puddles of thick, fresh blood ran through the cracks between the white cobblestones. Severed pieces of flesh and limbs lay in piles like butchered pigs. Carrion for the gulls and crows.

The last remaining thug dangled limply from where his hands had both been nailed to the false, barrel-door ... still alive, but unconscious.

A brutal message not even Sulam would be able to ignore.

Thirty-Four

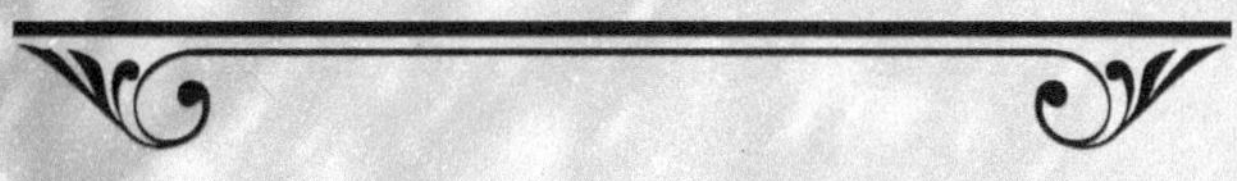

"Lie still and don't talk," Leruna snapped as she aggressively tucked me back into Roxus's bed.

I stared at her, the edges of my vision still blurry, as she propped me up on a stack of pillows so I could at least sit upright. That giant Holvradix fellow had carried me like a sack of flour all the way to Roxus's doorstep—an indignity I couldn't have imagined in my wildest nightmares.

Never again. Just let me die in the street.

Determined to keep at least a tiny fragment of my self-respect intact, I demanded to walk the rest of the way up the stairs and into the bedroom on my own. Granted, it had taken me a while, and I was a shaking, sweaty, half-conscious mess by the end of it.

Leruna was as mad as a wet hen, too. She scolded me with every step, warning me of all the damage I might do if I pushed myself too far too soon.

But I did it anyway, because spite was a powerful motivator.

So, yeah. Leruna was furious with me. And she had every right to be.

Stair-climbing aside, I'd taken off on my own, dragging my useless rear end all the way to Sulam's doorstep and straight into the trap he'd set. I'd created another huge mess that she'd been left to clean up. I had no right to say anything, even to apologize.

But I had to. She needed to know why. The reason mattered.

"Please," I managed hoarsely. "The hand—I-I thought it was—"

"I know," she cut me off. "I saw it. But it wasn't even a female hand, which I could have told you if you'd simply waited for me to return."

Oh.

Well. That ... would have been nice to know ahead of time, yes.

"Then why did you ask him if it was my sister's—?" I started to ask.

"Because I needed to know if he was going to lie to me, even with the barrel of my gun in his mouth. If so, then the rest of the interrogation was pointless," she interrupted again.

Right. That made sense, I guess.

Seconds passed in tense silence as she sank into the chair at my bedside again and immediately doubled over to put her face in her hands. Her curtain of dense, spiraling dark curls fell around her, brushing her lap and spilling down her back to her waist. Her shoulders flexed as she breathed, deep and slow, as though she were trying to collect herself.

I swallowed hard, trying to wet my throat before I murmured, "I-I'm ... sorry."

She didn't move or respond at first. Not until nearly a minute of that heavy, leaden silence had passed, and she finally pushed herself upright. Her eyes glistened, and her cheeks had flushed, as though she were battling down every shred of emotion before she even dared to look my way again.

"Why don't you trust me?" she demanded suddenly.

My pulse skipped a beat.

"After all of this, after everything I've done—everything we've been through—I deserved to know why," she said.

I stared at her, trying to scrape together words that made sense. But once again, all my thoughts tangled and knotted in my brain, too frayed to even make it to my lips.

I did trust her.

Er, well, for the most part. I knew she'd defend me. She'd put Sulam's thugs in their place. She'd defied him for my sake, not once but twice now.

I just didn't understand why.

Just because Violet had asked her to? Or because she felt sorry for me?

I didn't know. And the idea that all this had been done out of pity or as a favor to a mutual friend left a bitter taste in my throat. I didn't want or need pity. I didn't want to be babysat.

But was there any other reason for her to do this?

When I didn't answer, Leruna seemed to sink deeper into her chair. Her shoulders fell, and her head lolled back. She stared at the ceiling, her arms wrapped around her middle, as though she were thinking.

"I thought before it was simply because you didn't know me," she said quietly. "We weren't strangers, but we weren't friends, either. Now you know more about me than anyone else, except for my own family. Not even the high priestesses know I'm a Skyhart. Roxus suspects, I think. But we've never spoken about it. Perhaps he knows but has the good taste not to mention it. Or he's simply waiting for me to be the one to bring it up."

I opened my mouth, but the words died on my tongue.

Watching her, seeing the emotions flicker through her lovely sea-green eyes, made something hot and tight twist in my chest. A pain I didn't have a name for, although it seemed close to guilt or shame.

Both, I guess. But it was so much more than that.

I knew her secrets. Things that could ruin her. But she didn't know much about me, and I was still holding her at a distance. It wasn't fair.

I just didn't know how to fix it.

Minutes crawled by, and she didn't push for words. We sat in the silence, two islands with a roaring, raging sea between us. A gap I had no idea how to bridge.

Or even if I should.

Then Leruna blew out a heavy breath and stood. She let her fingertips drag along the edge of the bed, passing within an inch of my hand before she started to turn away.

"Kadfael is downstairs keeping watch, in case Sulam decides to retaliate right away," she said, avoiding my desperate stare. "I don't feel good about leaving Delthene alone here. Not until Roxus comes back, anyway. He and Violet have already been gone longer than Delthene anticipated, and she's beside herself with worry."

My throat throbbed as I swallowed that new information.

"If Sulam decides to make another move, we will be here. You may be able to drag yourself upstairs, but I doubt you can fight off more of his men if they decide to kick the door in," she murmured.

Good point.

"Rest. I'll see about bringing you some dinner later." She began to move for the door. To leave me here, stewing in this miserable, suffocating silence that slowly ripped me apart from the inside out.

I lunged at the last instant. Catching her by the wrist, I used what little strength I still had and held her firmly in place at my bedside.

"I *do* trust you, Leruna," I said, the words coming out

much shakier and more desperate than I'd hoped. "I-I've never had anyone fight for me the way you have. I don't know what to do with it. What to say. How to repay you."

"I don't want repayment, Declan," she replied firmly. "I want you to believe me when I tell you I am on your side. I want you to stop acting like you're in this alone. I want you to *see* me!"

Her voice caught suddenly, strangled with a sob, and she slapped a hand over her mouth to try and stifle it.

But it was too late. I saw her face seize, eyes shutting tightly, features scrunching bitterly before she managed to turn away.

Curse it all. I-I … I had done this to her.

I'd held her at a distance. And for what? Why couldn't I just drop these walls? Why did it feel like every step forward was just an excuse to backslide? To hide behind all those old habits.

Easy—because they were all that had kept me safe for so long.

Never fully trusting anyone, never being open, never letting anyone see the rawest, ugliest parts of me. It couldn't happen. I had to be a pinnacle of strength and confidence, ruthless and fit for the fight. Sulam needed to see that his favorite pet was still formidable. No cracks. No flaws.

Still bloodthirsty and indomitable.

And I hated it. Hated the performance. The man I had to become when I stepped into that pit.

Hated myself.

My stupid hands shook even as I threw the blankets off my legs and surged for her, my heartbeat slamming in my chest and turning my blood molten.

Leruna let out a sharp yelp of surprise as I seized her in my arms, wheeling her around and backing her against the wall suddenly. My chest heaved with halting, uneven breaths, half from the pain and half because I had no idea what I was doing. Her form was small and deceptively frail-looking, but there was strength in her hands as they gripped the front of my sweat-and-blood-stained tunic.

She blinked fast, puffing in fitful little breaths through her nose as she fixed me with one of those piercing, demanding glares. As though she expected me to know precisely what this meant and what I had to do next.

Gods, she was *so* wrong.

I wasn't entirely inexperienced. But I'd only handled a woman a few times in my life, and those instances had been the desperate, clumsy fumbling of a boy who didn't know any better. Coached by wine and adrenaline, I'd scratched that itch only to hate the sour, bitter flavor it left on my tongue for days after.

But this wouldn't be like that.

Leruna would demand better. The best I could give her. Everything or nothing. And that's what she rightly deserved.

That thought sent a bolt of wild, primal strength through me.

"I do see you, Leruna," I growled through clenched teeth, my hands pressed against the wall on either side of her head. "I see everything you've done for me. Everything you're risking. I just don't understand why—why go to all this trouble just to keep your word to Violet?"

"Is that really what you think? That I'm doing all of this just as some favor to her?" Her brow crinkled, nose brushing mine as her full lips pressed into a tense, uncertain line. Something pleading lit her sea-glass eyes like an unspoken prayer.

And a part of me must have heard it.

It drowned out the pain. Smothered all my common sense and made my instincts come alive, beastly and famished. Fully aroused.

This ... wasn't about Violet. It had never been.

Leruna had been lurking around the perimeters of my life long before that. Years, maybe. Waiting and watching over me. Giving me those potions. Bandaging me up.

Holding me together like an invisible thread stitched through all the broken pieces of my life.

But I saw it now.

I saw her. All of her.

And, gods, I needed her more than anything.

It happened fast—an instant that shattered over us like the breaking of waves against the fragile jetty built up between our lives. It crashed through me, drowning all the fear and doubt.

I seized the back of her head and dove for her, my mouth finding hers with ravenous desperation.

Her arms immediately wrapped around my neck as she pulled me in closer, lips parting for mine and welcoming me in. Her fingernails scraped my scalp as she twisted her hands into my hair. It pulled noises from my throat I'd never made before. Dark, dangerous, primal sounds that rumbled deep and made my blood rush hotter.

"You aren't well enough for this," she scolded between quick, feral little kisses, even as her hands worked to pull my filthy tunic off my shoulders and over my head. "You can barely climb the stairs, idiot."

"Good thing you're a healer," I said with a groan, every nerve lighting up like cannon fuses as she yanked my hair, pulling my head back far enough that she could bite at the side of my neck. The union of pain and pleasure as the edge of her teeth scraped my skin played on my sanity like fingertips on harp strings.

I'd sing whatever tune she wanted. Give her all of me. Let her take what she needed as greedily as she liked.

And, Gods and Fates, if this was how I died—so be it. Stack my pyre and bring the oil.

Grabbing her by the thighs, I forced my aching body to

cooperate through the haze of pain that hung like a foul mist in the back of my mind, warning me that she was probably right.

I'd almost died again today. Maybe I would tomorrow.

All the more reason not to wait.

I'd done enough of that. Of suffering. Of waiting to die without a single scrap of hope to cling to. The road at my heels was drenched in blood and pocked with pain. A legacy I couldn't escape.

But there was a new horizon in her turquoise eyes, shimmering like the sun on the sea. There was hope in the constellations of the freckles that flecked her warm brown skin.

And I wouldn't let it go. Not now.

Not until I tasted something soft, sweet, and utterly forbidden.

I lifted her off her feet and carried her, flinging her down onto the bed. The wooden frame groaned as I followed her down, prowling over her and seizing those pretty, deceptively dainty wrists to pin her arms above her head.

If my size or strength worried her, it never showed. All the light had gone out in her expression, replaced with a dark, vicious sort of hunger that set my appetite on edge. She would be every bit as vicious, merciless, and wild as the sea.

But she wouldn't let me die. Not yet.

Not until we'd both had our fill ... and then some.

Thirty-Five

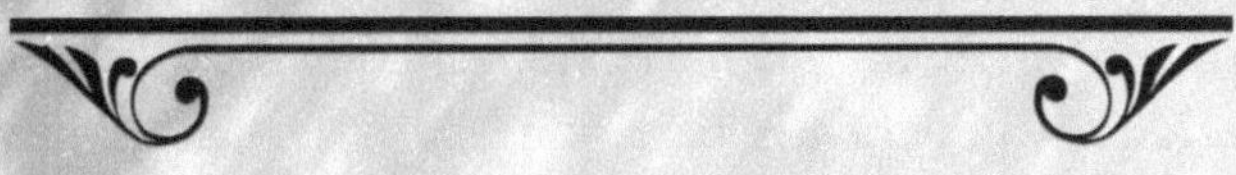

This was a *huge* mistake.

I knew that. I'd known it the moment I tasted her lips. Breathed in the gentle flavors of healing herbs that clung to her skin. Felt the endlessly soft canvas of her skin, tracing my fingers over every line of those beautiful tattoos ... and then following with my mouth.

Common sense, if I had any left rattling around in my skull, dictated that you didn't fool around with the beloved daughters of notorious, violent pirate-kings.

But, hey, I was already in over my head with one crime lord. What was another?

Worth it, that's what.

Maybe that was why, even with my body now vibrating with an agony that thrummed all the way down to my bones, I couldn't wipe an arrogant smirk off my lips.

Some things were worth the suffering—and I'd pay this price a thousand times.

"You're shaking. Are you in pain?" Leruna murmured, her head still resting on my shoulder, right at the crook of my arm.

All her long, gloriously soft curls splayed out over my chest and tickled at my neck.

"Tired," I admitted, refusing to let her hear even the tiniest hitch of withheld discomfort in my tone.

Lying like that, with her body so close and those strong, shapely legs draped over my waist, I could have been bleeding out for all I cared. I wasn't moving—or complaining, either, for that matter. Not when I could feel every breath she took. The radiant heat of her bare skin glided against mine with every tiny movement she made.

Delicious.

Gods, I'd probably just set recovery back a few more days.

But, again ... worth it.

Minutes slipped by, falling around us like warm summer rain. Soothing. Quiet. Slowly stifling the fire in my veins.

All the heaviness in my arms and legs ebbed away. My mind wheeled in circles like gulls on the updrafts. Restless but swept by the winds of everything that had happened—hand changed—in just a day.

"I thought it was yours, at first," Leruna said quietly, almost like she didn't want me to hear. "The hand, I mean. Delthene and I returned, and it must have been only a few minutes after you left. The door was open, and there was so much blood with footsteps smeared on it. I thought they'd nailed your hand to the door as a message to me. Then I saw the hair ... and I knew."

"I'm sorry," I apologized, knowing full well it wouldn't come close to fixing anything. "I should have waited for you to come back."

"Yes," she agreed. "But I understand why you didn't. I can't imagine what I'd do if I found Malina's hand nailed to a door like that."

"Malina?" I'd never heard that name before.

"My little sister," she clarified.

"You have a lot of siblings?" Before now, I'd only been aware of Elio, who was obviously younger, as well.

"Three," she said, and I could hear the thin, trembling smile in her voice. "Elio is seventeen. Then there's Malina. She just turned twelve. Noa is the youngest. He's only ten."

"And you're, what, nineteen?" I'd always assumed she was around my age. Maybe a touch younger.

"Twenty-one," she corrected.

Ah, so a year older, then.

"Your father must be nearly bald, trying to keep up with that many of you and manage a piracy empire," I chuckled.

She laughed, too. "I ... honestly don't know. I haven't seen him in years. Not since I left the, er, family business."

A strange, thick silence crept in and set a chill over my skin. The sense of a thousand unspoken words, withheld secrets, and worries, all seemed to whirl through the dim room like snowflakes.

I didn't dare make a sound. I couldn't. I had no right to pry into her personal life, let alone start interrogating her about what had happened with her family.

"You can ask me, Declan. It's okay," she said suddenly, like she could read my mind. Or maybe I just did a piss-poor job of not lying there looking awkwardly confused.

Yeah. Probably that.

I cleared my throat and shifted a little. "Why did you leave your family? Or was it, uh, not something you chose?"

"I did choose to leave," she answered softly. "I had to. I ... made a terrible mistake. I decided to trust someone I shouldn't have. It put them all at risk. It nearly killed my father. I was young and foolish, but I still couldn't bear to face my family after that."

Reaching for one of her hands, I wound my much larger,

thicker fingers through hers and stroked my thumb along her palm.

"I was born entrusted with a mighty gift that should have made me a powerful asset to my family's legacy. But I nearly destroyed them. I let someone I thought loved me twist everything up in my head," she continued, her words coming sharply. Angrily. "He made me believe they were all against me. That I didn't need them. That I only needed him. But all he wanted was my power. To control me. He wanted my family's legacy for himself, and by the time I realized it, it was almost too late."

She didn't have to say it—who that man had been to her, what he'd done to take her young mind and bend it to his whims, warping her vision of the world to suit his desires. It made my pulse thud harder, rage crackling on my tongue, as I held her hand firmly.

Like she was mine to protect.

It was a stupid, reckless thought. I couldn't even protect myself or my sister, let alone Leruna.

And given what I'd seen today, she might be the last person in the world who needed any protection. She could more than handle herself.

I was just an idiot—an idiot who wanted to mean something to her.

And maybe I did. Gods, I wanted to believe that.

"If it's any comfort, I have no experience or interest in captaining a ship. I'm not even that good of a swimmer. Can't float to save my life," I said, hoping to at least coax an exasperated breath from her. Something lighter than the intensity that wafted off her like heat from a forge.

Leruna blew out a breath that made her lips flap. "You're ridiculous."

Mission accomplished.

"So, uh, what power are you referring to, exactly?" I

hedged, not sure if this was something I should even dare prod at. "I've heard stories of the Skyharts, of course. Everyone has, probably. About what your family can do—summoning sea monsters and all that."

She sat up a little, hair falling like a luxurious dark curtain around us as her keen gaze searched my face. Then she took my hand and brushed along the tattoo right at the center of her chest.

The one of the coiling, mighty sea serpent.

The drakkon.

"My family has been blessed by Undae for many generations. When the War of the Stones ended, she gave us power over her oceans. Specifically, she gave us the ability to summon and control the drakkons. But as an oyster shell must have two halves to protect the precious treasure within, two individuals from my family must carry the gift," she explained. "Two stone-speakers. Two ships. Two drakkons. Two halves of one whole."

"And you're one of them?" I asked, trying to wrap my mind around all of that.

I'd heard numerous stories about the Skyharts, all terrifying, of course. But picturing this lovely little woman, who usually walked around in the soft robes of a healer, summoning a ship-devouring sea monster was ... difficult to imagine.

Even if I had seen her with the barrel of her gun shoved down someone's throat this morning.

"I am," she confessed, her gaze dipping away and her lips thinning some. As though that were a part of herself that she still hadn't come to terms with.

"That's ..." I couldn't find any words, so I settled for some impressed snorting, half-chuckling sounds.

"My youngest brother, Noa, is the other half. But he's only just come into his magic. It usually manifests in our tenth year. Undae is careful with her gifts. More so than many of the other gods who left their essences in the hands of mortals after the war," she explained, her mouth twisting to one side uncomfortably.

"But if you aren't there, with him, can he even use it?" I probed, still trying to understand it all. The notion that anyone could have divine power was still a foreign concept. I'd never seen anything like it.

Part of me hoped I never would. That seemed like the sort of thing you didn't get to walk away from unscathed, even if you weren't the target.

"To a degree, yes," she said. "He will still be able to command his own drakkon. He will learn to command the seas. To summon storms, and ... other things." Her words fell off, brow furrowing slightly.

She didn't expound any further as she settled back into her place under my arm with her head on my shoulder.

It suited me fine, though. She didn't owe me any answers. But it did help to understand her a little more. If someone from her past had used her or twisted her emotions just so he could have access to her power, I wouldn't blame her for being guarded. For not wanting to let her emotions slip beyond her control. For wanting to hide that part of her away beneath a healer's robes and a meek demeanor.

It must have made her feel safer, but not altogether disconnected, to serve in one of Undae's temples, instead.

I had to wonder if Undae was pleased to see her precious gift of power being held in reserve. Even the most benevolent of the gods and goddesses weren't known for their patience. Not when it came to their mortal servants.

Leruna was risking a lot, running from her destiny like that. Sooner or later, that tide would come in. She'd have to face it. And I'd be dead and rotting on the floor of Sulam's pit before I let her go through it alone.

I just had to find a way to fix this mess with Nora first. To get her free of Sulam's chains. To leave that fighting pit and everything it represented behind, once and for all. Then I could start over. I could try to build a life worth living ... with Leruna right at the center of it.

I'd find a way. I had to.

No matter the risk.

Thirty-Six

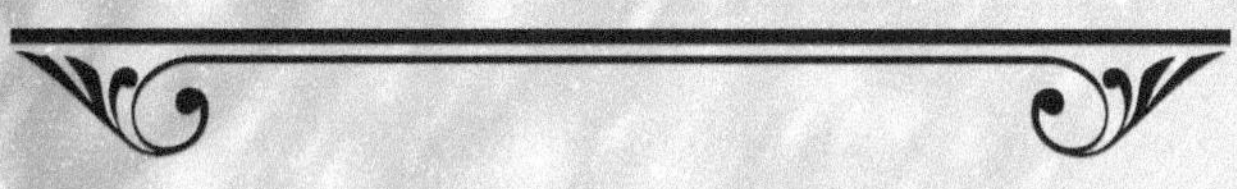

"YOU!" a voice like thunder boomed downstairs.

I tensed, my whole body immediately locking up solid as soon as my eyes flew open. My arm flung out to the side, reaching for Leruna. To make sure she was still there. Still safe.

Nothing.

Her side of the bed was empty. It wasn't even warm. She was gone.

Oh no.

My pulse took off as adrenaline poured through my veins, molten and turning everything red.

What was happening? Had Sulam's men come back here?!

Gritting my teeth, I threw off the blankets and shambled to my feet, starting for the door.

A thud and crash boomed from the floor below, loud enough that I felt the shudder in the floorboards under my bare feet. Another angry voice snarled, too muffled for me to make out the words. A woman was screaming. No—crying. Sobbing hysterically.

Oh gods. I had to get down there. Right now.

Staggering across the bedroom, I grabbed for the first thing I could find to use as a weapon—an iron fire poker from next to the small hearth in the corner. Good enough.

I burst through the door and out into the hall, sweat already slick on my skin as I started down the stairs. Each step sent sharp bolts of pain up my spine, making my vision swim and my breath seize in my throat, but I didn't stop. I couldn't.

Something was wrong. I had to find Leruna.

My knees wobbled, threatening to buckle when I reached the landing in the main sitting room on the first floor. With a shoulder against the wall, I gasped and wheezed, trying to blink away the dizziness. The hand gripping the fire poker shook so badly I nearly dropped it.

Not good.

I-I couldn't do it. I couldn't take another step. Not without falling.

"Declan!" a feminine voice cried out in alarm as I sagged forward, the whole world seeming to tilt with me.

Was that ... Leruna?

I couldn't tell. My ears rang and my legs finally gave. The fire poker slipped from my hand and clattered to the floor just before I fell.

A pair of strong arms caught me suddenly, and I sagged into someone's chest. Someone who absolutely reeked of animal musk.

"Fates, he's burning up," Roxus's voice growled sharply against my ear. He grunted and strained, struggling to lower my deadweight down to the floor. "How long has he been like this?"

"Nine hours," Leruna replied. "He was doing fine, but last night he started shaking and sweating. I couldn't get him to wake up. I've given him all the tonics I can. Anything more will poison him."

Nine hours? I'd been asleep for that long? Gods and Fates, what was happening to me?

No. This wasn't happening. I had to suck it up. I didn't have time for this.

"I-I'm ... fine," I slurred, barely able to make out the hazy outlines of three faces peering down at me—Roxus, Delthene, and Leruna.

"No. You're an idiot. An idiot with a scorching fever," Roxus fumed as he waved to someone else nearby, "Get over here and help, would you? We need to get him back in bed."

"N-No," I protested weakly. "I ... can walk."

"You can't even stand," Roxus said bitterly, hauling me into a sitting position so an all-too-familiar Holvradix man, Kadfael, could pick me up and throw me over his massive shoulder like a dazed lamb.

A dazed, completely naked lamb.

Gods, just end me. I'd never be able to live this down.

"P-Please ... what's happening? Is Leruna ... all right? I heard ... s-someone crying," I groaned as Kadfael dropped me back onto the bed I'd been borrowing for Fates only knew how long.

Roxus's bed, unfortunately.

"You heard arguing. Everyone in this house is perfectly fine, except for you," Leruna fussed as she worked with Roxus to prop me up, stacking pillows at my back. She glowered, avoiding eye contact as she covered me with a quilt and put a cool, wet washcloth against my forehead.

"B-But I heard—" I began to protest.

"Hush. Lie still. You've got a fever, and the healing remedies aren't working like they should. You're delirious and if we can't cool you down, we'll have to put you in an ice bath," she cut me off sharply, meeting my bleary stare for an instant. Long enough for me to see the raw, desperate terror flickering in her eyes.

"I'm still wondering why he's *here* and not at the *temple*," Roxus grumbled, standing back with his arms crossed and his brow set in a grim scowl. "This is hardly the place for him to receive the proper medical care."

"Because I refuse to endanger the other priestesses," Leruna snapped, casting him a cold glare over her shoulder. "You know as well as I do that Sulam wouldn't hesitate to attack them, even on holy ground. This place—you—are the only person he fears enough to stay at a distance."

"No. I'm not the only person. I'm just the only one you can stomach asking for help," Roxus retorted. "But now you've brought all the wolves to my doorstep. I come home from dodging Tibran assassins to find pirates in my living room, Declan nearly dead in my bed, and my housekeeper scrubbing blood from my front door. I believe I'm owed an explanation."

Ahh. So he *did* know about her, after all.

Leruna's expression went frosty, eyes closing tightly as her shoulders rose and fell in deep, angry breaths. "Fine."

"Let's discuss this downstairs. He needs quiet so he can rest properly. I can make a fresh pot of tea," Delthene offered, her tone pleading as she lingered in the doorway. She gave me a watery smile, blinking fast and hiding her hands in her apron as though she didn't want me to see all the blood smeared up to her wrists.

My heart sank, falling hard to the bottom of my chest. Gods, Roxus was right.

I owed him the truth.

"Sulam ... wants me ... dead," I blurted, gritting the words out through pained breaths.

"What? Why? You make him a lot of coin." Roxus straightened, his eyebrows snapping down into a deep, bewildered scowl.

I didn't know. And it took a while to explain that to him,

along with everything else that had happened while he'd been gone.

Things had been in a spiraling decline with Sulam for longer than that, of course. But the last two weeks had been exquisitely terrible, and now it felt like my entire world had been smashed and scorched to nothing. Sulam didn't just want my head, he wanted my public humiliation and suffering. He wanted my undoing to be messy and public.

And I had no idea why.

Now I was sitting in the ashes, my whole body shaking with fever and aching like I was slowly being stretched apart. My head throbbed sharply and my teeth chattered. The room seemed to spin every time I closed my eyes.

But I couldn't give in to any of it just yet.

Not until I knew what Roxus was going to do next.

The bed lurched as he sat down next to me, eyeing the way my legs hung off the end of his bed. A common problem for someone my size.

"Curse it, boy, you do know how to make a mess," he sighed and patted one of my knees.

"Can't you do anything? Can't you ask the Call to intervene? They could get to Nora. They could save her," I begged, my eyes welling as I stared at the one man who might be able to finally put an end to this. To set us both free.

Roxus held my stare, his thin mouth pressed into a thoughtful, tense line as he studied me. The scruff on his jaw had grown into a short beard, and there were heavy circles under his eyes. He still wore his ratty old longcoat, like he'd just arrived and hadn't even had time to change out of his traveling clothes.

"Declan, I can't force the Zenith's Call to intervene on your behalf," he answered at last. "Maybe I could have once, when I offered you a place within the Order. But you chose to be a mercenary. You chose to stay with Sulam. And with the way things are right now, Mistress Orvana is not going to want to provoke someone like Sulam. And she'd have my hide for a throw rug if I—"

"Why not? He's a monster! Everyone knows it," Leruna argued, cutting him off.

"He is. No one's arguing his morality. But his crimes are an issue for the city guard to handle," Roxus yelled. "You forget we are not mercenaries. We are a holy order with one mission: protecting divine artifacts that may be misused to the detriment of the masses. We protect the secrets of the gods, and our position has always been precarious and wholly dependent on discretion, which is precisely why we do not fight crime lords in the streets."

The room fell into tense silence, all eyes trained on Roxus as he rubbed his hand along his jaw and up the bridge of his nose.

"And now you've got one nailing bloody hands to my front doors," he sighed again, his voice softer and slurred with exhaustion. "Meanwhile, Violet and Axien are missing, we've received reports of assassins moving through Rienka in packs, and the Tibrans are waging a war against Nar'Haleen the likes of which we haven't seen since the War of the Stones. Sweet merciful Fates. I feel for you and your sister. Truly, I do. But you must understand my position here, Declan."

I did.

It was stupid of me to ask him to intervene. But I was out of all the good options. I only had stupid, desperate ones left now.

"I'm ... I'm sorry, Roxus," I murmured, my voice halting as I bit down hard against the trembling in my jaw.

"Don't be sorry," he said and patted my knee again. "I want to help you. Give me some time, all right? I can't ask the Call to intervene, but that doesn't mean this old bear doesn't have a few tricks up his sleeve. In the meantime, do as the lady says and rest. Heal. You're no use to anyone flopping around naked in my house, out of your mind from fever."

I ducked my head, staring down into my lap. My face burned—and it wasn't from the fever.

"You said Violet is missing," Leruna murmured quietly, one of her slender hands slipping around mine to grasp it tightly. "I thought she went on a mission? What happened? Did something go wrong?"

Roxus's entire demeanor darkened, his expression tightening with a furious grimace that made a muscle twitch in his jaw. A bear bristling for a fight.

He panned his gaze away, toward the door, brow knitted as he growled low, "I don't know. But I intend to find out."

Thirty-Seven

Dying was not an option.

Not yet.

I still didn't know if my little sister was alive, didn't know why Sulam was targeting me like this—why he wanted what was essentially my public execution in his pit even after all the years I'd worked for him without question or complaint.

It made no sense. But I knew better than to believe this was just some random act of malice on Sulam's part. He always had an angle. A motive that served him.

Somehow, my death would serve his machinations. I just needed to find out how ... before it was too late.

Lying in Roxus's bed, my body trembling with fever, I stared at the ceiling and tried to pick through all my memories. Everything Sulam had said. Everything that had happened in the arena.

The fight with that Tibran soldier. The Darksteel guard.

My stomach turned as the memories replayed, cycling over and over like a dark vortex in my brain. The sound of his skull cracking off the blunt end of a sword. The blood on the sand. The emptiness in his gaze.

I shuddered. I had seen men beaten to the brink of death in the pit many times, sometimes even at my hands.

But that had been different.

It had been murder.

I squeezed my eyes shut, swallowing against the hot sting of bile in my throat.

Sulam had chosen to bring a captured Tibran to his pit for execution. And he'd demanded I be the one to do it. It couldn't be chance. Sulam knew where my sister and I had come from. He knew we were Tibrans, too.

Was that why? Was it some kind of test? Or was he just trying to rattle my cage?

Regardless, the Zenith's Call couldn't help me or Nora. I doubted the city guard could do anything, either. Not against someone like Sulam, who ruled the underbelly of this kingdom like a prince perched high on a throne of blood and bone.

There was no one left to turn to. No hope of fighting my way out this time.

But Roxus hadn't kicked me straight out into the gutter, even after bringing crime lords, thugs, and pirates to his doorstep. Hopefully, his kindness didn't run out before I was able to walk around and manage on my own again.

I flinched as the door swung open suddenly. Roxus hesitated at the threshold, staring at me with his brow creased in concern and a big canvas travel bag slung over his shoulder.

"Sorry, boy. I thought you'd be asleep," he muttered as he shuffled in and shut the door behind him. "I need to get a few things."

"It's fine," I groaned as I sagged back into the bed. Sweating from the fever had left a damp place in the sheets and they clung to my skin as I tried to roll onto my side and shut my eyes again.

Rustling filled the awkward silence as Roxus dropped his heavy bag onto the floor and went rummaging through his armoire and chest of drawers. Was he unpacking? Or repacking?

I didn't dare interrupt to ask until I heard the cold scrape of a blade leaving its sheath.

Cracking an eye open, I watched him standing before his open armoire, eyeing a shortsword he must have pulled from somewhere inside it. The blade was short and straight, faintly leaf-shaped, but double-edged. The pommel was crafted in the shape of a snarling bear's head, and the crossguard was arced downward and engraved with interlocking runic bands.

A Vordegan blade if I'd ever seen one.

His eyes narrowed as he considered the weapon, his hard-lined frown reflected in the dark steel of the blade. His nostrils flared some, jaw tensing as he slipped it back into the old, battered leather scabbard before clipping it to the belt at his hip.

My stomach clenched hard and my mouth went dry. He was arming himself for battle.

Not a good sign.

"What's happening?" I finally dared to ask.

"Nothing, yet." Roxus flicked me a sideways glance as he strode past the end of the bed, returning to his open bag and pulling out pieces of leather armor. "But come nightfall, we'll be leaving."

My pulse skipped. "We?"

He didn't answer. He didn't have to. There were only two other capable fighters in this house right now.

Cold chills prickled up my legs and pinched along my scalp. Dread burrowed deep in my gut, twisting and wrenching like a barbed pike.

"Leruna is going with you." I winced, the words bitter on my tongue.

"Her idea," Roxus said sharply, as though he didn't approve but had already lost that argument. "And her Holvradix guardian. I don't know the fellow, but he does seem loyal to her. I suppose I have no choice but to hope he might extend that loyalty to me as well, albeit temporarily. Allies are thin on the ground, and the Mistress of the Call is unwilling to risk any more of her agents against enemies like the Ulfrangar assassins."

I froze at that word—*Ulfrangar*.

It hung like echoes from cannon fire in the room, sending out a shockwave that drained the heat from my body and sent a pang of icy panic straight through my chest.

The Ulfrangar were a breed of their own. Notorious, mysterious, and brutal in ways that had practically made them into myth. You didn't fight them. You didn't catch or arrest them. They were a poisonous vapor that snuffed you out before you even knew they were there.

There were no finer killers in all of Reatia. Once they had your name, you were as good as dead, and not even the gods themselves could save you.

Knowing they were on the hunt here, moving in the open where they could be identified, meant someone had made a very dangerous and expensive deal to hire their talent. I didn't even want to imagine why. But I was willing to bet my right arm it had something to do with the Tibrans.

Roxus must have felt the same way. He shook his head, making his shaggy dark hair swish around his collar as he muttered something about pirates and assassins with a few Rienkan profanities tossed in. He scrubbed his hand along his jaw and neck, something wearily resigned in the way he glanced over his battle-wares.

"You're going after Violet," I guessed.

He stopped, broad shoulders dropping some as he stooped down and picked up a studded, dark leather jerkin. His throat moved with a hard swallow and his expression softened, the hard lines of anger giving way to something like sorrow.

Or maybe worry.

"I am. She went on a retrieval mission with another young agent, the half-Avoran boy. It was supposed to be quick and simple, just a two- or three-day excursion to bring back an artifact. But there's been no sign of them," he explained. "Mistress Orvana already sent word to the family that was supposed to be meeting them to pass over the artifact. Apparently, they found one of their family members slain—the very one who was meant to rendezvous with Violet and Axien."

"Ulfrangar?" I forced myself to sit up a little, already piecing together my own theories as I watched him begin to buckle the jerkin over his tunic.

"I suspect so. We've now seen hard evidence that they are moving through the Southern Kingdoms, likely at the command of the Tibrans. They could certainly handle a slash-and-grab mission against two novice Zenith's Call agents without being noticed," Roxus said. "But according to the family, there were no other bodies found. The artifact was gone, but there was no sign of Violet or Axien anywhere."

I traced my tongue over the points of my teeth, thinking it over for a moment while he buckled on his vambraces and cuisses.

"Is it possible they got abducted?" I suggested. "I know the Ulfrangar don't typically take prisoners, but they also don't typically get sent to steal ancient artifacts—or run into Zenith's Call."

Roxus's mouth mashed to one side, his scowl deepening. His chest rose and fell, heaving in a deep breath as though he were steeling himself before he said the words aloud.

"That is what I'm afraid of," he murmured, his gaze

catching mine with an edge of quiet rage that made my skin prickle with fear. "I need to go and see it for myself."

Underneath those usually placid, cognac eyes, I could see the legendary war beast of Vordega lurking. It hungered for blood, determined to reclaim its cub by whatever means necessary.

"There's a lot about Violet you don't know, boy. A lot she's had to keep to herself, for her own survival," he rumbled low. "She's important to me, but she is also valuable to the Tibrans in ways you can't even fathom yet. I've done all I can to protect her from them, to keep her secret and spare her their special attention. But on our last mission, that secret was exposed. The Tibrans know about her now. And if they got the chance to take her prisoner ..."

His voice trailed off like the roll of distant thunder slowly fading to heavy, tense silence. He panned his gaze away, turning his focus back to fastening on matching leather greaves and slipping daggers into the sides of his boots.

"I wish I could go with you," I admitted, hating how pathetically weak and hoarse my voice was. "Dammit, I *should* be going with you."

"I know." Roxus didn't even glance my way as he started for the door, leaving his half-empty bag where it lay. "Leruna is giving Delthene instructions on your care. I'm sure she'll have some words for you, too, since you're awake. Say your good-byes, but keep it brief. Don't make this more painful than it already is."

My heart gave another agonizing twist in my chest at the thought of her leaving, most likely to fight Ulfrangar, without me. Yes, she was capable. She'd proven that several times over, and I'd yet to see her brandish any of her magical talents.

But still—Fates, curse it. I hated this. My jaw clenched hard, hands fisting in the sweaty sheets as I sat, stewing in the silence while Roxus's footsteps retreated out into the hall and down the stairs.

Time slipped on around me, passing like a blur while I battled the raging storm in my mind, until more footsteps approached. Softer and lighter, I knew it was her before she stepped into the doorway.

Leruna stood dressed in her healer's robes again, although I had no doubts she was probably armed to the teeth underneath them. Her beautiful face, framed in those spiraling dark curls, stayed eerily expressionless as we stared at one another from across the room.

Seconds ticked by with the lamplight dancing in her turquoise eyes. No words. Nothing but the yawning of a new, impassable chasm opening between us like a void straight to the abyss.

Gods and Fates. What if she never came back? What if I never saw her again? What should I say?

"Please don't do anything else reckless, Declan," she spoke at last, her voice so small and pleading it sucked all the wind right out of my lungs. "Please, just this once, stay here. Rest. Heal. I can't do this if I don't know for sure you're going to be okay."

All my frustrated anger shattered instantly, and shame rushed in like an all-consuming flood. My mouth screwed up so tight it made my eyes water.

I nodded slightly, unable to force any sound past the unbearable, choking tightness in my throat.

"Delthene will be looking after you, but you won't be defenseless. Roxus has reached out to some of his friends in the Zenith's Call. A Vindexori is coming here to stand guard. Apparently, he owes some sort of personal debt to Roxus. Something to do with mistreating Violet years ago," she went on, her eyes never leaving me. "Promise me, Declan. Promise me you'll stay here and let your body heal. I need to hear you say it."

"I-I ... promise," I gritted out, my voice rough and broken.

Leruna bowed her head slightly, eyes fluttering closed as though a weight had been lifted from those lovely, tattooed shoulders.

"Thank you," she whispered. "I will come back. You believe me, don't you?"

No. I didn't know what to believe, honestly. But I couldn't shake the sense of doom that seeped into my brain like a burning poison, spreading fear like sickness in its wake. If something went wrong, if she died because I wasn't there to watch her back ...

"I'm not your responsibility, Declan," Leruna said suddenly, as though she could somehow read my spiraling thoughts in just a glance. "Whatever happens, you need to understand I am not fragile. I can't be. Undae chose me to be her tempest, and for the first time in a very long while, I feel the pull of her tide. I have to do this. I'm meant to do it."

I didn't understand. Not even a little.

Why did this keep happening? Why was every single person I cared for always ripped away from me?

I hadn't been able to save my mother. My sister was still a crime lord's hostage. And now the woman I—

"I dreamt of her," she continued, her voice hushed again. Careful. Reverent in a way I'd never heard leave her lips before. "She sent me a dream last night. It was a vision of a terrible battle that went on for as far as I could see in every direction. There were many soldiers, all roiling together like a black ocean. And at the very center, they all parted and watched as three great beasts brawled—a white stag, a black wolf, and a red serpent."

"What does it mean?" I whispered back.

She shook her head slowly. "I don't know. But there was so

much fear. The soldiers wept as they watched. I could feel their terror. Their dread. Something awful is coming, Declan. We have to be ready. That's why I need you to heal. I need you to be able to stand with me."

My pulse thundered in my ears as I watched her shrink, turning away toward the hallway behind her with none of that light in her lovely eyes anymore. Whatever that dream meant, it had rattled her to the core.

Maybe Leruna wasn't fragile. Fair enough. I doubted the Goddess of the Ocean would choose someone weak-willed to be a vessel of her power.

But Leruna was still mortal. And she was right; I needed to be able to stand with her if that day of reckoning came. I could not fail her like I had everyone else.

I wouldn't—whatever it took.

"Goodbye, Declan." The words fell from her lips like shards of a broken prayer as she slipped away into the hall ...

... and took every last shred of hope and sanity I had left right along with her.

Part Seven
Violet

Thirty-Eight

I couldn't move my hand.

Sitting on the floor beside Axien, I fought with a strip of cloth I'd cut off one of the fancy pillows on the sofa. That monster had ripped a gash open down my forearm so deep I could see the white of bone in places. My fingers were numb, although I could still wiggle them a little. If I focused, I could almost make a fist.

I decided to take that as a good sign.

But the rest of my hand? It was basically dead weight. Moving my wrist or trying to flap my hand back and forth set off agony like acid poured straight into the wound.

A not-so-good sign.

I'd been cut before. I'd been slashed, stabbed, run through with a sword, and been subjected to a variety of other heinous torture. But this was ... not like that.

The burning from the wound made my vision dance with little bright stars, and my ears rang with a high, whining note that nearly drowned out everything else.

Fates, curse it all.

"I can help with that, you know," Axien offered, a hesitant edge to his voice.

"Augh! Fine." I let out a growl of frustration through my teeth and finally held my arm out in his direction, keeping my face angled away as I surrendered.

Axien said nothing as he scooted closer, looking much steadier and like his normal self as he got to work trying to bandage my wound. It wouldn't be pretty. But it had to at least get me by until we could get adequate medical help.

After an hour or so, he'd pulled himself together enough that he could sit up and move around. The coloring in his cheeks was better, and some of those eerie dark veins had faded —especially around his face. His breathing was slow, and he wasn't shaking or sweating.

I couldn't tell that he'd even taken any blows from the monster on our way out. But then again, if he had, it wouldn't be the first time he'd hidden injuries from me. He'd refused to tell me about being poisoned by a blade while we were scrounging around in the dark of the Avoran ruins, trying to claw our way back to the surface world.

It made me wonder what else he might try hiding—or why he'd even bother at this point. We'd seen the absolute worst in one another by now, hadn't we?

Stubborn idiot.

"This isn't good, Violet," he murmured low. The amethyst ring he now wore on his left middle finger flashed in the fire-light as he worked, but the stone looked a little dimmer than before.

"Our situation? Or the gaping hole in my arm?" I asked.

I didn't mean for it to sound sarcastic, but he flashed me an admonishing look, as though he found nothing about this situation even remotely funny.

"Both," he replied sharply. "You're lucky it didn't sever an artery."

"I'm lucky he didn't rip my entire arm off," I corrected, gritting my teeth as he tightened the bandaging to bind the wound closed as best he could. It took everything I had to hold still.

I couldn't do it, not without a shriek of pain and spewing a fountain of Viperi curses.

"Sorry about that." His tone had gone soft and cautious again.

"D-don't be," I groaned. "Just ... f-finish it."

He did. Axien wrapped my makeshift bandaging around my forearm again and again, four layers deep, before he finally tied it off. My shoulders shook, and the nape of my neck was damp with a chilled sweat.

"You okay?" His tone was cautious. Tense. Worried, even.

I nodded, not trusting myself to speak without stammering just yet. It wasn't like I had any other choice, even if I wasn't okay. Now wasn't the time to sit around, wallowing and whining.

We'd risked a lot and gotten nowhere. No closer to finding a way out. No closer to even understanding this place at all.

We were missing something. We had to be.

But what?

"So, the wings," I said, unable to keep an awkward tension from my voice as I cradled my freshly bandaged arm in my lap.

Axien sat across from me on the rug, the light of the fire crackling in the hearth dancing in the few feet of empty space between us. His expression steeled, closing up like a startled clam, as he stared down at the ring on his finger.

"They were from this," he said.

"I guessed as much." I tried to lighten my tone, to sound at least a little understanding and impressed. It was almost impossible while my pulse thundered with the pain that burned from my arm, sizzling all through my chest and down my spine.

Surely that creature's talons weren't poisoned, too.

No—I couldn't even entertain that idea. Not now. Not here.

"I think it's been siphoning magic from me and storing it," he went on, holding his hand up so he could consider the carved, silver details of the band in the firelight. "But as far as I can tell, it only summons those wings. Nothing else."

"Still handy, though," I observed. "You've been recovering a lot faster from using your magic. Is that something Vanora's helped you with?"

I tried to sound disinterested, like it didn't matter if he answered or not. He'd always been funny about discussing his powers. I wasn't sure if pushing him for details about what Curator Vanora had been doing with his training all this time was out of bounds for us or not.

It's not like we were, you know, friends.

"Not personally, but she's found someone else to guide me, in a manner of speaking," he answered cryptically, keeping his face angled away like he always did when he didn't want me reading the subtle cues in his emotions. "He sends letters with long lessons. I've never met with him in person, though."

I shifted uncomfortably, clearing my throat and trying to keep up my indifferent front. "Well, I'm ... glad it's working out for you."

"It's strange. The cold in that place made it hard to control my magic." Axien's handsome face drew into a thoughtful frown when he finally faced me. He brushed the tip of a finger over the small amethyst atop the ring, eying it with a critical little squint. "When I tried activating this thing, I was hoping for a boon or maybe something with fire. But all the power seemed to rush out at once. I couldn't control it at first. I could barely keep the wings moving how I wanted. I've never been all that skilled with my magic, but it's like something in that storm was interrupting my focus."

"Probably had something to do with running for your life while rapidly freezing to death," I mumbled.

His mouth tilted in a half-grin. "Maybe. Usually, Avorans are born with wings. A holdover from their past as divine beings and servants to the gods. Being half-blooded, naturally, I was denied that gift. This might do for compensation, though."

"Weird that an Avoran sorcerer would even have something like that, right?" I said. "Wouldn't he have had wings of his own? Why make a spare pair?"

Axien's lips pursed thoughtfully, head tilting to one side slightly, as though he were considering. "I'm not sure. That's ... a really good point, actually."

I grinned. "I have a few, now and again."

He chuckled and looked away, back toward the glow of the hearth. "Yes. But usually they're made of steel."

"Can't blame a girl for picking an area of expertise," I quipped, a tight breath seizing in my throat as I forced myself to stand.

My borrowed clothes were heavy and damp from where the snow caked on them had finally melted away. I'd abandoned the outer layers already, but the oversized wool tunic hung off my shoulder and gathered at my waist, where Axien and I had desperately synched everything together with the belt.

Gods, it still felt like I was one wrong step away from losing my pants every time I moved.

I shuffled back to the desk I'd rummaged through once already. Maybe I'd missed something.

Sinking into the massive, claw-footed chair, I flipped through the letters again. That name—Vesperus Theoclordan—marked each one either as the writer or the receiver. That must have been the name of the sorcerer who'd created, or at the very least used, this place.

Hmm.

I paused, holding one letter that was only a few lines long, written in Vesperus's curling, spidery writing. The message itself was vague, and while it was addressed to someone named Bellavora, there were no formal greetings or opening blessings that seemed to be the standard format for most of the other letters. Just six short sentences.

Do what you must, but I will remain at his side for as long as it takes. I drove him to it. I made us both monsters. I can contain this. I must fix him. I trust you understand.

The passage was blunt and to the point. Almost ... stubbornly insistent, like a snippet of an ongoing disagreement.

Or rather, it was unfinished.

I frowned, reading the passage scrawled onto the fine, soft yellow parchment over and over. It had been folded, but not sealed. A letter half-written and never sent.

Why?

Who was Bellavora? What had Vesperus driven someone —him—to do?

I made us both monsters.

That line stuck in my brain like a splinter, pinching and irritating. I'd only seen one monster here, so far. But it hadn't looked anything like an Avoran sorcerer.

What was I missing?

I stole a glance at Axien, watching his tall silhouette rise before the hearth. All broad, powerful shoulders, slimly cut hips, long legs, and leanly corded strength. He stood like a young god in bold relief to the warm, golden light of the fire. The tips of his pointed ears peeked out from beneath his dark hair that fell to just below his shoulders. Half of it was drawn into a braid that had been tousled wildly by the freezing, stormy wind.

Wind that had apparently thrown his magic all out of sorts.

I glanced back down at the letter again.

"Axien?" I blurted suddenly.

He turned some, glancing at me over one of his shoulders. "Yes?"

"You said before that you think that door can lead to multiple places, right?" I just had to make sure I had all my facts straight before I started coming up with wild ideas.

He ambled over with his hands on his hips, expression tinged with suspicion. "I am not a sorcerer, so I can only guess. But ... given what we've seen, I think so."

"How many places? You said it's a pocket dimension. A pocket isn't very big, though, is it?"

"Depends on the size of the coat," he retorted with a frown and leaned over to peer at the letter I still held. "If we're comparing the fabric of the universe to a coat, well, I'd say that's pretty large."

I snorted and held the letter out so he could read it. "What if ... this isn't a private study? What if it's sort of like a cage?"

"A cage for what?" he asked as his gleaming, ice-blue eyes quickly perused the letter.

"Oh, I'm pretty sure we've seen *what*."

Axien didn't reply, still scanning the letter as though he were reading it over and over the same way I had. Trying to peer through the tangled, swirling briar patch of Vesperus's handwriting and find whatever meaning was hidden beyond. He slowly rubbed a hand against the back of his neck, under his hair.

"You're suggesting that monster is being kept here on purpose," he said, as though he were processing the idea out loud, and dragged his hand down the sharp line of his jaw.

"That Vesperus trapped it here intentionally. That would explain why it can't breach the doors—both here and at the cabin. He must have spelled them against its power somehow."

"It would also explain why the storm messes with magic," I added quickly. "It would weaken the beast, just like it did you. Make its power difficult to control. Make it easier to get away from it, if you needed to."

"Not by much, though," Axien said with a resigned sigh.

"Doesn't have to be much. It just has to be enough that it can't outmaneuver a full-blooded Avoran sorcerer," I countered.

His eyebrows rose. I guess I'd made my point.

Too bad that made dread sink into my stomach with a queasy, rotting sort of ache.

"So let's say that is what Vesperus intended—that he made that pocket within a pocket to trap that monster. Why would he do it?" Axien reasoned. "Clearly, that thing isn't an Avoran elf or anything of the mortal realm. Its power made it seem more like something from the void. Something foul and evil."

"The letter says Vesperus made them both monsters," I pointed out, my tone hushed as I gnawed at the inside of my cheek. "Is it even possible to turn someone into a monster like that? Even with magic?"

Axien's expression skewed, head drawing back slightly with a grimace before he handed the letter back over to me. "I don't know. Gods, I hope not."

"We're talking about events that likely date back thousands of years. Remember, all this started with us in a crypt—an ancient Avoran crypt that undoubtedly dates to before the fall of their empire," I considered aloud as I gently placed the letter back onto the desk.

Axien's face paled. He looked down at me, brow drawn in a look of quiet horror.

"You think that monster is a beast of Vescor's making? The God of the Void?" he guessed in a hoarse, breathless whisper. "Fates, Violet. If that were true, why would an Avoran sorcerer trap it here?"

"I don't know. But the letter almost makes it sound like he thought he could cure it or something." I hated myself for pointing that out. Gods, I hoped I was wrong. What did I know about the finer details and rules of divine magic? Nothing.

But I did have a really awful, sinking feeling in my gut, and that pasty look of morbid terror on Axien's face was not encouraging.

According to the ancient texts, Vescor had done many gruesome favors for the Dire King Zarexius of Nar'Haleen during the War of the Stones, trying to tilt the odds in their favor. Everyone knew those stories; how he'd made my kin, the Viperi, to be his assassins. He'd made the switchbeasts to be his shock troops that could reproduce and spread like a plague upon the land.

But before that, Vescor had been the undoing of many a desperate fool. He had been birthed from the malice and desperation rampant in the world during the War of Falling Stars and had been known to strike bargains in exchange for his power—his favorite way of expanding his following. But I hadn't heard of Vescor crafting monsters or minions for anyone before Zarexius.

My stomach flipped, souring at the thought. Was it even possible?

He had been the eternally hungry God of the Void. The breath-stealer. The great devoured. He was perfectly capable and had proven that thoroughly before he was destroyed in the War of the Stones. And it wasn't beyond Avoran sorcerers to be tempted—especially during the War of Falling Stars, when their grip on the seat of power in the Southern Kingdoms was slipping. They were being forced to abandon their cities as the human kingdoms rallied against them, armed with weapons like my Spelldrinkers that had been specifically engineered to defeat them.

What if Vescor had made monsters that not even those old stories remembered?

I shuddered at the thought. Bitter chills climbed my spine, making my flesh prickle and my breath catch.

If I was right, then we might not be the only people trapped here with that monster. Vesperus might still be here, as well. Unless, of course, that pet he was keeping in the cold confines beyond the door had already slaughtered him.

But I hadn't seen any signs of that. No bodies on the ice. No blood in the snow. If time never passed here, then the evidence of his demise would still be there, wouldn't it?

I stared at Axien, my mind whirling with a thousand new, terrible questions. Things I didn't dare speak aloud. If Vesperus was still here, I sort of doubted he'd be pleased to have company. Gods, he might have been here and not realized how much time had passed in the outside world. Not just a month or a few years.

No, he had been in this place for more than six thousand years.

And now, we were trapped here with him... and his pet monster.

Thirty-Nine

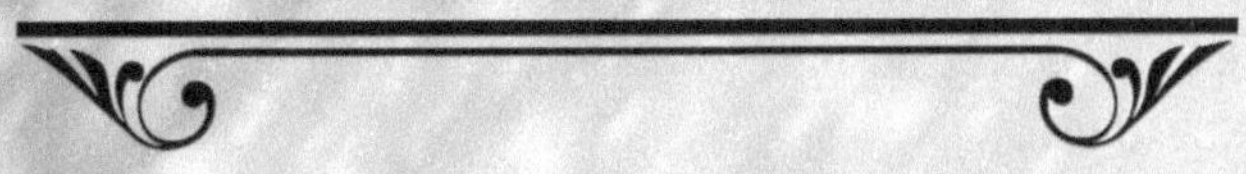

"Now look who's stealing stuff," Axien scoffed as I perused the shelves for anything else that might be useful.

"Shut up. It's just *borrowing*, remember?" I shot him a glare and wrinkled my nose.

We stared one another down from across the room, eyes narrowed, expressions pinched sourly. Neither of us blinked or dared to look away, just waiting for the other to flinch.

Then Axien burst out laughing and shook his head, turning his attention back to the bookshelves. He probably thought I didn't notice him going straight back to that box of magical rings and plucking the other two from it. He stuffed them away in his pocket and put the box back on the shelf.

Borrowing—hah! Like a former street urchin wouldn't know stealing when she saw it.

I rolled my eyes, biting back a smile before I got back to work.

"You danced beautifully tonight," he said suddenly.

I froze, heartbeat skipping, my hand hovering over the spine of a leather-bound tome.

“I know you were anxious about it, but you looked …” his voice trailed off, as though he couldn’t find the right word.

“Convincing?” I tried to finish for him, chancing a glance over my shoulder.

Axien stood across the room with his back to me, fidgeting around with artifacts on the shelves like nothing about this was unbearably awkward. Too bad the ends of his pointed ears were flushed bright pink.

Dead giveaway.

I couldn’t hold back a smile.

“I’d say so,” he agreed in a stiff tone before he cleared his throat a little.

“Glad I didn’t disappoint, then,” I quipped and went back to my own fidgeting, yanking that leather-bound book from the shelf and flipping through the pages.

Just useless political drivel.

“You never do,” he replied softly, something delicate in his voice that made my stomach flutter and flip. My face burned and my toes squirmed around in my borrowed, too-big boots.

We spent over an hour caught up in that strange silence, scouring every nook and cranny for, well, anything of value. Weapons, potions, more clues, an instruction manual on how to operate that stupid magical door—anything that might be of use.

“I’ve been thinking,” Axien finally spoke again, as if the silence were crushing in on him, too. “What would the Tibran Empire even want with this artifact? They sent Ulfrangar after it, which I think most would agree implies they were determined to have it. But what for?”

“Maybe they want to unleash that monster,” I suggested as I picked my way through another shelf lined with small wooden boxes. All of them contained some sort of jewelry item—bracelets, earrings, necklaces—but they didn’t glow blue. No magic.

"Maybe. It would certainly be effective on the battlefield," he agreed, but his tone held a tinge of doubt. "There'd be no stopping it, though. No reasoning with it. No controlling it. Even Zarexius struggled to manage the powers Vescor gave him. In the end, it was his own undoing."

"The Tibrans were collecting switchbeasts for some sort of research before," I reminded him, although I doubted he'd forgotten that after the mess we'd been through escaping them. "It could be that they want to research this monster, too."

When Axien turned back to face me, his expression had gone dark. His mouth was set into a hard, grim line, and his brows were rumpled together pensively as he stared around the room.

"Sanja didn't reveal much to me about that. I don't know how involved she was with it, to be honest," he said. "But we know this new tyrant, Lord Argonox, is obsessed with divine magic and harvesting artifacts that contain it. I suppose it's not much of a leap to think he might try doing the same with that creature. To figure out where it came from or how it was made so he could duplicate it or control it."

I shuddered at the thought. "Then we need to make sure that doesn't happen."

"Agreed." Axien let out a deep, unsteady sigh. "If we can't escape this place, if we're going to live out the rest of our days here, then we become the bulwark to make sure no one else comes in, especially not the Tibrans."

I snorted and cast him a smirk. "We could always just find a way to kill it. Problem solved."

He shrugged. "If we can. We probably should try that, anyway, right?"

"Yeah. But we'll need to come up with a better plan than running for our lives and hoping for the best," I mumbled and cracked open another box. This one was smaller than most of the others, but the wood had been stained deep red and was lined with golden-leafed details of moon phases, stars, and a very familiar symbol.

An icosahedron, just like the artifact itself.

My heart gave a jolt. My hands shook as I frantically opened the box.

Just another fancy necklace. Crap.

I picked it up, scowling at the fine string of pearls and sapphires.

And ... something else.

"A-Axien!" I flapped my good hand at him, calling him over.

He was at my side in an instant, peering over my shoulder at the marble-sized trinket rolling around in the bottom of the velvet-lined box. Another icosahedron—this one made of a solid piece of black obsidian glass. Each face was engraved with tiny lines of spellwork and meticulously inlaid with gold, not unlike the one that had hung in the vestibule.

Gods, it was like a miniature version of it. And it was glowing like a hunk of pure blue starlight.

"Magic?" Axien asked breathlessly.

"*So much* magic," I verified.

His throat bobbed as he reached for it, gingerly removing the glass icosahedron from its hiding place.

"I-I can feel it," he stammered, jaw tensing as he held it in his palm at arm's length, as if he were afraid it might suddenly explode.

A valid concern, given where we were.

"Feel what?" I pressed.

"A connection. To the door. To the artifact. It's like I can see it." He grimaced, chin dipping toward his chest as he squeezed his eyes closed. "It's ... a lot. Like a key."

"A key to the door?" I gasped, reaching to grab onto his other arm.

"No. Like a map key," he explained. A vein stood out against the side of his temple, and his jaw clenched harder. Sweat beaded on his brow while radiant blue light began to burn beneath his eyelids. Brighter and brighter, like someone had shoved hot coals into his eye sockets.

"It's ... gods, it's ... too much," he growled brokenly, voice hitching in pain. "I-I can't—"

I surged forward and seized the icosahedron, snatching it off his palm and staggering away from him.

Axien sucked in a wild, gasping breath, eyes opening again to stare at me in bewilderment. Then he cringed, shook his head, and pinched the bridge of his nose right between his eyes.

"Thanks for that. I don't know what happened," he panted, face flushing along his cheekbones and nose.

"You keep playing with the crazy sorcerer's dangerous toys, that's what happened," I scolded.

He flicked me a tired, half-grin. "Yes. But at least this one might be more useful."

I was about to point out that the last one had been useful, too. But Axien started for the door again, purpose in every step.

Oh no. Here we go again.

"What are you doing?" I asked, following him with the tiny icosahedron still clenched in my fist.

"Testing a theory," he said, squatting in front of the gilded knob and studying it for a moment. Then he reached to close a hand around it, shutting his eyes, and murmuring a phrase in the Avoran language I didn't understand.

Some sort of magic word?

It must have been, because the knob glowed blue under his palm, flashing brightly for an instant. Then the whole mechanism clicked almost musically, as though something inside it had changed or moved into place.

"I think I just figured out how to change rooms," he announced with a proud grin.

"You did the same thing before, and it landed us in the middle of a frozen prison with that monster," I reminded him.

He gave a conceding, half-nod, half-shrug. "Yeah, well, I didn't know what I was doing. I just picked a phrase that meant outside."

"Oh, and now you do know what you're doing?" I did my very best to sound as unconvinced as possible.

"I think so," he said and slowly rose to stand before the door, his hand still on that knob.

My heart gave a lurching, wrenching dive straight to the bottom of my stomach as he began to twist and slowly drag it open. Gods and Fates, had he lost his mind?! What if that thing was out there, just waiting for us to—

But instead of a blast of freezing wind, a rustling, warm breeze ebbed in through the crack in the door. The thick fragrance of moist, loamy soil and greenery filled my lungs. Something floral and sweet tickled my nose.

As Axien opened the door wider, soft sterling light spilled inward. The rustling of wind through leaves made my arms go slack at my sides.

It wasn't an icy wasteland.

It was a path straight ahead between two tall walls of greenery, almost like a hedge maze. A pale, full moon hung low overhead like a single sterling eye, lighting the way ahead to where the path split at a T.

Axien and I exchanged a wary sideways glance.

"What phrase did you pick this time?" I whispered as I took a small step closer to his side.

"I ... saw many rooms. They passed in a blur. Laboratories. Libraries. Places with shelves stacked with bottles and vials. One even looked like some sort of healer's operating theater. But there was one that had a big door. It looked a lot like the one in the crypt, so I just thought—" he rambled frantically until I cut him off. This was not the time for excuses.

"Axien," I repeated firmly. "What phrase did you pick?"

He licked his lips slowly, dragging his bottom lip through his teeth before he finally answered, "Portal. It ... it seemed to fit. We came here by a portal, didn't we? One that looked exactly like that. So why wouldn't the same sort of door lead us back out?"

I didn't know.

And clearly he didn't, either, or he wouldn't have been asking me.

Gods help us.

What kind of mess were we stepping into now?

Forty

None of this made sense.

I'd always been reasonably good at puzzles. Mazes were an easy logical exercise if you knew the right tricks.

But as Axien and I walked toward that first intersection, an uneasy chill slithered up my spine and made all tiny hairs on the back of my neck stand on end. Something about this place felt wrong.

Directly ahead, a tall statue of pure white marble stood bathed in the ambient moonlight. The sculpture of two opposing draconic beasts, their necks and tails intertwined, and their snouts nearly touching, loomed like an omen.

The Viepol, or the Fates as many called them, were a familiar sight. They were the keepers of the realm of the gods. The deciders of every mortal soul's final destiny. They saw through flesh and bone, down to the very soul of a person, and weighed their deeds for final judgement.

I'd walked past another effigy of them nearly every day since I'd first come to the Zenith's Call. The fountain in the main hall of Krin'Moir depicted them, as well. But unlike the grand fountain back at home, these were smaller—only about seven or eight feet tall.

"Which way?" Axien asked as we stopped before the statue, considering it with a tilt of his head.

"Doesn't matter as long as we pick a wall and follow it," I said, glancing behind us to find that the door we'd just come through was only barely there, the gold knob glinting through a wall of greenery that concealed the rest of it.

Once again, something stirred in the depths of my mind. An uneasiness I couldn't quite shake.

"You really think this is the way out of this artifact?" I asked.

Axien's shoulders dropped slightly. "I don't know. But we've got to try something."

Well, he was right about that.

I let out a deep breath, trying to exhale all the doubt and tension in one swoop. Forward was better than standing still. So, I seized his hand with my good one and tugged him down the left path through the maze.

"Why this way?" he asked after we'd been forging on for a few minutes, taking every turn and keeping one shoulder always to the left wall.

"I always pick left," I said.

We continued on, our footsteps crunching over the white pebbled pathway, until we came to another split marked by another familiar statue. Stopping before it, Axien and I stared at the depiction of a goddess with six feathered wings, her head crowned in stars and a veil covering her face. She held a long, slender blade in one hand and had one of her bare feet planted defiantly on a dragon's skull.

Clysiros, Goddess of Death.

"Not who I was hoping to find here," Axien muttered under his breath.

I frowned and glanced in both directions, wondering if I'd

chosen the wrong path, after all. Finding Clysiros on any occasion wasn't a good sign. But it wasn't a dead end, either.

Might as well press on.

I started to the left again, but stopped short when Axien didn't follow, his hold on my hand yanking me to a halt like a dog on a leash. I glared back at him, ready to argue about all the reasons keeping on the same left-sided wall was the best option if we were going to find our way out of this place—but Axien's face had gone pale.

His eyes widened, head slowly turning to look at me as he raised a finger in a gesture for me to stop and listen.

I held perfectly still.

A deep, sizzling, buzzing noise droned somewhere in the distance, growing louder and louder. Axien whirled to the right just as a faint, bluish light began to grow along the opposing pathway.

Oh gods. Something was coming. Something glowing bright blue.

The light intensified, and the buzzing hummed so loudly I could feel it rattling the roots of my teeth.

At the last second, Axien sprang like a startled stag. He dragged me behind Clysiros's statue and flung me downward, shielding my body with his as something huge rounded the corner and drifted past us.

A massive, lidless, glowing eye.

It hovered like a small star, so bright it washed out my vision and forced me to shut my eyes and turn away. The buzzing drilled through my skull, seeming to scrape at the insides of my mind until I was sure my ears must be bleeding.

Axien squeezed me tighter, his hold so fierce I could hardly breathe.

The floating eye drifted away, moving at a casual walking pace—even if it didn't have any legs. Or body. Or anything, really, except a single dark slit of a pupil.

The buzzing faded into the distance, retreating down the path we'd just come from and out of sight.

Axien's body sagged against mine with a ragged exhale. He pushed back, leaning out from around the statue in the direction the floating eye had gone.

"What in the abyss was that?" I whispered shakily, too afraid to speak at full volume just yet.

Even if that thing—whatever it was—didn't have arms and legs, I was willing to bet good coin that anything glowing with that much magic didn't need a body to do something terrible.

"I-I don't know," Axien panted as he staggered to his feet, leaning against the statue as his legs wobbled strangely. "But it ... it did something to me. I can't explain. It's like it drained away all my magic at once."

"What?" I hurried over to steady him.

He shook his head, still fighting for breath as he stared down the pathway where the floating eye had drifted. "I-I don't understand how something like that is even possible."

To be fair, a lot of this place shouldn't have been possible. I'd known that Avoran magic was ancient, powerful, and far beyond things that most of us mortals could even comprehend. But this?

This was just bizarre.

"What happens if we come across another one and there's nowhere to hide?" I asked, not expecting Axien to have any clue, but it was something we needed to consider. "There could be dozens of those things floating around in here."

His expression dimmed, falling with distress that seemed to snuff all the light out of his vibrant blue eyes. He didn't answer. But he didn't need to.

We might have to fight it. And for him, that meant no magic, at the very least; a death sentence, for an Avoran. Their magic was tied to the very essence of their soul—or so I'd read. Without it, they slowly starved.

That's why none of them left their only remaining city far in the north. After the fall of their empire, they had been driven out of many of their cities. Forced to leave everything behind, they'd begun rebuilding their strength in the kingdoms now called Maldobar and Luntharda.

But then came another war. A far worse one than ever before. So bad, in fact, that the gods had enacted a new law—the Law of the Stones—which had made all those ley lines of divine magic go dark and completely stripped away the flow of divine magic into the mortal world. It had starved the Avoran elves, and like plants denied of sunlight, they had withered and died in vast numbers.

To survive, what remained of the Avorans had fled to the only place left with enough magic to sustain them: a floating city that was said to sit right on the gods' doorstep—literally. The texts I'd studied had told of a portal that led straight into the realm of the gods, and that divine magic seeped from it like a winter's chill creeping in around a windowsill. It was enough to keep them alive, but not enough for them to thrive as they had before.

That portal was the Avorans' last lifeline, and they guarded it fiercely. Their lingering little sliver of a kingdom was absolutely forbidden to outsiders. No one went in, and the Avoran elves scarcely ever left.

Those that did ... well, it was supposed to be a death sentence for them. A slow starvation as their magic dwindled away.

For a half-Avoran, though? I wasn't sure if they'd be subject to the same fate. Being drained or overusing his magic had hurt Axien badly before. Fates, it had left him comatose and nearly dead. Maybe that meant it was the same, after all.

Now did not seem like a good time to ask, though. Not when he'd gone so green in the face, I thought he might vomit at any second.

"We move fast and quiet," I said as I reached for his hand again. "We listen for the buzzing. If it gets close, we run back to the closest hiding spot. Or we try wedging ourselves into the hedges."

Axien gave a reluctant nod and lightly squeezed my hand back. "Right."

"We can do this," I urged. "I know we can."

He wore that same tragic, goodbye smile he'd given me a few times while we were floundering around in the ruins of the Viperi city when he gazed down at me again. It turned my stomach to lead and made my blood rush as cold as glacier water.

"I won't let anything happen to you, Violet," he murmured. "One way or another, you will make it out of here."

All the little hairs on my body prickled, sending my nerves into a frantic whirling spiral as I stared back at him. I couldn't place it, and it made no sense whatsoever.

But somehow, I just knew ... he was absolutely sure about that.

Like he had already seen it happen.

Forty-One

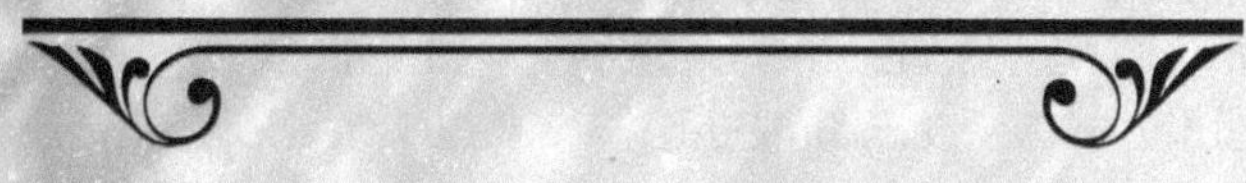

It was a mad race.

A sprint through the hedge maze with my left shoulder to the wall, marking our progress and making a mental note of every turn, every dead end, every place with an intersection with a corner that might make a good hiding spot.

Just in case.

The next time the buzzing hummed in the distance, we backtracked and ducked around a corner, hunkering down and waiting as another floating eye drifted past and continued on mere yards away. I held my breath, a hand over my mouth so I didn't make a single sound.

Axien tensed and grimaced, his face skewing with pain. But he didn't make any noise, either. Not even to gasp or hiss through his teeth.

So far, so good.

The eyes were all the same size, roughly ten or twelve inches in diameter, like a dinner plate. They made the same noise and moved at about the same pace. The aura of their antimagic field seemed to be about ten feet in radius.

That made things tricky, since the width of our hedge

maze pathways was a little less than double that. That meant that when one passed by, its aura filled the pathway entirely. There'd be no hiding from it or getting past it if one happened to block our path.

Part of me wanted to do an experiment—to find out just what the eyes were capable of and if they could be hurt or damaged. Maybe it was like popping a bubble. Or maybe doing anything to them would set off a big blast of power that would turn Axien and me into soot stains on the ground.

Seemed prudent to figure that out beforehand instead of, you know, in a moment of dire need.

But Axien did not like the idea of provoking them one teeny bit.

"We don't even know how fast they can really go," he growled bitterly as he stomped along beside me. "Even if you manage to stab one and start running away, they're not constrained by physical arms and legs to move. They might be able to glide faster than a flash of lightning. And then what?"

I pursed my lips sourly, saying nothing because ... well, honestly, I hadn't thought things out that far yet.

"What if we try setting up a trap, then? I provoke it. Try to stab it and run, lead it past a spot where you're lying in wait, and you try hitting it with a blast of your magic, hm?" I suggested.

He muttered a curse under his breath and looked away, probably rolling his eyes. "It's like you want to get killed," he muttered.

"I want to get out of here," I corrected.

"Then let's do it without provoking the giant floating eyeballs, shall we?" He flailed his arms angrily, grumbling louder this time.

Too loudly.

We froze, both hearing it at the same instant—the faint hum of that buzzing ebbing from around the next corner.

Axien began to turn, shifting his weight to sprint back the way we'd come. His arm snagged around my waist, as though he were going to try to carry me or fling me ahead of him.

But the buzzing turned into a blaring explosion of sound, like the low bellow of a battlehorn.

He staggered, letting out a sharp cry of agony.

A second later, it was upon us.

"YOU WILL NOT TOUCH HER!" Axien thundered as he braced before me, stance wide and arms thrown forward. A wall of crackling blue light formed before his outstretched hands like a shield.

The floating eye bore in, hovering before us and buzzing so loud it made my vision swerve and my brain throb.

"Stop it! We have to run!" I screamed as I seized Axien by the forearm, trying to pull him back.

But he didn't budge. Every corded muscle in his body tremored. Blood oozed from his nose as he bared his teeth in a crazed snarl. His chest heaved, face paling and the magical blue light of his eyes flaring.

The dark, purple-black sickly veins were already forming on the side of his neck.

Idiot! He'd completely drain himself like this!

Curse him, I had no choice.

Drawing the shortsword from Axien's belt, I dove around his magical shield and kicked into a sideways roll.

The floating eyeball was focused on him, arcing tendrils of strange energy from its center like bolts of pure light. They sizzled and snapped, hitting his shield and leaving singed holes. He cried out with every blast, shouts of agony that hit my brain like the bite of a whip.

He couldn't do this much longer.

No time to hesitate.

I sprang forward, spinning through a leaping strike that brought the steel of the blade down on the eyeball's center.

BOOM!

My vision went white as my body flew through the air, tossed like a ragdoll with my arms and legs flailing.

I hit the ground and rolled, finally slamming against something prickly. The hedges?

Everything seemed to spin in a hazy smear of color as I tried to blink, to move. My ears rang. My head throbbed.

Something thick and powerful snapped around my neck and began to squeeze.

Oh gods—what was happening?!

I gagged and gasped, clawing at the thick vine that clamped around my throat like a constrictor snake. It crushed tighter, and another vine snapped around my legs, pinning them together at my ankles. Another seized my injured arm, twisting and pulling. Strangling.

Crushing me alive.

I let out a strangled cry as the world went dark.

"VIOLET!" Axien's desperate shout shattered over me.

My body went numb as I choked and gaped, unable to get even the tiniest breath in.

A high-pitched shrieking and squealing filled my ears as a flourish of heat swept over my body. Fire?

I couldn't tell. I couldn't see anything.

"Damn you, let her go!" Axien roared, and the shrieking intensified.

Suddenly, the vine around my neck went slack. I gasped frantically, my vision returning in blinks and flashes as I sputtered in desperate breaths.

Axien crouched over me, his hands clenched on the vines and his expression contorted in pain. He bore in with his magic, channeling it through his palms so that they glowed vibrant blue and crackled with flames that danced between his fingers.

The vines recoiled at the heat and the hedges shuddered

behind me, making that awful screeching sound as he scorched them.

Whether it was the hedges themselves or some sort of camouflaged creature living in them, I couldn't tell. And it didn't matter. The instant the vines loosened their hold, I flailed wildly, clawing the rest of the way free and tackling Axien.

His arms immediately closed around me and together, we scooted and scrambled over the ground until we were out of the reach of the hungry vines.

"I-I ... hate this ... p-place," Axien rasped brokenly as he panted.

I gripped him tight, arms around his middle and face against his shoulder as I coughed and shook, still taking in as much air as I could. Behind him, the remains of the eye lay in the middle of the path like a shattered glass ornament.

So, stabbing it did work, after all.

It just set off a massive explosion. Not ideal.

"Are you all right?" Axien asked, still holding me against his chest with a hand on the back of my neck.

"Y-yeah," I croaked.

But I wasn't. Neither of us were.

We couldn't stay here. We had to move.

Right now.

His skin was cold and sticky with sweat, and his pulse hammered against my ear. Too fast. His whole body tremored as though he were vibrating, and when I pulled back, all the breath rushed out of me for a second time.

His eyes—their usual vibrant blue was flecked with gold like the light dancing in a cut gemstone. Blood ran from the corners of them like smeared, crimson tears. More ran from his nose and dripped from his chin.

My stomach dropped.

"S-sorry," he slurred and forced a bleary, relieved smile. Then his eyes rolled back.

He let out a low groan and slumped forward into me.

"No! Axien, you idiot, we have to get up! We have to run," I rasped hoarsely as I gathered my feet under me and tried dragging him up. "You have to move. I can't carry you!"

I jostled him. I smacked the side of his head.

No response.

A chorus of buzzing came from down the path behind us —so loud it made the ground vibrate and the air crackle with energy.

No—no, no, no!

That explosion had been so loud, too loud. It probably attracted every one of those floating eyeball things in the entire maze. They were coming for us. Searching. Moving fast.

We couldn't stay here. We had to move. We had to find a way out.

My pulse kicked into a frenzy as I dragged Axien to his knees, barely managing to drag him a few feet before I stumbled and collapsed onto my knees. He was too big. Too heavy. My injured arm throbbed with surges of agony so intense I couldn't close my hand fully.

"Axien, please, you have to get up!" I begged as my eyes welled and my rasping voice hitched with a sob. "They're coming!"

The buzzing roared like thunder around us. So loud it squeezed at my brain like someone wringing out a washcloth. It came from everywhere.

Sprawled before me on the ground, Axien's chest rose and fell with fast, shallow breaths. His face ashen, dark veins spidering over his throat and cheeks. I couldn't move him. But, gods curse it, I would not leave him here.

The glowing aura of the floating eyeballs approached from the path ahead. Whipping my head around, I spotted the same encroaching glow coming from the path behind us. Both directions were blocked.

There was nowhere to run. Nowhere to hide.

So I threw my body over Axien's, flattening us both on the ground with my head right next to his. I shut my eyes tightly ... and waited for the end.

Forty-Two

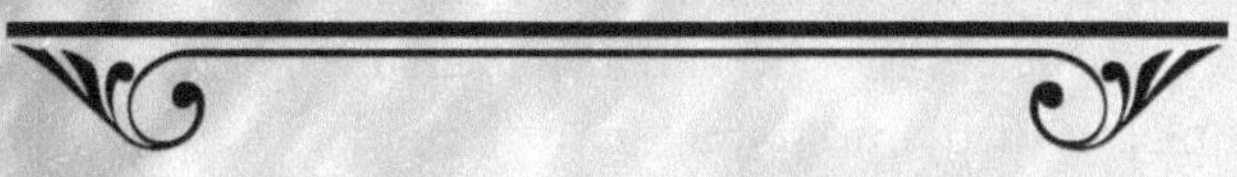

I didn't dare to look.

Or breathe. Or even think.

They might hear it. They might see me move.

Playing dead—no sound, no movement—that was the only option. The only chance we might have.

But I couldn't stop my pulse from racing as I lay covering Axien's body with my own. Swells of cold poured through me, my blood rushing like icy sludge, as I held my breath.

My skull vibrated as the buzzing from the floating, arcane eyeballs filled the narrow path. They hovered all around, their warring frequencies sending pangs of agony through my brain. I clenched my teeth, daring to squint one eye open just enough to see four of them circling the area around us.

Searching. Waiting.

One hovered right over us, so close I could feel the heat radiating off the orb's smooth, glassy surface.

But it didn't seem to see us sprawled out on the ground like two corpses. It didn't even pause to take a second look.

My mind whirled, trying to process what that meant.

Gods and Fates, what if ... what if they couldn't see

anything that wasn't moving? Just like the statues, they weren't triggered by anything stationary and silent. But why?

If Vesperus had been the one to place these things here, he'd probably designed them this way on purpose. He had set them loose in the maze like security sentinels that could only hear loud noises and see objects moving. It was oddly specific.

One thought of that horrible monster trapped in the frozen wasteland beyond the magic, changing door made all the pieces snap into place in my mind. The way it had screamed so loudly. The way it moved to pursue us.

These had been put here to keep that monster out of whatever lay beyond this maze. A last line of defense in case it somehow managed to breach its frozen prison.

Clever, effective, and deadly.

I might just like this Vesperus fellow, after all.

One by one, the floating eyeballs drifted away, probably going to resume their pre-orchestrated patrol paths through the hedge maze. When the last one finally sailed around the corner and out of sight, I finally dared to suck in a ragged breath.

I shakily lifted my head, moving slowly and searching both directions just to be sure.

But there was nothing. Even the buzzing had faded back to silence.

We were in the clear.

I flopped my head down onto Axien's chest and lay there, draped across him, while I tried to recompose myself. His heartbeat thumped, strong and steady in my ear. His breathing had slowed some, and a little of the color was rushing back to his face.

A good sign.

"I'm just gonna ... lay here for a minute ... or ... maybe ten," I wheeze-panted quietly, not expecting him to even hear.

"Me, too," he replied in a rough, strained whisper. I

flinched in surprise as he shifted beneath me, draping one arm over my waist.

I blew out a sigh and let my much smaller body relax into his, feeling every single place where we touched like the caress of sun-warmed sand. Something about it felt so familiar.

Familiar—and safe in a way I'd never been before.

We lay there, sprawled on the ground unceremoniously like a pair of fresh corpses, as minutes slipped past. With my head settled on top of Axien's strong chest, feeling the rise and fall of each breath he took, I let my eyes roll closed and my mind sink into restless silence like a lukewarm bath.

It might have been relaxing, but my injured arm throbbed fiercely, the sensation sending waves of trembling heat up into my shoulder. Probably a bad sign. I'd spent enough time around Leruna to know that if I went too long without proper medical treatment, the risk of infection would sharply increase. I might even wind up losing my arm altogether.

Not ideal. I was pretty fond of that arm—I'd had it as long as I could remember.

After a while, Axien finally stirred beneath me. He let out a growling groan and reached up to scrub the heel of his hand against his forehead.

"Fates, m-my head is killing me," he said.

After what I'd seen him do with his magic, not to mention all the blood now dried on his face, I didn't doubt it.

"You're recovering a lot faster than you used to," I murmured and shut my eyes again.

I could hear that stupid, arrogant smirk in his tone as he slurred, "P-Practice makes perfect. Arcane recovery is a necessary skill if I'm going to keep working with you."

I pursed my lips in a scowl but didn't retort. I didn't have the energy to go another round in a verbal joust with him. But he must have been feeling a lot better if he was already taking jabs.

For whatever reason, realizing that made my scowl twist and warp into a bitter little smile. He'd pushed himself to the limit twice now on my account—risked his life for mine. And it wasn't hard to jump to the wrong conclusion about why.

Especially since he'd already kissed me once, even if he'd claimed it was just some sort of repayment.

"We need to get moving again," Axien murmured at last, his voice steadier now.

I blew out another sigh, hating that I had to move. Every single part of me ached. I'd be mottled in bruises from being thrown by the blast of that exploding eyeball. It had sent me skipping over the ground like a stone on a pond, and I was lucky I hadn't broken anything.

"Ready?" Axien's arm moved where it was still draped over me, his hand sliding up my spine. It sent a wave of warm shivers through me so suddenly my breath caught. My face burned and I bit down against the urge to spring off him immediately.

Calm. I had to stay calm. Collected. Confident and fully in control.

"Yeah," I managed to squeak, heat tingling in my cheeks as I pushed off him and stood. "So, um, you should know that if we come across those things again, we just have to hold still and not make a sound."

"Sure. If you can manage it," he teased as he slowly got to his feet. He wobbled some as he straightened, expression seizing with discomfort.

"As I recall, I wasn't the one who gave us away last time," I grumbled halfheartedly. "You're the one who started yelling."

"Yelling? Hardly. It was an impassioned exclamation, at best," Axien said, still sporting that vulpine grin that made me want to shake him.

I narrowed my eyes, wondering if it would be worth it to

gut-punch him. It would slow us down even further. It might even make him pass out again.

Definitely worth it.

He just chuckled quietly and hobbled stiffly over to pick up the shortsword that had been blown out of my hand when the glass eyeball exploded. A low hiss of pain slipped through his teeth as he stood again, slipping the blade back into his belt.

"Can you manage? We can take a few more minutes, if you need it," I said, keeping my gaze pointed away so he didn't read too much into that suggestion.

He feigned a startled gasp. "Was that concern? For me? I am truly touched."

"Never mind. Let's sprint the rest of the way," I muttered, but it only made him laugh again. That rich, deep, infectious sound sent tingles through my chest all the way to my toes.

My mouth twisted to the side as I studied his profile—the way those dark, purplish veins had receded to the normal warm bronze hue of his skin. The smug arch to his brows and roguish, crooked grin he wore made his half-elven features seem sharp and enticingly unpredictable. As though he were secretly scheming, but only the gods knew what he was really up to.

Probably not that far from the truth, honestly.

"I'll be fine," he said, resting a hand on my shoulder for a moment as he shuffled past and started onto our chosen path through the maze.

With one last look at the shattered remnants of the eyeball still scattered across the path like shards of gleaming glass, I turned and jogged to catch up.

Keeping to our original plan, I made sure to mark the left wall as our line to follow as we pressed on into the maze. With each twist and turn, something cold and prickly knotted tighter in the pit of my stomach. A feeling I couldn't shake that made prickles rise on the back of my neck.

A feeling like being watched. Or maybe hunted.

I didn't like it one bit.

My teeth on edge and my head on a constant swivel, I kept my senses trained all around us for the slightest hint of any buzzing sounds that might be coming our way. But there was nothing. No sound other than the crunch and scrape of our footsteps.

As we came to another intersection, my steps slowed as I caught a glimpse of a white stone statue of Tykeron standing just like all the other gods had been in pearly white marble. He appeared as an impish little boy with the lower half of a fawn, curled horns peeking out of his curly hair, and long ears that looked more like a goat's than a human's or elf's.

My steps dragged to an involuntary halt as we drew closer. I'd never seen a statue of him like this—looking like a child rather than a regal adult. Somehow, it seemed to better suit all the stories I'd heard about how much he loved mischief and trickery. Even the way he leaned into a crooked staff topped with clusters of grapes was lazy and arrogant—befitting of a young god who loved to stir up trouble with mortals.

But that wasn't what made me pause and frown at the statue. While he held onto his staff with one hand, Tykeron's other hand held out a bejeweled, solid gold goblet. It shimmered and sparkled, resting in the statue's smooth stone hand, looking like something a king or emperor might sip from.

Weird.

None of the other statues had anything jeweled or metal on them. Why was this one different? Because this was supposedly his—Tykeron's—puzzlebox?

Or was it for another reason?

The young god's statue grinned widely at the path straight in front of him. Or maybe he was smiling at the chalice he was holding out toward it. I couldn't tell which. Both pointed in the same direction.

My gaze followed his attention along the path to our left.

Oh gods.

My breath snagged in my throat as I snatched Axien's hand, yanking him to a stop just as every muscle in my body locked up at once.

There, not two hundred feet ahead, the path between the hedges ended abruptly before a pair of tall, arched doors of the same carved, milky-white stone as all the statues. Lush green vines snaked across it and draped down from the top, lightly obscuring the relief of dozens of eyes engraved into it.

The end of the maze.

I stared at the long path that stretched between us and the door, something cold and heavy settling into the pit of my stomach.

Something about this place just felt ... wrong. Too easy. As though the entire maze was now holding its breath, just waiting for us to take that next step. Hoping we would.

I didn't like it one bit.

The path was wider here. And all those eyes engraved into the doors looked a little too much like the hovering ones that had nearly killed us. Even the stones paving the ground were bigger and wider, more perfectly placed than the ones in the rest of the maze.

All of it screamed one thing in my mind like a chorus: trap.

"Finally," Axien breathed and started tugging me forward down that final path.

"Wait," I protested, digging my heels in.

"What is it?" he asked, pausing again.

I didn't know. I couldn't explain it—the gnawing in my gut that told me something wasn't right.

I frowned at him, my exhausted brain working overtime to

try to come up with a way to put that feeling into words. The sense that we were missing something important.

I just didn't know what.

Axien's brow creased as he studied me in silence for a beat, then his jawline hardened. He eyed the path again, the door covered in eyes, and the statue of the smirking young god with his shiny, jewel-encrusted cup.

Then his gaze found mine again, and his throat moved in a hard swallow.

"Stay here," he ordered.

"What are you doing?" I demanded.

He didn't answer as he prowled cautiously forward, glancing back and forth between the eye-covered door and the statue of Tykeron. When he reached the edge of that better-manicured path, Axien crouched down and brushed his fingers over a few of the white stones that paved the ground. His features darkened, becoming contemplative and masterfully focused.

Then he slowly stood and stretched out a foot, tapping the nearest stone on the left side of the pathway with the toe of his boot.

Axien wobbled as the stone immediately crumbled away like dust under the pressure, flinging his arms out wide to keep his balance.

Then a low, buzzing hum rumbled from the far end of the pathway as the largest eye engraved into the very center of the doors lit up brilliant blue.

I opened my mouth to cry out, to warn him, but in an instant an arcing beam of crackling magic exploded from the eye, hitting him squarely in the chest and blowing him backward—directly into me.

No time to duck. No time to dodge.

Axien slammed into me and we both hit the ground in a

heap. All his body weight crushed down onto me, and the stench of seared flesh filled my nose.

"G-gods!" I gasped frantically, trying to wriggle out from under his much larger body. "Axien?"

No answer.

Oh, gods, please ... no!

"Axien, are you all right?!" I panicked, grabbing his shoulder and shaking him.

He let out a shuddering groan and whimper at the contact.

Alive. Thank the Fates, he was alive. But his clothes were ... sticky.

Something thick and wet oozed through my fingers and I drew my hand back, my heart in my throat as I saw dark, scorched blood smeared over my palm.

Oh no.

Axien's body shook as he dragged himself off me, hissing curses through his teeth as he flopped onto the ground and rolled onto his back.

I sprang up immediately, rushing to his side and gaping in horror at where that beam of raw magical power had seared straight through his clothes. His upper right arm and shoulder were laid bare, the flesh bubbling and burned.

Tears welled in my eyes as my entire body locked in paralyzed horror that held me in a chokehold. I couldn't speak. I couldn't move.

"I-it's fine," he growled weakly.

It wasn't—not in any way, shape, or form. He was burned badly, and we had no medical tools. I didn't even have any water to pour over it to stop the burning.

"Axien." His name left my lips in a broken sob as I reached toward him, my shaking hands halting over his wound as I tried to think of something—anything—to do to help him.

"I'm o-okay, Violet," he lied again, forcing a thin, twitchy smile that shattered me to the core. "It's g-gonna be fine."

It wasn't. Not even a little.

What could I do? How could I help him?

A warm hand touched my face, jarring me from my shock. Axien cupped my cheek as though it were something precious, a thumb tracing the corner of my lips.

"We're getting out of here," he swore. "Help me up, okay? We'll figure it out together."

I swallowed against the sobs still caught in my throat, trying to force down all the fear that turned my body to stone and my brain to useless sludge.

I couldn't lose it. I couldn't fall apart when he needed me.

He needed me steady.

Pulling the kitchen knife from the side of my boot, I started cutting away pieces of my oversized clothing, patching together makeshift bandaging to cover the burns on his upper arm and shoulder.

There wasn't time to do it properly, so we just had to wrap it over his clothes and all. It was horrible and sloppy, not to mention terribly unsanitary, but there wasn't any other choice. Not here.

Right now, we had to stay focused. The door was right there. We had to get the hell out of this nightmare of a labyrinth and back to the real world.

But first, we had to find a way past this deathtrap. There had to be some way to reach those doors without being fried alive. A trick or something we just hadn't figured out yet, just like with those floating eyeballs that could only detect us if we made noise or moved.

There was an answer hidden here somewhere.

And by all the gods, I would find it.

Forty-Three

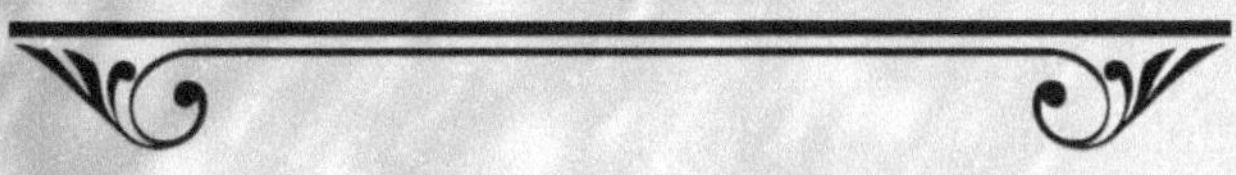

"It's a riddle," Axien said quietly, voice hitching in pain as he hobbled toward the statue of Tykeron before us.

What?

I looked again, studying the graceful marble effigy more closely. But I didn't see it. Not until Axien tugged me closer to the statue, pointing to the goblet where small lines of swirling Avoran script had been etched into the rim. A simple phrase that I had mistaken for filigree at first glance.

"The only safety is in his sight," Axien read aloud.

I turned, following that gleeful grin on Tykeron's cherubic face straight ahead to the doors. There, along that line, every second or third row of white stones was in perfect alignment with the statue's gaze.

I frowned. Was that really what it meant? That we could only walk on those stones? It couldn't be that simple, could it?

"Stay behind me," Axien warned as he moved forward, herding me behind him with an arm.

"Are you insane? We should test it first!" I protested. "For crying out loud, your clothes are still smoking, you idiot!"

But it was too late.

Ignoring my squawks of protest, Axien strode straight down the center of that path, choosing only those specific stones to walk on.

One step.

Nothing. No buzzing. No searing beam of energy from the eyes on the door.

He took a deep breath and took another step onto the next stone.

Still nothing.

At the third, he stopped and turned back, waving me after him with that frustratingly handsome grin that looked a lot like the one on Tykeron's statue.

I sagged, all the energy and tension seemed to drain out through my heels as I watched him continue. No fear. No second-guessing.

Gods, was he dense? Or did he really just not care if he died?

Maybe that was an argument better saved for later.

Moving carefully, I started following his path one stone at a time. The first few were easy. We only had to hop over one or two rows of square white stones to keep directly on the path between the statue's gaze and the doors.

But halfway down the passage, the center-aligned stones became smaller and a lot farther apart. Axien had to leap the distance, stumbling and wheeling his arms to keep his balance while I waited for my turn.

I could stick the landings easily, since I was smaller. But jumping that far was a challenge. My legs were shorter, and I couldn't get a running start to help make up for my lack of height. A dangerous gamble with every step.

At the next-to-last stone, I eyed the jump and tried to plan out my technique.

"If only one of us had *wings*," I growled as I coiled my legs beneath me, eyes fixed on my landing point.

"Somehow, I doubt that sort of cheating would be rewarded in this scenario," Axien retorted. "And since I've already been incinerated once, I'd rather not be the one to test it a second time."

Ugh. Fair point—especially considering the same sorcerer who had the rings also made this place. And given the fact that the monster he was trying to contain here had wings, as well, Vesperus had probably thought of that already.

Going through the walls was clearly not allowed. The strangling vines had gotten that point across extremely well. Flying over the maze would probably get us struck by holy lightning again or smashed by a divine meteor.

"Want me to come back and toss you?" Axien baited when I hesitated, still gauging the next leap.

I gave him a one-fingered gesture with my good hand and braced myself, focusing on the strength in my thighs and calves. The angle of my jump. The way I needed to thrust all my weight at once, and then land without taking a compensatory step on the other side.

Gods, this sucked.

"Come on," Axien coaxed from his stone, a few rows past the one I had to jump to. "You can make it."

I sprang forward, arching through the air and trying to move my arms to get as much forward momentum as possible. Too much.

Oh gods—way too much!

I landed and immediately pitched backward, my balance off and my heel sliding off the back of the stone.

My stomach dropped, heart lodging itself somewhere in my throat as the earth behind me immediately crumbled away and revealed an endless dark void directly below.

What the—?!

I dropped into a crouch, pitching my weight forward and hunkering down as cold terror shuddered all the way through me from head to foot. My pulse hammered against my ribs as I gaped at Axien in mute horror.

If we couldn't make the jumps, if we stumbled or took a wrong step, then we would fall into that yawning darkness below. A drop that might as well have been an eternal abyss.

Certain death.

I shut my eyes tightly, hissing curses through my teeth as I fought to get control. To push the fear down. To focus. Quiet my mind.

"Violet," Axien said firmly, never breaking eye contact with me. "Breathe."

I stared back at him, my heart pounding sloppily as I drew in a deep gulp of air and slowly released it.

"Good girl," he coaxed. "Now, do it again. Then get ready to jump to me."

What? Jump to him? And what? He'd catch me in mid-air? With an injured arm and shoulder? Not likely.

I eyed the gap between us, weighing the options. He was only one stone ahead of me now. But the space between my stone and his was nearly ten feet—an even bigger leap than the one I'd just taken.

He was right. I couldn't make it. Not and stick the landing.

Panic took me in a chokehold tighter than those throttling vines.

"You can do it, Violet," he urged, stretching both hands out toward me.

I nodded shakily, drawing my legs underneath me again and placing my feet as far apart on the stone as I could without going over the edge.

"Now, focus," he coached, that smoldering gaze relentless on me. "Feel your feet. Your calves. Your thighs. Think through the movements. Don't overshoot it."

I let my eyes roll closed, feeling the slow return of strength to the lower half of my body. The flex of my muscles, drawn tense like bowstrings. I had to do this.

I would do it.

"I *will* catch you," Axien reminded me, his eyes steady upon me when I looked at him again. "Now, on my count. One ..."

I steadied my breathing, arching my back and pouring all my energy into my legs. Into the way I had to move up and forward.

"Two ..."

I flexed my toes in and out, feeling the slip and slide of the too-big boots and how they weighed me down. Curse it, I should have just taken them off. Too late now. Besides, for all I knew, there'd be another tundra on the other side of those doors.

"Three ..."

I bowed my head, forcing my mind to go silent. To pull all the frayed threads of courage holding my battered, wicked soul together taut again.

One last time.

"JUMP!"

With a feral cry, I sprang outward with all my strength.

My arms flailed in circles, and I drew my legs in close to my torso, angling myself straight for Axien's open arms as I sprang forward. My body sailed like a projectile flung from a catapult through the air straight for him.

And the whole world seemed to slow.

Axien's expression steeled, teeth bared and eyes blazing with relentless determination as he reached for me. Braced. Ready.

Oh gods, what if I hit him too hard? What if he stumbled? What if he dropped me, or we both fell, or—

BAM!

I hit him square in the chest, my nose crushing right into

his collarbone. Axien's arms closed around me tightly. He staggered back on one foot, letting out a grunt as he immediately dropped forward into a kneeling position to keep his balance. With my legs clamped around his waist and my arms squeezing his neck, I gripped him like a squirrel on a tree trunk.

If we fell, we fell together. If we burned, we burned together.

Then everything was still. No sound except for our ragged breathing.

"Gotcha," he gasped, voice tremoring with pain.

All I could do was let out a whimper, just to let him know I was still alive. Still breathing. Still coming to terms with this never-ending nightmare.

"One more left," he panted against my ear, still holding me close. "I think you'll need my help again this time."

Undoubtedly, even if it stung my pride a little.

Axien gently put me on my feet in front of him, both of us wobbling as we struggled to keep our footing on the same small paver stone. Ahead, the final leap would put us at the wide landing slab for the doors. But the gap was even bigger than before. Ten feet, at least.

Too far for me to jump, even if I didn't have to worry about stumbling.

I traced the edge of my teeth with my tongue as I studied it, my mind spinning through scenarios and strategies that might get me there without being zapped or falling to my doom.

Behind me, Axien loosed a deep sigh and murmured, "I ... I could always toss you."

I whipped my head around to glare at him. Seriously? With that injured shoulder?

His mouth mashed into a half-hearted, cringing smile.

"You know, like an acrobat toss. I can hold your feet, give you a bit of a boost, and you can jump it."

"And what about you?" I countered. "Can you jump that far?"

His brows rumpled together, jaw working from side to side as though he hadn't considered that problem.

"Probably," he decided aloud.

My brows rose. "Probably?"

He gave a wincing smile. "Yeah. Most likely."

"I'm not betting your life on a probably, Axien," I growled.

"I can get close enough to catch the edge with my hands, I think. Then you can pull me up the rest of the way, yeah?"

Gods help me. This man ...

Too bad I didn't have any better ideas. If he did miss the landing and fell, at least he had wings. He might be able to make it to the edge before something else horrible happened—like taking a magical beam to the chest from that carved eyeball at point-blank range.

I shuddered at the thought.

"Ready?" he urged, already shaking out his hands and arms in preparation.

"I hate everything about this plan, for the record," I muttered as I turned back around, facing the doors.

"Noted." He chuckled as he dropped down into a squat and grabbed me by the calves. "It's got to be one fluid motion, all right? I pull up and get my hands under your feet. You crouch, and as I stand, I'll toss you. You have to jump at the same moment."

"Like an acrobat," I grumbled.

I could hear the smirk in his voice again. "A lovely, graceful, agile acrobat."

"You're such an ass." I bit down hard, my pulse already

pounding frantically. It sent waves of adrenaline through my body, making my stomach spin and my hands shake.

This was insane. We couldn't do it. What if he got stuck? How was I supposed to help him? I couldn't catch him. I didn't even know if I could drag him over the edge with my injured arm.

"On my count again," Axien said as his grip on my legs tightened.

My head went dizzy, bright spots dancing in my vision as I stared at the doors—directly into that unblinking stone eye that could burn a hole straight through me. What if it did anyway? What if hitting that landing set off all the eyes on the door and we died anyway?

"A-Axien," I started to protest, my voice trembling as fear throttled all the breath from my lungs.

"One," he started counting again.

No. Not yet. I wasn't ready. I-I couldn't do this!

I would fall. Or stumble. Or something awful would happen if I did make it. We'd both be burned alive.

But it was too late. He wouldn't back down. He wouldn't let me hesitate or stall.

Axien counted down, and on three, he hoisted me up as though I were weightless.

I had no choice but to follow his lead, to spring into the open air as he launched me skyward.

A feral scream ripped from my throat as I aimed straight for that door, body tucked in as tight as a cannonball. The world turned to gray haze, all time seeming to slow to a crawl as I flew.

The door came closer and closer. The landing was right there. All I had to do was extend my legs and brace for it. If I hit the door's surface, maybe it would be okay as long as I didn't bounce back and off the ledge.

I could do it.

I had to.

I would *not* die here.

I stretched my legs out, waving my arms to prepare for landing. To hit that hard stone ledge and smack face-first into the door. At the last second, I shut my eyes and braced for impact.

Only to feel the splash of sudden, frigid cold over my body like I'd jumped headlong into the icy depths of a frozen lake.

Forty-Four

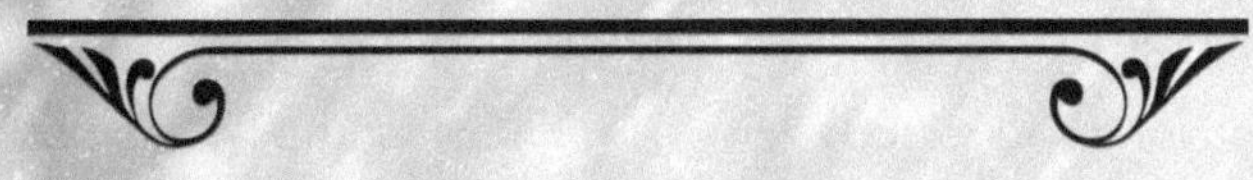

I was falling—falling too fast.

Too far.

Plummeting through cold darkness until, at last, I hit something solid. I staggered and tripped, falling to my hands and knees on what felt like ... carpet?

I dug my fingers deep into the plush wool fibers as I wheezed and panted, my head still spinning. Shakily, I lifted my gaze to stare around a broad, spacious room draped thickly in shadows.

Only the dancing firelight from a large, looming marble hearth on the far wall illuminated the space, revealing the silhouettes of lavish furnishings. Claw-footed chairs with tall backs crouched close to the fire. One was much larger than the other, but both were surrounded by stacks of books.

More heaps of scrolls, sheets of paper, and pages covered in scrawled handwriting were scattered about like autumn leaves. Massive oil paintings hung on the walls, depicting the ghostly faces of two handsome young men.

Two *Avoran* men.

I stared at them, my heart a throbbing lump in my throat.

They were so similar, like reflections of the same person with a thin, wistful smile, long red hair, and discerning golden eyes. One appeared slightly older, his jawline harder and more defined. The other still had a boyish softness to his features, and something secretive seemed to tease at the edges of his mouth.

Brothers, maybe?

With Avoran elves, it was hard to tell, since they could live for so long and scarcely age a day. They might have been father and son. Or cousins.

Peeling my gaze away from the portraits, I scanned the room again.

And I saw it, not twenty paces away. It loomed on the wall directly opposite those huge paintings, as though both men were keeping constant vigil over it.

A massive white stone door.

My breath caught with a ragged, broken sound.

It was exactly like the one from the crypt. Same markings of entangled branches and the draconic twins, the Viepol. Same phrasing engraved above it.

Tears welled in my eyes, blurring everything to a smear of deep, shadowed colors. Gods and Fates, we'd found it.

It was the door—the way out. It had to be.

Gathering my feet beneath me, I started to move—to stand—when something slammed into me from behind and sent me sprawling back onto the carpet with an explosion of purplish-blue light.

Axien hit me like a projectile, his body crushing down onto mine with a loud grunt of pain, all magical wings and flailing limbs. We lay in a breathless, tangled heap, his head on my stomach and his arms and legs fanned out like a starfish. He tensed, expression seizing as those glassy, magical wings melted away.

"Didn't make the jump, did you?" I rasped.

"N-not ... quite." He coughed and sputtered, gritting his teeth as he clenched his fists as though willing himself steady through the pain of using magic again so soon.

"I told you it was a terrible plan," I fumed quietly, still stifling sniffles.

"W-worked, though," he gritted out. "You okay?"

"I was fine till you crushed me again," I said, puffing a few deep breaths in and out to try to collect my sanity.

He barked a hoarse, strained laugh and lifted his head to squint at me, fresh blood running from his nose.

Well, at least he hadn't lost his spirit.

"If you don't mind, I'd appreciate it if you didn't bleed all over my wool rug," a deep, masculine voice suddenly purred through the gloom.

A voice speaking flawless Avoran.

Panic coursed through me like a jolt of electricity, sizzling through every muscle and setting every nerve on edge immediately. I sprang to my feet and reached for the knife in my boot.

Axien grabbed my wrist, forcing me to stop. He shook all over, weaving on his feet as he forced himself to stand and face the direction of the voice.

I followed his gaze, tracking it to one of the tall, lion-footed chairs pulled close to the roaring fire. A hand rested lazily on the arm of the largest one of them, the fingers glittering with an assortment of jeweled rings. A pair of legs stretched toward the glow of the flames, as though the figure reclining in that chair had just thrown themselves haphazardly into it.

When we didn't answer, the figure blew out a scoffing breath and stirred.

All the wind rushed out of me at once as the back of the chair moved, parting down the middle soundlessly. No ... it wasn't the back of the chair.

It was a pair of wings.

The silhouette of a tall, slim man with impressively broad shoulders rose from his seat, his back set with two large, black-feathered wings. The tips of his long primary feathers brushed the floor behind him as he stepped toward us with a staggering gait. Every other step seemed to wobble unsteadily, and his large wings shifted to compensate and keep his balance, as though there were something wrong with his knee.

"Who are you?" The man's tone bristled with agitation as he bit sharply on each word. "How did you come here? How did you breach my arcane shield?"

Axien tensed beside me, his jaw working as he stared back at the figure as though trying to steel himself for another fight. His arms flexed, fingers splayed wide and veins standing out against the backs of his hands.

Whoever this man was, we couldn't afford to assume he wasn't a threat. I couldn't even see his face thanks to the contrast of the shadows against the glare of the fire, but his eyes pierced through the near darkness like two smoldering blue coals.

Eyes that glowed with ancient, divine power ... Just like Axien's, only brighter. Stronger. Boundless and intense in a way that made me wonder if he could see all the way down to the bottom of my warped, wicked soul.

He stopped only a few yards away, those glowing rings of molten blue light moving over us one at a time. Then, with a sweep of his hand, all the lamps in the room sparked to life, and we were bathed in ambient light.

I squinted and recoiled, blinking to adjust to the sudden change.

Then my mouth fell open.

I'd never stood in a king's parlor, but I had to imagine it had to be something like this.

The golden trim and moldings, all carved to look like the faces of the gods and interwoven with leafy branches. Long embroidered drapes poured like waterfalls of rich color from the ceiling to pool on the floor. Statues of winged figures adorned in gold, bronze, and platinum armor stood vigil in every corner like frozen sentinels.

The man looming before us wasn't a king, though.

"Lord Vesperus?" Axien asked, speaking in Avoran.

"I am." The winged man straightened in acknowledgment.

What? This ... No. That couldn't be right.

One glimpse at the man's face made my heartbeat stammer to a clumsy halt, and I drew back a step. Not that it would do either of us any good. If he wanted to hurt us, I doubted there was anything Axien or I could do to stop it.

After all, Vesperus Theoclordan was a full-blooded Avoran sorcerer. A being of power beyond what anyone in our world could even fathom. If all the tales and texts were true, he was closer to being a god than a man—even if he didn't look it.

He didn't resemble either of the men in the paintings that hung on the wall nearby, although he had the same steeply angled jaw, deeply set eyes, and long, deep red hair.

Rather, he looked like a shattered version of them.

Deep, severe scars sliced across his face—which had probably been handsome, once. Now, it was as if his face were a smashed porcelain mask that had been haphazardly glued back together, the lines of the fractures still crude and plainly visible. The thick, raised white scars pulled one corner of his mouth downward in a perpetual frown, split one of his defined brows, and cut across the long bridge of his nose.

Beneath the scars, he could've passed for a man in his late twenties or even early thirties. He might have even looked like the figure from one of the paintings hanging on the wall to our right.

But I didn't dare take my gaze off him to check, not when

those eerie eyes narrowed on me like he could smell something wrong in the air.

Or something wrong with me, rather.

"What are you?" Vesperus demanded, his gaze dragging up and down my body slowly, as though I were a puzzle he couldn't quite solve.

I tensed, sucking a sharp breath through my nose as cold terror flushed through my veins.

Vesperus's head tilted to one side slowly, those huge wings unfolding behind him as though bristling with uneasiness.

"You are not human. Not elf," he said. "Your blood ... it has the same smell. The reek of the void. Of Vescor."

"My lord, I suspect there is much of the world we come from that is unknown to you," Axien spoke quickly, his voice caught between trembling pain and earnest determination as he took a step closer to my side.

Vesperus leveled that same smoldering, appraising glare upon him, eyes narrowed with suspicion.

"You are ... a half-blood?" Vesperus asked, as if the idea were completely baffling.

Axien's shoulders cringed slightly, drawing up toward his ears as though the words were a slap to the face.

"I am," he replied. "My name is Axien. And this is Violet."

Vesperus blinked in surprise, seeming to hesitate for a moment before he spoke again. "I suppose that explains how you were able to come here in the first place. What house name are you? Did your mother survive the birth? Was she human? Or was it your father?"

"I-I'm not sure." Axien shook his head, seeming to shrink before the angelic man like a child caught out of bed too late. "My father was Avoran—or, at least, that's what I was told."

"He did not claim you?" Vesperus frowned disapprovingly, crinkling those scars along the corner of his mouth.

"Even after you survived gestation by a human female? I suppose that is why you are wingless, as well."

Axien made a few choking sounds that might have been the beginnings of words, then hung his head low and shook it again. His face flushed deep red, and a muscle in his jaw twitched as he clenched his teeth.

My heart gave an agonizing lurch in my chest, seeing him shamed like that before one of his own kind. Gods, I hated it.

Axien had absolutely nothing to be ashamed of.

But I didn't know what to say, either. How did you explain to an ancient stranger that you were the pre-planned product of a secret organization that bred rare courtesans for rich nobles? Especially when it had all happened in a world, in a time, that this sorcerer might never be able to comprehend?

When Axien didn't reply, the sorcerer's eyes cut straight to me for an explanation.

"It's complicated. For time's sake, let's just say he never got the chance to meet either of his parents in person," I said, stumbling over the words. I'd never spoken this much Avoran out loud, and I probably sounded like a babbling little kid.

Out of the corner of my eye, I saw Axien's shoulders relax again.

"It's very strange. Half-human, no wings, and yet you also retain the ability to channel divine magic. Even if you are a half-blood, your father should have been pleased to at least have you as a squire in his court," Vesperus mused, settling his weight on his back foot as he gave Axien another head-to-toe, appraising stare. "I suspect your mortal flesh is a poor conductor for your magic, however. Is that why you are unable to regenerate your injuries?"

Axien leaned away, face paling as he seemed to shrink under the sorcerer's scrutiny. "I-I ... I don't know, my lord."

"You don't know?" Vesperus repeated, as though that

answer was wholly insulting. "You did not care to learn? Did your tutors fail you so miserably?"

"I never had tutors. Not until recently," Axien explained, his head bowed.

I frowned, bristling again. "Listen, you need to understand you've been tucked away in this artifact for a long while. The world is very different now from the one you remember. There are no tutors who teach people how to use magic. Not anymore."

Vesperus stopped short, his brows slowly lifting as he glanced between us again. The hard edges to his expression seemed to soften somewhat, as though he hadn't considered that might be the reason we looked strange.

"How long?" he asked, his tone much quieter.

Oh boy.

"How long?" Vesperus demanded, his tone sharper and tinged with a quiver of anxious rage. His wings spread wider, filling the space with midnight feathers.

"Six thousand years," I replied, unable to keep it from sounding like an apology.

Silence swept over us so suddenly, my stomach dropped and my body went cold. My heart pounded sloppily, but I didn't dare move or chance another sideways look at Axien. Not yet.

Not until we knew how he would take this news.

At first, Vesperus didn't move. He seemed to have stopped breathing altogether and just stood there, staring at me as if I'd suddenly grown a second head.

Then his throat bobbed as he swallowed thickly, wetting his lips with a sweep of his tongue before he looked down at the floor between us. His wings relaxed, falling limply at his back until they splayed across the floor behind him like a long train of ebony feathers.

"I see," he murmured, and there was no mistaking the brokenness, the utter anguish, in those two simple words.

"Are you trapped here?" I had to ask.

For our sake, I needed to know. If the powerful sorcerer who had apparently built this place couldn't escape it, then what chance did we possibly stand?

None.

"In a manner of speaking," Vesperus answered cryptically, turning away to stare despairingly at that large stone door. "I knew time must be passing in the material world. But I had no idea it would ..." his voice trailed off to heavy, somber silence. It seemed to drench the entire room like bitter rain, deepening the shadows that wavered in the firelight.

Axien and I swapped a wide-eyed glance, my mind already whirling with a new storm of questions. Hadn't Vesperus realized how long he had been here? Gods, what did that mean for us? Fates, how long had we been here?

It had only felt like hours—half a day at the very most! But what did that translate to in the outside world? Months? Years?

My good hand clenched into a trembling, sweaty fist at my side. We couldn't linger here. We had to get out. We had to get through that door and return to the real world—now.

"I think we should have a discussion, Lord Vesperus. There's quite a lot you've missed," Axien said carefully, his hand seizing mine as though he could sense my inward spiral into panic.

A discussion? Had Axien completely lost it? We didn't have time for a discussion!

The sorcerer eyed us again, gaze lingering on the bleeding, makeshift bandages we'd tied over Axien's clothes, the dark veins now readily visible along his neck and hands, and the blood caked around his nose and cheeks.

"I believe you're right," he replied as he slowly nodded and raised a hand, passing it slowly over Axien's form with his palm glowing brilliant blue. "But I won't have you sitting on my furniture in this state."

A shiver coursed through the air, making my pulse skip and my skin prickle. My stomach fluttered as the sickly dark veins on Axien's body melted away, vanishing from all the places they peeked out from under his clothes. He staggered back, sucking in a sharp breath. His eyes went wide, and he gripped a hand to the center of his chest, gasping and panting as all the color seemed to rush back into his features.

Gods, I hadn't even realized how ashen he'd been until that moment, when his cheeks shone healthy bronze again and his eyes blazed with brighter clarity.

He stared down at his hands in stunned silence, then frantically began pulling at the bandages on his shoulder, revealing clean, healed skin beneath. His burns were gone. There weren't even any scars left behind.

All his injuries were completely healed.

"I can't do anything for your attire, I'm afraid," Vesperus mumbled as he turned and hobbled away from us, back toward the pair of chairs pulled close to the fireplace. "Or your ... *companion*."

He bit at that last word, as though it were the only nice one he could come up with when it came to me.

Great. Well, at least he hadn't gone with a racial slur. Granted, he probably didn't know any, since my kin had been created after he'd already been confined here for a few thousand years. He really had no idea what I was.

Probably best to keep it that way for as long as possible.

"But she's hurt, as well," Axien protested, following Vesperus with a desperate scowl. "That monster you've got locked away with the frozen lake, it—"

"I am aware," the sorcerer cut him off sharply, pausing to level a resolved frown at my injured arm. "Unfortunately, there's nothing I can do about that. Do you think I *chose* to look this way? Wounds from him cannot be touched by magic, no matter what I ..." Vesperus stopped short, his expression snapping into a strained grimace as though he were fighting back an emotion that threatened to punch through his mask of calculated calm.

I winced, realizing now where all those scars on Vesperus's body must have come from. The reason he couldn't heal them like he had Axien's injuries. Those must have come from his attempts to destroy that monster and failing over and over again.

"I have spent quite a long time trying to discover a way to dispel the dark power that infects him, but to no avail," he finished at last, his gaze softening on me before he turned back to his chair.

"Is that why you're here? Locked in this artifact?" I pulled my injured arm closer, holding it against my chest as I followed from a distance. "You're trying to find a way to destroy that creature?"

Vesperus let out a stiff grunt as he settled back into the same chair we'd found him in, folding his wings behind him. His sharp, handsome features twitched with discomfort as he reclined and straightened one of his legs. At last, his whole body seemed to relax beneath his fine silken robes.

"No," he replied, opening those eerie, glowing eyes to meet my stare with a look of pure, soul-deep anguish. "I am here ... because I was trying to save it."

Forty-Five

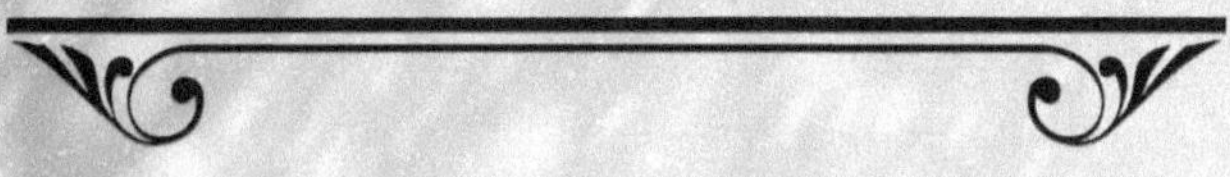

None of this made sense.

Vesperus had been here, living in this little pocket-dimension, of his own free will? Because he wanted to *save* that abyssal-looking monster that had nearly butchered us on the frozen lake?

By all the gods, *why?*

My mind raced, trying to piece together some sort of explanation that made sense. The words from that letter replayed, flowing through my thoughts and ensnaring me wholly.

Do what you must, but I will remain at his side for as long as it takes. I drove him to it. I made us both monsters. I can contain this. I must fix him. I trust you understand.

I turned, looking up at the pair of portraits hanging on the wall. The two young men—probably brothers—were placed there as if in a memorial.

And one of them sat before me now, scarred almost beyond all recognition.

But where was the other?

Unless ... Oh, gods.

"It's your brother." The words slipped past my lips in a breathless whisper. "That monster is your brother, isn't it?"

Vesperus's chin tipped down toward his chest, his gaze half-lidded as he murmured, "My younger half-brother, to be precise. His name is—was—Leomarr. I doubt very much he remembers it now, though, so he will not be offended if you don't address him by it."

"What happened?" Axien asked as he moved closer, standing right at my side.

"You say it's been six thousand years," he said with a snort. "I am surprised you cannot guess. Does the Lord of the Void not tempt desperate souls, still? He is a young god, but his power is growing as more are drawn to him. He preys upon the desperate and downtrodden, yes. But he feasts upon those driven with greed and ambition, or even a lust for recognition. He is, after all, the God of Hunger."

His wings shifted as he puffed a deep, weighted sigh and rubbed a hand along his chin, seeming to reflect on that.

I had to let it sink in, too. Hearing him talk about Vescor as though he were still around, Fates, it was enough to turn my insides to queasy mush.

"Vescor's power is a double-edged sword. Whatever is given, more must be taken in repayment," Vesperus continued. "Leomarr was always the more ambitious between us. The one more likely to take risks. I suppose he felt he had to, being born a wingless half-blood, like you. His power was all but insignificant compared to mine, and our father treated him poorly for it."

Axien's expression tightened, his throat moving as though

he were swallowing back all the emotion that threatened to smash through his mask of calm.

"It pained me to see him neglected, and in my effort to instruct him, to encourage him to work harder in his tutoring, I … drove him straight into Vescor's sight." Vesperus sighed and shook his head slightly. "He turned a good young man's desire to make his father proud into an unquenchable thirst for superiority."

"And this was during the war?" Axien pressed, his mouth a firm, uncertain line. "The one we call the War of Falling Stars?"

Vesperus gave a coughing chuckle. "If you say so. My, what a romantic title for a feud that claimed the lives of thousands —perhaps even millions of our kin."

I shifted my weight uneasily. I didn't dare to tell him it had wound up costing a lot more than that, in the end. It had cost his entire race the downfall of their empire. Or, the beginning of it, at least.

"I built this artifact, as you call it, as a private study place for my brother and me, so I could teach him. Our father's house was blessed by Tykeron, and my power permitted the creation of such pocket-dimensions, as you call them," Vesperus continued, motioning to Axien with another wave of his hand. "The same way your bloodline is touched by Milontos, God of All Future. A mighty house; I could sense it on you right away. No doubt you've some equally mighty gifts that stem from it, even if you are half-blooded."

I blinked, trying to process that information. Axien's bloodline was tied to Milontos? What did that mean? Sure, I'd seen Axien use a fair amount of his magic. But what sort of mighty gifts was he talking about?

Something more than shields and flinging fire?

Axien had gone completely still beside me, his face empty of anything except a hollow stare that stayed fixed right on

Vesperus. All that new, lively color drained from his features, and little by little, his shoulders hunched and curled inward, head bowing low as he seemed to cave in on himself.

It was as though he'd been stripped completely bare and left to stand there, frozen and exposed.

"You ... um, you should know that Vescor was destroyed," I interjected quickly, trying to change the subject. "There was another war, a much worse one. The gods got involved, and the Avoran Empire fell after the ley lines all went dark. There are only a few Avorans left, but they stay far away from the rest of the world, deep in the north."

Vesperus sat in silence for a few moments, his expression unchanging and his gaze dancing and flickering as brightly as the fire in the hearth. Then the unscarred side of his mouth tilted in an ironic, almost grim smirk.

"So, we fell to our hubris," he scoffed. "How fitting. My people have always fancied themselves superior in all aspects and believe that is why they are rewarded with divine magic. How humbling it must have been to see their empire crumble when that magic was taken away. All that supposed superiority counted for nothing in the end."

He shifted in his seat, expression slipping into a pensive frown for a minute or two. Then he looked back to Axien, motioning to him with another small wave of his hand.

"Well, if things in the world are now so dire for our kin, then I suppose you've noticed a change in your abilities since you entered my artifact, hm?" His mouth bent in a smile that made the corners of his eyes crinkle some, as though that were his attempt at a joke. "Since this pocket-dimension lies outside the fabric of mortal and divine reality, I had to bring a source of divine magic here. You must have seen it when you arrived."

I had to think about that. We'd seen a lot of weird stuff since we'd been sucked into this place, after all.

"You mean that glass icosahedron?" Axien asked, brow knitting thoughtfully. "The one suspended from the ceiling?"

"Indeed," Vesperus confirmed. "It contains a well of divine power. Standing in a realm fed by it must be the closest thing you have experienced to the world as I knew it. Have your magical talents improved since coming here? Perhaps you've noticed you don't tire as easily, or can recover more quickly?"

Axien's eyes went wide.

So that was why ...

"Can you use the ring, as well?" Vesperus nodded to the one Axien had found in the study—the silver one that had granted him those magical wings.

He nodded shakily, eyes as big as two glowing blue moons. The hand that wore the ring slowly curled into a fist at his side, almost as though he were afraid our host was going to demand that he give it back.

"I made it for Leomarr, since he was born wingless. Not having wings is a shameful thing among our people, as it usually means they were cut off as a severe form of punishment." Vesperus let his head slump back against his chair with another deep, weary breath that made his broad chest rise and fall. "I'm pleased someone has found a use for it. Keep it, if you wish."

"We, uh, we borrowed a lot of other things, too. Sorry, we just ... were trying to survive," I said, wincing.

Borrowed? Hah. More like we'd looted his entire study.

Vesperus arched an eyebrow at me suspiciously. "Are you able to use any of them?"

Heat tingled over my cheeks and I shook my head.

"I see." He made a face and clicked his tongue like he wasn't surprised at all by that.

"Right. Well, look, we really need to get out of here. As soon as possible, actually," I pressed, flicking Axien an earnest glance. "Can you tell us how?"

"I can." Vesperus's expression darkened with an ominous frown and he sank deeper into his chair. "But it will do you no good."

My heartbeat stammered. I squeezed Axien's hand tighter, my lips already numb as I dared to ask, "Why not?"

Vesperus didn't move, sitting as eerily still as one of the many crumbling statues of ancient Avoran warriors I'd seen countless times in the ruins of their empire. Then he blinked slowly, those bright eyes seeming to dim as his brows drew together in a deep, anguished furrow.

His chin tipped down, and he took a deep breath before he finally answered. "When Leomarr began to fall to the effects of Vescor's curse, I lured him into this place and fixed new, specially crafted wards upon the door. I had to make certain he could never escape—not until I'd found a way to cure him. Leomarr himself has the only key that will unlock the door back to the material realm."

"You mean we're locked in here with him?" I snarled, my pulse pounding in my ears like a war drum. "Why would you give the only key out of this place to that monst—"

Axien gave my hand a sharp tug, as though trying to jar me out of my rage. His expression had gone as cold as Vesperus's, but there was something calculating in the way his jawline went stiff and his own gleaming eyes narrowed slightly.

"You say he has the only key," Axien pressed. "Then to get out, we must cure him ... or kill him?"

"Correct." Vesperus's expression seized slightly, as though that thought caused him real pain. "That was my intent in giving it to him anyway. If I could not cure him, then I would be forced to confront him—to confront my own failure—to leave both him and this place behind."

A beat of heavy, tense silence crushed in around us while that harrowing truth settled around my heart.

"Curing him isn't an option," Axien said, his tone low and

forbidding. "In all this time, you've obviously tried that and failed. Based on what I've seen, there is very little of your brother left in that monster at all."

Vesperus's eyes snapped open, his gaze as molten as abyssal fire, as his mouth twitched at a defiant frown.

"But what is left of him, whatever power Vescor implanted in him, is far more dangerous than you realize," Axien continued quickly, his shoulders firmly squared and head held high. "You must understand, Lord Vesperus, this isn't just about us. We came here as part of a greater cause—one that threatens the material realm with a new war. And now that I've seen your brother and witnessed the power of this place, I think I finally understand why this artifact was targeted."

Vesperus sat forward in his chair, squinting curiously between the two of us as his glare of rage dissolved to bewilderment.

Too bad I had no answers for him. I stared at Axien, trying to piece together what he meant. Had I missed something? Or was this some lingering secret from his time serving Sanja he hadn't shared?

Obviously, the Tibrans really wanted this artifact. They'd been willing to subcontract to the Ulfrangar to get it, which didn't come cheap or easily.

But why?

I stood, my heartbeat nothing but a frantic, distant thump, All the heat slowly drained out of my body as Axien explained. He told Vesperus everything—about the Zenith's Call. About Tibrans and Lord Argonox. About the rarity of pure divine magic and our encounters with the minions of that would-be tyrant who was fond of warping it for his own machinations.

And like the cracking bite of a whip across my back, it hit me. The ugly truth that I'd been staring straight in the face the entire time.

It wasn't the artifact itself Argonox wanted ... not really.

"I believe our enemies desire this artifact because of what you managed to do here," he said, lowering his voice as his tone strained with desperation. "Lord Argonox is obsessed with what Zarexius managed to achieve when it came to crafting new, deadly monsters and magical weapons. He delights in experimenting on anyone or anything he can find that has even a fleck of divine power. He has engineers who have managed to unlock many of the secrets of how to transfer that power from one being or object to another."

I gulped against the rising knot caught in my throat. How did he know that?

Had he been experimented on like that?

The idea drove rage like a white-hot spike straight through the center of my chest. I bit down hard, tearing my gaze away from his and glaring down at the toes of my borrowed boots.

Calm. I had to stay calm. We'd talk about it later.

We had to.

"By locking yourself in here with a unique source of vast magical power and a fragment of Vescor's power, you've created one object that contains what the Tibrans want the most," Axien murmured. "In a world starved of magical power, the icosahedron is invaluable."

Vesperus's face paled. His gaze held Axien's, wide and horrified, as his mouth drew into a tight, twisting grimace.

"Right now, as we speak, it is extremely likely that this artifact is already in their hands. The assassins who pursued us had no other competition for it," Axien urged. "We were the only ones sent to retrieve it. Not even the Zenith's Call knows the true value of this artifact, otherwise I'm sure we wouldn't have been the ones charged with its safety."

Oh, gods, he was right. My stomach rolled and I fought back the urge to gag that burned in my throat like hot sulfur.

What if we were already too late? What if the Ulfrangar

had already handed the artifact over to the Tibrans? What if, by some miracle, we popped out of this artifact only to tumble to the ground right at Argonox's feet?

I shuddered, new panic swelling in my chest like a surging, icy tide. We had to get out. Whatever it took—we could not waste any more time.

"Please," Axien begged, his voice shaking. "Please help us get out of here before it's too late."

Vesperus didn't move. It didn't even seem like he was breathing anymore.

Silence fell like a deep winter's snow, freezing us all in place.

"You're asking me to kill my little brother. To give up my entire life's work—to give up on him," Vesperus said at last, his tone hardly more than a thick, broken whisper.

"I'm asking you to save him from becoming a monster enslaved to the heel of a mad tyrant," Axien countered. "Because if we fail, if the Tibrans break into this artifact, there will be no stopping them. They will come like an unending flood. They will butcher us like cattle and do whatever it takes to seize control of this place. They will try to capture you, as well, and ... a-and ..."

His voice halted and he swallowed hard, seeming to choke on whatever horrible thought or memory came after.

Nightmares I'd only barely glimpsed during our mad escape from the Viperi city.

Vesperus didn't speak. He sank back into his chair, his large black wings seeming to fold around him tighter, almost as though he were trying to shut himself off from us and everything else.

A terrible choice he couldn't escape ... despite six thousand years of trying.

I held my breath, watching the ancient elven sorcerer scowl into the dancing light of the flames in his hearth.

A second passed. Then another. Maybe another ten years for the outside world. Who knew?

Beside me, Axien still gripped my hand, his much larger, callused fingers wound through mine.

"Leomarr will not give up the key easily. You're going to need finer weapons and armor than what you've scavenged from my cabin," Vesperus growled suddenly, his tone hard-edged and beastly as he gripped the arms of his chair and slowly pushed himself up again. "Come, little guardians. Let us do battle."

Forty-Six

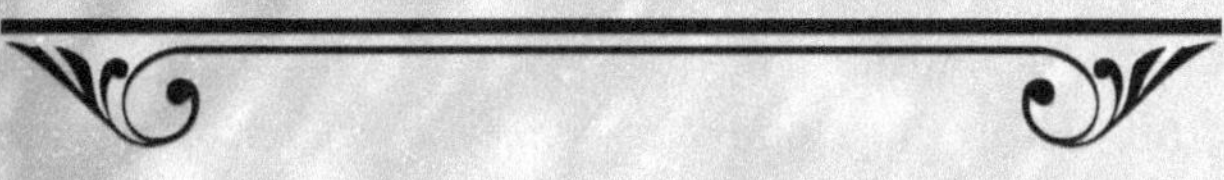

There was no turning back.

Not now. We'd come too far. Fought and bled. There was no other path than this.

We had to find a way to put that monster down and escape this artifact, even if that meant carving our path to freedom through the mire of its blood.

My head raged with memories of our last encounter with it—the slice of its claws through my flesh, the screech that threatened to split my head wide open like a melon. My heartbeat raced so fast it made my vision spot as dread soaked me down to the marrow of my bones.

Even with an Avoran sorcerer on our side, I couldn't fathom a victory. Not against a beast like that. Escaping it? Sure. We'd gotten lucky once. We might be able to manage that again.

But finding a way to actually kill it?

I stole a glance at our new ally, wondering at all the deep, jagged scars that marred his face and neck. Clearly, he hadn't fared much better when he had faced it. What chance did we stand now?

Moreover, when it came down to it, was he really going to kill what was left of his little brother for our escape? What if he changed his mind?

Clearly, there wasn't much, if anything, of Leomarr left in that monster. It didn't reason. It didn't speak. It was reckless hate embodied.

But Vesperus was bound to want to find some fragment of his brother still inside it.

I nibbled at the inside of my cheek, considering every angle I could fathom. We needed a plan. We couldn't afford to stumble into this half-aware. We needed a real strategy, or the Tibrans might crack this artifact open to find three new corpses left to rot on that frozen lake.

Axien must have known it, too. I felt it like a subtle pressure between us as we followed Vesperus deeper into the labyrinth of his artifact. He wouldn't even glance my way as we approached another, smaller door hidden behind one of the tapestries—the same wooden one we'd been using to navigate between previous "rooms."

If you could call a hedge maze and frozen waste rooms, anyway.

The golden knob glowed and rattled at a wave of the sorcerer's hand, sending chills prickling all over my body. He didn't need the little map key to know his way around, and he didn't hesitate to whip the door open. Holding it ajar, he stood aside and motioned for us to step through ahead of him.

The gloom of the next room swallowed us whole, leaving Axien and I stumbling across the dark stone floor until Vesperus followed and gave another flick of his wrist.

Immediately, hanging chandeliers of tangled dark iron sparked to life, revealing an open space lined with long, flat tables and walls lined with an assortment of cabinets, shelves, and display stands.

Glass vials and flasks in all shapes and sizes stood on intricate silver stands, connected with delicate tubes. Some were suspended over flickering candles that heated vividly colored liquids. Others were corked and set aside, or crowded onto shelves alongside hundreds of large, identical jars of powders, herbs, and raw materials marked with labels in curled Avoran lettering.

"Alchemy," Axien breathed the word reverently, his hand slipping out of mine as he moved farther into the room, taking it all in.

I drew in a shaky breath, cringing at the strong acrid odor that hung in the air. Something about it reminded me a little of Leruna's healing tonics—a potent mixture of herbs and chemicals that left a bitter film in my mouth.

"I dabble," Vesperus said with a shrug, as though the large laboratory were just a side-hobby he'd almost forgotten he had. "There was a time when I believed I might create a draught that could cure Leomarr's condition."

"And you keep weapons in here, too?" I asked, leaning in to get a better look at one of the jars that held hundreds of tiny little bones.

"What little I have, yes," the sorcerer replied, striding past us to a row of display mannequins covered by long black drapes. "I never fancied myself a warrior. But I have some of our family pieces on hand."

My breath caught as he pulled the sheets of inky fabric away from the first two, revealing full suits of Avoran battle armor that shone in the dancing candlelight. Both were crafted of the same bluish-silver metal and had been inlaid with golden details that spiraled along the curves of the gauntlets, breastplates, pauldrons, and cuirasses. Every inch of them had been polished to mirror-like perfection, shining like quicksilver without a single scratch or blemish. Like they'd been finished yesterday and never worn.

I stared up at them, admiring the way the gold inlay

mimicked feathered wings along the outside of the gauntlets and down the backplates. Spines bristled on the knuckles and outside forearms of the gauntlets, each one plated in gold—a balance of beauty and lethality.

Too bad neither of them would even come close to fitting me. They'd clearly been made to fit a man's body.

A much larger man.

"You will take Leomarr's," Vesperus announced, motioning to Axien. "He was of a similar stature."

Then his bright, moon-glow gaze fell to me, his mouth scrunching thoughtfully before he strode down the line of mannequins to the last one.

"You, on the other hand, are very small," he mumbled unhappily before tugging the fabric cover off, revealing a sleeker, more understated suit of dark, graphite-colored armor. It had far less of the fine, luxurious details. No golden inlay or intricate engravings. If anything, it looked like practice armor.

But it did seem a lot smaller than the others.

"Don't worry. She more than makes up for it in viciousness," Axien quipped from down the row of armor, where he'd already begun changing. "Just give her something sharp and she'll find a way to gut someone with it."

I rolled my eyes.

Vesperus didn't seem convinced, though. His gaze was incredulous as he reached to pluck the helmet from the top of the display, turning it over and brushing his fingers over a few scrapes in the metal.

"This was mine when I was a lot younger. It will still be far too big, but certain pieces might suit temporarily," Vesperus explained, his tone almost apologetic as he put the helmet carefully back.

"I can work with it. Heavy armor was never really my style, anyway." I shrugged and stepped forward, beginning to work the gauntlets, pauldrons, and poleyns off the mannequin.

My thoughts ran wild, tangling and coiling over battle plans and strategies as the chamber filled with the rustle and clatter as the three of us changed into battle hardware. I had no idea what Vesperus might be capable of in a fight. But we had to stand a better chance if there were three of us.

Fates, I hoped so.

I spat a curse as I fought with the straps of the pauldrons, my injured arm throbbing fiercely as I twisted to get the buckles fastened in the right places. Closing my hand sent sharp pangs of agony all the way up to the base of my skull. My vision spotted and I sagged forward, bracing against the cabinet as I gathered my sanity and tried to breathe through it.

Gods, I ... I didn't know how I was going to do this. I couldn't grip a blade with that hand. I could barely feel my fingers. Sure, it was decently bandaged, but just trying to move and force my hand to cooperate only made the pain worse.

How was I going to fight?

"Let me do it," Axien demanded suddenly, his voice so close it sent a jolt of alarm through all my frazzled nerves.

I turned and found him standing behind me, fully dressed in all that gleaming armor like a young god. Every inch of polished, sculpted silver fit his lean, muscular frame and followed the sculpted contours of his body as though it were a second skin.

He'd pulled half of his lengthy dark hair back into a messy little bun to keep it away from his eyes, making his pointed ears more obvious. Except for the lack of wings, anyone might have assumed he was a full-blooded Avoran.

A mighty sorcerer of old.

My breath caught and heat flooded my cheeks. My gaze instinctively dropped to the floor as he moved into my space and began working the pauldrons into place on my shoulders.

"They're, um, way too big," I stammered stupidly. "Well, all of it is, I guess. But I've never worn heavy armor like this."

"Will they get in the way of swinging a weapon?" he asked.

I didn't know. Probably, given my recent string of luck.

And worse, my throat closed and I couldn't even choke out an excuse. Not with him looming over me, fingers sliding under my hair to move it out of the way while he checked the crossed pauldron straps on my back.

"Violet, I know you like to be right smack in the thick of things, but ..." he began, his brow creasing in an uncertain frown while he worked. "Please don't do anything reckless. Not this time."

I drew back and shot him a bewildered stare. Seriously? Had he lost his mind?

I scowled, giving him my shoulder as my temper kindled, hot and prickly in my chest. He had seen me fight Tibrans, switchbeasts, even my own kin. I wasn't some novice. I could handle myself in a fight, even without magic.

Or ... the full use of one hand.

"You want to talk about reckless?" I hissed. "Reckless was getting blasted and nearly blown in half by that eye-door. I don't need you to babysit me like some rookie. Just because you got assigned a solo mission first, that doesn't mean I'm any less qualified to—"

"This has nothing to do with my pride or your skill as a fighter! It's ... it's because if the choice comes down to killing that creature or saving you, I'm choosing the obvious," he snarled loudly, cutting me off. "I'll choose you. I'll always choose you—monster, Zenith's Call, and Tibrans be damned."

I stared at him, mouth hanging open, while he gave a few more hard tugs on my pauldron straps and moved on to checking the ones on my vambraces.

Silence filled the air between us like a reeking swamp fog. My throat burned like I'd swallowed a fistful of hot coals.

But I couldn't speak. Not yet.

Gods, what did he even mean by all that? Was this some kind of confession? Or … or was I misunderstanding it? Was this going to wind up being another favor-for-a-favor transaction like the last time?

I couldn't tell. Even after all this time, I couldn't read him. Every time I thought I knew what to expect or what he felt, it wound up being another layer of misdirection or misunderstanding.

It wasn't fair, especially when it seemed like he always saw straight through me.

Letting out a slow, heavy breath, I forced myself to swallow back all the anger that burned like hot bile in my throat. Arguing with him wouldn't fix anything.

I had to try reasoning with him.

Gods help me.

"We have to work together for this to work, Axien," I tried again, forcing my tone to quiet. "Like it or not, I think we can all agree that none of us will walk away from this if we aren't on the same page. We need a plan—one that includes everyone."

He didn't reply, his jaw working from one side to the other as he went on adjusting my armor.

I put a hand against his breastplate, right over his heart. When he still didn't stop, I slid my palm slowly up until I grasped his chin and forced him to look back at me.

"You don't have to protect me. I'm not fragile," I reminded him calmly. "You know that."

"This is different, I-I …" Axien stopped short, his breath coming in quick, defiant puffs as he locked his smoldering, glowing gaze downward and refused to look me in the eye.

"Okay, look, I know last time was a mess, and we almost got ourselves killed. Which is why I'm willing to *humor* your assistance," I teased gently, hoping to at least crack through that unnerving, twitchy frown he wore. "But we know what we're up against now, and as long as Vesperus doesn't decide to get sentimental and betray us, maybe we'll actually stand a—"

Axien seized the back of my head, fingers digging deep into my hair as he drew me up onto my toes suddenly and pressed his mouth fiercely against mine.

Everything stopped.

My thoughts, sanity, nerves, even my vision upended all at once. My knees went rubbery, my mind went blank, and my stomach dropped like a knot of lead straight to the soles of my shoes.

I stood frozen in his grasp, my heart pounding like it might punch right out of my chest, as his warm lips moved against mine with feverish force.

Oh gods. What was happening? Why was he doing this now?

And ... why did he taste *so* good?

The heat of Axien's breath fanned across my cheek as he deepened the kiss, a swipe of his tongue against mine sending a rush of tingling energy through every inch of me.

I started to reach for him. To let my mouth open wider, yielding to his. Wanting more. Needing to explore him the same way.

Axien immediately pulled back, ripping away from me with a ragged gasp, covering his mouth with a hand.

"S-sorry," he stammered, his expression contorting in pure agony before he whirled around and stormed away without another word.

I watched him go, hands clenched into fists at his sides. He didn't even glance back as he retreated to the display stand where he'd gotten his armor and started taking weapons off the rack behind it. His features twitched angrily, face flushed dark red as he slammed a pair of longswords into place on his belt.

All I could do was gape, my head spinning. My lips buzzed with heat from his ... outburst. They felt strangely sensitive. Almost swollen, and, well, *kissed*.

Embarrassed heat sizzled through my body. My pulse skipped and stalled, so erratic it made my vision swim.

What ... what was that? What was going on with him? Was he just afraid? Was this some warped attempt to vent his frustration because we had to go back into that awful, frozen nightmare all over again?

Or was it something else altogether? Something I didn't understand?

Whatever the case, he couldn't keep doing this. He couldn't keep pulling me in and then shoving me away. Hot and cold. Jerking me back and forth and making excuses. I wouldn't be used. Not like this.

Not by him.

It had to stop. It would stop.

I would get an explanation ... one way or another.

Forty-Seven

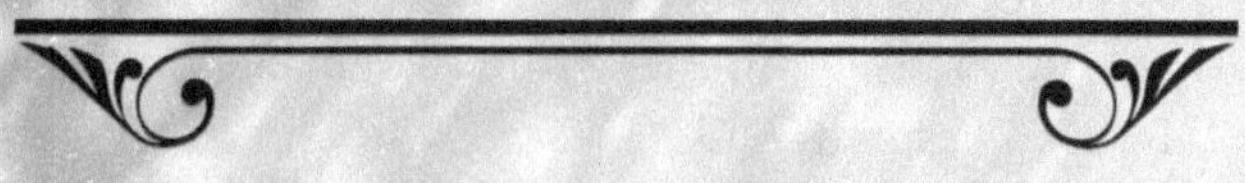

He wouldn't get away with this.

Not again.

I started after Axien in a furious march, bristling like an angry alley cat. He could yell, throw a fit, or default to teasing like he usually did. It wouldn't matter.

I would have an explanation for why he kept jerking my feelings around, toying with me and acting so ... so ... WEIRD!

"Here, this is for you." Vesperus stepped into my path so suddenly, I almost slammed into him. It was as if he had materialized out of thin air, holding a slim, curved shortsword in his hand like he wanted me to take it.

Apparently, he was either oblivious to what had just happened or he didn't care. Either way, I bit back the urge to shove him out of my path.

"What is this?" I frowned as I eyed the weapon resting in his palm. The scabbard was no less intricate than the rest of his collection, shimmering with chips of inlaid jewels and silver filigree.

"A gift," he replied simply. "I trust you can handle a blade well?"

"Well enough," I agreed as I took it. "Is this another one of your childhood toys?"

The metal sang beautifully as I drew the sword from its sheath and gave it a quick flourish to test the weight. It spun easily over my good hand, perfectly balanced from hilt to tip—not that I expected anything less from Avoran craftsmanship.

"Hardly," Vesperus said. "I learned early on that I was not destined to be a soldier of any skill, much to my father's disappointment. That didn't stop him from gifting me weaponry in the hopes I might find something that suited me."

"Not an alchemist. Not a soldier. What exactly did you do before you locked yourself away here, hm?" I quipped as I slid the scabbard through my borrowed leather belt.

"Well, I am fond of books." The Avoran man shrugged, making his black wings shift as his wide shoulders moved. "And I dedicated a fair amount of time to tinkering and crafting new spellwork in my youth. I very much enjoyed gardening, too, I suppose."

Wow. Well, that explained the weird hedge maze. So, we were going into battle with an ancient Avoran gardener.

Fantastic.

What could possibly go wrong?

I stared at him, willing every shred of my strength to keep from letting my emotions show. Now was not the time to have a full-on, raging mental breakdown.

Then it hit me like a runaway fruit cart—an idea. Probably the worst one I'd ever had. Or maybe the best.

Only one way to be sure.

"Vesperus, you created those floating eyeball things in the hedge maze, too, didn't you?" I asked, stepping closer and reaching for his arm to get his attention as he began to turn away.

"The gazers? Yes, I did," he confirmed. "If Leomarr ever managed to breach his containment, I wanted to be sure he would not make it here—to the passage out of the artifact."

"Is there any way to move them? To take them with us into the fight?" I couldn't hide the excitement in my tone.

"Well, yes. I can redirect them." He made a thoughtful face and rubbed at his chin. "I'm not certain how well they will function in the cold, however. Arcane cold tends to dull the effects of all magic, which I had hoped would slow the progression of Leomarr's condition."

Ah. Well, that explained why he'd chosen to lock him in a frozen tundra.

"If they can weaken him, or even just distract him, we might actually stand a chance of getting that key. You're sure he still has it, right?"

Might as well be sure. No point in risking our lives on a guess if there was any chance he had hidden it somewhere else.

Vesperus nodded. "I'm certain. He wore it on a chain about his neck. Or rather, one piece of it."

My entire body sagged, weight slumping into my heels as I stared at the grim-faced sorcerer. I had seen something glowing on the monster's chest when we had last encountered it. Just a tiny pinprick of magical light—but it was there. Gods, we'd been so close and hadn't even realized it.

But that wasn't what sent my teeth on edge as I took a furious step closer to Vesperus and planted my hands on my hips.

"Only a piece of it? Where's the rest of it?" I demanded. "Why didn't you mention this earlier?"

Vesperus glanced over his shoulder toward where Axien was most definitely eavesdropping, his expression pinched and sour as he fidgeted with his armor and weaponry.

"It didn't seem prudent since you already have it in your possession. It appears as a small gem, or icosahedron, as you called it before. It fits into the handle of the key. You need both to activate the spellwork that opens the exit door," he explained.

At the mention of it, Axien stopped and turned slowly toward us with his eyes wide.

I hesitated, my hand shaking as I reached into my pocket and drew out the tiny, twenty-sided gemstone. Its magic glowed like a tiny blue star in my palm, no bigger than a marble and probably about as mundane looking to anyone else.

But it was a crucial piece of our salvation.

Gods, I'd never been so glad we looted a stranger's study.

Now all we needed was the piece that monster carried. And a whole lot of luck.

"It is an interesting idea," Vesperus mused as he studied the tiny stone in my palm and went on rubbing at his sharply angled jaw. "You are correct. Using the gazers to distract or restrain him somewhat might provide an opportunity to take the key with minimal risk."

"We'll have to be fast about it," Axien mumbled as he finally sauntered over to join us. "The gazers are effective, yes, but not indestructible. She was able to take one down with a single hit."

"Yeah. And then it exploded and nearly killed us," I reminded him.

He gave a conceding shrug. "That might not be such a bad thing if the monster is the one doing the hitting."

True.

"I believe these may be useful, as well," Vesperus announced as he pulled a few small glass flasks from his pockets.

Each one was roughly the length of my thumb, shaped like a teardrop with a wax-sealed stopper to keep the liquid contents from leaking out. A few held something viscous and red, and the others contained what looked like a thick, black sludge.

Strange.

He handed a pair to Axien and me, one of each color, and kept the rest for himself before he explained, “Red is fire, black is a noxious smoke. Take care that you throw them far away from you. The explosion is quite volatile. It would also be best if they did not detonate together … or in your pockets.”

“This is what you call dabbling?” Axien asked, his tone dubious as he pocketed his flasks.

Vesperus’s wings ruffled slightly as he straightened, his scarred face flushing across his cheekbones. “For an Avoran, yes. Explosives have a fairly basic alchemical composition.”

“It’s exactly what we need,” I said as I stuffed the vials into the inside breast pocket of my coat. “We can’t just storm in there. That monster isn’t stupid. We barely escaped it last time, and we weren’t even trying to fight it head-on. This time, we need to be deliberate. We send the gazers in first as shock troops. Stun it, if we can.”

“Then we make our move,” Axien agreed, his gaze smoldering with focused intent. “Vesperus and I will keep it distracted from above, draw its focus, and once we have it down, you strike. Cut that key off its neck and run. We’ll fall in behind you, keep the monster off your back, and try to make it to the door. If we have to fight it to the death, I’d rather do it with an exit at my back.”

I crossed my arms, cocking my hips to the side and tilting my chin up in defiance. “Sounds reckless, if you ask me.”

“It is.” Axien tensed, brow drawn into a bitter scowl as he looked away. “Unless you tell me you can do it. Then it’s a calculated risk.”

I smirked, watching the mixture of conflicted emotions dance across his shining, ethereal eyes. A quiet storm he barely kept tethered as he finally fixed me with a smoldering, half-lidded glare.

"I can do it," I said.

"You'll only get one clean chance," Vesperus added, doing a much worse job of disguising his doubt in my capabilities. "If you miss or fail to secure the key, a second attempt will likely be costly."

I cut him a scorching glare of my own. "I said I can do it."

"She's fast," Axien chimed in, flexing his hands and adjusting the winged silver ring on his finger. "Faster than either of us, even on our best day. If she says she can do it, she can."

His words landed like a weight on my chest, knocking me breathless for a moment. Did he really think that?

Or was he just talking me up to Vesperus so our new sorcerer-ally didn't try to make me sit this one out altogether? Either way, the comment made my face flush hot and I had to look away.

"I hope you're correct," Vesperus murmured, still sounding unsure as his gaze traveled over me one last time. Probably marveling at what a frazzled, slapped-together, injured, hot mess I was in his borrowed clothing and armor.

Fine. I didn't exactly look like the embodiment of death's cruel edge, right now.

I didn't have my proper fighting leathers, my weapons, or even my own shoes. But I'd make do. I had to.

Our only way forward was through that monster's claws, so either I pulled this off, or we might as well hand this artifact and all its power over to Lord Argonox and the Tibrans ourselves. There was no other choice.

Do, die, or doom the world.

My specialty.

Forty-Eight

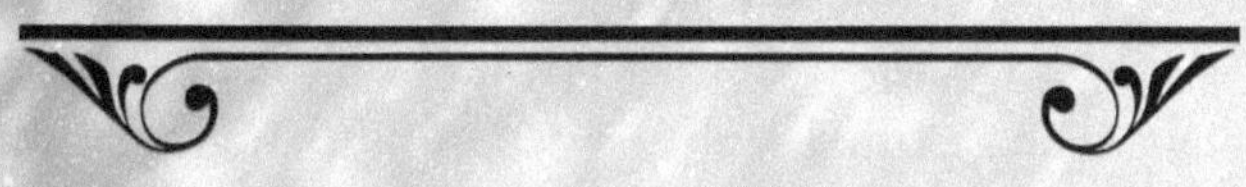

"We go on my count," Vesperus said, flicking a sharp look back at Axien and me.

Standing before the door in the hedges with a line of five floating eyeballs right behind him, I could hardly hear him over the buzzing of each one of those gazers. Being so close to them practically made my teeth vibrate, and I made sure to keep a few feet back ... just in case one of them decided to go rogue.

I'd be taking no unnecessary chances today.

Vesperus already had a large, elegantly curved scimitar clenched in one fist, and his body was braced against the solid wooden surface of the door. His other hand gripped the golden knob so tightly his knuckles blanched, and his wings were tucked tight against his back.

"Ready?" he asked.

Not even a little. I twisted nervously at the ring on my hand—the one Axien had given me as a gift.

"Do it," Axien snarled low, baring his teeth.

Vesperus shut his eyes tightly, jaw flexing as he clenched his teeth in a grimace of dread. Then his mouth set. His nostrils flared, and his glowing eyes slowly opened. The knob glowed to life under his hand, and the shiver of magic climbed my skin like frosty fingertips.

Vesperus flung the door open wide, and a gust of icy wind blasted my face like an icy slap. It stung my eyes and made my breath hitch, face immediately burning as I turned my nose into the wintry onslaught of sleet.

The wind snagged and whipped in Vesperus's long, dark red hair as he gestured with a sweep of his hand and a shiver of his magic. The gazers obeyed immediately, drifting forward into the tundra and disappearing into a vortex of darkness flecked with whirling snowflakes without hesitation.

Then Vesperus forged out after them, blade at the ready. With his shoulders thrown back, he stepped off into the snow without a word.

"You're sure you can do this, right?" Axien called down to me over the wind, bits of ice pinging off his armor.

I shot him a venomous glare, silently daring him to ask me that again.

"Good. Just checking." He smirked, winking one of those glowing eyes before he turned to follow Vesperus.

Idiot.

I gave him ten paces before I slipped out of the door, too. Crouching down right beside it, I pulled my coat tighter around my ears and pulled a length of cloth over my nose and mouth so I could breathe more easily. Snow stuck to my eyelashes as I squinted ahead, watching the two men prowl onto the frozen lake with the five gazers hovering just ahead of them.

So far, so good.

But where was our quarry?

That monster, Leomarr, was here somewhere. I had no doubts about that whatsoever. We just couldn't see him yet. It could move fast and without making much noise, and had snuck up on Axien and me twice already.

Knowing that it was probably observing us—hunting us—lit a burning coal of rage in my chest.

Vesperus and Axien continued on, venturing farther and farther out onto the ice until, suddenly, Vesperus stopped.

My senses opened, instincts igniting and setting my teeth on edge. I switched to my heat vision so I could keep a closer watch on their movements, marking every subtle gesture. Every step. Every head turn.

Vesperus glowed far brighter than Axien, probably something to do with using magic to warm himself against the bite of the wind. He surveyed the battlefield ahead of us, gaze seeming to linger temporarily on the distant glow of the tiny cabin's windows across the lake. His expression twitched, as though the sight were uncomfortable.

Bad memories? Or good ones?

Either way, he turned his focus back to the lake, glowing eyes constantly moving and large, feathered wings rustling in the fierce wind.

Axien stood eight paces behind the sorcerer, his every step a smooth, calculated prowl forward. I'd gotten much more familiar with his body language, but I'd never seen him this on edge.

Axien stopped, standing stiff and tall as he studied their surroundings. A bulwark of armor against the howling winter storm, he fixed his gaze on the ancient sorcerer ahead of him. His fingers flexed on the grips of the two longswords he held, weight shifting slightly from one foot to the other.

Ready to move at any instant.

Meanwhile, Vesperus panned his gaze back and forth, expression still locked into that unyielding frown. Ahead of him, the gazers fanned out in perfect formation like floating, glowing pearls of vibrant blue light on the ice.

My heartbeat began to slow, slipping gradually into the steady, calm rhythm that honed my focus. The rhythm that let the chains slip off that burning, thrumming, angry heat buried deep in my soul. The part of me that loved this.

The Viperi part.

A wicked smirk curled across my lips when Axien's entire body suddenly tensed. Vesperus, too. They turned slightly, exchanging a wary look.

Then the ground rumbled faintly under my feet.

It was here.

Close—but still out of sight.

I bared my teeth, that seething rage kindling brighter and sending waves of heat through my veins and out to every single one of my fingers and toes. My mind stilled as I searched the whipping, snowy wind for anything out of place.

A ripple of darkness, deep and formless, moved on the ice. It seemed to swallow all of the weak light around, forming a curling, churning void that stood out prominently to my heat-vision.

But Vesperus and Axien didn't react.

Oh, gods, they didn't see it!

I opened my mouth to shout. To warn them. But the sound snagged in my throat as a deafening *BOOM—CRAAACK* shook the ground and sent me bouncing off the door at my back.

Fractures snapped and buckled across the surface of the frozen lake, fanning out like a spider's web around Vesperus and Axien.

The two men wobbled and shouted, calling to one another as two huge, black vines burst up from beneath the ice. They twisted and coiled, bristling with thorns like spear tips, as big around as tree trunks, and slammed back down onto the surface of the lake.

A snarl like thunder rumbled through the wintry hellscape

as a huge, clawed skeletal hand reached through the fissure in the ice. Then an arm, and a bony, spined shoulder emerged. The wretched beast's wings burst from the ice with a shower of freezing mist, its huge, rotting shoulders now supporting three, bleached bone heads.

Gods and fates, it was huge! More than twice the size it had been before!

And those black vines—they weren't vines. Each spiny, writhing growth connected to the monster's back like a tentacle of bone, wood, and rotting flesh.

I sat, utterly paralyzed, gaping up at it.

Wh-what had happened? How had it suddenly gotten so much stronger?

Had Axien and I caused this somehow?

The monster twisted and wrenched its hindquarters free of the ice, landing before Vesperus and Axien with a *BOOM!*

It considered them with six, red pinprick eyes, then the middle head let out a screaming shriek that immediately put me on my knees. My vision scrambled, and the coppery flavor of blood filled my mouth, as I gripped my ears, desperate to cover them.

But it didn't work.

That noise, the scream, was everywhere. In my flesh. In my bones. Crawling under my skin like a parasite. Raking over my brain like rusty nails down slate.

I-I couldn't escape it.

"NOW!" Axien's voice roared over the chaos.

Vesperus kicked skyward, his black, raven-like wings flared against the storm like an avenging dark angel. Axien's form rippled, wreathed in bluish-purple light that coiled around him and solidified into a pair of gleaming wings. He took off like a shining comet, following Vesperus as all the gazers began to converge on the monster below.

The five floating orbs encircled the beast, hovering and

blaring their warning like a cacophony of doomsday trumpets. Then their pupils widened, and tendrils of blinding, white-blue light arced and snapped out at the creature.

The monster screeched again, recoiling as each lash from the gazer's magical assault ensnared a bony spine, bare femur, rib, or wing digit. The contact made the beast's body shudder and shake, as though it were being paralyzed.

Or cooked alive like a frog hit with a lightning bolt.

"The heads—we must cut off the heads!" Vesperus shouted as a mote of flame poured from his outstretched hand.

On cue, Axien spiraled downward, his arcanely crafted wings drawn in like a diving falcon, a flask of that red liquid gripped tight in one hand. Less than ten feet from the monster's head, he hurled it headlong at one of its open eye sockets and zoomed skyward again.

BOOOM!

My heat-vision went white as Vesperus's blast of fire hit like cannon fire, striking that spot and detonating the flask. My ears rang and I staggered, barely keeping my feet as the explosion rocked the ground beneath us and sent shards of ice and black bone flying in every direction.

The monster screeched, reeling as its tendrils slammed the ground and writhed in the air. Its bare, tattered wings flapped uselessly as it keeled forward, smashing against the frozen lake and sending out another web of fractures.

The surface of the lake was blown to pieces like a shattered mirror. Hunks of it floated and bobbed, bumping and buckling against one another. One misstep would send me plunging to an icy death.

But I couldn't hesitate. This was it.

My one chance.

Even from a distance, that tiny fleck of light shone in the creature's sternum like a chip of moonlight. Dark, coiling, inky clouds of its power whirled around it like a hurricane as the monster flailed, but that spot still shimmered brightly.

I snapped to my feet and sprinted forward, wind snatching in my hair and burning my cheeks and forehead. My vision teared, forming freezing crystals on my eyelids. My pulse boomed in my aching eardrums.

My oversized boots hit the surface of the lake and made the slab of ice teeter, but I didn't stop. Forward. I stepped lightly, moving fast, and made sure I didn't give any of the floating hunks of ice time to flip before I was long gone.

My lungs ached as my feet flew, springing ahead and leaping the gaps between the drifting ice. Landing in a crouch, I kicked off again. Ducking and weaving with the motion of the ice slabs, I wove a path directly for the monster.

Faster. I had to keep moving. No slowing down. Only forward.

One of the beast's spined tentacles swung right over my head, passing like the mast of a ship with a wave of sulfuric heat that hit my face like a blast from a volcanic vent. It filled my lungs with the stench of rotten eggs and decaying flesh, and I wobbled, coughing as my throat burned and my eyes watered.

BOOOM!

A scream ripped past my lips as the tentacle suddenly slammed down behind me, smacking off the big floating hunk of ice where I stood. It sent me flying like a projectile straight for it, arms and legs flailing.

Oh gods—I was going to hit it! Or hit the ice. Either way, the landing would be brutal, and I—

"Gotcha," Axien panted in my ear as he snatched me straight out of the air, swooping low enough to set me back on my feet again.

We faltered as all three of the monster's skeletal heads shrieked in unison, sending out a blast of bone-splintering sound that made my brain rattle in my skull and warm trails of blood ooze from my nose. The frozen lake rippled under the shockwave, sending us both rocking onto our heels.

Explosions reported somewhere off to the left, lighting up the storm with flashes of light as it took a successful swipe at two of the gazers. The arcane eyes imploded on impact, and I recoiled back against Axien's side.

"We have to hurry!" he shouted, grabbing me under the shoulder and hauling me to my feet. "We can't hold it down much longer! It's now or never!"

"Just keep it distracted!" I yelled back.

Axien nodded, his body braced for another takeoff. Dark veins already spread across the hollow of his throat, spreading toward his face like a sickness against his darkly tanned skin.

He was pushing it again, probably compelled to keep pace with Vesperus.

I had to hurry and get this done.

With a flourish of those gleaming, magical wings, Axien was gone—streaking for the monster with his palms glowing and sparking with magic. I bit down fiercely, watching him go, still tasting the burn of bile, blood, and sulfur on my tongue.

Tearing my gaze from him, I glared up at the towering monstrosity and locked onto that single glowing spot embedded in its sternum.

A guiding star.

Our only hope.

I spat on the ground and spun my blade over my hand, testing the strength of my grip before I took off again. Rage like hellfire blazed through my body, numbing away the bite of the wind, the throbbing of every bruise, and the thrumming ache in my injured arm. None of it mattered—only this.

Only the hunt.

Only victory.

Forty-Nine

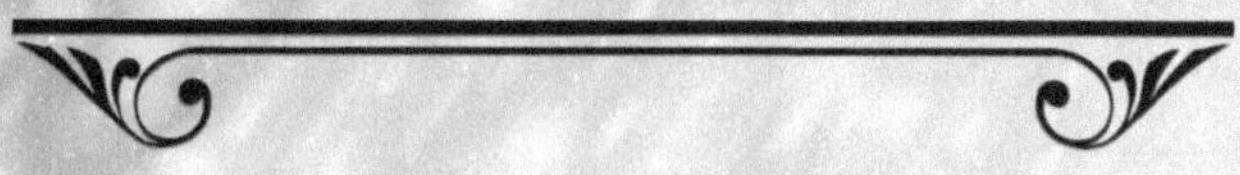

Our plan had one flaw.

I realized that as I scurried between the beast's legs like a cockroach, springing from one slab of ice to another, dodging its thunderous steps, coiling tentacles, clawed hands, and whipping tail. A deadly dance I knew I couldn't keep up for long.

But climbing the wretched, putrid thing?

I skidded to a halt, gaping up at the sheer size of it. It must have been fifty feet tall.

And I was ... very much on the short side.

Granted, I hadn't realized the thing would more than double in size in such a short time. Before, it wouldn't have been an issue. Or, at least, not one I couldn't deal with.

This was definitely a problem now.

And I was fresh out of ideas.

I hissed a curse, ducking frantically as one of the gazers went soaring behind me, buzzing and blaring that horn of alarm as it continued to attack the creature. I glared at it, the heat from its spherical body practically making my eyelashes curl.

WHOOOM!

All the breath tore out of my lungs as one of those massive, vine-like tentacles slammed into the ice only feet in front of me. It smashed the gazer, and the arcane device detonated like a powder keg.

In an instant, I was flying through the air again. I hit the ground yards away and rolled, pain searing through my body as my skull cracked off the ice. My vision winked in and out. My head spun.

Then the hunk of ice began to tilt under my weight.

No, no, no!

I floundered, delirious and half-blind, trying to balance my weight on it so the slab of ice didn't flip with me on top. My ears rang, and my injured arm throbbed.

Overhead, the monster let out another deafening scream that made my spine curl and my brain throb as if it might explode just like that gazer. The world slid out of focus again. Every muscle vibrated and trembled, as though that monster's screech was ripping me apart from the inside.

Then I heard him—a male voice crying out in agony over the rush of the wind and the buzz, boom, and rumble of battle.

My eyes flew open just in time to see the monster's massive, clawed hand gripping Vesperus like a freshly picked carrot. The sorcerer squirmed in its grip, blood leaking from the corners of his mouth as the creature crushed him.

He couldn't escape. Not without help.

I had to do something—right now.

Like ... that reckless idea Axien had warned me about.

Willing my trembling body to move, I dragged myself to my feet and pulled my own red flask from my pocket. Thank the gods it hadn't detonated when I hit the ground.

Putting the corked end between my teeth, I rushed for the nearest of the monster's hind legs and drew the shortsword from my belt. Every nerve in my body sang with agony as I raised it over my head with both hands, blade angled down.

A wild, furious scream tore from my lungs as I drove it into the creature's hooved hind foot with every shred of strength I had.

The blade sank deep, sliding into the rotting flesh just above its hoof.

The monster pitched and screeched, dropping Vesperus immediately and turning all its focus to me.

Excellent.

I gave my weapon a brutal twist, just for good measure, and left it embedded deep in the creature's putrid flesh before I staggered back.

"VIOLET!" Axien's cry of panic and horror broke over the rage of combat.

Wherever he was, it was too late.

The monster's massive hand descended on me just like it had Vesperus, snatching me up. I made sure one of my arms was kept loose—my good hand able to grab the flask out of my mouth—as the ground fell away, leaving my stomach somewhere down below.

The monster held me, all three of its skull-faces considering me at once. I glared back, squeezing the flask in my shaking fist.

I wheezed through my teeth as the creature began to squeeze, my eyes welling. My bones bent, sending waves of agony all through my body. But I didn't squirm. I refused to scream.

I stole one last glance down at its exposed sternum, and a manic, wretched grin spread over my lips.

After all, why climb—when you can fall?

"See you in hell," I seethed and chucked the flask at the middle skull-head. The glass flickered in the weak light as it spun end over end, soaring the distance between us and slamming right into the monster's open maw.

BOOOM!

The detonation blew my hair back. The monster pitched backward and staggered, faltering on its wounded foot. It shrieked again, its upper body now wreathed in smoke and shards of bone that flew in every direction.

Its grip on me loosened. I fell, sucking in a wild breath as I plummeted through the freezing, open air.

BAM!

I slammed hard against the exposed bone of its chest, seeing stars and frantically gripping onto anything I could as the gigantic beast began to twist and buck, clawing at the flames that boiled out of the empty eye sockets and mouth of its central head.

I hung on for dear life, the wind and motion of the monster whipping my body back and forth. My injured hand screamed, too weak to hold on for more than a second or two.

That's all I needed.

My gaze landed on that bright speck—only a few feet above me. So close. I could just make out the outline of something narrow and metallic, like a twisted piece of silver filigree.

The key.

Another primal scream tore from my throat as I forced my arms to pull. Higher and higher. Hanging from my one good hand, I stretched out my other as far as it would go. A foot away. Then inches.

I kicked, my fingers slipping on the slimy, rot-slicked bone. My injured hand fumbled, clumsy and numb.

So close.

Almost there.

With a final, desperate pull, I heaved myself upward. My fingers closed around the object, fingers digging into the soggy, soft rot that surrounded it like wet clay. It made a wet, sucking, *sluuuuuurp* as I wrenched it free.

I-I had it! Oh gods, I had it!

I opened my mouth to scream—to cry out for Axien. I could let go. I could fall. He would catch me.

He always did.

Beneath my grasp, the monster made a strange, low, vibrating gurgle. The reel of the rot blasted in my face as the fleshy mess around me began to ... melt.

My good hand slipped on the sternum bones as they shifted abruptly. Dislodging.

Crumbling.

I fell amidst an avalanche of rot, necrotic ooze slapping at my face and hissing against my skin. The sharp edges of bones slashed at my arms and legs.

I tried to yell. To cover my face and head with my arms. It had to stop. We would hit the ice.

The broken ice.

A sudden burst of intense cold met my body, consuming me. A cold that paralyzed. That made every joint lock up solid so I couldn't even try to claw my way out.

I was sinking into it, deeper and deeper. Until there was no more sound. No more up or down. Nothing but that soul-crushing cold that dragged me down, down, down ...

Down into the endless dark.

FIFTY

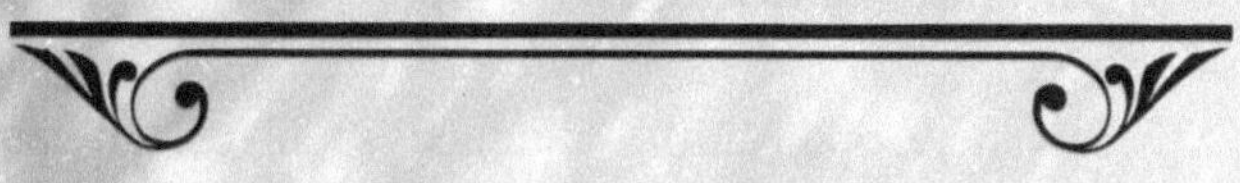

"I've got you. You're okay. Almost there," a shaky, deep voice whispered in my ear.

Axien.

The world hung in a foggy gray haze all around, but I knew him. His voice. His warmth. His smell was everywhere, filling my nose with the familiar hints of cedar, eucalyptus, and anise. His arms gripped me tightly as I bounced and jostled, held in an embrace with one of his hands grasping the side of my head as though to hold me steady against his shoulder.

Were we ... running? From what? Was the monster still chasing us?

Gods, what had happened?

My thoughts seemed to slosh like watery cold porridge in my skull with every step he took. I couldn't force my eyes open any wider or make my arms and legs move. I hung, every part of me limp, heavy, numb, and ... wet?

Had I fallen in the water?

I-I didn't know. I couldn't remember anything but the

darkness. My hands clenched and my teeth chattered as my entire body convulsed in violent shivers.

"Get up, Vesperus," Axien snarled suddenly, his breathless tone tight and frantic. "On your feet, man! We have to get to the door!"

The door?

Oh. Oh, gods. *That* door!

The key!

My eyes flew open and I flinched as all the memories rushed in like a crashing wave against a reef.

I caught a glimpse of the frozen, stormy wasteland around us before Vesperus was there, weaving on his feet with an arm wrapped around his middle. Blood ran from his mouth and dribbled off his chin, staining his teeth pink as he grimaced and shambled after us. Every step left a smeared crimson trail in the snow behind him, and his wings dragged along limply.

The monster was—gods—I couldn't see it anywhere. Had it fallen beneath the surface of the lake?

Hunks of ice still floated in a jagged patchwork of white against the dark surface of the water. But there was no sign of the creature anywhere.

Dread burrowed deep in the pit of my stomach, wrenching and making my pulse beat wildly. Adrenaline ran hot and acrid in my veins. Wherever that monster was, it didn't matter. We had to get out.

Now.

Once we were through that door, anything that happened here was none of our concern.

"D-did she get ... the key?" Vesperus asked, his voice broken and halting with each staggering step.

"We can worry about that later!" Axien snapped, stopping before the wooden door. His expression twitched and seized, dark veins spreading from his neck down over his cheeks.

Vesperus slammed his hand down onto the knob with a

hiss of pain. It glowed brightly, sending a current of magical power through the air before he twisted and ripped it open.

All three of us fell through the open doorway, scrambling, crawling, and shaking. We hit the ground on the plush, cozy warmth of a finely woven wool rug, and Vesperus wasted no time scrambling to shut the door again.

As soon as it banged shut, the howl of the wintry wind stopped, replaced with the gentle crackle of flames in the hearth. No snowfall. No ice.

No monster.

We were safe—back in Vesperus's living room.

With his back against the door, Vesperus sat with his legs and wings splayed out. His face was drawn and pale, all his fine armor was smeared and speckled with blood. His long red hair hung in tangled, wind-tousled locks that were caked with snow.

But he was alive.

And so were we.

"Is it dead?" Axien asked hoarsely, still gripping me tightly against him. "Did we kill it?"

Vesperus shook his head. "I-I'm ... not sure. We certainly w-wounded him. But he's a c-creature of the void now. I've no idea wh-what he's capable of. Perhaps he c-can regenerate, given enough time. But I-I ... I don't know for certain."

"Let's hope you're wrong, then," Axien grumbled and flopped onto his back.

"Indeed," Vesperus murmured, his expression twitching with little grimaces of pain, as if each breath stung. "What of the k-key? Did she get it? You s-aid she was capable."

"We also assumed the creature would be half that size and without giant, earth-shattering tentacles," Axien growled back. "You never mentioned it could grow and change like that! I never would have sent her off on her own if—"

"Sh-shut ... up, b-both of you," I rasped.

They both stared at me, glowing eyes wide in shock.

I tried to sit, pushing away from Axien's chest. Heat stung my skin where the icy wind had left it raw. A weak whimper rattled through my teeth as I forced my wounded arm to move and my hand to open, revealing the piece of twisted silver metal resting in my palm.

It didn't look much like a key, to be honest. More like an ornate, metal filigree frame roughly three inches across. The empty spot in the center was obviously meant to house the little icosahedron we'd found in the study, and the entire thing shone like it was made of pure blue light.

"She did it," Vesperus gasped in awe.

"I said I would, didn't I?" I cut him a frazzled glare. "And now I want the truth."

Vesperus flinched, his eyes narrowing as though he were silently warning me against my next question.

Too bad. We'd come too far—suffered too much—to indulge his privacy anymore. He'd come clean, or I would carve the answers out of his flesh.

"Why did you really trap Leomarr in here? What's wrong with him? What power did Vescor give him?" I questioned, instinctively drawing my injured arm closer to my torso.

The wound, the one Leomarr's talons had carved into my flesh, burned and throbbed even in the bitter cold. It felt like white-hot nails under my skin, spreading up my bicep and into my shoulder now.

Vesperus blinked slowly back at me, his expression emptying of anything but a cold, dejected despair that seemed to drain all the color from his features. His eerie, glowing eyes gradually drifted down to my arm, mouth tensing into a hard frown.

"Despair," he replied simply. "Vescor gave him ... despair. A powerful weapon to crush the resolve of any enemy. But Vescor did not warn him of the effects of such a thing. How it only spreads and grows, infecting the darkest parts of a person's heart, even the person wielding it."

"That's why you implanted the key in his chest," Axien murmured, shaking his head. "You tried to implant hope in him."

"Tried and failed. The void-god's influence over him was already too great. I thought ... if I had more time, perhaps I could come up with a better solution. So, I brought him here, where I could contain the spread," Vesperus said, his head slowly bowing toward his chest. "Here, he wouldn't be destroyed by our father or the Anointed Legion before I had a chance to help him. Here, we would both have a chance to make it right."

Vesperus clenched his arm around his middle, almost covering a place where the shining steel of his breastplate was bent inward. Blood oozed from that area, but with his arm in the way, I couldn't tell how badly he'd been injured.

"But Leomarr's curse grew quickly—he became too powerful. It consumed him. His mind, his body ... it was gone. And the more we fought, the more damage he did to me, the stronger he seemed to become," he said, his tone wavering with half-contained sobs. "As despair spreads, it grows in strength."

My heart gave a sharp, frantic twist in my chest as chills swept up my spine one vertebra at a time. Something in his tone, in the way he said those words, set all my senses on edge.

Leomarr had damaged me, too.

Was that the answer? Was that why he'd suddenly become so much bigger and stronger? Why his body had warped?

I glanced sideways as Axien shifted, his brow furrowed in deep thought.

His mouth quirked to the side as he confessed, "During our first encounter with him, that monster nicked me with a blast. You healed it, so I didn't think anything of it."

"I'm pleased I got to you early." Vesperus's gaze found me again, and I couldn't resist the urge to shrink back.

Because no one had ever looked at me like that before—like they felt nothing but deepest, purest sympathy for what was about to happen to me.

"But in her case, I am truly sorry I could not do the same," he whispered.

Axien stiffened, expression suddenly going blank.

"What do you mean?" he demanded.

"She may draw her blade for this order you both serve, but as noble as her intentions may be, she is still a being of Vescor's own blood. I can sense it in her." Vesperus shifted, hissing a sharp breath of pain through his teeth as he tried to stand. "Just as I now sense the seed of his despair growing within her heart. It seems she is fertile ground for his darkness to spread rapidly, as you saw how much Leomarr's form had already changed."

"You're saying the reason he had become so much more powerful was because of how he injured her?" Axien stood, too. His hands shook in white-knuckled fists as he glanced wildly back and forth between Vesperus and me.

"I am," the sorcerer confirmed as he began shuffling stiffly across the room, leaning against furniture as he went to stabilize himself. "And now that she bears his curse, it will grow and spread through her, just as it did through Leomarr. She will become a creature of despair."

No ... that wasn't ... that couldn't ...

The world around me went blurry as tears welled in my eyes. I stared at Axien's foggy outline, mouth open but unable to draw in even a scrap of air.

G-Gods. I was ... I was going to become like him?!

No.

NO!!

"NO!" Axien thundered suddenly, a ripple of power

crackling off his body and spreading out like a flash of heat. His face twitched, drawn in a glare of pure rage as he faced our host. "She will not become a monster."

"How do you know?" Vesperus demanded sharply as he turned back to face him, a corner of his mouth curled in a half-snarl. "Have you seen it?"

Axien recoiled like he'd been punched across the nose. His face blanched and his chest rose and fell with fast, frantic breaths. He held still, not even blinking, as Vesperus wheeled back around and continued hobbling across the room toward the carved relief of the massive door.

The door that led out of this wretched cage of secrets.

"There are no answers here that will help her," Vesperus admitted as he ran a hand over the empty relief at the center of the magnificent carving. A place in the carefully chiseled filigree where the piece still clenched in my fist would fit perfectly.

The ancient sorcerer glanced back at me, all his scarred features steeled with a look of earnest determination. His glowing golden eyes seemed to bore straight through me, seeing down into the twisted depths of my soul where that curse, Leomarr's curse, was already growing.

Festering in my heart like a wound that wouldn't heal.

"Whatever hope of overcoming this you may have lies beyond this place," Vesperus said, holding out a hand toward me, beckoning me closer. "You must go. And when you are back within the material world ... you must swear to me that you will make sure this artifact is never allowed to fall into the wrong hands."

"Of course we will." I stood shakily, barely able to feel anything below my neck as I staggered toward him with all the grace of a toddler wobbling to the outstretched arms of a parent.

The toe of one of my too-big boots snagged on the dense,

wool carpet. I started to topple forward, but Axien appeared at my side and held me steady. Together, we moved closer to the looming door, leaning into one another and shuddering in a tangled-up mixture of hope, fear, and dread.

My hands trembled, bruised, bloody, and smeared with black necrotic sludge as I dropped the empty filigree and icosahedron into Vesperus's waiting hand.

"You must promise me that you will take this artifact and cast it into the sea, so that it will not be found again," Vesperus insisted with a brittle smile, fitting the icosahedron into the hollow space at its center with a soft click.

I frowned at him, reading between the hard lines of his pale scars and the weary frown that played over his thin lips.

"You're not coming with us," I realized aloud.

"No," he confirmed in a consoling whisper. "I'm afraid not."

"But ... but why?" I started to protest, seizing him by the arm as he moved to slip the filigree into place on the door. "You could come back with us! You could stay with the Zenith's Call, or—"

"I was made for a different world, little one," he interrupted gently, putting his free hand over mine and letting his glowing eyes fall closed for a moment.

As though cherishing the contact. Savoring.

So he could remember it for the next six thousand years.

"Promise me," he repeated quietly.

"I-I promise." The words were so bitter on my lips. I had to squeeze my eyes shut to swallow them down.

"Whatever you were made to be, I am pleased to see you have chosen a different path," he said, casting a quick look behind me to where Axien stood, watching in tense silence. "There is darkness within you, yes. But there is fire, as well. See that you do not lose it. It may be all that saves you from despair."

I gasped and stammered, trying to speak as I drew back from him. But my lips wouldn't form anything but garbled, strangled, frantic sounds as tears flooded my eyes.

One of Axien's arms found its way around my shoulders, pulling me against him as we watched Vesperus press that silver filigree key into place on the door. Just like the one in the crypt, the engravings glowed to life, spreading outward and filling the room with ethereal light.

"Hurry now," Vesperus urged.

Axien started toward it, but I couldn't force my legs to move. My heels were stuck fast, like I'd been melted to the ground. I couldn't drag my gaze away from him—the slim, towering shape of the Avoran sorcerer who watched us with eyes alight, and his dark wings folded close around him.

He was injured—probably a lot worse than he was letting on. He'd said before he couldn't heal himself of injuries that came from that monster. Would he ... die? Suffer slowly alone in this place until the Harbinger came for him?

Could the Harbinger even find souls in a pocket-dimension?

I didn't know. But whatever happened with his soul, I couldn't do it. I couldn't let him suffer like that. Whatever else he was, Vesperus was a good man. He'd done everything he could to save his brother.

He deserved mercy.

I slipped the poisoned ring from my hand, the one Axien had given me, and forced it into his palm.

"If it comes to it," I whispered, forcing his fingers to close around it and squeezing his hand in both of mine. "One prick of the barb and it will end quickly. No suffering, I promise. One brother has already suffered far too long in this place. Don't share that fate with him. You don't deserve it, whatever you think."

Vesperus stared down at me, his expression a skewed

mixture of surprise and grim understanding. He nodded once, then took a single step back. The smile that spread across his somber, scarred features cut me straight to the core.

Because it was real. It made his gleaming eyes shine brighter with a kind, gentleness I'd never seen before. It squeezed at my heart and threatened to twist it straight out of my chest.

"We need to go," Axien murmured against my ear, beginning to nudge me on.

Little by little, I edged forward. Closer to that door.

Closer to the waiting world beyond it ... and whatever new nightmares awaited us there.

An inch from it, I froze again, every muscle locking up as solid as granite as my heart pounded and my knees shook, threatening to buckle.

"We have no idea what's going to be waiting for us on the other side of this door." I couldn't stop my voice from shaking, or my mind from flashing between all the worst-case scenarios.

Being surrounded by Ulfrangar in that ancient crypt.

Being deep in Tibran territory, surrounded by enemies.

Or being somewhere completely unknown and realizing hundreds of years had passed, and everyone we'd ever loved was gone.

My mouth screwed up, tears streaming down my face. My entire body trembled as I gripped Axien's arm like a life preserver.

"You're right," he replied, hugging me tighter so my back was pressed firmly against his armored chest. "But we do know what's waiting for us if we stay here: an eternity of not knowing. Of waiting to see if the Tibrans ever try to come here. Of never even having a chance of seeing Roxus, Delthene, Vanora, or anyone else again. Of wondering what kind of life we missed out on."

My tears left warm trails on my cheeks as I stared into his knowing smile. Something about it—about the way his brows turned up slightly and his mouth wobbled at the corners, was all wrong.

It was ... sad in a way I didn't understand.

"There's a destiny waiting for you beyond this door, Violet. I wouldn't be able to live with myself if we didn't chase it together, for as long as we can," he said, his hand reaching to guide mine closer to the surface of the door before us.

How do you know that? a voice like a jagged, fractured echo of my own hissed through my mind.

I sucked in a sharp breath as the wound on my arm throbbed, sending another current of prickling heat up to my shoulder.

"Have you seen it?" Vesperus's voice boomed like distant thunder, entangled in that snarled, broken tone.

No. Axien couldn't know for sure. He was just hoping.

And I knew, as both our hands pressed against the surface of that magical door and felt it give way to the vast expanse of time and space beyond ... that reckless hope was all we had left now.

Fifty-One

We landed on a cold, slate-tiled floor.

Or, Axien did, anyway.

He let out a wheezing cough of surprise as he hit flat on his back. A second later, I slammed down squarely on top of him, bouncing off his chest and sprawling over his middle like I'd just been bucked off an angry horse.

He let out a groan and shifted, reaching for his crotch, where I'd unfortunately landed with the point of my elbow.

Oops.

"S-Sorry," I stammered, quickly squirming off him.

"S'fine," he whimpered, clearly not fine.

While Axien rolled onto his side, still gripping himself and wheezing, I took a quick look around while reaching for the knife tucked into the side of my boot—the only weapon I had on me now.

We'd made it. Gods and Fates, we had made it out of the artifact.

Now the most important questions were glaring down at us like the heat of the midday sun: where and when were we?

Neither of us moved or made a sound. My heartbeat was

wild as thunder as I carefully took in the details of the open, luxurious chamber where we were sprawled on the floor.

A wide desk behind us seemed to be made from a solid slab of marble, and there, faint streams of silvery moonlight ebbed in through the huge, arched windows to the right. No fire burned in the fire pit in the middle of the room, mere feet away from us. A pair of carved wooden doors on the far side must have led outside, and the fragrance of wine and tobacco hung thick in the air.

Wherever we were, it was late at night ... and we were alone.

Or so I assumed.

"I think ... I think we might be in the Southern Kingdoms, still," I guessed, keeping my voice down as I studied the lavish furnishings.

"Well, that's good news," Axien replied quietly. "Are you hurt?"

"I'm okay." I frowned around the room, unable to shake a strange tickle in the back of my mind. The sense that something about this place was familiar. Had I been here before?

No—that wasn't possible. Before Roxus took me in, the nicest place I'd ever stood in was the Brood Father's estate. Since we weren't hundreds of feet underground, this wasn't the same house.

So why did the hint of incense in the air make all the tiny hairs on my body stand on end?

I squeezed the hilt of my knife harder, searching all the scattered, dark corners of my memories for one that fit this haunting puzzle.

"I'm going to take a look, stay down," Axien whispered as he slowly rose to his feet, his glowing gaze scanning the room. He turned, considering the huge marble desk behind us—then, faster than a viper's strike, he snapped a hand out to seize something off the edge of it.

The artifact. Tykeron's Puzzlebox.

More like Vesperus's Prison Cell.

I blew out a shaking breath as he handed it to me, and I quickly stuffed it into the pocket of my too-big coat. We definitely could not afford to leave it here, wherever here was.

Nowhere good, according to the gnawing ache of dread in my belly.

I kept my eyes trained on the windows and every dark corner as Axien prowled the length of the room, stepping over exotic, animal-skin rugs and hedging around squatty velvet sofas. He paused before the wooden double doors, holding a hand up in my direction as a signal to stay still and quiet while he carefully twisted one of the knobs.

Axien opened the door a tiny crack, barely enough to squint through, then slowly pulled it open farther.

I held my breath, my pulse pounding so loud it throbbed in every one of my toes.

Then he slipped out of the door altogether, disappearing into the hall, and leaving the door slightly ajar.

Oh—freaking gods—what was he thinking?!

I started to move, to chase after him, but as soon as I got to my feet, Axien swept back inside and silently shut the door again.

"Good news or bad news first?" he whispered, his face pasty as he panted.

I blinked at him, still fighting the urge to throttle him for leaving like that. Had he completely lost his mind? What if someone heard him? Or worse—saw him!

"Good or bad?" he asked again.

"Good," I growled low. Maybe some good news would bring me back from the brink of blind fury.

"We're still in Rienka, and as far as I can tell, not much time has passed. There's a window at the end of the hall overlooking the street, and I don't see any Tibran soldiers or banners flying. Nothing's burning. No corpses in the street," he answered quickly.

My shoulders relaxed a bit, my grip on my knife loosening slightly. Well, thank the gods for that. Maybe we'd only been gone months instead of years.

"And the bad news?" I pressed.

"Bad news is ... I'm fairly certain we are on Kosaar." Axien's expression twisted uncomfortably. "In Sulam's family estate, to be precise. The Caldera is right outside. Granted, all of it is empty at this hour. But I'd bet good coin he's got no shortage of hired muscle patrolling the grounds."

Reality crashed into me like a landslide.

Gods, no wonder this place smelled familiar. I'd recognize Sulam's reek anywhere. But worse, this meant he was directly involved with the Ulfrangar and the theft of the artifact from the Ragentrudes. Either he'd been subcontracted to see it done, or he was directly responsible for it.

Either way, it did not bode well.

"We need to get out of here," I whispered, wheeling around to consider the room again. The windows were large—the sort meant to be decorative. They wouldn't open, and breaking them would make too much noise.

We had no choice but to take our chances outside this room.

"I agree, but first ..." Axien prowled past, returning to the large marble-hewn desk.

He rummaged around in the papers stacked onto it, pilfered through the drawers, and opened every scroll or book he found.

"What are you doing? We need to go," I hissed.

"We found the artifact here, completely unguarded," he countered without pausing his frantic search. "That means two things: Sulam is entirely confident that either no one knows it's here or can reach it even if they did know about it.

I'm betting on the former, given this room isn't crawling with guards."

I put a protective hand over the lump in my coat pocket where the artifact was now tucked safely away. "And? What's the other thing?"

"If he's comfortable enough leaving something that valuable sitting on top of his desk, he probably has other things hidden here he would prefer no one know about." Axien straightened suddenly, yanking something out of the bottom drawer of the desk and holding it up to the sterling moonlight.

A cylindrical black leather case closed with a series of three small, delicate locks.

"What is that?" I asked, creeping closer as he inspected the case.

It couldn't have been twelve inches long, and roughly half that in diameter. But the trio of locks were extremely intricate, held in place and apparently fused to the metal body of the case hidden beneath the oiled black leather.

Whatever this was, Sulam didn't want anyone else opening it.

That was more than reason enough for me to try.

"Wait," Axien protested as I reached for it, his frown traced with concern. "I ... I recognize this mechanism. It's a Tibran design."

I stared at him, unable to make a sound.

"There are small vials of acid inside. If we tamper with it or try to force it open, they will break and destroy whatever is inside," he explained. "Crassus's wife—the woman who owned me—used something similar to correspond with people she didn't want him to know about."

My mind crawled with questions like spiders escaping a jar, each prickly one making my body stiffen in disgust. What was Sulam doing with something like this? What was inside that he didn't want anyone to find? Was this something he'd gotten from the Tibrans? Or was it just a coincidence that he was using the same sort of device to relay information he didn't want anyone else to see?

I slowly traced my teeth with my tongue, feeling the places where my pointed incisors had once been while I stewed in those thoughts.

We needed to know what was inside that container. We needed to find a way to open it without destroying the contents.

Axien must have arrived at the same conclusion, because he flashed me a fierce, smoldering glare of defiance as he shoved the canister into the side of his belt.

The heavy thud of footsteps and metallic clunk armor beyond the chamber doors made us both freeze suddenly. A pair of muffled voices echoed in the hall just outside, coming closer and closer. Males, judging by the deep tones.

Guards?

Or Sulam?

I bit down hard, anger flaring from somewhere deep in my chest. Whoever they were, it didn't matter. I'd cut them down like chaff.

My grip on the knife, still resting in my good hand, tightened until my fingers throbbed. I jerked forward, focused on the doors. Ready to fight. To kill.

Axien snapped an arm out, catching me by the shoulder and holding me still. He slowly shook his head, pressing a single finger to his lips.

"Wait," he mouthed silently. "We move as one."

I bared my teeth at him. Fine.

We held perfectly still, all focus on those double doors not twenty paces away.

The voices grew louder. Closer.

The footsteps scuffled right outside, and I could see the

shadows of two pairs of feet moving, eclipsing the light under the door.

I held my breath, poised. Waiting—my eyes trained on the movement beneath the door and the slightest twist of the polished doorknobs. My pulse pounded low and steady, every muscle tense and every instinct silently screaming in my brain like a wild horse on a tether.

Ready to draw first blood ... and last.

Fifty-Two

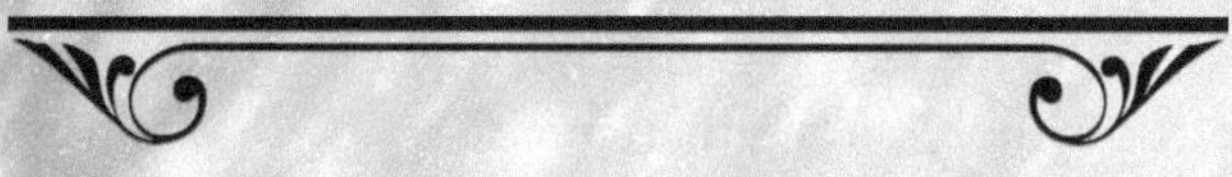

There was no stopping it.

We would fight.

Or we would become yet another one of Sulam's victims.

One of those golden doorknobs rattled faintly, beginning to twist, and fury ignited in my brain like a lit cannon fuse. My blood was fire in my veins, roaring so loudly I couldn't hear anything else.

I sprang the length of the room without a sound, Axien right on my heels. Whirling apart at the last second, I pressed my body against the wall on one side of the doors while Axien did the same on the opposite.

No sound. Only wicked efficiency.

We exchanged a steely-eyed glance and nod. No need to talk.

As one of the doors swung open, Axien drew his longsword and I dropped low into a crouch, knife still at the ready.

The guard entered the room—one step, then two.

Axien struck like a coiled viper, bringing that longsword

around in a brutal sweep aimed at the base of the guard's neck. The man let out a gurgling cry, already slumping to the ground as I bounded past him, hitting the next guard head-on and driving my feet into his chest.

He staggered back, waving his arms to keep his balance and crying out in alarm.

Curse it—someone would hear. I had to end this quickly.

Rushing the second guard again, I sank my knife into the side of his neck, hitting that crucial artery. I twisted myself around him, wrenching him to the ground and locking my legs around his torso to pin his arms before slamming my empty hand over his mouth to stifle the noise.

He pitched and rolled, trying to throw me off. But only for roughly a minute. His movements quickly grew sluggish as thick, dark blood pooled on the marble floor beneath him.

He slapped helplessly at my legs, then, with a shuddering breath, went still.

I looked up, eyes narrowed on the place where Axien had just finished dragging his kill into the office chamber. He wasted no time and seized my fallen guard by the heels, dragging him away as well and leaving a trail of dark crimson behind.

"Someone will have heard that," Axien warned as he joined me in the hall and shut the door behind him.

"Let's move," I agreed and stood, flexing against the thrumming pain from my injured arm.

Together, we darted forward down the length of the hall, passing the window Axien must have looked out earlier to determine where we were. Sure enough, the looming, bowl-shaped structure of the Caldera rose above a sea of smaller buildings with windows alight in the dark like a sea of flickering stars. The colosseum was empty, and the surrounding streets were deserted, too.

No sign of invading armies or pillaging.

So far, so good.

Judging by our aerial view of the city, however, we must be at least four floors high in Sulam's family estate. Less good. We had to get down to street level and out of this place as soon and soundlessly as possible.

Axien and I skidded to a halt at the end of the hall, faced with an open intersection where three other hallways met. The sound of shouting echoed from the one to the left—guards calling to one another to sound off. They were trying to figure out who had made the distress call.

We only had seconds. Minutes, if we were lucky.

"Come on," Axien urged, taking the hall to the right and sprinting headlong down past rows of doors.

Dead-eyed portraits of primly posed nobles stared down at us from heavy gilded frames. Generations of Sulam's family, all bearing those same dark, shark-like eyes that showed nothing but a deeply rooted malice. Too bad there wasn't time to burn this whole place down.

At the end of the corridor, we paused again to consider our next path. More halls, all dimly lit with sconces and flickering candles. More portraits and mounted animal trophies stared after us, glass eyes glittering and fanged mouths agape.

We turned and twisted through Sulam's house, the echoes of guards intensifying as the alarms were raised and a series of high-pitched horn blasts filled the manor. They'd found the bodies in the office.

They knew we were here. They'd be closing down all the exit points, locking down the entire estate, and anticipating our attempt at an escape.

Adrenaline flooded my body and drove my legs faster, the lengths of my borrowed coat billowing behind me as I ran alongside Axien. Every breath scraping raw in my throat. Every muscle quivering, exhausted, and ready to buckle.

But I couldn't.

Because I was steel pulled fresh from the fire. I would bend, I would sharpen, but I would never, ever break.

Down a flight of stairs, we took another hard turn, delving deeper and deeper until we arrived at a wide vestibule that stood open on one side, lined with large, pear-shaped alabaster columns. The rush of free, faintly salty night air filled my lungs and chilled all the sweat on my skin. The weight of the humidity settled into my bones, as familiar as the pull of the ocean's tide.

This was it—our way out.

Almost there.

Almost home.

Beyond the huge columns, a courtyard spread out around a central fountain and rippling pool tiled in chips of glass that sparkled in an array of gemstone colors. The sky hung wide and unobstructed overhead, dotted with stars and smears of faint, milky purple. A sliver of moon hung like a shard of curled glass, pouring light over us.

Real instead of some arcane illusion.

As soon as we sprinted into the open area, another chorus of shouts went up from all around the courtyard. Guards rushed from the shadows, storming for us with blades drawn and crossbows aimed. We ducked and dodged, arrows pinging off the cobblestones as we ran for the opposite end of the courtyard—away from the main estate and looming structure of the Caldera.

Toward freedom.

So close.

Axien stretched out a hand to seize mine, dragging me along as he ran faster. His face had gone pasty with desperate terror, and his fingers clenched around mine so tightly I could feel the thud of his pulse in his sweat-slicked palms.

Faster. Just a little farther. We could make it. There had to be a gate leading out of this place somewhere nearby. We just had to find it.

Then we could—

Axien and I lurched to a halt as we rounded the fountain, still dodging crossbow fire. With the gurgling fountain at our backs, we stood staring down the outer perimeter of the courtyard. Lined with a tall, wrought-iron fence nearly twenty feet tall, it offered a broken view of the street and sleeping city beyond.

There, at the very center, was the gate. It stood open already, making way for the majestic black carriage pulled by a team of six gray horses parked right in the middle of it.

A host of twenty armed men stood around it, facing us and waiting with their weapons levelled. They didn't move an inch or make a sound as the carriage door opened and Sulam stepped out into the night, the wind licking at the long, fur-trimmed cloak he wore. His dark eyes glittered, considering us with that oily grin that had haunted my dreams for so long.

My knees locked up solid. All my insides turned to mush.

Beside me, Axien sucked in a sharp breath and drew me closer, trying to put himself between me and the host of enemies before us as though to shield me.

"Well, well. I was afraid I might arrive too late and miss all the fun," Sulam sneered as he swaggered forward, his group of guards parting for him to pass like a wall of leather and steel. "The Ulfrangar were so sure you had both been absorbed in the puzzlebox, but I admit, I had my doubts. After all, these ancient relics can be so finicky. What's to say it hadn't just vaporized you both on the spot?"

His smile widened, showing crowded, tobacco-yellowed teeth. He wasn't denying any of it—that he was involved, that he'd been working with the Ulfrangar, that he'd wanted this artifact either for himself or for the Tibrans.

"I've never been so pleased to be proven wrong," he added

and gave a small bow of his head. "It would have been a much harder sell on just the promise that the artifact also contained you two. Now, I can charge whatever I want for the pitathi-traitoress and the half-Avoran seer. And with you two out of the way, securing the others will be all the easier."

My heartbeat skipped, mind racing at the sudden realization. The others ...?

Did he mean Roxus? The Tibrans had tried to take him before, so that made sense.

But who else were they targeting?

And why had he called Axien a seer?

What was all this for?

What did the Tibrans or their mad tyrant possibly stand to gain from harvesting people like us? I could understand easily enough why they wanted the artifact. Vesperus's arcane device—the puzzlebox—would throw open the doors of endless possibilities with its source of divine power.

But why did he need us? Why not just kill us outright? Were we truly worth that much to Argonox?

Why?!

"Oh my, have you truly not realized it?" Sulam snickered, seeming to enjoy my bewilderment as I glanced frantically between Axien and him. "After that nasty business with the switchbeasts in that nest of your kin, I'd assumed you were clever enough to have put it all together."

I tensed, my mind reeling as I considered all those broken pieces scattered through my mind. Bits that didn't seem to fit together or make sense.

Tagged switchbeasts. Cages filled with people like Roxus and me. A thirst for a consistent source of magical power. And ...

Leomarr. The letters. Vesperus had been corresponding with someone before he'd locked himself inside it with his brother.

Someone who had apparently known about Leomarr's affliction.

No ... was it possible? Had they somehow known what was locked in that artifact with all that power?

My throat closed. I blinked hard, eyes welling as the truth took me like a fist around my neck. My injured arm gave a sudden, sharp throb, and more waves of those itching, stinging chills swept through me like stinging ants under my skin.

When it came to engineering new horrors, Vesperus hadn't just given them all the power they would ever need ...

He had also given them the perfect source of special insight into infusing innocent people with Vescor's dark power.

And now I had brought solid evidence that it worked right to Sulam's feet. I was walking proof that it might work, with that gaping wound bound on my arm likely infused with Vescor's curse.

Sulam wasn't going to let either of us leave this place unless it was in chains.

Something inside me snapped—a thread I hadn't even realized was pulled well beyond its breaking point. That itching, tingling heat coursing up my arm intensified, spreading through me and setting my body ablaze with a sudden, overwhelming surge of strength and steadiness.

I'd been born a wicked little monster.

But I'd be damned to the deepest pit of the abyss before I died bound to anyone's heel.

One look at Axien's face, at all his fine elven features steeled in a resolve that matched the molten venom already pumping like mad through my veins, and I knew: there was only one way out of here now.

And that was a path soaked in blood.

Fifty-Three

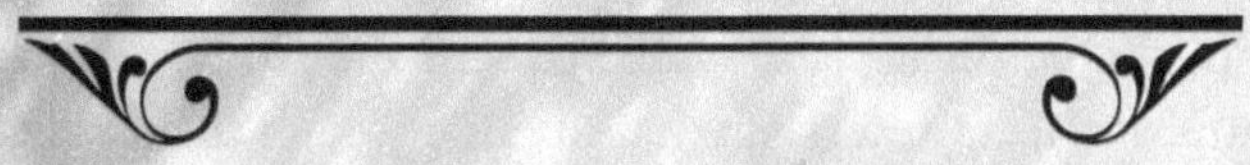

Surrender was not an option.

I knew that as I slid apart from Axien, blade already spinning over my hand. I only had one weapon, one good hand, one second of surprise, and one chance.

But I'd never felt anything like the fire that roared in my body.

The *TWANG* of dozens of bowstrings all firing at once cracked in the air, and Axien bared his teeth like a lion as he widened his stance, palms glowing and eyes flaring with divine power. One sweep of his hand sent a curtain of white-hot flame arcing around us, incinerating the bolts and giving me time to dart in closer while our enemies reloaded.

I met the first of the guards, dipping easily under his sluggish strike and jabbing my knife into the gap between the front and back of his cuirass. Spinning behind him, I kicked out the back of one knee, and jabbed the blade in again—feeling the surrender of soft flesh right at the side of his neck.

He fell, and I swiped the shortsword from his hand before his lifeless corpse ever hit the stone.

One down.

Countless more to go.

But we didn't have to kill them all. We just had to kill enough to carve a path to that open gate.

I waited, dipping around wide swings and stabbing strikes, until about eight of them surrounded me before I ripped one of Vesperus's alchemy vials from my pocket and smashed it onto the ground at my feet.

Instantly, thick black smoke choked the air. My attackers began to wheeze and stagger, fumbling through the dark. One hard blink and I could see them all as clear as day. All the glowing heat of their bodies betrayed them as they flailed around me, even in the pitch dark of the smoke.

Easy prey.

I sprang between them like a lunging serpent, the edge of my blade finding neck after neck until the stones were slick with blood. I sprang from the cloud of smoke, spattered crimson and seething.

Before me, three of the guards were already advancing. One with a greatsword, and two with handaxes.

I snarled, feeling the roiling heat in my blood rise like an infernal tide. More—I would kill more of them—until the night was filled with the chorus of their screams.

I darted forward again, light on my feet, and dropped into a backbend as the greatsword swung past. The massive blade sailed over, missing me entirely with a deadly low hum. But a weapon that size couldn't be turned for another strike quickly. He was committed to each swing, needing several seconds between them to recover.

More than enough time.

I'd deal with the other two first.

Leaning and weaving, I whirled around the swings of that massive sword as I caught the first handaxe-wielding thug in an upward parry. One twist of my shortsword wrung the weapon from his grasp, and I slammed my elbow upward into his chin. He let out a curse of pain and tried to seize me by the hair.

Mistake.

When his arm reached for me, I grabbed it and gave a violent twist and upward strike with the blunt end of my blade. The crack of his elbow brought him to his knees, and the slice of my dagger under his chin ended things just as the greatsword sailed past again.

My body burned in the throes of it—the dark symphony of battle. The coppery tinge of blood in the air. The dying cries of the wounded. The slick of sweat on my palms and the occasional sting of a crossbow bolt nicking my flesh.

It drove me closer and closer to the edge of no return. Of seeing only a world of flame and blood. Of wanting nothing else than to lose myself in it for an eternity ... because in that wicked symphony, my soul sang.

I dropped the second axeman just as quickly, stacking body after body on the cobblestones with the *BOOM* and *SIZZLE* of Axien's magic at my back. The carriage horses bucked and fought their tethers, shrieking in alarm at every burst of his arcane fire.

Then, through the fray, I heard him.

"You really think this is how it will end? With you carrying my head back to your friends? Don't be stupid, girl. I owned you the second I found you half-dead in that desert, still clinging to your mother's corpse," Sulam ranted, his voice touched with the slightest hint of panic.

Good.

He would fear me long before I let him die.

I whirled, searching for him through the smoke, fire, and flashes of steel. Another arrow zipped past my head so close the fletching brushed my cheek, but I didn't even flinch.

"I've indulged your rebellion, played your little games, but

I will bring you to heel—you and that thick-skulled mongrel will serve your purpose!" Sulam shouted.

I stopped, his words striking a chord off-key to the symphony.

Was he ... talking about Declan?

"Oh, I see. You thought this was all about *you?*" Sulam cackled, sounding closer.

Too close.

I whirled, my blades levelled, just in time to catch another attacking guard that burst from the curling cloud of smoke in a frantic parry. The impact rattled my bones and set me on my guard, barely able to time a quick sideways feint to avoid his second swing.

"Selfish little wretch, don't be ridiculous," Sulam's voice slithered through the air, so greasy with delight it made my stomach turn. "I thought I'd lost my chance when my men went too hard on his sniveling little sister, but as it turns out ... he's a far better choice for a vessel."

Wh-what?

Was he talking about Nora? Declan's little sister?

My heart dropped, falling somewhere near my heels as I whirled again, searching the smoke for him. I'd cut his forked tongue out myself for even daring to speak about—

"It's a good thing you stood by and did nothing while they beat her to death, hm? Otherwise, I might have let him die in that pit long ago and wasted all my effort on the wrong sibling." Sulam's voice seemed to be everywhere. All around me—inside my head—every word like the touch of his putrid fingers over my brain. There was no escaping it.

No escaping him.

I staggered back, fumbling and dropping my shortsword as I scrambled to cover my ears. To stop it. To shut him out.

No—stop, stop, *STOP!*

"He will be a fine, resilient vessel once I've broken him just right. The life he has now? He owes it all to you, pitathi," he laughed. "And that young, sweet, tender sister of his ... owes you her death. Did you watch them take her? Beat her? Did you listen to her scream? Did she call out for you in the end? Or did she whimper and snivel like her brother all the way to the bitter end?"

I saw it. Flashes of it, like bursts of lightning popping in my mind. The rain. Running while the voices laughed and chased us. Getting closer and closer ... until she tripped.

And fell.

And I left her there.

I left her there for them to find. I hid away and watched. Watched them find her. Watched them hurt her until ... until ...

A scream tore from me, erupting from the foundations of my being. It exploded through my body, leaving searing paths of agony and fire across my brain, and sending out a shockwave that cracked the cobblestones like chalk. Thick, thorny vines of black burst from the ground all around me, lashing out in every direction.

I felt them like extensions of my own will, moving and writhing along the ground. Fast and ruthless, they ensnared the guards one by one. Squeezed them. Crushed them. Broke their bones and split their flesh.

But not his.

Where was he?

Where was *SULAM?!*

I screamed again, letting that burning spread through me until there was nothing else. Only fire, and anger, and ... despair. Deep, cutting, wrenching despair settled into my chest and took root quickly. I couldn't stop it. I couldn't resist the way it twisted through my heart.

I had failed Nora.

She was dead because of me. Because I'd been a coward.

Young, terrified, and unable to fight off so many of Sulam's men, yes. But still a coward who had watched her suffer and die and done absolutely nothing to stop it.

It was my fault.

My fault.

MY FAULT!

"VIOLET!" Axien's cry sent a sudden pang of cold through me.

I froze, my gaze instinctively searching the entangled bodies all around for him.

O-oh no. Had I hurt him, too?

I-I wouldn't—I couldn't!

Gods, where was he?!

A hand clapped over my eyes suddenly, and everything went dark just as strong, callused fingers wove through mine and forced me to drop the dagger.

"It's okay," Axien's voice breathed in my ear, deep and steady. "I'm right here. I've got you."

The roaring, crackling flames in my soul dimmed. The heat subsided. My body trembled against his, but I could feel the thump of his pulse against my back as he held me close against him.

Safe.

I was safe ... as long as he was there.

Axien.

My Axien.

He was still with me ... to whatever bittersweet end awaited us now.

Fifty-Four

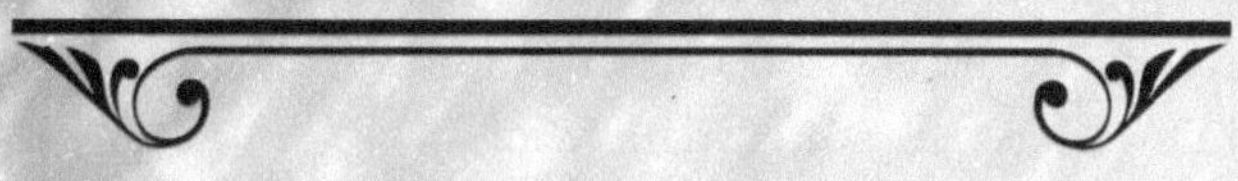

"Take her now! Don't let her get away!" Sulam's voice called like an echo from the shadows. "No lethal shots! We need her alive!"

"Listen to me, Violet," Axien spoke, his lips brushing the shell of my ear and his words drowning out everything else. "I'm going to move my hand, and you're going to open your eyes. But you're going to look at me—me, and only me. Understand? Nothing else."

"O-okay," I whimpered, but I could already feel my will crumbling.

My body trembled, knees quaking so much I could barely stand.

"Deep breaths," he coaxed as his hand slid away from my eyes and the smeared colors of the night flooded in. Reds. Blacks. Gray-ish purples.

I squinted, blinking hard and coughing, as the world seemed to spin slowly into focus. I caught a glimpse of an armored body, its arms and legs twisted all wrong, with something awful jutting out of its mouth like a pike of black thorns.

Wh-what was that? Oh, gods, had I—

"Hey now, take it easy," Axien murmured, his face eclipsing my view and his arms sweeping to lift me off my feet. "It's just you and me right now. Okay?"

I tried to move, to put my arms around his neck. But one of them wouldn't move. It hung limp, and I stared down at where something black had soaked through the bandages wrapped around my forearm. It ran down my arm, dripping from my fingers like thick, dark ichor.

"Hand her over, boy," Sulam's voice cracked like a whip in the cool night air. "And maybe I'll consider letting you go. I do enjoy the hunt, after all."

Axien's body tensed, but he held me tight. His expression flickered between a quiet, smoldering anger and a nearly desperate terror. But he never looked away. Never trembled.

"You will *never* touch her," he snapped defiantly.

Sulam's chuckle rolled like thunder through the courtyard. "Oh, I'll touch her plenty, boy. And for your insolence, I'll make you watch."

Axien's face seized in a twitching snarl of fury. His arms went solid around me, braced and preparing, as his eyes flashed brighter with arcane fire.

Then the roar of a beast tore through the night, shattering around us and making Axien's features go slack in alarm. His gaze darted away for the briefest instant as he turned, facing the sound. His brows drew upward, creasing and quivering. His mouth mashed into a frantic, pleading line.

His eyes welled.

"What's happening?" I had to know. If I couldn't see it, if I couldn't look for myself, then he had to tell me.

"It's him," he gasped brokenly. "It's Roxus. He's come for you."

Fifty-Five

My whole world crumbled away like the surf slowly devouring a sandcastle.

Bit by bit, grain by grain, it dissolved under the crashing rumble of battle.

All the weary, fractured pieces of my consciousness slipped and slurred, fading into a star-streaked haze as Axien began to run—still holding me like his life depended on it.

Maybe it did.

The roaring of a furious war bear mingled with the screams of men, the clash of swords, and the occasional concussive crack of gunfire. The acrid odor of black powder stung my nose. It consumed us from every side, as if we were trapped in the eye of a hurricane.

"Hold on. Just hold on, Violet," Axien said, repeating it like a prayer as his hot, panting breaths puffed into my hair.

I tried.

Pressed against the warmth of his body, I willed my pulse to match his. To keep feeling the rhythm of his pulse. To keep sucking in slow, steady breaths of the salty night wind.

The noise of battle faded behind us until, at last, his pace slowed. Axien staggered to a stop and pitched backward, resting against a wall in some dark alley and shutting his eyes tightly. His expression seized and twitched, those dark veins standing out against his tanned skin on his neck and jaw.

So much magic—so much of himself torn and broken—all for us to survive.

"We're okay," he panted hard, shaking his head with his weight still against the wall. "We're gonna be fine now. He wasn't alone. There were others fighting with him. He can win, and then they'll find us here. Roxus will smell us out." He barked a thin, cracking, slightly manic laugh. "He always does."

No argument there.

I had no idea how Roxus had found us at Sulam's. I didn't even know how long we'd been gone while we were trapped in that puzzlebox. But in whatever time had passed, Roxus hadn't forgotten about me. He'd been waiting. Or searching. Or both.

And he'd come just in time.

Axien let out a hissing grunt of pain as he slid down the wall, still holding me as he sank into a sitting position with me in his lap. His arms went slack around me, and he blew out deep breaths through his mouth that made his cheeks puff.

"I'm just gonna take a breather right here," he said, his voice slurring a little.

"Okay," I replied and let my head rest right in the crook of his neck. My eyes rolled closed as I let the feel of him fill all those broken places in my soul.

Time dragged as we huddled in the shadows, him fighting for breath while I struggled to stay conscious. I had to keep my eyes open. Focus. If it came down to it, I needed to get on my feet again. I needed to be able to run, at least.

Then, somewhere in the distance, the familiar voices of Roxus and Leruna called out to us. Looking for us in the night. Following our trail.

Axien was right—they'd find us soon.

And whatever came after ... gods, I couldn't even begin to fathom it. Had they killed Sulam? Was he finally gone?

Or was this nightmare just beginning?

"They're here!" I jolted slightly as Roxus shouted over us.

Cracking an eye open, I forced a bleary smile as he bent down and put a rough palm gently against my cheek.

Thank the Fates, he didn't look any different than before we'd left. No older. No shabbier. Just the right amount of scruffy old bear-man I'd always known.

"Pass her to me," Roxus gritted the words as though biting back emotion.

Axien didn't protest and shifted his position to pass me into Roxus's waiting arms.

"Can you walk, boy?" he asked as he adjusted my weight and put a hand over my head like he was cradling a child.

"Y-yeah. I think so," Axien said.

"Good. On your feet, then. We've got a boat waiting and no time to spare. Sulam gave us the slip, but you can bet your last copper he'll be on our heels within the hour," Roxus warned. "Follow me. And whatever you do, keep your head down. This place is crawling with spies."

Burying my head into Roxus's worn old coat, I breathed in deeply the familiar sweet musk of his tobacco. My fingers gripped the threadbare fabric, and I peered over his shoulder to meet Axien's worried stare as he followed only a pace or two behind.

As the corners of my vision began to blur and slip into hazy darkness, he gave me that awful, thin smile that never reached his glowing blue eyes.

The smile that hid everything he truly felt.

Fear. Dread. Anticipation of what might be coming for us next.

Because even though we'd fought with everything we had, it wasn't enough.

Sulam was still alive.

And we still weren't safe.

Fifty-Six

There were four arrows sticking out of me.

I stared down at them, ears ringing as I took in the strange sight of three black-feather fletched arrows sticking out from my legs—two in one thigh and another poking halfway through the meat of my calf. Shots that must have been intended to put me on the ground so I couldn't run away.

I had another stuck in the back of my shoulder, but I hadn't felt any of them hit me, let alone punch through my flesh. Even now, watching Leruna check each one with practiced speed and efficiency, the pain seemed strangely faraway. Like it was someone else's body being turned and inspected.

I barely winced at the numb, achy twinges whenever Leruna pulled one free. She worked fast, fingers flying to pull each arrow out one by one in the weak light of a single lantern. The only lantern burning down here.

I stared at it, watching the little candle dance inside four walls of grimy, yellowed glass.

I'd never been on a ship before. At least, not one like this. Not a real, two-masted vessel with an actual bunk area below deck. We'd used little ferries to pass between the islands plenty of times, but they moved slowly and used oars to glide through the swift currents between Rienka's many islands. They weren't made for the open ocean like this one.

Lying on one of the narrow bottom bunks, I watched that one lantern hanging off an iron hook sway gently back and forth as the ship rocked at its moorings. This ship had room for twenty people to sleep, but now Roxus, Axien, and I were the only ones waiting down here.

Thanks to his borrowed armor, Axien hadn't taken any hits from the crossbows. Leruna muttered something about how my thick coat had spared me the worst of the damage, since none of the arrows had punctured all that deep. Flesh wounds.

I was lucky.

Then again, Sulam had shouted to his men not to fire lethal shots at me. Maybe they'd all missed on purpose?

I didn't know. I still didn't even remember being shot. It must have happened when ... when everything went red.

I shuddered, looking over to where Axien sat on a bunk across the aisle. He'd taken off all that fine Avoran armor and left it in the pile on the floor at his feet. Underneath, his tunic was drenched in sweat and speckled with pink dots of blood.

My blood.

It must have seeped under his collar somehow when I had my arms around him.

"She needs to rest. The wounds from the arrows are fairly superficial, but that gash in her arm is worrisome. I'll take a closer look once we get to the temple," Leruna said as she stood, wiping her hands and rolling up her bundle of medical tools. "I'm going on deck to speak with the captain again. We should be underway soon. Stay here and keep quiet, for now."

"Thank you," I rasped as she began to step away.

Leruna paused, glancing down at me with her fair face

framed in thick, windswept dark curls. I'd known her for years, been treated by her on countless occasions, but this was the first time I could ever remember seeing her not wearing her healer's robes.

She'd swapped them for a pair of fitted leather trousers, heeled boots, and a billowy white tunic worn under a tightly laced blue corset. Not exactly the usual uniform for a priestess of Undae. The pair of blunderbusses slung across her hips on a wide belt studded with what looked suspiciously like small vials of black powder wasn't standard-issue, either.

And the tattoos peeking from above the sweeping neckline of her blouse?

I'd definitely have to ask her about all that later.

For now, she was right. We had to lie low, keep quiet, and wait for the worst of the storm to pass.

"I'm glad you're safe, Violet. I'll be back as soon as I can," Leruna said, her words clipped and her tone reserved. "Get some sleep, if you can. We should be back to Sol'Karr in a few hours."

A faint smile pricked at the corners of her mouth as her turquoise eyes darted around, landing on each of us briefly before she turned and hurried above deck. Her footsteps retreated, and a cold, tense silence closed in, filled with only the rhythmic creaking of the ship as it lolled in the waves.

With Vesperus's heavy wool coat draped over me like a blanket, all I could do was stare at that swinging lantern, tracking its sway back and forth. I strained to hear anything that sounded even remotely like combat or distress coming from the upper deck. But as the minutes slipped by, everything settled into a strange, lukewarm calm.

My thoughts ran in circles like a hound chasing rabbits, retracing every moment. Feeling the weight of each one settle over me until my chest grew tight and my breathing hitched. Buried somewhere in the pockets of that coat, Vesperus's artifact thrummed with power. And he was still locked inside it with that monster. For him, maybe it had only been a few seconds.

But for us—

I flinched as Roxus's hand suddenly came to rest on my shoulder. He stared down at me, earthy brown eyes and deep-set features lined with worry. I hadn't noticed him shifting to sit closer to me on the cramped little bunk.

"How long were we gone?" I asked, my voice thick and hoarse.

"Almost three weeks," Roxus replied quietly.

My breath caught, and I stared at him, my mouth open.

Three weeks?

It had only felt like we were trapped in that artifact for five hours or so. Maybe a day, at the very most, but that felt like a stretch. In that place, time seemed ... irrelevant. The rooms didn't change. The fires in the hearths never died. The stupid man-eating hedges always bloomed. The snowstorm never subsided.

That prison might as well have been eternal.

Maybe it was.

"We started searching for you five days ago," Roxus continued, leaning forward to rest his elbows on his knees. "The Ragentrudes weren't much help. The only one of them who saw what happened was found dead at the scene. We scoured the crypt for two days, looking for some clue of what had happened. We did the same at the inn where you stayed. Found all your belongings, but no sign of foul play."

"We never even made it out of the crypt. The Ulfrangar jumped us there during the ball. But we were pulled into the artifact before they could do anything to us." Axien let out a slow, shuddering breath where he sat on the bed across from mine, rubbing a hand along his jaw to the back of his neck.

"They must have taken the artifact directly to Sulam after that."

"We thought they'd taken you, too. But it took us a while to pick up their trail. The Ulfrangar are nothing if not brutally efficient. Thankfully, Sulam is less so. We found enough evidence to convince Mistress Orvana to sanction surveillance on him." Roxus reached into the inside breast pocket of his coat and took out his favorite long wooden pipe, turning it over in his hands while he spoke. "We assumed he was holding you hostage in his estate until he could pass you off to the Tibrans. So we had to wait until he had left to make our move."

"Let me guess, you were watching that fancy carriage trot by when all pandemonium broke loose inside that manor?" Axien's dry chuckle caught in his throat and turned into a cough.

"Alarm horns blaring, guards running around like a bunch of panicked hens." Roxus smirked and put the pipe between his teeth. "Took us a bit to sort out where you were exactly. At least ... until we saw the explosion in the courtyard."

"Better late than never," Axien said.

Roxus's expression contorted some, skewing with his mouth twisted to the side around his pipe, the way he always did when he was using chewing on it as an excuse to think. He dug around in his pockets again, fishing out a tin packed with fragrant dried fruit and tobacco, before he finally leveled an earnest stare across at Axien.

"I owe you for this," he muttered around his pipe.

Axien blinked in surprise. "For what?"

"For looking after her. And bringing her back to us in one piece." Roxus tipped his head toward me slightly.

I scowled. He'd always been terrible at thank-yous. But I wasn't dead—I was lying right here!

"I don't need a babysitter," I growled.

"Nope," Roxus agreed as he busied himself packing tobacco into his pipe. "But a voice of reason never did you any harm, now did it?"

I scowled harder. Really?

"You don't owe me anything, Roxus." Axien gave another hoarse, uncomfortable chuckle. "I invited her to work with me. And as far as ... everything else. Well, I knew what I was getting myself into."

Roxus's eyes flicked to him again, fixing him with an intense stare that only lasted for a second or two. Something shifted in the air between them. A sense of knowing that I didn't understand.

Whatever it was, though, Axien just hung his head and looked quickly away.

Roxus shifted in his seat, clearing his throat before he lit his pipe. He took a few long, deep puffs from it, blowing fragrant rings of purplish smoke into the air.

"You should know, things at home have changed. The situation with the Tibran Empire has only worsened. Nar'Haleen has fallen. The emperor surrendered to Tibran rule in an effort to stop the bloodshed, but the damage is beyond words. And now, given this ... situation with Sulam, I think we can expect Mistress Orvana to close ranks swiftly," he said at last, keeping his voice low.

"Close ranks?" I pressed.

"She'll want to withdraw all her agents to the temple grounds. Perhaps even into Arx Eburna itself," he explained. "With Nar'Haleen's navy now at Argonox's command, it's not a stretch to assume Damaria will be next to fall—and Rienka along with it."

A hard, painful lump lodged in the back of my throat.

Our home, *my* home, would fall to the Tibrans?

"That's ridiculous! We can't just hide out like cowards and

wait for them to—!" I started to protest, but Roxus cut me off swiftly.

"We don't fight in wars, Vi. We're not soldiers," he said, his tone heavy and stern. "We guard the secrets and artifacts of the gods. We keep them from falling into the hands of those who would abuse them. But we do not take up arms and fight against armies. Our purpose extends beyond the quarrels of thrones and crowns, whether they choose to respect that or not."

Argonox certainly hadn't. He was targeting us directly—with Sulam's help!

How could we not fight back? How could we just stand by and hide while Rienka burned? This was different. This was our kingdom.

It was my *home*, whether it wanted me or not.

"Empires rise and fall like ocean tides," he continued as he stood, shaking out the lengths of his ragged old coat. "If we're lucky, we'll see this one break against different shores and balance will be restored, but that choice isn't ours to make. All we can do is what we've always done—keep to our oath. Protect what we can and who we can."

I sucked my teeth, tongue writhing against all the bitter words I wanted to scream until my throat bled. It wasn't right. We could do something. We should do something.

But Roxus was right. I'd sworn an oath—given my word. I wore their mark on my skin.

And I wouldn't forsake it.

"Sometimes, serving a higher purpose means accepting that not every battle is yours to fight." Roxus's gaze caught mine as he shuffled past, making his way to the steep stairwell that led above deck and leaving a curling ribbon of that fragrant pipe smoke in his wake. "But that doesn't mean we don't have our own part to play."

Fifty-Seven

I couldn't sleep.

My soul stirred like a dark whirlpool, restless and treacherous, even after our ship slipped free of the harbor into the swift, dark waters that would carry us back to Sol'Karr. Back home. I couldn't force my mind to focus on that—on seeing Delthene, sleeping in my own bed, or the taste of a home-cooked meal.

My body ached. Every muscle felt twitchy and overstretched, quivering with the echoes of adrenaline that chilled me to the marrow. All the places I'd been hit with arrows had finally begun throbbing fiercely. And my arm, gods, it burned.

None of Leruna's salves or tonics had helped. The shadowed expression of concern she'd worn while inspecting and cleaning it still made my stomach turn and flip. She seemed baffled by the dark, necrotic ooze that seeped from it, and interrogated both of us thoroughly about what had done this to me in the first place.

But, gods, how could I tell her? Should I tell anyone what had been inside that artifact? Even Axien seemed reluctant, watching me out of the corner of his glowing blue eyes, as though searching for some indication or for me to take the lead on how to handle this.

Too bad I had no idea.

Eventually, I would tell Roxus. I had to. Maybe he would have a better idea of how to handle it.

Not yet, though. Not here. Once we were back in Arx Eburna, safe and out of Sulam's reach ...

Then I would tell him everything.

Flashes of Sulam's leering face struck my mind like tongues of lightning. I flinched, trying to squeeze my eyes shut. I clenched my fists in the thick wool coat draped over me, twisting it through my fingers.

Nothing helped. Nothing got his delighted sneer out of my mind, or drowned out his vile, hissing words. They snaked through my mind, choking me slowly. Repeating again and again.

"Did you watch them take her?"

I cringed, rolling onto my side and curling my knees toward my chest as my freshly bandaged arm throbbed harder.

"Did she call out for you in the end?"

Had she? I-I didn't remember. Had she even known my name?

It was so long ago, and no one in Sulam's house had ever called me anything except pitathi—at least, not that I remembered.

I didn't know.

"Remember, this was a mercy."

My eyes flew open wide, body jolting at the whisper of a different voice that curled through my mind like a wisp of black shadow. It sent frigid chills over my skin, prickling every tiny hair on my body at once.

Chrysa.

Had she known about Nora somehow? Is that what she'd meant all along? That I had deserved a far worse fate than bleeding out slowly on the ground, her blade punched through my body like a pike?

Maybe she had been right. Maybe I had deserved worse.

Staring around the near-dark of the ship's bunkroom, I could barely pick out the shapes of Roxus and Axien sound asleep. Axien was curled on his bunk across from mine, breathing deeply. He'd used so much magic in such a short amount of time. He had to be exhausted.

Roxus had taken up a post by the doorway, however. With his head bowed to his chest, he sat with his back leaning against the wall and his longsword sheathed across his lap, hand resting on the grip. Ready to fight at a moment's notice.

It wasn't hard to imagine he'd been running himself ragged searching for us.

He snored faintly, never even stirring as I scooted to the edge of the rickety wooden bunk and slipped my arms back into the roomy sleeves of Vesperus's long wool coat. Wrapping it around myself like a robe, I picked my way quietly across the creaky wooden floors toward the doorway. My bare feet made it easier to stay quiet as I slipped past Roxus, up the stairs, and out onto the ship's deck.

The briny wind blasted my face and tangled in my hair as I walked the deck, stealing a glance up to the quarterdeck, where a few sailors were gathered around the wheel. A few more lounged on the deck, but paid no attention to me as I made my way to the bow and leaned against the railing.

I stared out across the dark waves, vast and ever-shifting, sparkling with touches of sterling moonlight. The ominous shapes of islands passed in the distance, flecked with warm spots of light from the cities that clustered on the steep cliffs. Temples stood on treacherous mountaintops, their braziers making the limestone pillars and high walls shine like gold.

I'd studied maps of Rienka's many islands for the last three years. I knew them all by heart, but right then ... I had no idea which islands they were.

I didn't know where I was.

Part of me didn't want to know.

My hand drifted into the deep pocket of my borrowed coat, wrapping around the familiar shape hidden within it.

The icosahedron was heavier than I'd expected as I drew it out and held it like a fist-sized egg in both hands. I turned it slowly, inspecting all twenty of its finely adorned sides, each with a different symbol inlaid in swirling gold filigree. All that glittering finery made it seem so deceptively fragile—but I could see beyond it.

The entire thing gave off a brilliant blue aura of magical power, just a hint of what was locked away inside.

My lungs clenched, fingers squeezing it harder.

Vesperus was still in there. For him, it had probably only been a minute. Maybe less. He'd been injured worse than he wanted us to know. He might even be dying.

But he'd insisted that once we were outside this artifact, we had to make sure it was put out of reach to people like Argonox and the Tibrans forever. He'd made me promise.

And I would keep my word to him, just like I intended to keep it to the Zenith's Call.

No matter how utterly wrong it felt.

"You don't have to carry this burden, too," a deep voice spoke behind me suddenly.

I fumbled, almost dropping the artifact on the deck as I turned to find Axien approaching. He hadn't bothered putting his boots back on. His features squinted slightly in a sad, knowing smile as his hair blew around his face.

He nodded to the artifact in my hands.

"You carry so much on those lovely little shoulders. But you don't have to carry it all," he said, holding out a hand.

I eyed him, wondering for an instant if he had some sort of

ulterior motive for wanting me to pass the artifact over to him. Didn't he trust me with it? Or was he worried I wouldn't keep my word?

He moved closer, standing before me. I had to tilt my head way back to hold his gaze as he murmured, "I heard what Sulam said to you."

My pulse gave a shivering, wrenching skip. I drew back slightly, bumping against the railing as I scrambled for words. For some sort of explanation other than the truth.

That I was responsible for what had happened to Declan's little sister all those years ago.

"I know you keep secrets. I also know what it means to carry the shame of someone else's death," he said, his hand still open to me. "There are a thousand burdens we might carry, but that one is always the heaviest. I know I can't take the weight of that burden from you, even if I tried. But this one," he said, and tapped the artifact with his finger. "This one I can. So let me carry this for you, Violet. Not because I owe it to you. Because I want to."

My eyes welled as I watched the way his steady, calm smile dimpled one of his cheeks. The way the warm sea wind tousled his hair over his brow and cheeks. The way his gaze darted to my lips before that soul-splitting sorrow ignited in his eyes again.

He kept secrets, too. Vesperus had hinted at his bloodline's tie to Milontos. Sulam had called him a "seer." I didn't understand what any of that meant, and I had a suspicion that Axien wouldn't tell me, even if I asked. Not yet, anyway.

And yet, it didn't matter. It was already far too late.

Roxus had taught me trust for trust ... and Axien already had all of mine.

"You're the only one keeping score, Axien," I said as I placed the artifact in his open palm. "I don't keep a tally. Not when it comes to people doing me favors."

He hesitated, his throat moving and his jawline going suddenly tight.

It took everything I had to hold back an exhausted sob as a twitchy, embarrassed smile fought its way over my mouth.

"Especially not with people I care about," I added, the words slipping out before I could even think to hold them back.

Axien's expression went slack. He leaned back slightly, recoiling as if I'd just slapped him or spat in his face. His chest heaved and shuddered, breath halting between erratic gasps as he gaped down at me.

O-oh no.

Was that ... wrong? Should I not have told him that?

I'd never ... well, I'd never said something like that to anyone before. Had I crossed a line? Even if it was true, and it was, maybe I shouldn't have—

Axien didn't even look away from me as he hurled the puzzlebox artifact over the side of the ship, casting it out into the dark waves before he surged for me. His lips found mine, tasting faintly of sea salt, as he wrapped his arms around me and held me close.

I gripped him back, flinging my arms around his neck and drinking in every tiny place our bodies touched. His bigger, warmer, stronger body seemed to close around mine like a protective shield as his mouth hungrily roamed mine. Every puff of his warm breath against my skin and swipe of his tongue along mine sent shivers all the way down to my toes.

There wasn't an inch of him I didn't want.

And there wasn't a part of me I wouldn't give him.

Bathed in the starlight, Axien pulled back just enough that our noses brushed and he could look at me eye-to-eye. His hands settled at my waist, holding me with his head bowed to mine.

"Violet, there's ... there's something I need you to know,"

he whispered, his voice desperate and pleading. His expression drew into a terrified grimace, as though whatever came next would be his undoing. "I—"

I pressed a finger over his lips to silence him, letting my forehead rest against his with my eyes closed.

Whatever came next, if it was going to hurt him, I didn't want it. Not yet. Not here.

This memory would be sweet. It would be perfect.

It would be ours alone.

Little by little, his body slowly relaxed again, understanding passing between us like the soothing caress of the wind. He let out a deep, unsteady breath as he drew me in again, arms pressing me against his chest so tight it was as if I'd been swallowed whole.

"Whatever happens now, please remember, you are never alone." His deep voice thrummed so close, his chest pressed right against my ear, so the sound permeated every corner of my mind. "I am *always* on your side."

It soaked down to the foundations of my soul like sweet, warm summer rain.

"Oh, I will. Especially if Mistress Orvana finds out what we just did with that artifact," I whispered, tilting my head back again to flash him a daring smirk.

"Well, the way I see it, no one else here even knew we had it. But if they get suspicious, well, you're the only witness to my accidentally dropping it overboard," he quipped. "What's she going to do?"

"She could kick both of us out," I reminded him.

"I suppose." Axien laughed and shrugged. "But since the only other Avoran sorcerer I know of just sank to the bottom of the deepest bay in the world, she's going to have a hard time scraping up a replacement."

I arched an eyebrow. "And what about me?"

He drew me in close again, hands sliding up my shoulders

to cradle my face with that delightful, infuriating vulpine grin playing over his lips.

"Oh, you're mine now, little viper," he warned in a throaty growl. "And I am a greedy, selfish sorcerer. If Mistress Orvana even dares to try to take you away, I promise, the Tibrans will be the very least of her problems."

FIFTY-EIGHT

There was no time for hesitation.

"Once we get back to the house, we need to move fast," Roxus warned as soon as we stepped off the boat at the docks in Sol'Karr.

"Do you need my assistance packing? Or should I go to Arx Eburna and report back about what's happened?" Axien asked, his shoulder lightly bumping mine as we shuffled onto the docks.

"Go and find Vanora. I'm sure she'd like to know her new tandem is still alive," Roxus said. He flicked a suspicious, squinty glare between us, like he'd picked up on a shift in our ... interactions.

Like the fact that we weren't snarling or sniping at each other anymore.

I cringed, toes curling inside my boots as I squeezed the strap of my bag, which thankfully he'd retrieved from the inn where Axien and I had stayed right before going to the Ragentrudes. All my belongings were intact—and most importantly, I had my Spelldrinker daggers belted back to my thighs.

"I need to return to the temple," Leruna announced,

standing on my other side with her billowy healer's robes thrown back over her other clothes to hide the weapons and leathers from plain sight. "The high priestess deserves to know why I've been absent, even if I cannot tell her the full truth of it. She might be understanding if she knows it pertains to you."

Roxus gave a quick, devious little smile and nodded. "Indeed. You can tell her I've been suffering greatly. She'll forgive your absence."

I pursed my lips, trying to sort out what he meant by that. Why would the High Priestess of Undae care if he was the one injured? What difference would it make if it was him instead of anyone else?

Unless he knew the high priestess personally, of course. Or had been involved with her somehow—

Oh. Oh, gods, ew. *EW.*

Had he fooled around with the high priestess? Seriously? When?!

No, never mind, it was better not to know.

I grimaced, flashing a look to Axien to see if he'd picked up on that, as well, but he was too busy sucking his teeth to keep from grinning.

Only Leruna seemed equally disgusted and stared at my scruffy mentor for a few long, uncomfortable seconds.

"Lecherous old bear," she muttered, her lip curled as she turned away.

Roxus just chuckled. "We were all young and reckless once. Just watch your back. We're not the only ones Sulam will be watching now."

"I'll keep that in mind," she said, already walking away.

We stood, watching her pale robes and long mane of dense, dark curls disappear into the early morning crowds. It wasn't until I'd lost track of her amidst the throngs of sailors, deckhands, and shoppers that I realized ... she wasn't heading toward the temple.

Hmmm.

Was there someone else she was going to see? Or was she taking a different path to get there?

I gave Roxus a questioning glance, arching an eyebrow.

He just shrugged and tipped his head in the other direction, gesturing for us to follow.

The sun hadn't fully risen, but the fishermen were already unloading their first hauls of the day. They dumped nets full of slim, silver fish onto the docks, where workers quickly sorted them into barrels or tossed them back into the water.

The reek of fish, chum, sweat, and sour brine stung at my nose and saturated every breath as we wound through the crowds, pushing past early-morning shoppers from the local restaurants, taverns, and merchants looking to buy enough to feed their customers. The thick, humid air filled with shouts for prices, pounds, and haggling. The routine this district repeated day after day, without fail.

But I couldn't relax or let myself sink into it. Not when Roxus moved onward with a purpose, a hand resting on the pommel of his sword half-hidden beneath his coat. To anyone else, it might look casual or like a nervous habit.

I knew better.

I kept my gaze moving on the crowds around us, senses reaching for anything out of place while we made our way off the docks. Axien stayed right at my back, so close I could hear the soft clink of the Avoran swords that hung from his belt. He'd packed away the armor into his bag, though.

Probably for the best since an ensemble like that was sure to attract a lot of attention.

My feet knew the path from the bustling harbor inland, along the curved, steep sidewalks all the way to the narrow house on the corner where I'd spent the last three years. Roxus's house.

Somehow, seeing it now, it felt so ... small. Unassuming.

And strangely exposed.

Roxus knocked three times before he opened the front door and stepped inside. Strange—but, then again, he'd probably needed to take measures to keep Delthene before he left.

I followed him in, already slinging my heavy bag off my shoulder so I could dump it just inside the door.

A scowling face suddenly appeared in front of me, emerging in the shadows with beady, cobalt blue eyes narrowed suspiciously.

My blood rushed, instincts taking over immediately. I drove a knee into the male figure's gut, letting out a scream of rage before diving forward and hitting him with full force.

We flew backward, hitting the ground with me on his chest, my blade already at his throat before I realized ... Gods and fates, I knew that stupid, squinty scowling face.

"Varren!" I hissed through bared teeth. "What are you doing here?"

Dressed in his usual black Vindexori leathers, Varren lay under me with his weapon half-drawn and his teeth bared back like we were two snarling wild dogs, ready to brawl to the death.

"Vedra'tavas!" he seethed back, spewing a furious Damarian curse like he was spitting poison. "I was invited, you feral little wretch."

"Do you have any idea how close I was to slitting your throat?" I snapped as I stepped off him, spinning my dagger over my hand in a flourish before I slipped it back into its sheath at my hip.

"No closer than usual," he growled and rubbed a hand at his neck, scowling when he discovered a smear of blood from a tiny nick the edge of my blade had left in his skin.

"I invited him here," Roxus muttered as he shuffled past, not even giving us a second glance on his way into the sitting room to shrug off his coat. "We needed the extra security while I was away."

I blinked back and forth between them, fumbling for words and trying to make sense of it. Extra security? And he'd called on *Varren* for that?

"Because of Sulam?" I guessed, holding out a hand to help pull Varren back to his feet.

"Something like that," Roxus replied. "Get packed. I need to speak with Delthene. She ... isn't going to like this."

"I'm going to Arx Eburna," Axien announced from where he lingered in the doorway. "Vanora and I will be waiting for you there. I'm sure she'll want to be present when you speak to Mistress Orvana."

"All right." Roxus's wide shoulders rose and fell with a deep, resigned breath—as though that was a chore he had already begun to dread.

Well, that made two of us.

Before he could turn away, I grabbed the sleeve of his tunic and dug around in the pockets of my coat. I handed him a fistful of Vanora's fine jewels and winced, noting that some of them were bent. They must have gotten crunched during one of our battles.

"Tell her I'm sorry about ... well, these. And the dress," I murmured.

Axien gave a parting nod, carefully tucking the jewelry into his own pocket, and ducked out, shutting the door behind him. I locked it, just for good measure.

"Anything happen while I was gone?" Roxus muttered as Varren and I made our way into the sitting room.

Varren straightened immediately, assuming what I could only assume was a formal, attentive stance with his hands in fists at his side. We weren't at Arx Eburna, but if he'd come here on orders, then he was at Roxus's disposal.

"Nothing out of the ordinary until last night," Varren reported. "That big elven fellow returned here late, gathered their things, and left. He wouldn't say much except that you'd found them and were coming back here soon."

Huh? Big elven fellow?

Was he talking about Declan?

Roxus rubbed at the thick, dark stubble on his chin and jaw as he stared at the low table where two cups of tea sat, both empty. A beat of silence passed, and I could see the tension rising in the way Varren's brow slowly creased with a furrow, and a muscle twitched in his jaw.

"Hang around for a few minutes, would you?" Roxus said at last. "We're going to move to Arx Eburna. Delthene will need help carrying her things. I can't leave her here unattended."

I swallowed hard as bile burned at the back of my throat. Delthene wouldn't take this well. She hadn't liked it when Roxus had left because of the Tibrans. This news—that she had to leave her home again—might break her.

"Go and fetch her for me, if you don't mind." Roxus blew out another breath, running his hand along his jaw and through his shaggy hair.

"Of course," Varren replied quickly. He made a formal show of clasping a fist over his chest before turning on a heel and leaving the room, disappearing into the kitchen.

"Be gentle with her," I warned as I started for the stairs to begin my own packing.

Roxus caught my gaze, his mouth already tight in an uncertain but curious frown.

"She told me about what happened before," I clarified. "About how you met. She was beside herself after you left. I'm worried about her, Roxus."

His expression softened as his gaze drifted away from mine, landing back on that pair of empty teacups.

"Yeah," he murmured in agreement. "So am I."

Fifty-Nine

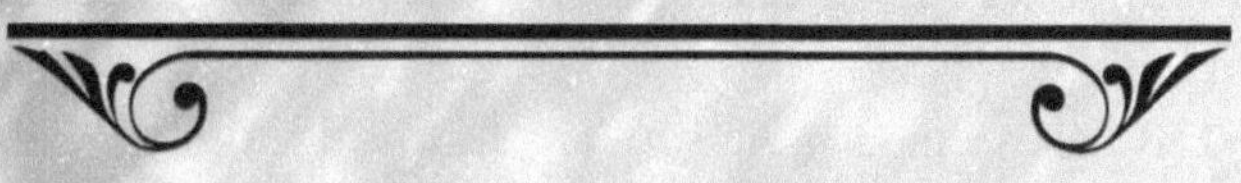

There was a huge man on my bed.

I barely made it a single step into my bedroom before my entire body jerked to a violent halt. I froze in place, staring at the shape of a large, young man sitting on the edge of my bed, staring down at his scarred, battered hands.

My heart hit the back of my throat as hard as a closed-fist punch. All the air rushed out of me in a ragged gasp.

Declan looked up slowly, those sad, tired eyes meeting mine for the first time in ... gods, I didn't even know how long. It felt like an eternity since we had seen one another.

Maybe even a lifetime—one I'd desperately tried to forget.

"Sorry to come in uninvited," he said quietly, "Just needed to talk."

Oh gods. Did ... did he know? Had someone told him already?

No—no, that wasn't possible. Axien and I were the only ones who had heard anything Sulam had said. And surely Sulam wouldn't sell out his own evil plan to someone he was trying to manipulate with it?

I-I didn't know.

So I couldn't speak as he slowly stood and made his way toward me, moving stiffly as though it were painful. Every step made his expression seize slightly, and he kept one arm close to his torso, almost protectively.

It made me glance him over again, paying more attention.

He looked ... terrible, actually. Even worse than before we'd left.

His face seemed more sunken, and he'd lost some of that brawn. One of his hands was bandaged securely—Leruna's work, no doubt. I'd worn enough of her medical dressings to recognize the knots she used to tie off the outer layers.

His skin seemed somewhat ashen, and dark circles ringed his eyes. The faint, greenish hints of old bruises mottled his features, especially around his nose. Fates, had he broken it again?

I probably didn't look much better, though. My too-big, borrowed coat was filthy, and the clothes underneath were still damp with blood. I desperately needed a bath before I even bothered with a fresh change of clothes.

But I couldn't do any of that. Not with him standing there, showing me that crooked smile that squeezed at my heart like someone ready to rip an apple from a tree branch.

He didn't know.

He wouldn't be smiling at me like that if he did.

"I'm glad they found you," he said. "Everyone was really worried. I, uh, I've been here for a while. Not in your room, specifically. I've been in Roxus's. But ... you should know some things happened while you were gone."

My mouth opened, but I couldn't muster a sound. I stood there, blinking at him stupidly as he stopped in front of me—a towering figure to my barely five feet. Even weaker, even injured, he could crush the life out of me. He should have.

I deserved that and worse.

"I can't go back to the pit," he confessed as though he were ashamed. "Not because of, er, this." He motioned to himself, namely his bandaged arm. "I got my butt handed to me pretty good, yeah. But it's more than that. I'd never considered how I was going to get myself and Nora out of this situation permanently. Obviously, I can't keep doing it forever. And now—"

"Declan, I ..." The words died in my throat, stinging like I'd tried swallowing a mouthful of urchins. His face went blurry as my eyes welled. I had to look away, gulping in frantic breaths, as I fought to swallow the pain down.

I had to tell him. He had to know. His sister was dead, had been dead for years, and I couldn't let him keep walking around believing anything else. It was cruel. He needed to know the truth—that Sulam had been blackmailing him to fight and risk his life in that pit under false pretenses.

Threatening him with the death of someone he loved who had already died long before.

I had no idea how Sulam had managed to convince him that Nora was still alive. There was no telling what lies and machinations that disgusting man had spun to keep Declan submissive. But I knew the truth of it now.

And he should hear it from me.

It was the right thing to do.

... I was just the wrong, wicked person.

"What's wrong?" Declan asked, moving closer and reaching for me like he was afraid I might faint or something.

I cringed back, staying out of his reach. I couldn't let him do it. I wouldn't let him comfort me, not after what I'd done.

"What happened?" he pressed, frowning now. "Where's Roxus? Is he all right?"

"He's fine," Varren spoke behind me, seeming to appear out of nowhere.

I hadn't even heard him climb the stairs.

"But you need to get out of her room and let her get to

work. We're leaving soon," Varren announced, his tone firm as he kept himself positioned behind me as though he thought I needed his protection or something.

Gross.

"Leaving?" Declan glanced between us, confused.

"Yeah. It's not safe here anymore. So she needs to get packed up, and you need to get your things together, too. Roxus wants all of us out of here as soon as possible." Varren crossed his arms, his expression staying stony and superior as he stared down the much taller elf in front of us.

He was either completely fearless or way dumber than I'd ever given him credit for.

Ironically, those two traits often ran parallel.

"Where am I supposed to go?" Declan began to argue, his thick shoulders already going tense and straining the seams of his thin, white cotton tunic.

"The temple of Nai'Pol." Varren smacked his lips as though he wasn't happy about that. "Apparently, you are now under the protection of the Zenith's Call. Roxus won't say why. It's above my rank, apparently. You won't be permitted into Arx Eburna proper, since you aren't members of the order, but you'll be allowed to stay on the grounds for your safety."

Ahh. So that's what had him all bent out of shape.

"It's because of Sulam." I decided to clear the air as I side-stepped around Declan, heading for my armoire so I could find some clean clothes that actually fit.

"Sulam?" I could hear the startled scowl in Declan's voice without having to turn around and see it. "What about Leruna? Is she coming, too? Gods, would someone just tell me what's going on?"

"He's involved with the Tibrans. It's complicated, and not something we need to talk about here." I sighed deeply, glad to have my back to him so he wouldn't see my face screw up as I forced the words out, biting angrily on each wretched one.

It wasn't a lie.

But it wasn't the truth, either.

I couldn't say what needed to be said now, though. Not with Varren standing there with all the tact and intelligence of an angry llama.

"Unless you both want to carry the image of me naked in your brains forever, get out. I need to change," I fumed as I threw off the wool coat and started kicking off my boots.

Neither of them said another word, and by the time I turned around, the room was empty, and the door was shut.

Good riddance.

There were way too many difficult, stupid, chatty men in my life.

Knowing Roxus wanted us out of here likely before nightfall, I rushed through packing everything I cherished into my bag. There wasn't much, to be honest. I'd never been one to collect things, but Delthene had lavished me with a few fine pieces of jewelry, combs, and trinkets she insisted girls needed. I packed those, a few books, letters, and my favorite pieces of clothing into a larger bag.

Gibb meowed and scratched at the door while I redressed, sticking all three of his furry orange feet under the door in protest. I guess this was the time of day he preferred to nap on my bed. I hadn't even considered what Delthene was going to do with her grumpy old cat until then.

Roxus would have to sort out how we could take him with us. It was bad enough that Delthene was being forced out of another home. She shouldn't have to give up her cat, too.

With all my belongings packed, I threw my bag over my shoulder and staggered at the weight. I guess I'd accumulated more things than I realized. I steadied the load, then made my way to the door.

Gibb wasn't outside the door anymore by the time I opened it, but the sound of his restless cries echoed in the stairwell as I started back down to the sitting room.

"I can carry that, if you want," Varren offered, his tone stiff and awkward as he met me on the next landing, his arms still crossed, and his expression still pinched and sour.

Or maybe that was just how he looked these days.

"Are you kidding?" I arched an eyebrow at him, trying to find some reason or angle behind his kindness.

"Roxus said you were injured in the fight with Sulam," he offered, unable to meet my gaze. "I said he must have brought a whole army if you actually got hurt."

I blew an exasperated snort through my nose. Idiot. He'd certainly at least heard of me getting smacked around and nearly killed several times in all these years. The talking heads in Arx Eburna loved new gossip about their least favorite agent —Roxus's horrible little pet monster.

Not that I expected any less. But why would Varren even care?

Unless ... he'd noticed how upset I was with Declan. Was this an attempt at trying to cheer me up? Gods, I couldn't decide if that was sweet or disgusting. Either way, it was terrifying.

We did not need to start saying sweet things to each other. Nope. That was not us.

"He did bring an army, actually," I said.

"*Pffft.* Sure. How many?" Varren asked, sounding genuinely curious.

"How many were there?" I gave him my very best, toothiest, menacing, and slightly insane smile. "Or how many did I kill?"

Varren shuddered and shook his head. "Forget I asked," he muttered and stomped down the stairs ahead of me.

"It was more than ten," I called after him, following him down to the first floor.

"I said forget it!" he yelled, waving a hand back at me.

I smirked, wondering at the back of his stupid head—which was a little on the flat side, if you asked me. His mother should have turned him more when he was a baby.

"Ready to go?" Roxus called as we entered the sitting room. He stood along with Delthene, her angry cat now tucked under her arm, waiting by the door. They only had a few bags each, and Declan didn't seem to have anything apart from the change of clothes on his back.

I eyed each of them, noting Delthene's red, puffy eyes and the deep lines of worry around Roxus's mouth, before I finally nodded.

"No, but there's no other choice, is there?" I muttered bitterly.

"Unfortunately, no," Roxus said, putting an arm around Delthene's slim shoulders and drawing her closer to his side. "But we'll get through this. It's just a precaution."

For now, I thought angrily as I headed straight for the front door.

He couldn't guarantee how this would end. Sulam could very well burn this entire house down for spite after what we'd just done at his estate. If we weren't here, he might not bother. But there was no way to know for sure.

I didn't dare point any of that out, though. For Delthene's sake, I kept my mouth shut and a tense smile plastered to my mouth while I held the door open for them to leave. For her, I'd stomach this with as much grace as I could muster.

I owed her—the woman who'd become like a second mother to me—that much and more.

Even if it hurt to stand there, smiling while we shut the front door and locked it one last time. Not knowing if we'd ever get to come back here. Not knowing if it would still be standing the next time I walked this street.

I'd never truly had a home before I set foot into this place three years ago. Leaving it now made my insides cramp as though I were rotting from the inside out.

One way or another, I had to come back here. I had to set things right. I had to find a way to deal with Sulam. He deserved far worse than death after everything he'd done to us.

And somehow, someday, I would find a way to make him pay.

Sixty

"Gods, girl, I've never seen anything like this." Kaedan, Arx Eburna's lead healer, frowned as he examined the wound on my forearm.

I winced and squirmed on the white medical cot as he gently wiped at the foul, black ichor that seeped from the jagged slash from my wrist to my elbow. Leruna had tried stitching it, but every prick of her needle set my whole arm ablaze.

I couldn't leave it gaping open, though. Even if the actual bleeding had stopped, it wept that thick, sticky dark fluid. It had already soaked the layers of bandages Leruna had put on it last night.

So, now Kaedan would take a turn at closing it, one grueling stitch at a time.

"The flesh is extremely inflamed and irritated," he murmured, leaning in and carefully tracing the outline of it with a damp, clean washcloth. "I may need to sedate you in order to close it."

"That's fine." I couldn't hide the relief in my voice. The idea of trying to sit still while someone else poked it with a needle over and over ... gods, it was enough to make me want to faint.

I was no stranger to pain and suffering, but this wound wasn't like the others I'd suffered. And worse ... tendrils of dark lines had begun to spread from it like curling briars branded into my skin. The sight turned my insides to icy slush, and Vesperus's words rang like tolling temple bells in my mind.

"I now sense the seed of his despair growing within her heart. It seems she is fertile ground for his darkness to spread rapidly."

Gods, I prayed he was wrong.

Axien had been adamant that I wouldn't be afflicted like Leomarr had been. That this wasn't a curse. That I wouldn't become a monster.

But how could he or anyone else know for sure? Wouldn't Vesperus have the best idea of it, since he'd dealt with Leomarr all this time?

I shuddered at the thought and turned my face away as Kaedan set about mixing up a sedative tonic.

"You might not fall asleep, but you'll be too drowsy to fight me off," he warned as he handed me the slim glass filled with a fizzing, bluish liquid. "Try to drink it all in one go, if you can."

I did, and the effects were almost immediate. My head swam, and I slumped back onto the cot, watching the ceiling slowly spinning overhead. Everything from my neck down became a numb, tingling afterthought. And in that blissful haze ... exhaustion found me at last.

I hadn't slept in days, even before our mission had dragged us into that puzzlebox. There wasn't an inch of me that wasn't wrung out, bruised, and battered.

A few slow blinks, and I was gone. Lost to the haze of the tonics and a deep, mercifully dreamless sleep.

Hours must have passed, because by the time I snored

myself awake, Kaedan was gone and my arm was throbbing angrily beneath new layers of fresh, tight bandaging. The candles on the bedside table had burned down to nubs, and someone had spread a thin quilt over me.

I sat up on one elbow, squinting around the dim chamber. All the other cots were empty, and the door was closed. But through the gloom, two brilliant spots of glowing magical light glinted like stars, focused right on me.

"Have you been standing there the whole time?" I blew out a deep sigh and rubbed at my eyes. It cleared my vision enough to see a slash of white teeth from a wide, roguish grin even before he pushed away from the wall and sauntered toward me.

"I enjoy watching you snore and drool on yourself." Axien spun on a heel and sat on the cot beside me.

I couldn't muster a glare or a biting response as I lurched upright, dragging myself into a sitting position next to him with my injured arm cradled against my stomach. I scrubbed at my face, rubbing my eyes with the heel of my hand.

"The healer said you likely needed the rest and to let you be," he offered, his tone apprehensive as he eyed my bandaged arm. "How do you feel?"

"Like I've been dragged behind a speeding horse," I said. "You should have woken me. Did you already speak to Mistress Orvana?"

"I did." He laughed softly. "It's fine. You needed the sleep."

No argument there.

"Roxus came and went a few times, but he's got his hands full with getting Delthene and your large pit-fighting friend settled in," he continued. "After he came with us to speak with Orvana, of course."

I grimaced.

"And? How did she take the news?" I pressed.

"That we lost the artifact? Or that Sulam is most likely conspiring with the Tibrans?" He sagged forward, resting his elbows on his knees. "About as well as you can imagine."

"I should have gone with you to tell her. I'm sorry," I murmured.

"Don't be. Frankly, I'm flattered you trusted me to do it all on my own," he teased and bumped his knee against mine. "At any rate, I'm happy to spare you her wrath now and again. She can't afford to stay angry at her only sorcerer."

Tense silence filled the soft candlelight that flickered and danced around the room, making the shadows quiver and setting all my nerves on edge.

Because I needed to know. I had to.

There was no simple way to crack that topic open.

"Did you tell her what Sulam said? About ... about Declan and ..." I tried to begin, but my throat closed and all the words died on my tongue.

Axien dragged his bottom lip through his teeth slowly, expression thoughtful for a moment before he finally answered. "No. She did ask about your mental state, though. Apparently, the healer here is concerned. You're not as full of venom as usual, in his opinion."

"And what did you say?" I scowled at the floor.

"I told her the truth. That you're exhausted and so am I. That what happened in the artifact was extremely taxing on both of us, and since our ancient Avoran host wasn't able to heal you, you're likely far worse off than I am," he replied. "I told her you needed some time to rest. And then you'd be back and ready to find all manner of new ways to make life difficult for the rest of us."

I flicked him a sideways glance, wondering at how he made it all sound so routine and mundane. Not at all like we'd spent a day fighting tooth and nail for our lives against a monster the likes of which this world hadn't seen in six thousand years.

That we'd narrowly survived. That it had carved its mark into my flesh forever.

A mark that might claim my life, according to Vesperus.

"I keep thinking about what he said. About Leomarr's curse. About how it spreads," I whispered, just in case someone was eavesdropping nearby. "And this wound ... Kaedan said it's infected strangely. What if Vesperus is right? What if that monster implanted me with Vescor's curse, and—"

"You're going to be all right, Violet," Axien interrupted.

I bristled and shot him a glare. "How do you know that?"

"Because you're far too stubborn to succumb to an infection and what happened to Leomarr wasn't a curse. You saw him as plainly as I did. Vescor's magic possessed him. Made him into that thing. It wasn't a curse; it was the doing of a long-dead god," he said matter-of-factly.

I shook my head slowly, sliding my good hand over to trace the lines of bandaging around my forearm, right over the wound. Beneath all that sterile padding, it still throbbed sharply. That ache spread through my body like a shockwave, over and over, burning and distracting me from everything else.

"I feel it, Axien. Like bugs crawling under my skin," I confessed. "Something isn't right."

Axien put a hand over mine, his much larger fingers now adorned with three new rings. Vesperus's rings sparkled, glowing with that faint, magical blue hue only I could detect.

"Even if it had somehow transferred to you, Vescor is gone. The ley lines are dark. There's no magic to feed it. It has no choice but to fade. Just give it time," he said.

I tried to swallow. To push it down. To will my expression to indifference. But ... but I couldn't. Everything twisted inside me like a tangled mess of a thousand worries and wrongs I could never resolve.

It was crushing me from the inside out.

My mouth screwed up, eyes welling. I turned my face away so maybe he wouldn't see it.

Axien's hand closed around mine and tugged lightly, coaxing me to face him again. "What's wrong, Violet? Talk to me."

"You heard what Sulam said? About Declan and ... and his sister. It was true. All of it," I blurted, leaning into him suddenly and hiding my face against his arm. "And I have to tell him. He needs to know that she's been dead all this time, or he will try going back to that pit to fight again thinking he can save her. He will keep letting Sulam torture and kill him slowly, all for a ghost. For someone *I* murdered—"

"Stop it. Don't ever say that again," Axien cut me off sharply, seizing my chin in his fingers and forcing me to meet his gaze. "What happened to her; I can't even imagine the horror of it. Or of seeing it. But you were a *child*, Violet. Whatever else you were, you were a child just like she was. Her fate was not your responsibility. And her death ... it's not your burden, either. Don't let Sulam convince you it was."

"But Declan needs to know—!"

"And we can tell him in due time," he countered quickly, giving me no time to argue. "But for now, let it alone. Declan won't go back to Sulam. He can't. He's chosen a side now and he knows that. He's staying with Delthene in the dormitory apartments on the temple grounds. First and foremost, you rest. You recover. And then we talk to Declan, preferably with Roxus present."

"You think he'd try to hurt me?" The words were bitter on my tongue—mostly because I already knew the answer to that question.

"I think Declan has been a slave to his baser instincts far too long," Axien murmured, his hand sliding from my chin to my cheek. "He's been forced to communicate with his fists rather than his words, thanks to Sulam. It's the language he will likely default to in a rage. But if he dares put his hands on you in anger, I'll burn the soul from his chest without remorse. And I know that would ... disappoint you."

"You really think you can take him in a fight?" I arched an eyebrow, unable to disguise my doubt.

Sure, Axien was a sorcerer of sorts. But Declan was ... a force of nature. I'd seen him beat too many men within an inch of their lives with his bare hands to ever doubt that.

Axien's eyes narrowed slightly, features sharpening into a smoldering glare as he carefully tucked some of my hair behind my ear.

"I let him strike me once, because I thought it was justified. I'd handled you too roughly in our little bout in the pit," he said. "But I won't suffer his insolence against me again. My blood knows his."

Right. Because the Avorans and the Holvradix elves had a special hatred for one another—apparently even among their half-breeds.

"Your blood would be disgusted at the very thought of you defending a *pitathi's* honor," I reminded him.

Axien's gaze caught mine, molten and fierce in the candlelight as his hand slid to the back of my neck and drew me in closer. So close his lips brushed against the sensitive skin around my ear while he whispered, "Whatever you are, you are *mine* now, Violet. I don't intend to surrender you easily. Your honor is the only thing worth protecting."

I shivered against him, eyes fluttering closed as his mouth pressed against the side of my neck. One long, slow, famished kiss that ended with his teeth lightly grazing my flesh there. A kiss that would leave a mark.

A kiss that claimed.

It set every inch of my body on fire instantly.

"Lie back and try to sleep again. Mistress Orvana has called a meeting ... and I'm certain she'll want you there for this one," he murmured as he slowly pulled away, licking his lips like a wolf after a feast.

Really? He wanted me to just ... fall asleep? After *that?!*

I gaped at him, my face still burning like someone had lit my hair on fire, as he stood and started for the door without another word.

"You're really leaving? Now?" I managed to wheeze as he opened the door.

Axien paused, his back to me. His wide shoulders flexed, rising and falling with hard breaths as he stood there. His hand still gripping the doorknob clenched so hard veins stood out against his knuckles. He gripped it like he was clinging to it for dear life.

Or like it was the only thing keeping him from coming back to finish what he'd started. One push, one word, might bring him back like a raging summer storm. And a vicious, wicked part of my heart desperately hoped he would.

"I have to, Violet," he bit off each word with sharp brutality as he started out the door again. "For your sake ... and mine."

Sixty-One

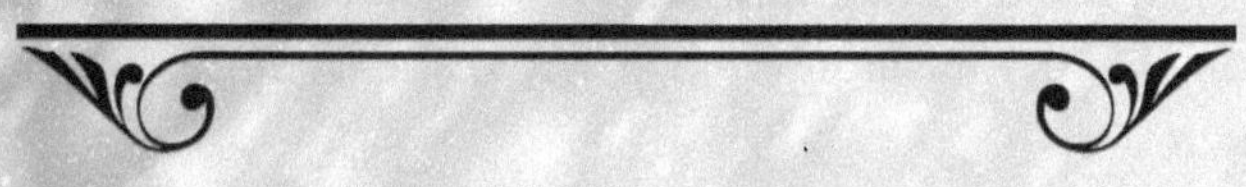

It was worse than we thought.

Sitting in one of the green velvet-backed chairs positioned around a wide, circular table, I checked every detail of my posture and expression. It took everything I had to school my demeanor to calm, collected indifference—especially when Axien recounted the details of what we'd been through in Tykeron's Puzzlebox.

This wasn't just a simple debrief. This was a full-blown inquisition now.

Upon hearing what had transpired at Sulam's estate, no one was surprised when Mistress Orvana called for all the elders and senior agents to meet. I was a little thrown, however, when she insisted that Axien and I also be in attendance.

Yes, we'd been the ones to discover a lot of this information, but there wasn't much more either of us could tell her that she didn't know.

So why invite two green tandems to a meeting like this?

I had no idea, but I'd had an awful, aching knot in the pit

of my stomach ever since Axien had warned me about it. Even now, three days later, I couldn't shake it.

Sitting with my legs crossed and my shoulders back, I stared coolly across the company of other Zenith's Call agents who were a lot older and more experienced than I was. That heavy, sinking coldness shivered through me.

It numbed everything except my right arm—the place where Leomarr's monster had flayed me open like a freshly caught perch.

That place still ached and burned like it had only just happened. Kaedan had done his best with it. But no matter how they wrapped or stitched it, the wound festered. It refused to heal. It leaked black ichor and spread those odd-looking dark lines across my skin that faintly resembled vines. They almost reached my elbow, now, and Kaedan was completely confounded by them.

I kept the wound covered with bandages, not wanting anyone else to notice. Whatever it was—a curse or just a wound that never fully healed—I couldn't deal with it right now.

There were bigger, far more important problems to solve.

My toes squirmed in my boots while Axien debriefed the panel of elders around us, relaying moment by moment everything that had happened. The crypt. The Ulfrangar. The monster and power hidden in that artifact, and then the sorcerer responsible for both. He chose his words carefully, and I picked up traces of Vanora's phrasing now and then. She must have coached him thoroughly before this.

Good. We couldn't afford to trip up at the finish line.

I knew better than to open my mouth or give anything further than what he wanted. Some things we had to play close to the chest, especially since we'd granted Vesperus's wish and cast the artifact into the sea.

Mistress Orvana might have even agreed with that decision, given what came next.

"We emerged in an office, and quickly deduced we were in Sulam's private office at his estate in Kosaar," Axien said, his voice steady and firm with resolve. No uncertainty. Only facts. "We searched the room quickly, since the implication of finding this artifact in his possession after our encounter with the Ulfrangar suggested he might be in collusion with them."

"That's quite a stretch," one of the elders, a stern-faced man with a close-cut beard, interjected suddenly.

All eyes turned to him, and a spark of rage kindled in my chest. I'd seen him in passing, of course. But we hadn't exchanged words in years. Not since I'd first darkened their doorway.

He was Naveen Decillus, overseer and commander of all the Vindexori guard. Varren's superior. And by the sound of it, sure to be my new best friend.

"How do we know Sulam would not have returned it to us? Perhaps he meant to and simply did not get the chance?" Commander Naveen cut an accusing glare my way, making no mystery of who he thought the real villain of this tale was.

"Perhaps I'm mistaken, then." Axien fixed the man with a relentless stare, his eyes darkening ominously. "Is it the habit of prominent crime lords to hand over valuable, powerful divine artifacts they find to the order in a gesture of goodwill?"

Silence.

"If so, I was not aware of it. So I thought nothing of searching the rest of his office for further evidence," Axien continued, waving a hand as though dismissing Commander Naveen altogether.

"And it is good that you did," Mistress Orvana spoke, giving the commander an equally disapproving scowl as she rose from her seat and spread out a thick roll of crinkled, weathered parchment.

It must have been twenty or thirty pages deep, each one stained and frayed as though it had been through an ordeal just to wind up in that curled stack.

"Axien and Violet retrieved this correspondence from a secured container in Sulam's office," she announced, motioning for the other elders at the table to take it and inspect it if they wanted.

Many of them did, pulling pages from the stack and examining each one with narrowed eyes, confused expressions, and whispers before passing them around.

"The container itself was of a uniquely Tibran design," Mistress Orvana continued, producing the black round case and setting it on the table as well. All three complex latches were open now, and she took her time explaining to the elders how it had taken her finest artificers three days to disarm and open it.

"Devices like this are reserved for only the most sensitive of material, since failing to disarm the locks properly would destroy the documents within," she said. "I've only seen such things used in royal settings where secrecy is of the utmost concern, and rarely outside of Tibrus."

"Are you suggesting Sulam is working with the Tibrans?" another elder, a delicate-looking woman with half-moon glasses perched on the end of her nose, gasped.

"No," Mistress Orvana replied evenly. "I'm suggesting he's working for them."

"Ridiculous!" Commander Naveen scoffed. "Mere speculation! How could you possibly know? None of this is even legible!"

Was ... was he freaking kidding?!

I slowly ran my tongue along the sharp edges of my teeth, counting the seconds so I didn't give him the fight he seemed to want.

"Very true, Commander. But this seal is difficult to

mistake, is it not?" Mistress Orvana conceded as she took up one of the pages, tapping a finger at the bottom right corner where a faded red watermark was inked into it.

I quickly looked down at the page that had just been passed to me. It bore the exact same seal. They all did, in fact. Pages upon pages with the Tibran insignia inked into them.

But that was about all I could tell about them because, unfortunately, Commander Naveen was also correct.

The rest of the marks on the page were a hodgepodge of irregular shapes and designs; all strung together in nonsensical patterns. They weren't words. Fates, it didn't even look like a real language.

"I believe what we have in our hands is of vital importance," Mistress Orvana said, lowering her tone. "As we speak, I have already assembled a team of curators who have transcribed the documents in perfect detail. They are working to decode these documents for us."

"To what end?" Roxus spoke next, slouched in his chair with his arms folded over his chest and his expression the picture of stony forbiddance. "If we are correct and these documents implicate him in Tibran schemes, what will you do? He has already tried to kill members of our order—myself included."

"Because you lot broke into his estate in the dead of night?" another elder chimed in angrily. "I doubt if anyone seated at this table has any love for Sulam. We are all aware of what he is. But to provoke him is reckless. It only makes our already difficult situation more impossible."

Roxus bristled in his chair, his tone heavy with a growl.

"The artifact was found in Sulam's private office, under guards who were willing to kill us to keep it. That fact alone warrants concern," Roxus insisted.

"Concern at what? A businessman defending his own home?" Commander Naveen scoffed.

"If he is facilitating the theft of artifacts and feeding them to the Tibrans, then our situation is already impossible," Roxus shouted suddenly. "We already have to contend with Tibrans and Ulfrangar, but if Sulam is aiding them in any way—"

He stopped short, mouth snapping shut and breathing hard through his nose as Vanora placed a hand on his arm.

As elegant and poised as a freshly bloomed lily, she considered the document lying before her on the table through long lashes before she flicked her gaze back up to Mistress Orvana. Her opaline eyes shimmered in a thousand changing colors as she pursed her red-painted lips and slid her hand carefully down Roxus's arm before taking up a piece of crinkled, battered parchment and perusing it.

"It could take many weeks, months even, to decode this," she surmised.

Mistress Orvana's expression flashed with frustrated anger before she finally admitted, "Yes. It is astoundingly complex."

Vanora's brows rose slightly.

"Then you will need to do better than a team of curators," she said. She placed the page back on the table and slid it toward the Mistress of the Call with one slender, perfectly manicured finger. "The shortest distance between two points is always a straight line. To break a Tibran war code, you will need a Tibran."

A rush of unsettled murmuring went up around the table like the hissing of wind through dry leaves. Only the four of us —Axien, Vanora, Roxus, and I—stayed silent and still as we stared at Mistress Orvana. Watching. Waiting.

Hoping she could do something about this discord before it tore the entire order apart from the inside.

But after several minutes of her elders and senior agents arguing and exchanging verbal jabs across that table, her proud stance seemed to shrink somewhat. Her features fell slack with exhaustion, and she blew out a slow, controlled breath as though she were trying to recompose herself.

She quietly stacked all the Tibran-marked papers into one pile, rolling them up before she waved a hand to the room and announced, "As soon as we learn more, I will call another meeting. Until then, those of you who live outside Arx Eburna are encouraged to at least fall back to the temple grounds. Dormitories will be opened for you. We take no chances now."

"That's it?" Roxus snapped. "We need actionable plans, Orvana! You can't ask us to just sit here and wait for the next terrible thing to happen!"

"We have no choice!" she shouted back, slamming an open hand down onto the table with a *BAM*. "If you are unhappy with these instructions, then you are welcome to join Rienka's city guards, as I'm sure they will need assistance very soon."

I flinched.

Everyone at the table hushed and went still, staring at her in shock. I had to wonder if she'd ever checked Roxus like that in front of them before. She'd always bent to his stubborn outbursts before.

This, apparently, was her hill to die on.

After a beat or two of heavy silence, Roxus looked away. His mouth bent bitterly, and his features scrunched into a furious, half-snarl. But he didn't retort.

Not this time.

"You are all dismissed," Mistress Orvana murmured quietly as she began to turn away.

But then her gaze halted squarely on me, eyes smoldering with cold fire.

"Except for you, Violet," she said bitterly. "I will speak with you alone in my office. Now."

Sixty-Two

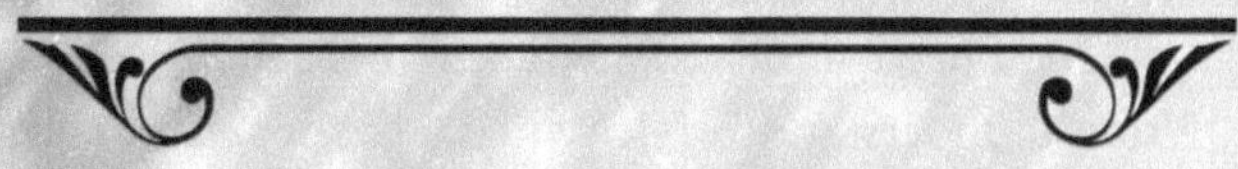

She had never used my name before.

At least, not that I could recall. She had lots of names for me—most of them derogatory. But if Mistress Orvana was using my name to address me in front of all the elders in Arx Eburna ...

Gods and Fates, this really might be the end of the world.

I stayed silent as I followed her into her office, circling the only chair positioned on the other side of her desk before I dared to sit in it.

She didn't speak either, her mouth pinched into a tight, thin line as she shut the door behind us and locked it. I tracked her movements, measuring each step and flicker of expression as she crossed the room, strode behind her desk, and dropped the stack of papers onto it.

"I know what you think of me," she said as she let out another deep breath. "You think I am cruel and unfair to you. That I despise you, even after all you've already done for the order."

My mouth clamped shut, hands gripping the arms of the chair like it might suddenly try to buck me off the seat.

What was she saying? What did this mean?

What did she possibly want from me?

"I am cruel because I know where you came from. I am unfair because of how many of our agents your kin have tortured and killed." She placed her hands on either side of the stack, resting her weight against her desk as she fixed me with that smoldering, cold stare. "I despise you because, in spite of what you are, I need you. Now, perhaps, more than ever."

"I don't understand." I frowned, meeting that ruthless look with one of my own.

If she'd invited me here in hopes that the solitude would make me squirm, she was sorely mistaken.

I preferred things with no witnesses.

"Curator Vanora is correct. We have fine scholars here. But what we don't have is time. We need this code broken and these messages translated in days, not weeks." Mistress Orvana tapped the stack of papers in front of her. "What you and that boy found could be the key to sparing Rienka a gruesome fate, and with it, our order. We cannot abandon the vault here. My fear is that Sulam knows this. Whatever the Tibrans do when they arrive here, we will not flee. We cannot. There are things inside that vault that cannot be moved except with great peril. While Argonox might risk it for his own gain, I will not. I will ask my agents to honor their oath. I will ask them to die defending it."

My throat jumped, hands going sweaty on the arms of the chair.

"But if we can supply any insight or advantage into the Tibrans plans, I intend to give it to Damaria's king and the city guards here," she said. "We need to know what these pages say. We need someone who can break the code. We need a Tibran who is willing to do it for us."

It hit me like an arrow to the forehead.

I slumped back in the chair, staring at her in horror. I only knew of one Tibran. One person who might have any insight whatsoever into Tibran plans and codes.

And, disgustingly, she was tied directly to me.

"Chrysa won't do this," I whispered. "She won't help me."

"Maybe not," Orvana countered. "But she may help herself. Three years in Necrolis Prison is sure to feel like three lifetimes. If we offer her freedom, perhaps she can be persuaded. But this will have to be done very carefully."

I stood slowly, meeting her eye-to-eye and waiting for her to get to the point.

"No one can know what we're doing." She kept her voice hushed—hardly more than a whisper audible over the crackle of the flames in her office's tiny fire pit. "Not who she is or why she's here. And if she makes even one false move that might endanger this place or any of the agents within it, I need to know she will be dealt with swiftly and without remorse."

Ahh. So that was why she needed me.

A wicked pitathi to hold Chrysa's leash.

It made me sick to my stomach.

"Just so I'm understanding this for the madness it truly is —you want me to break Chrysa out of Necrolis Prison, bring her here without anyone noticing, and somehow convince her to help us break Tibran codes to thwart the very army she used to be a part of?" I put my hands on my hips, angling my stance with a haughty confidence I knew she'd hate. "And if she refuses, or tries to betray us again, you want me to kill her?"

Mistress Orvana silently studied me for nearly half a minute, her dark eyes searching mine as though she were silently scooping through all the putrid depths of my heart in search of any kernel of goodness.

"Yes," she said without even the slightest hesitation. "That's exactly what I want you to do."

Gods.

My heartbeat took off in a flurry, and I stared after her,

trying to scrape my jaw off the floor as she rounded her desk again and began opening and closing the drawers as though she were looking for something.

She couldn't be serious … could she? This was a joke. A very bad, poorly timed joke.

Or a test.

Either way, it was insanity.

I had seen that prison a few times, and it was a fortress on its own. Not to mention how many guards must be inside it. Even if she was serious, and even if I thought I could convince Chrysa to hear me out, there was no way I could ever get into that place undetected, let alone—

Mistress Orvana dropped a heavy roll of hair-thin paper bound in old, tangled twine onto her desk in front of me.

"Blueprints of the prison," she announced. "You'll need them."

Gods, Fates, and all things holy. She was serious!

"I-I don't know if I can—"

"You don't have a choice," she cut me off sharply, sliding the blueprints toward me. "Either you do this, or everyone in this ancient fortress will die defending it. Although I'm told Argonox has a special appetite for unique individuals like Axien and Roxus. So perhaps they might be reserved for a fate far worse than death."

My stomach lurched, bile burning at my throat as I shakily reached out to take the thick scroll of blueprints.

I had no choice. She knew that.

Neither of us did, really.

"You will do this because it is the only way to save them," she warned. "And you will do it, because you are the only one who can."

"You seem so sure about that. You're ready to bet everyone's lives on it," I argued. "But I know what people say about that prison. I've seen it myself. It's a deathtrap just to reach it, let alone dream of breaking out of it. But you want me to do that and more—with a passenger in tow."

Mistress Orvana straightened, levelling a stare upon me that was as relentless and unforgiving as the razor-edge of my daggers. It froze my blood, making my pulse skip and stall.

I might as well have been two inches tall as I stood before her, gripping that bundle of blueprints to my chest.

"It's true. It is the most brutal place in the Southern Kingdoms," she admitted. "There is nowhere else like it. It is a cage for this world's vilest, most dangerous criminals. Some have said it could even hold a god. But the only question that matters now is ... can it hold you?"

The corners of her mouth curled into a knowing, ruthless smile—the same sort of smile my mother had given me, many years ago, before my very first kill.

A smile that saw me. That *knew* me.

That believed in the wicked little monster I was deep down at my core.

It set my blood on fire and my teeth on edge. It kindled the wildfire in my chest, awakening a brutal appetite that wanted —needed—to feed.

I drank it down like the sweetest poison.

"So? What, then? You're going to have me arrested again?" I tilted my head to the side, considering her as a vicious smirk brushed my lips. "Want me to scream and sob while they drag me away in chains?"

Her eyes narrowed dangerously. "Nothing so dramatic. As I said, if we are to do this, then it will have to be done as swiftly and discreetly as possible. I trust you can manage that."

"Haven't you heard? Discretion is my specialty." My smirk widened, and I folded the blueprints before tucking them into my belt.

"Let us hope so." Orvana snorted, turning away and striding a few restless steps closer to the edge of her fire pit.

"I need a day to prepare," I said, already moving for the door. "Three if you actually want this to work."

She nodded wordlessly, and I took that opportunity to unfasten the lock and reach for the knob. My mind already spun with plans and schemes, things I'd need to gather, and how I was going to break this news to the others.

Roxus wasn't going to like it one bit.

"In more than a thousand years, no one has ever broken out of Necrolis Prison," Orvana's quiet, prayerful tone caught me like a chokehold.

I froze, still gripping the doorknob tightly.

Slowly, I turned to look over my shoulder and found her already staring at me, the firelight dancing in her eyes like dark mirrors.

"But then again ..." she whispered, "I don't know that a Viperi has ever tried."

GLOSSARY OF TERMS

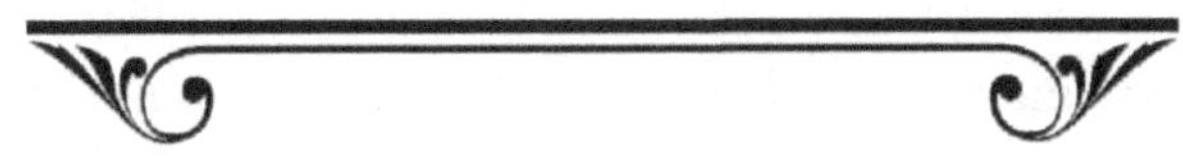

ADIANA – Goddess (or godling, specifically) of the Moon. She is considered a young goddess and is highly revered by the Lunostri elves. Symbolized by the panther.

ARX EBURNA – A prominent stronghold of the Zenith's Call located on the island of Sol'Karr in the small kingdom of Rienka, where the Mistress of the Call resides.

AVORA – Once a powerful empire of divinely-touched elves that stretched over the majority of Reatia. Their beauty and magical power was considered unrivaled, and they were the children of Enais. They fell from power after the War of Falling Stars, and now has limited territory in the north that is strictly guarded from outsiders.

CLYSIROS – Goddess of Death. She is revered as the guardian over the realm of the dead, judge of souls, and the prison of stars. Symbolized by the jackal.

CURATOR – Zenith's Call agents who specialize in dealing with ancient artifacts and texts.

DAMARIA – A vast human kingdom that specializes in agriculture and mining of precious gems. It was once a part of Nar'Haleen, but was divided and developed into a separate kingdom at the behest of Emperor Tashaar to appease his twin sons who did not want to share the throne upon his death. Since that time, Damaria has been fiercely independent and refuses to merge with Nar'Haleen once again. This refusal sparked the War of the Stones, which saw Nar'Haleen mount massive military efforts and enlist several of the gods to try to reclaim the land.

DEXTRUM – Active Zenith's Call agents who are sent out on missions, usually with a combat threat. They must be skilled in all areas, but may choose a specialization that makes them better suited for certain missions.

ENAIS – Foregod of Present. Symbolized by a golden three-pointed star.

ETERNAL HALL – A specialized area of Arx Eburna reserved for training and testing new prospects for the Zenith's Call.

HOLVRADIX – A race of hardy, war-like elves from the north known for their immense stature and physical strength. They have long warred against the Avoran elves, and care little for the world beyond their icy homeland.
ITANUS – Foregod of Past. Symbolized by a right hand.

KRIN'MOIR – The main hall of Arx Eburna. It features a

large ancient fountain depicting the two Fates, or Viepol. The waters of this fountain are considered highly sacred.

LUNOSTRI – A race of elves from Nar'Haleen who roam the vast desert in nomadic tribes. They are considered fierce warriors and keepers of ancient religious rites and knowledge that predate the War of the Stones.

MAGISTER – A senior agent of the Zenith's Call with greater than twenty years of experience.

MILONTOS – Foregod of Future. Symbolized by a golden eye.

MISTRESS (OR MASTER) OF THE CALL – The elected leader of the Zenith's Call who makes all major decisions regarding the order. He or she rules with the help of a council of six elder magisters from strongholds throughout the world.

NAI'POL – A large joint-temple complex on the island of Sol'Karr that houses prominent priests and priestesses and is dedicated to the entire pantheon of Reatia.

NAR'HALEEN – A vast kingdom to the east that once spanned the entirety of the southern region and was rivaled only by the Avoran Empire. It was divided into two halves (Damaria and Nar'Haleen) by former Emperor Tashaar to appease his twin sons. It remains the prominent power in the south, boasting military might and a rich mining industry of precious metals, but continues seeking to regain its lost territories through brute force.

PALIGNO – God of Life. He is known as a benevolent but

mysterious god, who first seeded life upon Reatia and often referred to as the shepherd of the wild. Symbolized by the stag.

PATRON – Dextrum agents of the Zenith's Call who are actively training new recruits, referred to as prospects, and overseeing their education.

PITATHI – A slur word used to refer to Viperi. In Nar'Haleenan, it translates literally as "dirty snake."

PROLEUS – God of War. He is a stern but fair god who values justice, mental and physical fortitude, and honor. He is often referred to as the father of humankind. Symbolized by the wolf.

PROSPECTS – New recruits still going through their training and trials to join the Zenith's Call. These may be children or young adults, but seldom are older than eighteen years of age.

RAJINNA – An ancient humanoid race highly gifted in magic. They are said to have been the first children of the goddess Astaris, making them one of the five peoples first created by the gods. Their skin colors are diverse, but all have shared features of horns, fang-like incisors, and tails. Their lifespan is far longer than the average human, ranging between 1,000 to 3,000 years.

REATIA – The known world (see map at the beginning of this book).

RIENKA – A small, newly-formed kingdom that has declared its independence from Damaria. Ruled over by five merchant lords who call themselves the Trader's Guild, it is known for its many islands, rich trade ports, and vibrant tapestry of cultures from throughout the world.

SIVANTH – A magical boundary wall created after the War of the Stones by the gods to separate the divine and mortal realms.

STEMMA – Ancient Avoran currency touched with magic. They are frequently used by the Zenith's Call as calling cards or identification markers.

SUROTRIX – The "Keeper of Whispers" that resides in the Vault of Whispers at Arx Eburna, overseeing the most volatile and secret archived documents and items for the Zenith's Call. This is considered a high honor that demands a lifetime of loyalty, and chosen candidates must have their tongues removed.

TANDEM – Pairs or partners of dextrum agents within the Zenith's Call that work side-by-side on missions.

UNDAE – Goddess of the Sea. Often referred to as the great mother, she is known for her changeable moods, love for adventurous souls, and beauty. Symbolized by the hippocampus.

URSINAAR – Bloodline of ancient Vordegan warriors who have the inborn magical ability to transform into a large bear. They are considered the most powerful and brutal of all Vordegan fighters.

VESCOR – God of the Void. Symbolized by a black spiral.

VIDRATHIAN STEEL – A prized and rare metal mined by

the dwarves of the Whitecrown Mountains and forged by the Vordegans into weapons. The metal has the unique ability to absorb magical energy, sparing the user from its effects if wielded in the right way. Vordegan warriors train their entire lives with these mystical weapons, learning to deflect or even redirect magical assaults with them.

VIEPOL – A pair of powerful god-like beings said to embody fragments of Avgior's shattered essence. They guard the boundary of the Sivanth, judge the souls of the mortal world, and take on the appearance of dragons. They are also known as the Fates.

VINDEXORI – Agents of the Zenith's Call who specialize in combat and are used as guardians or foot soldiers to protect certain sites, temples, or artifacts.

VIPERI – The ill-regarded offspring of Vescor. They are an ancient humanoid race that dwells in the caverns, cave systems, and long-forgotten ruins of ancient cities far below the surface world. They are vicious, highly skilled fighters and have no love for anything outside their subterranean realm. They are known to have pallid complexions, pale hair, red eyes, and fang-like incisors.

VORDEGA – A small, isolated kingdom to the west that is ruled by brutal, warlike tribes of humans said to be gifted at thwarting magic. They were known as the most efficient forces against the Avoran elves during the War of Falling Stars, but rarely deal with other kingdoms.

WAR OF FALLING STARS – An ancient war between the Avoran elves and the human kingdoms of Tibrus, Vordega, and Nar'Haleen. As the Avoran Empire expanded across

Reatia, it absorbed and enslaved a great many other kingdoms, showing particular hatred and disgust for humans. The human kingdoms allied against them, resulting in a brutal conflict that lasted nearly 800 years. The human kingdoms managed to drive back the Avoran Empire in a costly victory that left both nations forever diminished and broken.

WAR OF THE STONES – An ancient war between Nar'Haleen and Damaria that became interwoven with the affairs of the gods thanks to Emperor Zarexius's blood pact with Vescor. Many of the gods chose sides, and the result was catastrophic. The war left the landscape eternally scarred, many races of peoples nearly extinct, and two of the gods themselves were destroyed. To see that no such war ever took place again, the gods all made a pact to seal their power behind a mystical barrier called the Sivanth. Their influence would be tempered through sacred stones with a mortal individual acting as their mouthpiece.

ZAREXIUS – Emperor of Damaria during the War of the Stones who made a deal with Vescor, the God of the Void. He is also known as the father of the Viperi, as he was given leadership over them after the fall of Vescor.

ZENITH'S CALL – A secret society of scholars, assassins, mercenaries, historians, and priests that formed after the War of the Stones. They are sworn to protect the secrets and artifacts of the gods and those who worship them.

A Special Thanks To …

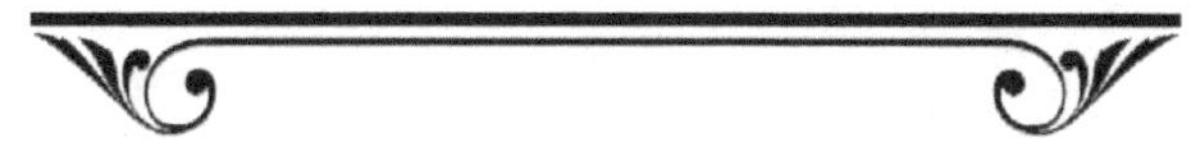

My Tiktok family, especially the My Book Boyfriend podcast, Coop, Posative Potato, Mr. E, Harrow, Wilton, Natalie, Footenotes, Book Dragon, Amara, Trophy Husband, Kristen, Henry, and SO many others who gave their time, energy, and support helping this series blossom. I'll never be able to express how much having folks like you in my life has changed my entire outlook on publishing! Here's to many more books and successes all around!!

Heather, Khara, Emily, Alicia, Ashlee, James, Wilton, Laura, Jennifer, Lori, Rue, Tricia, Cheryl, Kailyn, and all of my author friends who have shown up over and over to give me support, words of wisdom and comfort even when I am fully spiraling. I couldn't have made it this far without you!

And once again, my AMAZING Beta team!!! Thank you so much for taking the time to make sure these books are ready for the world.

My lovely artist, Lulybot, who has created such wonderful pieces for these books! Thank you!

My outstanding editor, Cameron, for all her hours of work helping me perfect this story to make it shine!

Philippians 4:13

Books from Nicole Conway

THE DRAGONRIDER CHRONICLES

Fledgling

Avian

Traitor

Immortal

THE DRAGONRIDER LEGACY

Savage

Harbinger

Legend

THE DRAGONRIDER HERITAGE

Hunter

Betrayer

Successor

Godling

Sojourner

Pathfinder

Paladin

Eternal

MAD MAGIC

Mad Magic

Vicious Vows

Wicked Ways

SPIRITS OF CHAOS

Scales

Wings

Hearts

EMPIRE OF BLADES

Born of Shadow

Oath of Moonlight

Cage of Secrets

Curse of Thorns

www.ingramcontent.com/pod-product-compliance
Lightning Source LLC
LaVergne TN
LVHW040824090826
845145LV00001BA/23

* 9 7 8 1 9 5 2 5 5 4 3 1 5 *